HYPERBOREA

⟶ TRAITOR'S PATH ⟵

by

E.M. Zolotor

Zolotor Publishing

CONTENTS

HYPERBOREA

TRAITOR'S PATH

PROLOGUE

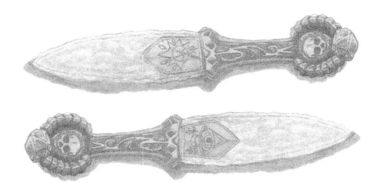

LEAVING THE NEST

Caldus rounded his back to loosen his muscles, but it only cracked the scabs where they had whipped him. It was a whipping he'd never forget. A month had gone by, dark and alone, and still, he felt his wounds hinder him.

"Not like that." A gruff criticism came from Domin Strat's bearded mouth. "Bring the knife across when you swipe, not up! You want them to dodge into your other blade as you stab in." He cuffed Caldus on the back of the head even though he had swiped only a few degrees off of an ideal attack. The blow wasn't as painful as the whipping had been and no worse than the dozen other swipes delivered by Strat every day during their lessons.

Domin Strat demonstrated by bringing his right hand across an imaginary enemy's face with a dagger held in reverse grip and stabbing his left hand up into an abdomen with another blade. He grunted for the two boys, both eight years old, to go again.

PROLOGUE

Caldus faced his training partner, Bray.

He swiped his hand viciously as Domin Strat had done. Bray feinted away, but Caldus' wooden dagger caught Bray in the cheek with enough force to leave it bruised. Caldus didn't bring the second blow to fruition as Bray whimpered.

The teacher's strike caught both boys this time as Domin Strat imparted them with knowledge.

"I did as you said," Caldus protested.

Domin Strat gurgled in the back of his throat and spat a thick stream of saliva.

"You didn't deliver the second blow," he said and turned to Bray, who was clutching his tender cheekbone. "You know what you did. Your opponents will be a lot faster than Caldus out there." He gestured past the high, ice-covered mountain peaks of Necogen with a fur sleeve. "When you leave these walls to work for the clan, you won't find timid attackers, slow targets, or wooden weapons. There's only *kill*, and you must decide who's doing the killing." Caldus stared where Strat's finger pointed and sighed as he imagined successfully escaping Necogen and not having a back full of soon to be scars. For today he was stuck on the training grounds of the Nest, as it was called. High above the foot of the mountain, the Nest was a region flat enough for the heart of the village to reside. However, this Nest was one made of crags and peaks of the Southern Sepeleo Mountain, which hid it entirely from the rest of the Cor Land, the main continent, on Hyperborea.

The boys drilled hundreds of more times before Domin Strat released them.

"Get some food," he barked.

LEAVING THE NEST

The boys bolted away eagerly, but the rough hand of the domin caught Caldus by the back of the neck and broke open more of his wounds.

"Not you." Domin Strat sat the boy down.

Caldus avoided eye contact, but his chin was tilted by the callused hand so he couldn't look away.

"Not many get the idea to leave before their assignments," Domin Strat referred to the day boys of the clan reached twelve years of age and completed their training by dueling their classmates with real blades. The victor kept their daggers and became assassins for the Necogen clan. "You did. You've already been punished, but if I see you staring at the walls like that again during lessons…I'll have you whipped again and thrown in the icebox for another month."

Caldus remembered the last thirty days he spent inside the box made of wooden stakes. The cell had no floor; only cold stone and patches of ice on the rock of the mountain peaks. The wind that blew through the wooden walls of the icebox had a bite only those sentenced to the cruel fate knew. The walls of Necogen didn't block the mountaintop gusts for those punished.

"I won't, Domin Strat." Caldus shivered and tapped his foot anxiously.

Domin Strat dismissed him with a brush of his fingers, and Caldus went to meet his sister, Jezca, who would be finishing her training for the evening. Around the corner, Bray was waiting for him.

"What was it like in the icebox?" Bray asked with an eager bluntness. "I bet it was cold!"

Caldus eyed the talkative boy. "It was as cold as you can imagine." He closed his eyes and was in the icy cell again. Its slatted

PROLOGUE

walls pressed in on him. He was trapped in the confined space and punctured by a wind so cold he could barely breathe.

Caldus opened his eyes. "And suffocating." That part wasn't from the temperature; instead, it was the squeezing walls that haunted him. He tried to break away from Bray, but his training partner followed.

"They say you was the first in nearly twenty years to leave the walls before his assignment," the boy pressed the topic.

Caldus took a detour on his way to the other side of the training grounds. He turned corners sharply as he walked through the Necogen temple. Still, Bray followed.

"Strat warned us every day while you was in the box not to think of anything so stupid as you did. Hit us extra each day as a reminder too..." Bray's voice trailed as he followed on creaky floors and through hallways of carved walls and ceilings. Ornamental engravings of eyes and serpents hidden throughout leafed patterns covered the walls. It was the only building in the whole village that was so adorned.

They entered a small room with a golden case at the center. Both boys slowed and gawked at its contents— as did every boy of the village who had ever passed it. Caldus saw himself in the glass display. Training knives and Strat's blows had bruised his face. His ears still needed some growing into, but he wasn't too far from handsome. His light blonde hair was a color he was proud of, and his jaw had a masculine square shape. Bray was quite the opposite. The glass showed a faded reflection of Bray's poorly shaven head: stubble rose at different heights in patches on his scalp.

Behind the reflections and glass rested a pair of twin daggers belonging to Amon, the fabled founder of the clan. The sunken eye-holes of skulls decorated the hilt, and large inlaid jewels were at the end of each iron handle. They were some of the most valuable manus stones—of the amgrite variety and a deep enough red to be called animus quality. That was the highest grade of amgrite stone and could amplify Soul Energy many fold.

Caldus let his reflection linger over the weapons and dissolve into the blood-colored gems—not that it mattered. All the desire in the world would not make him a wielder. Domin Gron had said he had powerful Soul Energy, but he was incapable of manifesting it. Even after a month in confinement in the icebox with nothing to do but attempt wielding, he still could not bring forth a single bead of Soul Energy. Thus, the domins tutored him in the art of daggers and daggers alone. He would learn and master every technique Necogen possessed and never learn the techniques of wielding. Bray had long since fallen behind him in skill, and Domin Strat had to dig deep within his angry heart to find the smallest of reasons to strike Caldus. His assignment day was on the horizon. He envisioned Amon's daggers in his hands on that day—but they were only to be possessed by a Wielder of supreme talent that Necogen hadn't seen in hundreds of years. Perhaps his sister could have earned them if she had focused on the art, but daggers was not her discipline.

Bray looked breathlessly on the artifacts but didn't forget to pester. "What was it like?"

"What was *what* like?" Caldus whispered without breaking his awed stare at the weapons.

"Beyond the wall. What was out there?" Bray whispered back as a keeper of the Necogen temple passed through the room and gave them a scolding look.

PROLOGUE

Caldus turned to Bray and muttered, "Wouldn't know. We were out there less than half an hour before they caught us. Barely made it through the north entrance tunnel." He stomped away bitterly.

They shouldn't have escaped through the village entrance. They should have run faster. They should have done…something…anything else to avoid being caught. He dragged his nails against carved railings as he marched on to meet his sister. She had caused fewer problems in the icebox and gotten out ten days earlier than him. They had told him that she accepted her whipping without resisting. Caldus wasn't one to take punishment standing still, and he'd have extra scars to show for it.

Over his shoulder, Caldus noticed Bray wasn't following him this time.

The mess of a boy did call out one more question, "Where are you going, Caldus?"

"To the manus shrine."

"Why?" Bray squeezed his eyebrows together.

"To ask for guidance…to pray…" Caldus said hollowly with no conviction.

Bray snickered, "Yeah, right; you don't pray or take advice from anyone, let alone the manus gods."

Caldus struck his knuckles on every carved creature that sat atop the railings he passed. *Thunk. Thunk. Thunk.* Each one cried out a dull wooden noise as he hit them. Bray was right. He didn't take advice any more than he had needed to get by. He certainly didn't pray, but neither did anyone else in the village. It was mostly two generations above him and a few of their descendants who still held the old ways of praying to the manus soul stones.

Thunk. Thunk.

LEAVING THE NEST

He was going to the shrine. That much wasn't a lie.

Caldus descended a final flight of stairs before crossing the inner courtyard of the temple to the shrine antechamber. The doors had no handles. They were already ajar and ready to receive him.

Thunk. Caldus cracked his knuckles on the heavy beams of the doorframe as he entered.

Inside he found Jezca.

She only nodded to him and tilted her head down the hall that led to the shrine.

Caldus gave the carved walls one more solid rap with his knuckles as he passed it. *Thunk.*

Slam! The wind seized the door and hurled it into the frame as he took his first step. A carved eye within a diamond border met him when he looked back. He put his fingertips to the closed door. A decent effort didn't even budge it.

"Come on, Caldus," Jezca insisted lightly.

He followed her down old, faded stairs; he felt the carved eye on him as he descended.

"How are the wounds?" Jezca asked. She had the same well-defined jaw as her brother, but her high cheekbones turned the lines into an attractively feminine feature.

Caldus winced as he walked but said, "Fine. They'll heal soon. Yours?"

"They keep reopening in training, but it doesn't matter. I've been studying in the hall of scripts while I've been waiting for your release. I think I have a way, but our best bet is tonight," Jezca whispered.

"Tonight?" Caldus asked a bit too loud and hushed himself, "That's a quick turnaround." He laughed.

PROLOGUE

Jezca warned, "They're watching us. The domins probably know we're here right now—"

"To pray," Caldus snickered.

"And that's exactly what you'll tell them. To pray for guidance because of our poor decisions."

Caldus nudged his sister. "So, what did you learn in the script halls?" He knew the tomes and scrolls of the hall were full of recorded secrets. Most of those were wielding knowledge.

Jezca didn't answer.

They exited the hallway and were on a cliff face. They followed the roped ledge, leaving footprints in the snow powder of the nearly untraveled walkway. Above and across and below and all around, cabins protruded from either side of the chasm. Sloped roofs covered in white were strung across the rock and embedded into it. These structures made up the hidden village of Necogen. Balconies and halls extended from cabins, and rope ladders were as common as stairs. Every window glowed a warming yellow that pierced the gray-purple light outside. The thought of fires inside the mountain quickened Jezca's steps. Caldus hurried to keep up, but the wind didn't bother him. The past month had tempered him to it like a smith's anvil tempered steel. The wind had made his skin into a tougher form.

Soon they were alone inside the manus shrine.

Traditional torches lined the walls in an alternating pattern. Every light that bore a flame was separated by torch handles with low-quality condlucite stone in the prongs. The gems had the visual appearance of a chunk of flawed glass. Any condlucite of value had a bluish tone, but that made torch stones more accessible and widely used throughout Corland.

LEAVING THE NEST

Jezca waved a few fingers, and a pinkish-gray Soul Energy sprang from her fingers and drifted from stone to stone, lighting them in a series of white crystal glows. The shadows receded and revealed two shrines at the head of the room and rows of pews before each. The shrines themselves were carved from the stone and were one with the floor. They sprang up in gently curved bases with runes carved on every side. Atop each base was an open-faced box with a roof. Within the left one were flecks of the highest amgrite stone of animus quality; they glittered a scarlet hue. Inside the right were shards of the purest condlucite stone of anima quality. The few pieces that were in the miniature stone temples were worth more than anything else in the village—save the larger chunks in Amon's daggers. There was no need for guards in the shrine room; the shards sunk below the surface of the gray rock. It would take hours of scraping with proper tools to remove one fleck.

Jezca bowed before the anima shrine first and made an offering. She imparted her Soul Energy to the stones as she bent down, and the little temple flashed like a lit tinder. The gentle glow now blinded Caldus and Jezca with the deepest saturation of aquamarine. After a few seconds, the Soul Energy dimmed, but upon inspecting the stones, Caldus could see the light refracted internally in each shard just as brilliant as before. It was as if she had charged the anima stones.

Caldus had never been to the shrine before, but he had learned that anima quality stones were nearly permanent storage for Soul Energy. Some of the domins and scripts even claimed a large enough anima stone could have strange and fantastic powers.

"Close your eyes," Jezca commanded.

PROLOGUE

Caldus managed to roll them up into his skull with exasperation before squeezing his eyelids shut. Through the black of his shut eyes, a wave of red penetrated his retina. The light was so intense that he saw crimson shapes dance on the wall even minutes later. This was the animus stone. The domins had not lied—it amplified Soul Energy for short periods. As his eyes adjusted to the room after the flash, Caldus could see the smoldering glow in the shrine was already dimming.

With her offerings made, Jezca knelt before the anima shrine. "Pray," she commanded.

Caldus sat back irreverently against the pew and crossed his arms as his sister practiced her faith. He would take no part.

"I said pray, Caldus. I made enough offering for both of us."

"You know I don't believe in these lumps of rock. We're here to talk about our plan not—"

Jezca stood and let her umber brown eyes do the talking for her. They were fierce and entrancing below her nearly white-blonde hair.

Caldus swallowed as he tried to hold his ground with a shaky voice, "I said I don't believe."

"*I do.* So, kneel."

"It doesn't do anything. You know it. I know it." Caldus gestured to the still glowing rocks.

Jezca hadn't blinked and didn't let up her strong, but hurt stare at her brother. "It brought Mom back *every time. Every time* that I asked the manus stones to bring her home safely."

Caldus turned away and looked stubbornly at the torches on the wall. "Well, it didn't work the last time. She's been gone for three years."

Jezca blinked, taken aback.

LEAVING THE NEST

She slapped her brother harder than intended.

"I...I just missed my prayers once. The domins had worked me so hard that day. So much that...I fell asleep early the night she left for her mission...I....and she...*pray Caldus!*" she uttered steadily and stood up straight. "Sometimes, you need something to believe in. Tonight, we certainly will."

Caldus knelt before the animus shrine, stunned. His face stung with a pain he had never felt before. The pain tingled and mixed with guilt for nearly half an hour until his sister finished.

The silence throbbed with Caldus' cheek until finally, Jezca turned to him.

She whispered, "Tonight is the night. It must be. It's when they won't expect it, and I can sense snow coming."

A nod was all Caldus could muster at first, embarrassed for the disrespect he had shown their mother.

His sister had a strange ability to sense all sorts of things. Some domins had titled her a prodigy of awareness, and weather predictions were only the beginning of it. Jezca could see all kinds of revelations.

She continued, "I found maps of the South Aisle Mountains in books that even the domins of the script-hall hadn't gone through. They were left in the unrestricted halls. I've been searching for them for over a year, and four nights ago, I found them."

"What's in the maps?"

"Petramon, the Monte capital. If the maps are accurate—it's only two day's travel down the mountain." Jezca let hope show as her folded hands shook with excitement.

Caldus curled up one side of his lip and sighed. He let his straw blond hair fall over the pew as he moaned, "That won't do us any good if we can't get past the walls of the Nest. Last time was a

PROLOGUE

complete failure. It's as hard to escape as it is for outsiders to find the village." They both knew it was impossible to find Necogen. The only entrances were tunnels in the mountain peaks, and the only signs of the village from the outside were a few enormous vertical drop-offs that sentries walked.

Jezca curled her lips up, confidently. "That's not the only thing I found in the script hall. A few months ago, I found a book in the section for advanced wielders—"

Caldus cut her off, "How did you get in there without old Domin Gris catching you?"

Jezca only smiled. "I was careful. You have to listen to your surroundings to know when he's making his rounds, and read by the light of your own Soul Energy. Point is, I think I'm ready to use a new technique that'll help us get out of here. I just need you to trust me." She put each of her thin pale hands on Caldus' shoulders and made him commit to her plan. "Promise me: you'll do as I say tonight; without question and without hesitation."

There was something in her voice, like the edge of a sharp blade, which made Caldus understand how real the scheme was becoming. "Jezca, I promise. We'll leave here tonight. We'll escape to Petramon and then find out what happened to Mom." His pale blue eyes locked with hers, and he whispered with a hint of fear, "They'll kill us this time if they catch us."

After that, everything blurred for Caldus. Time moved in a euphoric slowness without memory. He remembered the details of the plan: where he would meet his sister and when, but it was more like the facts had been planted in his head. He didn't recall hearing them.

He was terrified, but remembered bumping into an old domin with loose hanging skin that neither of them had recognized. The

LEAVING THE NEST

old man had chastised Jezca for bringing a non-wielder, an ostaka, to the manus shrine. She assured him she made the proper offerings and that they only wanted forgiveness and guidance because of their past mistakes. The old domin hadn't liked that answer much, but he didn't seem in the mood for any explanation.

Caldus remembered feeling like icy water was melting off of rooftops and landing on the back of his neck. *Did the domin overhear their talking? Would he tell their teachers that they had been alone together?* His spine tensed as his thoughts ran uncontrollably. He didn't remember what Jezca said to get past the old domin of the shrine, but now he sat in the barracks and listened to a bird through the window. It whacked a shell against the mountainside, trying to get at the meal that curled up inside. Each time the shell clacked against the mountain, Caldus nearly jumped from his cot. He didn't need to worry about staying awake. The bird, the uncomfortable cot, and the overwhelming anxiety prevented him from even blinking. He fixated out the window at the shell that was slowly being broken open.

The boys of his age slept around him, twenty-two in all, as he worried about leaving without waking all the other assassins in training.

The bird finally cracked the shell.

Caldus knew what he must do as the purplish spiral of protection split open and the bird found its dinner. It was still too early to meet Jezca, but another idea possessed him. He was the most agile boy of his age and the quietest. There was no sense in worrying. His peers were the least threat to him, especially with what he was about to do. Effortlessly, he rolled out of bed without as much as a creak. He buttoned on his black tunic with brown fur trim and fastened his leather belt buckle with a pattern of two

PROLOGUE

pillars around a symbol, much like the one for Hyperborea: two circles with ridged tails that formed a greater circle. The tails on this belt buckle weren't connected into the larger shape but instead wandered into the pillars. The design was from a people long since passed and turned to legend his mother had said. It was the only thing she had ever brought him back from her missions. Gifts were not allowed, and so he had told everyone he had made it himself; down to the set of runes scratched into the reverse side.

Caldus pulled up his hood so that the fur trim tickled his cheeks. He placed his hands on the open window sill and launched his feet out the opening, turning his body to face the wall as he fell through the window. His fingers held on long enough to slow his drop but released the wooden ledge early enough to prevent collision with the wall as he fell from the barracks.

Anxious hands felt the empty sheaths on his belt where daggers would have gone after his assignment day; his index finger penetrated the emptiness of the plain leather scabbards. He figured he would earn his daggers well enough tonight. Only the victor kept his blades after the brutal dual of assignment day, but tonight he would be the victor over the entire village of Necogen.

Specks of snow landed on Caldus' lips. Jezca's vision had been right.

Caldus met Jezca an hour later on the west side of the village. They stood atop a dusting of white, far from the entrance tunnels to the north or south. It made him question his sister's plan, but he had promised her in the shrine to act without hesitation tonight. He tried to stay behind her discreetly, but Jezaca's eyes saw all.

Jezca clamped onto Caldus' wrist, and she swept back the short cape of his tunic to reveal the source of color that had caught her eye in the moonlight. "Caldus!" She nearly raised her voice above a murmur at what she saw.

Two ruby red animus stones split the darkness on either side of her brother's waist.

"Why do you have those?" she hissed, pressed against a wall under the shadow of a rooftop.

"I wanted a weapon for when we get outside the walls," Caldus said with a fake coyness.

"So, you thought Amon's daggers, *the most valuable things in the village*, would be your best option? How did you even get them?"

Caldus mimicked his sister's confident smile from earlier, "Like you said—I just listened. When the domin on duty walked away, I stole a blade, and then used it to crack the case to get these."

Jezca nearly smashed her brother with a fist, "They'll kill us for sure now."

"They'd kill us anyway. What does it matter?" he said.

Jezca knew he was right. She let out a foggy breath. When the condensed moisture dispersed from her face, she focused on the ladders that led up the west wall. They moved silently in the shadows of the courtyard until there was only a moonlit stretch between them and crags of the drop-off. It was over a one-hundred-foot climb up the inside of the wall to the walkway.

The layer of snow that was forming on the ground worried Jezca; there would be footprints. She waited without words. Caldus hid beside her patiently. The temperature and weather numbed his anxiety, and he was sure he was ready for whatever his sister planned.

A minute passed, and Caldus' fingers began to stiffen inside his thin gloves.

PROLOGUE

The snow continued to fall, frozen seeds from the sky that suspended time in a mask of pinholes.

Finally, two sentries made rounds past the ladders in heavy fur boots. The Necogen men managed to barely leave an imprint on the snowfall. The sentries passed and turned around a jut of mountain that created the perimeter around the Nest of the village.

Jezca grasped a rung of the rope ladder that ascended up to the top of the village drop off. She took a calculated first step onto the planks of the right ladder. Caldus mimicked his sister putting his right hand on first and planting his foot, but for every rung his sister found and pushed off of through the increasing snow, Caldus stepped up two without looking. He was halfway up the wall before long and Jezca was still moving past the quarter mark. Her moves were more aware and careful, but it slowed her.

Caldus looked down. It was a dizzying height, especially as he watched the snow drop down on his footprints below. They had left a set of tracks from the last building to the wall.

He was nearly to the top, but Jezca was only half way as the guards came back around. His entire body tensed and he looked to his sister.

Jezca waved him up frantically as the first guard noticed her.

"You! Get down from there." He barked in deep surprised groan. It was probably the first time he had ever seen someone on the wall during his tenure.

Caldus peaked over the edge of the walkway once he had heaved himself onto it. Jezca had their full attention. He doubted they had ever seen him, let alone what he had stolen from Necogen.

LEAVING THE NEST

Jezca held onto the ladder with one steady arm and swung away from the wall. She reached a gloved hand down to the guards from her high position.

The guard hollered again, "No, climb down. Don't jump, stupid girl!" He spoke without realizing the intent of her movement. By the time his eyes widened at the dull rose glow of Soul Energy, it was too late. Jezca cursed when the second sentry turned and ran. She wasn't skilled enough yet to catch a sprinting target in hindered visibility, so she continued up the ladder. This time, she proceeded up much more haphazardly. A slick of ice on a rung nearly sent her to join the sprawled guard below, but she had kept hold with her hands and quickly found her footing again.

On the walkway Caldus questioned her with a fearful frown, "What did you do? You didn't kill them, did you?"

"I did as the domins taught me. The other got away. He's sure to wake the others so we have to go now!" She answered as breathless from surprise as from sharp winter air. Somehow it hadn't been as bad as she expected. She had been raised for it after all. Now, it was her life or her captors. She would choose hers and her brother's every time without fail.

Caldus leaned over the wall with his hands on his head. "By Amon! What did you do," he breathed hysterically. "They'll kill us now. You can be sure of that," he said. The sight of the drop on the other side of the wall dizzied him. It was well over six hundred feet of mountain face before even a slight slope for footing was available.

Jezca grabbed Caldus' tunic and pulled him in close. "They'd have killed us anyway." She nodded to the daggers he had stolen and then released him and threw up both hands. The motion reminded Caldus of their situation. They were as good as dead if they didn't get away.

"And where are we supposed to go now that you got us stuck up here?"

Jezca found balance and sank into a deep squat at the brink of the walkway. There was no railing or wall. Anyone meant to be up there for sentry duty would have well trained feet, and all trying to scale the wall would certainly not.

"I learned a new technique in the script halls. You said you would obey without question—"

Caldus protested what she was proposing, "Jezca…"

"Caldus get on my back now if you don't want to die."

"Jezca I—"

"Now!" she screamed loud enough to wake anyone near the west wall of the Nest.

Caldus knew he had no choice. He said he would not question and he did not intend for that to be a lie to his sister. He wrapped himself around her neck and back as she shifted her weight forward.

"Hold on tight," she whispered with words that exited her mouth in a visible fog.

She let her feet slip off the edge.

They fell down the enormous wall that hid Necogen.

Wind and snow cut their faces.

Down they rushed.

Down.

Down.

Caldus' belly lodged in his throat when they first jerked up.

Jezca created rose-colored platforms beneath her feet, but they were immediately shattered as she fell through. Still, they slowed the fall and Jezca made more platforms. She hadn't accounted for the added weight of her brother when she had practiced Soul Step as shown in the texts of the script hall.

She created another and another, releasing small bursts of Soul Energy from the platforms as she began to compensate adequately for her brother's weight.

It wasn't enough. At least not enough *and* in time.

The base of the slope rushed to meet them.

A rapid flash of murky pink Soul Energy burst in succession as Jezca stamped at the air desperately.

Thooompf!

They struck the powdered rock and slid down the icy slope.

Before pain, before dread, there was only the sense of the unknown.

Caldus and Jezca could only wonder if they were still alive in this world or if they would be born again in another. All was unknown as the base of the mountain imposed upon the young siblings.

CHAPTER ONE

NEW WORLD PRECIPICE

The feeling came over Eos in a fleeting pulse of the unknown, like being born again. His exile was over, and he had defied the odds to make it so. The Mitad, Ares, General Braxton; he had refused to let any of them impose their wills on him.

This moment was his reward.

Pink and lime-colored light bathed the snow around him in a warmth that was not physical. It was a warmth of fulfillment, like when he rescued Maxima and embraced her. It was a warming of the soul, and Eos reveled in it.

After all, he had earned it. A lifetime of separation from his homeland, years of slave labor, and three months of fighting, struggling, training... sweating... bleeding... He had earned his freedom to return to Hyperborea. It was time to cross the irreversible line into the world of wielders. All these emotions and experiences swelled to the surface of down payments towards his dream. They brimmed about until a crimson light flowed unstoppably from Eos' black, cursed hand.

The light shot to the sky and mingled with the Northern Lights; it was a spattering of stardust among a canvas of stars. It returned down into the open vial, a relic known as the Mellizo Glyph. It brought with it some of the green majesty above, and the Soul Energy crashed into the vial.

Eos had to reassure himself again of the truth. As Aizo had said, there was no guarantee of what they would find on Hyperborea, but it was enough to know that he was going home.

"Hold on to the glyph!" Aizo urged.

Eos grimaced to keep the small rectangular artifact in his clenched hand. The downward force of the energy filling it was dragging his arms towards the snow at his feet.

Maxima placed her hands around his. Together they supported the Mellizo Glyph in the ceremony to open the gateway between Earth and Hyperborea. They held it until the brilliant light stopped swarming into the tiny vacuum-like opening. Maxima closed the cap.

The engravings on the glyph glowed.

The two circles that sat side by side with tails forming a larger ring came to life first. Then the ridges around the outer circle followed, and the glow spread to the archaic runes that covered each side of the white stone. It pulsed one final time like a lighthouse signaling a lost ship, piercing the sky with its call.

Eos looked up to see that a small moss-covered cave, no deeper than a closet, had appeared behind Maxima, and it contained only a staircase that descended beneath the ground.

CHAPTER ONE

Aizo put his hand on the wall of the cave. "It's been far too long since I've walked down these stairs."

"Where will they take us?" Maxima asked.

"To the Guardians of the Gate. Earth and Hyperborea are separate worlds. Between them exists a gateway that you've revealed with the glyph." He shifted uncomfortably off his wrapped leg and leaned up against the stone.

Eos went first and stepped down beneath the surface. He found, to his surprise, not darkness below, but light. There was a loud *hurr* of static, white noise. When he put his foot down on the final stair, a splash of warm water dampened his boots.

To his front was a waterfall that poured into a lake. He was standing beneath it on a large bluish-green stone with others like it sitting above the surface of the water to each side. They led out from underneath the torrent of water in a circular walking path.

Eos followed it.

As the curtain of water was left behind, Eos was greeted by air that smelled lightly of honey and a touch of burning wood. He found himself on a pointed cliff that jutted away from the waterfall. Its narrow shape and gradient guided the water of the lake to spill off each side. He followed the path across the water and planted his foot onto grass.

He waited for Maxima, who was now on the rock stepping stones. Aizo was not far behind, but Eos could tell the deep gash on the middle-aged man's calf was limiting his mobility as he hobbled to keep up.

The three of them looked ahead to the pointed end of the cliff. Two white and gray, marble pillars rose to the sky and towered over the entire strip of land. Their rectangular shape slanted at the top, nearly forming a point between the two. Runes, engraved scenes, moon and sun symbols decorated the entirety of the massive pillars. The two obelisks seemed to scrape the heavens and much of the detail was lost to the human eye on the upper levels. They stood, planted on a platform of the same marble material with a staircase at each end.

"That's the gate to Hyperborea," Aizo murmured in a hushed awe at the sight.

"Then what are we waiting for?" Eos strutted ahead. "I've been waiting my whole life for this."

They climbed the stairs on the left which made a right turn up onto the main platform. The Guardian of the Gate stood between the two pristine towers of white.

Aizo directed them in a low whisper, "Go on. You two first, I'll catch up."

Eos approached the Guardian, whose skin was lightly tanned and so smooth it nearly hid his age. A bald head and white beard told otherwise. The Guardian gave of the feel that he was nearly as ancient as time itself. He raised a hand to Eos and gestured for him to come closer with a thin finger. With the motion, rose the dark orange robe which he wore and the deep purple sash that was tied around his waist and thrown over his right arm.

Once in front of him, Eos hesitated to speak. "Will you take me to Hyperborea?"

The sage-like man nodded in the smallest of movements while looking on the boy.

"So, I'm finally going home," Eos whispered in disbelief. The moment held a surreal silence only distinguishable by the strange smell of burning and honey.

The Guardian leaned into Eos, "That is for you to decide."

CHAPTER ONE

He raised the drape of orange and purple before Eos in a motion that seemed to possess all the power the universe could offer. Then, the finger tapped lightly on his forehead.

Eos looked up at the man. His beard was gone, and his face was longer. The smell of burning wood prevailed over the honey. Unsure what to do next, he turned to Maxima and Aizo, but they were gone. Only the stretch of grass leading to the waterfall was there. Its water surged, much like before, but it traveled from the bottomless fall below the cliff into the lake. From the lake, the water flowed toward the sky. The waterfall that hid the cave was traveling in reverse.

Eos whipped his head back to the Guardian. He smiled kindly at Eos. Behind him, an indiscernible distance away was a blot of land—the cliff he had just been standing on. Between them floated another smaller landmass, but it was all too far away to make out.

The Guardian kept his pointer finger outstretched, in the same way when he had tapped Eos.

Maxima appeared at his fingertip. She stepped aside and took in the reverse waterfall as Eos had. Finally, Aizo came to the other side of the gate.

"Thank you," Aizo bowed his head to the Guardian. Eos and Maxima glanced at each other before doing the same.

Words struggled to leave Aizo as his happiness replaced the years of loss and imprisonment. The crazed look that Eos was accustomed to crossed Aizo as he said in a cracking voice, "Well, Hyperborea is waiting!"

They made their way around the waterfall and up the staircase, stepping out into misty skies that tasted of salt and loomed in a blue-gray. They stood on a tangle of roots, each thicker than a man's body. Eos placed a hand on the giant tree next to him, amidst the forest. It rose hundreds of feet until the trunk morphed into the mist that hung over the area. Vines grew up the trees, and glowing fungi clung to bark, emitting a dim blue glow from under their caps that reflected off the water.

Eos and Maxima took in the ecosystem below their feet. Through the tangle of thick roots, the briny water that had a glow of its own. From far below the surface, jewel-like moss shimmered a bright emerald. The water refracted the light and danced with life.

"Where are we?" Eos marveled.

"Mmmm," Aizo grunted and nodded to himself. "Off the northwestern coast of the main Hyperborean continent of Corland. An isolated spot in the Sepeleo Mountains, and one that's difficult to find. The Guardians use these locations to discourage most from traveling between worlds. They like to keep Earth and Hyperborea separate. We're standing above what some call the ancient Emerald Pools. A valuable, herbal moss grows below these roots, but it's nearly impossible to get to."

Maxima breathed to take it in, "It's so beautiful, Aizo."

Behind the thick mist, the face of mountains could be seen all around them. Aizo's eyes looked as if a sheet of glass formed over them. Then that sheet melted into liquid as the incredible atmosphere of the Sepeleo Mountains welcomed him home. Standing here wasn't just a homecoming for the siblings; it was also a moment that Aizo had written off as nothing more than a dream on some dark days in General Braxton's prison. He forgot everything around him and reached out over the water with both hands. The emerald glow wavered on his sleeves from the water and tinted his face. As Eos looked closely, he saw Aizo's lips and cheeks were shaking with an intensity that he had never seen. The

CHAPTER ONE

man's fingers slowly went limp, and he pulled his hands back from over the water.

Aizo wiped his eyes and sucked in through his nose to halt the sentiment, "Mysterious and dangerous. This is one of the most exotic places in all of Hyperborea. There are rare instances of nature, the land, and its creatures having interactions with Soul Energy. Everything here falls into that category. It's best not to wield until we are out of the heart of the mountains."

Left of the mound of roots on which they stood, a yellow eye with a slit pupil rose from the water. The eyelid was made of albino scales, and a similar nostril protruded up two feet from the eye. Eos nearly warned Aizo, but the creature re-submerged no sooner than Eos opened his mouth.

Aizo laughed and patted the bald top of his head. "Best to stay on the paths created by tree roots. Wouldn't want you to get eaten so close to Anondorn," he referred to the capital city of Anite, a northern territory of Hyperborea, as he walked along the mangled wooden platform and shimmied around the trunk of a tree to the other side.

Eos and Maxima followed at a slower pace. They observed every detail of the spectacle around them. Birds no different than those of Earth chirped from the tree branches above. The branches intertwined into a hanging canopy that a glowing fungus was overtaking. It created a spotlight over the water where the cyan from above met the emerald below.

"Which way are we going?" Maxima asked softly.

Aizo tilted his head and looked through the trees at the mountain walls around them. "Based on where we stand now…I couldn't say." He carried on, then stopped, and looked back at the slightly disturbed Bellator siblings. "Not to worry. Your father left us a map in a hidden chamber nearby. Talus and I used to visit there when we were younger. We'd come to dive the Emerald Pools and hunt for moss." He began to lose himself to fond memories. Eos could see them overcome by other recollections as his eyes dimmed. "Talus said the map would guide us to the safest return location."

The glowing ponds grew less frequent, and the roots and vines that they walked on gave way to the mountain.

"The places where Soul Energy interacts with the world," Aizo grunted as he limped on his wounded leg. "are called Sacrum-Crypts. They are the great wonders of our world. However, the world outside of them is more mundane; not all that different from Earth in some ways."

The Sacrum-Crypts enthralled Maxima. "Were those pools Sacrum-Crypts?"

Aizo threw back his head and gave a hearty laugh from his belly. "Much like the roots we are walking on, the Sacrum-Crypts spread their roots. Those pools are only the fingertips extending out."

"So, there's a bigger body of water? Is that where we're going?" Eos asked.

Aizo nodded. "Exactly, but we shouldn't get too close. The Sacrum-Crypts usually have dangerous protectors near them— Crypt Keepers."

Maxima's eyes widened. "Monsters?"

Aizo couldn't contain another laugh. "Your imaginations are running wild, I think. I'm talking about spirit like animals. Beautiful creatures, but dangerous…and not too different in appearance from those of Earth—" Aizo's wounded leg nearly collapsed

CHAPTER ONE

underneath him, and Maxima caught him before he fell into the swampy waters below.

Eos jumped in and yanked Aizo back up to balance.

"Eos careful with his leg! I had him. You should let me—" Maxima said with irritation.

"You couldn't handle his weight. I wanted to make sure he didn't fall into the wat—"

"I had it under control," she scowled. "You can't just force him onto his injured leg like that."

Aizo leaned his weight on Eos and Maxima both as he stood back up and combed the sides of his head, where he still had hair, with his fingers. "I just lost my balance, no need to argue...*hmmph siblings*," he chided.

Maxima urged him, "Let's stop and tend to your leg."

"No, we are too close. After we get the map...I need to know where the map is leading us." He trudged on, recklessly fueled by the idea of returning home.

Minutes later, they came upon a crumbled gate of sorts. In its glory, it must have been more than one-hundred feet high. Now, most of the structure was falling to pieces and submerged under the swamp-water and vines. Enough of the sand-colored stone remained for Eos to recognize that he was passing through the missing door of an arched passageway.

Eos and Maxima stared at the ruined city they had entered. Moss covered domed structures with keyhole windows, arched bridges, and protruding balconies filled the pass between mountain walls. They were missing substantial portions of walls, or sunken at a tilt so that their long balconies were more like spires, and all of it was engraved with ancient curling symbols or patterned with cobbled sandstone. They could only see what wasn't entirely consumed by vines. Eos could only guess they were walking over a small percentage of a once-great city.

Aizo led them through keyhole tunnels, over piles of ruins, and across vine paths that rose above the water level. It was all Eos and Maxima could do to keep up while spinning in circles to take in the abandoned civilization around them.

"Aizo, what is this?" Maxima asked in a whisper.

The hobble-and-limp pace that Aizo moved with, ceased.

"Something you should know about Hyperboreans is that they keep excellent history. There is modern history, and there is ancient history. But," his voice rose to a wily tone, "there is also missing history, eh? This place is forgotten by the civilized world. Missing from books and scrolls. Forgotten in historians' lore. Before the ancient history, I reckon."

There was a long pause as Aizo breathed heavy, labored breaths.

"Talus…and Ramath…and I…we discovered it. Nothing about it in any libraries. It doesn't exist in books or scrolls. 'Course no one comes this deep into the Sepeleo."

"Why is that?" Eos asked.

"The corcinths, of course," Aizo said no more and limped on.

Not long after, they came upon a great chunk of wall that leaned above the waters, covered with intricate engravings of a six-pointed star with horned lion-like creatures at each vertex. In the center was an ornate sun icon with a crack at the center. Dark carvings flooded into it…or from it. Eos couldn't make it out well enough. Time had worn off much of the wall. Below the sun, was a crescent moon that seemed to hold the same dark engravings in its concave form.

CHAPTER ONE

Aizo stood still and huffed wildly. The prospects of the map and the pain in his calf were the only thoughts his brain could process.

"We're here," he said and walked behind the wall.

The siblings followed, somehow struggling to keep up with the injured man. He passed through an arch in the wall of the mountain itself. They entered a chamber that was ankle-deep in stagnant water. The darkness in the room was held at bay by an emerald glow that hung in the air. The source was a circular exit hole a quarter-mile down.

Aizo lit the small circular chamber with an orange Soul Sphere. Each of them stood on the platform in the center of the water-filled room. "It's here." Aizo held his light over a wooden chest. The orange energy swirled above it, casting shadows that danced with his anticipating heartbeat.

Maxima opened it and pulled out a rolled scroll of parchment tied by a thin string. She spread it on the raised area near the chest.

"This is a bag of currency," Aizo produced a bag of coins that clinked as he set it down. He showed the siblings the coinage of Hyperborea's Corland. "Bronze Jital." He revealed a small bronze piece with a cross punched out of the center. "Silver Dirhem." He displayed a large silver piece with an elsu decorating one side. Eos recognized the bird of the Anite kingdom; it was the same form his Soul Energy manifested as. More than that—he knew it as the same coin his father had left with him. He had lost in sands of the North American Sector desert back on Earth. He was tempted to ask for it and hold it, but the urge subsided. He would meet his father in person soon.

"Most valuable of all, the Gold Sol. We have more than enough to feed ourselves on the way back to Anondorn." He dropped a brilliant coin bearing the symbol of Hyperborea between feather wings into the bag. All the coins had detailed minting and warranted a better look, but Aizo quickly tied the bag to his waist and switched focus. He smoothed the paper Maxima had spread out. "And this is a Wielder's Map. The maker created it to show us our path. A truly rare skill to find." He let the energy from his hand fall to the map. His Soul Energy stained it like ink.

Eos watched as the lines on the paper glowed orange with Aizo's expertise. The triangular peaks, shaded carefully to resemble mountains, started to glow first. The mountains came from the western sea and nearly divided the top third of the continent entirely, save for a small gap near the middle of Corland. The landmass as a whole ran further north and south than it did east and west.

The ink didn't merely stop with the glow. This was a wielder's map. The black turned orange and then rose from the paper. The mountains became three-dimensional holograms of Soul Energy that depicted the world. Amidst the blossoming map was a line more vibrant than anything else.

Aizo traced it with his fingertip. "This is the path Talus has left to us." A tear left the corner of his eye, and he cried out a Hyperborean expression, "By the Great Soul. There's hope still." The thick finger that followed Talus' map north guided Eos' eyes until it rested on the city of. Anondorn.

Aizo choked out words, "That is the Anite Kingdom's capital. It still stands. If nothing has happened to Talus since he left this map, then there is still hope for Hyperborea." He rolled the map back up. "Follow me. I want you to see this."

They exited the other end of the chamber.

CHAPTER ONE

Eos had to shield his eyes from an emerald glow as he left the dark room. He stepped onto a balcony that protruded from the mountain face, overlooking a grand lake. The lake shone with a living pulse that refracted in the rolling fog above it. It looked as if a million living organisms were communicating under the water with nothing but jeweled light, and the mist above was recording the messages.

Maxima was awed yet again. She put her hand on the railing of a staircase that seemed to lead infinitely down to the lake. "A Sacrum Crypt!" she cried out. "This is the source of the emerald pools we passed before. Oh Aizo, can we please go down?"

Aizo's eyelids spread open until the whites of his eye were exposed, but not in admiration. He backed away slowly and retreated into the shadows of the map chamber. A slow nod of his chin pointed the Bellator siblings to the disturbance. At the mountain crest, on the opposite side of the lake, the fog shimmered, but this light was blue. As the mist drifted, it momentarily revealed a lion creature. It was bigger than a lion on Earth, with muscular shoulders the size of a man's head and a majestic mane that shimmered a dull blue. Most distinct of all was the pair of curled horns that turned up from its head.

Eos struggled to swallow at the powerful sight. "Crypt Keepers..."

The gray horns shone blue for a second as if threatening, and the trio withdrew from the balcony. As they made their way for the entrance of the ruined city, Aizo explained, "Those are the corinths. Remember, I told you that there were a few rare creatures that could interact with Soul Energy? Corinths are that class of animal. Males' horns can harness Soul Energy when threatened."

NEW WORLD PRECIPICE

Eos summoned platforms of crimson energy beneath his feet. "Then, let's not give them time to feel threatened."

Aizo shook his head. "Females calm the males by negating Soul Energy. They've caused nasty falls to those Soul Stepping through the mountains...not to mention it attracts them. They don't wander too far north from the lake, and we're headed north. Best to make our way by foot."

Eos released his Soul Energy and settled onto the vines.

They moved quickly out of the mountain pass. Eos turned and looked one last time at the ancient structure from the lost period of Hyperborean history. The gates of the sunken city fell beneath the water's surface; the vines gripped at the remaining structures and held the city's secrets under the surface.

Aizo refused to stop traveling until they were an hour northeast of the Sacrum Crypt. For the first time in a long while, Eos' mind had the freedom to wander...and to recount the events that happened over the past few days. The Sepeleo mountains broke from the ocean, and Hyperborea became more familiar as Aizo had mentioned; beautiful, but mundane compared to the fantastic emerald pools. Green ridges rolled from the ground into spine-like crags covered in vibrant moss and trees.

Eos kept losing sight of the beauty around him. His thoughts cut to the battle they had fought against the ominous group calling themselves the Mitad. His struggle with Ares had been an epic test of his newly evolved wielding ability, and Ares had demonstrated a level of danger that was unlike anything he had ever experienced. The beastly form of energy the Soul Chain had transformed into haunted the back of his consciousness.

It was strange. Eos had all these things to ponder, and yet his mind didn't focus on the fearsome might of Ares that he would

CHAPTER ONE

likely face again nor the fact that they shared the same curse mark—he had asked Aizo about it while they slowly made their way. Aizo claimed to have no more insight than Eos, but the identical mark worried him. The pattern that covered Eos' entire arm was also on a Mitad member, his half-brother no less.

They hiked in quiet. The three took longer routes to avoid steep inclines for Aizo's sake, but now they had no other way. They came to the end of a valley where an uphill of loose rock was their only option. Aizo put an arm around each of the siblings, managing to hobble up the slope. Maxima tested her footing with each step, dragging behind Eos, who dug his feet into the ground and charged ahead.

General Braxton filled Eos' mind as they went. Not the Mitad, or Ares, or his curse mark—it was Braxton. The man he hated more than anyone, the man who treated Eos and Maxima as slaves and bargaining chips, the man who was the dictator of the North American Sector, had been reduced to weakness and uncertainty, bleeding to death on the snow by Dr. Kurt Fleischer. Eos was certain General Braxton had deserved it, but somehow, he got little satisfaction from the knowledge that he had died with fear in his eyes. It only made him recall the soldier he had destroyed during the rescue mission with Colonel Kane. It reminded him of Major Clark and the price that had been paid to obtain information about Hyperborea. He had come to peace with all of these high prices, recognizing them as tragedies he couldn't undo, but everything had consequences now. As enormous mountain peaks and walls of rocks dwarfed him, he couldn't help but feel the stakes had risen significantly. No one was safe in this new life journey he was on.

They made it around the crag of rock that had been in their way and began their descent down the other side. The journey down was no easier than it had been to climb up with the weight of supporting Aizo and three different paces traveling down the loose rock.

They reached level ground again and continued towards Anondorn.

Eos wondered if being on Hyperborea offered safety or meant the stakes would be even higher now. He shook his head, pushed out the thoughts, and focused on being grateful. He was with his sister again. After months of fighting for freedom, they were reunited.

Eos smiled and threw an arm around his little sister.

"Hey, hey, what's this?" Maxima teased. "Has finding Hyperborea gotten rid of your moodiness?" She gave him a playful jab to the ribs.

Eos smirked. "We've only been here for half a day. I'll find something to brood about soon."

Maxima hugged him back. "You better not. You got what you wanted. We're going to meet Mom and Dad! Besides, you'll never have anything over Ares when it comes to brooding."

Eos went rigid and grew quiet at the mention of Ares.

Then he said, "I suppose he has something to be angry about now that he lost both Mellizo glyphs and us."

Maxima nodded, "I'm not sure what to make of him. He's clearly unforgivable...but something about him makes me think he's not all bad. Maybe just troubled...like he—"

"Maxima, that's enough. He's as bad as they get. The Mitad is the furthest from good that I've ever felt." He had goosebumps just thinking about the spear-wielding Mitad officer, Tessio, and what he had done to Major Clark.

CHAPTER ONE

Maxima nodded and pulled her shawl up to her lips and bit it. She once would have conceded completely, but she hesitantly countered. "I...I know he took me away, but he took me away *from Braxton*. He taught me Soul Step. He's bad, but there's something more to him."

"No." Eos was resolute. "He's the reason we were separated from our homeland for twelve years."

Eos had had enough talk about their half-brother. They didn't have an opportunity to discuss it further.

"*Agghh*." Aizo cried out weakly and crumpled to the ground.

Immediately, Eos was at his side. Maxima went straight to his injured leg and saw the bandages were soaked through.

"After everything I've been through, I'm afraid...I won't make it because of my leg." Aizo stared blankly at the sky.

"Is there anything we can do?" Maxima asked.

"No. If only we had made it to Anondorn. The Sanofem, revered healing woman, would have been able to save my leg."

"Let me at least rewrap it," Maxima said as she inspected the soaked rags around his calf.

"And there has to be something around to help get you to these healer women," Eos added.

A gentle head nod showed Aizo's agreement. "Go to the rocks and find a red moss if you can. We'll use it to pack the wound and numb it."

Eos sprinted off.

Maxima undressed the injury. "These Sano—whatever you called them..."

"Sanofem," Aizo returned with a weak voice.

"What do they do to mend wounds?"

NEW WORLD PRECIPICE

"They…use Soul Energy. To wash…to purge…to restore tissue…accelerate healing."

Suddenly, images of Eos at the floor of the generator back on Earth came to Maxima. She hadn't been helpless then, and she wouldn't be now. Eos had leapt great distances ahead of her at Soul Wielding. She wouldn't let herself fall behind in usefulness. She closed her eyes, exhaled softly, and held her palms out.

Sapphire light emitted from her hands, and her Soul Energy drifted down around Aizo's calf.

A cooling numb sensation took over his leg.

When Eos had fallen, it had been different; he had overexerted himself, but she had to try something for Aizo's leg…she hoped it would work. Maxima enveloped his injury and began creating a tide of energy as more sifted down from her hands.

Aizo's glazed eyes sharpened. "Incredible…" he murmured, and blue energy swirled around his lower leg and shone brightly. The pain eased considerably.

Eos found a single patch rust-colored moss growing in a crevasse of stone. He extracted it carefully into his cupped hands and returned to find Aizo propped up on his elbows, looking across his body at Maxima.

"That wasn't the technique of the Sanofem, that was something …different, and yet similar. I'll have to take you to the healers when we arrive. They'll be very interested in you. Mmmhh, very interested." He then noticed Eos and took the moss into his own hands. He put a bit in his mouth and pursed his lips. "Metallic and bitter. This is the right one."

He packed it into his wound and had Maxima rewrap it with fresh strips of cloth.

CHAPTER ONE

The sun was falling low now. A fog was sliding in as Maxima and Eos helped Aizo to stand with an arm around each sibling. He hopped on his good leg, then tenderly put weight on his injured one. It held for the most part. "It'll be slower going now." He grunted and nodded them on.

Neither sibling moved.

He eyed his footing carefully and grunted again as he took a limping step with his arms still around Eos and Maxima. They didn't come with him.

He looked back and followed their locked eyes.

A corcinth stood majestically at the cliff. It looked down at them with a marred face. Its horn was broken off on one side. Its dull blue mane was missing a large patch that instead had a scar. This scar left him without fur across much of its muscular gray torso. There was no pupil to its eye on that side. This corcinth had been gravely wounded.

The gray and blue, oversized lion-creature stepped through the mist to the very edge of the mountainside. The silvery veil of fog parted as its heavy paw crossed it. Dozens of blue gleams came from within the haze, and an entire pride of corcinth emerged behind their injured leader.

Aizo let out a shocked gasp.

A leader of one of the most fearsome wielding beasts had been seriously injured. Now they were on the move and too far away from the Sacrum Crypt. Aizo had known them to venture south into the Corleon nation. There were tales of a time when they roamed the Monte territory as well, but the mountains thinned out this far north of the Sacrum Crypt. The corcinth never left their mountains.

NEW WORLD PRECIPICE

"Something," Aizo struggled to swallow, "…has gone poorly. Whatever did that to the corcinth—we should be very afraid of." His tone was drastic and full of untamable fear.

The scarred beast made a pulsing beacon out of its single horn that was far brighter than all the other members of the pride. It slowly lifted its mighty paws, strode back, and turned away. The majestic beast disappeared with the low swing of the blue fur at the end of its gray tail.

CHAPTER TWO

STRAY APART

Morning light broke through a stone framed window of castle Alasedis. A burly, six-foot-tall man looked out at the sunrise in copper-trimmed leather boots that belonged to someone with a giant's proportions. At the far end of the room, a woman's shadow sprawled back against the wall from the chair she sat in, imposing over the area.

Talus had managed to finish his council meeting early. He looked left at his wife, Terrava, who sat with concern etched in her face. The stiff black collar of her dress tightened around her neck, giving her a further stiffness.

"Accept it, Talus, Ramath hasn't contacted us in a year," she said with a flip of her hand over the arm of her chair. Her dark blue sleeve guided Talus' eyes. He followed the motion and took in the striking looks of Terrava. Her jet-black hair fell on silver woven patterns on the shoulders of her dress, which opened up in a triangle of skin on her center chest. His gaze held there for a shorter time than it used to, and he followed a long blue stripe down her midsection in pointed pieces of fabric.

Talus turned his head away from his Queen and looked over his right shoulder and out the window.

"He would never betray me. We grew up together...trained, conquered, and kept peace together!"

Terrava countered, "And you grew apart as well. He is a member of the Mitad now."

"He's *our only* source on the inside."

Terrava adjusted the silver circlet on her head that held a single anima stone at its center. "Yes, *if* he's still *our source.*"

Talus focused on the gem amongst silver leaves and dark hair but whipped his attention back to the window. After some time, he decided, "Something must be preventing him from reporting."

"That something is likely his loyalty."

Talus looked at Terrava, then at the billowing clouds as the wind whistled against the stones of the window sill. He turned left to his wife and then right again, stroking his auburn beard that separated into three heavy braided strands. Gold hexagonal ties clamped the strands, and all three met at a thicker link near his clavicle. The beard fell over a breastplate of silver, crested with a golden elsu: the swift bird of the Anite Kingdom.

It had been a year. That much was true.

Right. Left.

Right. Left.

He settled down and leaned on the sill and looked out at the clear day.

CHAPTER TWO

"You've grown so cold and distrusting, my dear. I will give Ramath more time."

Terrava's face fell more stoic. "Has the world given me a reason to be anything otherwise? I'll obey my King's wishes, but we cannot afford to be soft. The conclave will wait no more than another month. Then we must act accordingly."

A grunt was Talus' return. It was fair, and he could ask no more. "If I had only stopped it. If I had been there." He paused as he went back in time. "When they took you. I'd like to think you wouldn't be so cold."

"We've been over this," Terrava sighed. "There is nothing more that could have been done. You rescued me. I'm forever grateful that I came back alive in your arms. It's pointless to dwell on what's done. We can only plan for what's next."

"I'd like to think you still believe," Talus said.

"In?"

"People, goodness...them."

"*Let this go,* Talus," she said bluntly. There was a commanding and powerful edge in her voice.

Talus rolled his neck against the fur that padded the collar of his uniform and popped his knuckles. "No. I feel them out there from time to time, on days like today. They're alive."

"I scream inside every day about what horrors befell them on Earth." Terrava's thin hands shook on the armrests of her seat. "But after twelve years they aren't coming back. Invest in the future. You're dwelling back then. The world has moved on from our happy days. Ares is our only living child—even if he isn't your blood, and even though he stabbed us in the heart."

The white puffs of cloud broke as a noble bird soared toward the castle. It declared its arrival with a loud cry. Talus' messenger elsu had arrived. It dove in at nearly a hundred miles an hour until it beat its wings to brake. It was a creature that even the fastest Soul Step couldn't match.

"It seems Hariban Brasidas' report has arrived. I'll let you know what his scouts have found about the Mitad's movements when I see you tonight in our meeting with Hariban Goridas." His mind went over the current missions of all his haribans, the highest-ranking leaders in the Anite military, as he took his leave of Queen Terrava.

Talus sat at the work desk in his personal quarters. He brushed two massive fingers against the elsu messenger, and it purred as he petted its gold-tipped feathers. The white bird lifted its leg for Talus to remove the scroll.

"What have you brought for me, Hermios?" He removed the parchment, unrolled it, and set weights on the corners. The words it contained were a collection of meaningless rambling about the sights Hariban Brasidas was taking in during his mission. *The mountains seemed greener than the years before; however, there was less wildlife. The village population had grown at twice the rate…*

There was no point in reading the front. He drew a drop of golden-red Soul Energy to his fingertip and let it fall onto the scroll. The ink glowed momentarily with a foreign Soul Energy but recognized the intended reader. The ink began to bleed as if water had spilled over the precious scouting report. With a golden finger stroke, he spelled out the password: *ASHVA*. The ink drew back into legible shapes and revealed the true message.

Shaking his head, Talus continued to pet Hermios as he read. "No good, my friend. No good. Krogs are advancing in the mountain ranges. A Mitad mirza has been spotted further north than usual. What am I to do?" He furrowed his brow. The Mitad

CHAPTER TWO

officer ranks for wielders were: viziers the lowest officer position, mirzas above them, and emirs below only Vistomus and Saida. Which of them held more power, he couldn't tell. A mirza testing territory…he could just keep a careful eye on him for now…so long as an Emir wasn't with him giving the command.

Talus rolled up the scroll and tapped it against the table. His dutiful woes were a mere distraction from his personal ones at the moment.

"They're alive, Hermios. I can feel it, can't you?"

Hermios rustled its clean feathers in a flutter of soft golden blurs. It nuzzled against Talus' fingers repeatedly.

"I haven't forgotten your reward." He produced a handful of seeds and scattered them on the table. Hermios pecked away at the feast. "I just wish she'd believe too. I still admire her skills as a wielder and her beauty…that has not changed. I fear the Terrava I loved lost a part of herself when she was taken away. The rest was ripped apart when Ares…I'm sure you're tired of hearing the same babbling, Hermios."

Talus spilled his Soul Energy into the well of ink. He picked up a quill and began on a new piece of parchment:

Old Friend,

Your silence worries the conclave. I still hold belief in the value of your position, but the others need reassurance of your loyalty. Any response would appease them.

Hoping you're in good health,

Talus

STRAY APART

He sealed the words with the letters *VIRLARBO* spelled in Soul Energy and tied the letter to Hermios' leg as the sentences scrambled into a message about famine in a neighboring village.

"Thanks for listening, my little friend. I know I'll see them again, whether in this life or the next." Hermios dropped a seed at the edge of the table near Talus. "You know I don't have a penchant for those seeds like you."

Hermios did not break the stare but only nodded toward his offering.

Talus chuckled and swallowed the gift.

Soon a golden streak painted the sky and he was left alone in his office.

∞   ∞   ∞

An orange moon hung low in the sky over the desert remains of the old civilization that was once the United States. The moon distilled an amber color over a short piece of raised highway. The structure stood on concrete beams that were disappearing into sand and rubble below, and the ends of the segment of road drooped down in sagging vines of rebar and concrete debris.

Ares ascended through the heavy orange night and climbed on platforms of his Soul Energy that he created beneath his feet. He stomped slowly upwards while Tessio followed behind him quietly. As they neared the lip of the highway, Tessio caught Ares' eyes. Ares gave him a brotherly nod that urged himself to proceed just as much as Tessio.

The feeling of failure percolated in Ares' skull. The two men knelt humbly before Lord Vistomus Fulmen on the raised table of the old world. He chose this highway turned monument to the past as a ceremonial location. Here he carried out promotions, delivered orders, organized plans with his Soul Wielder officers, and carried out punishments for failures.

"Rise, Ares." Lord Vistomus ordered in a dangerously persuasive voice, and Ares stood. Lord Vistomus' bald head reflected the eerie moonlight as if he was magnetizing the night's attention to him. "Your failure is beyond measure. Not only are our chances of swaying the Bellator children diminished, but they'll soon be under the influence of their father. The glyphs too." Lord Vistomus spoke of his losses with no anxiety. His words held a perfect calm as he drank from a teacup. He created a platform of blinding white Soul Energy. It seared Ares and Tessio's eyes with its violent apparition.

Lord Vistomus set the cup on the floating platform and loomed over Ares.

Ares tensed his jaw and bore his chastisement.

"Worse still, Bellia is injured, the weapons are trapped here on Earth, and our campaign on Hyperborea is halted—"

"You think I wanted this outcome?" Ares asked through pursed lips.

A deep pressure surrounded him. Lord Vistomus looked Ares over with his garnet eyes. He held back very little presence of his Soul Energy. The energy saturated the platform, and it took effort for Ares to breathe in the thick air. He tried to speak again, but the bald man did not let him.

"The only possible benefit of this whole event is that General Braxton is dead. With him out of the way, the North American Sector will be frantic." Then Lord Vistomus' voice went ghostly as if a spirit was speaking through him, "Your lack of results leaves me questioning you...you, my son born from darkness—bred to bring war and destruction. Yet, now I am unsure of you."

It was as if another person was speaking to him. Ares couldn't keep silent, "My devotion to the cause is not in question here. I am loyal to the Mitad; loyal to you. We were simply not prepared for Aizo. He was stronger, smarter than you described. And Eos had somehow learned partial Severance. To question my loyalty is—"

The wide nose of Lord Vistomus flared, and his pencil-thin lips disappeared to show teeth that were dulled to a blackish hue. A crackling sound rumbled amid the soul-dense air. "I did not permit your tongue to wag! It's not your loyalty in question. It's your effectiveness."

The poison bubbled in Ares again. It burned at his chest and brain so that he could not think straight. "I should have retrieved the glyphs and defeated Aizo myself. There'll be no more mistakes. I will protect Bellia next time! This, I swear."

Kadadoom!

The crackling solidified as a bolt of branching white lightning tumbled from the air. It found its path to the ground through Ares and struck him where his trapezius attached to his neck.

His knees buckled, but Ares didn't let his feet fail. To do that would be admitting his unworthiness of his Mitad rank of mirza. It hurt...he was sure it hurt, but the pain of his failure was greater. Only the smell of cooked flesh confirmed the wound even existed. It was only a mild punishment from his master. Ares knew it was the slightest display of the man's wielding power.

"I see your attachment to her. Don't think you can hide anything from me. *I know.* This relationship will only breed weakness, *and you are useless to me weak*," Lord Vistomus said in an unwavering tone. "I wish to discuss your waning use no more. I

CHAPTER TWO

know you won't let me down again, Ares. I trained you too well for anything else."

Ares knelt once more and bowed his head. "I will not fail you." He started to leave, but Lord Vistomus stopped him. "No, I want you to witness unwavering dedication. To learn from your subordinate how to achieve results. Watch."

Tessio was still prostrate with his fist on the ground. The x tattooed above each knuckle and the rings of ink tattooed on every finger pressed into the crumbled asphalt.

"Tessio, when I brought you into the fold, you were a criminal, a slave laborer, but I have not seen such promise since young Ares."

"Thank you, Lord Vistomus. I only carry out your orders."

Lord Vistomus returned to his floating teacup and took a drink with a murmur of relief as he swallowed the liquid. "You slew a witness during our arms deal without hesitation. You fought beyond reasonable expectations against one of the greatest wielders of our age, Aizo. You did so while Ares, your mirza, pursued his emotional desires in battle rather than fulfilling his duty. These show me you rise above the other vizier. Perhaps, you have the making of a mirza. There is one empty seat, but still…you were part of the failed plan to retrieve the glyphs, and you failed against Aizo in the end. I need proof of your conviction. I need to see you won't be driven by emotion like Ares."

With impassioned eyes, Tessio clasped his right forearm before Lord Vistomus. "My skin is a testament to my identity. I am Mitad. I know no other life. I have killed the old ways." He pulled down his sleeve to reveal a tattoo of a dagger piercing into a cracked gemstone. "I killed my faith in anything else."

STRAY APART

"And you chose wisely in doing so. I know you are a valuable member of the Mitad, but I need to witness your resolve to lead." Lord Vistomus turned. A violent, pulsing white stairway of Soul Energy formed. It led up to the drooping end of the platform from the sand below. "Niall, bring him here." He called down to the bottom of his Soul Energy stairs.

A gaunt, crooked faced man climbed the stairs with overly particular steps, dragging a bound prisoner behind him. He spoke with a heavy rasp that was lined with a hard to place European accent. "Yur prisoner, Lord Vistomus."

Ares looked the prisoner over. Instantly he knew what was to be done. The bound victim's face looked much like Tessio's: as if it had been whittled from a block of wood too hastily. Their wavy hair was the same straw-like color.

Tessio did not move, did not speak, did not flinch, but his pupils dilated like chasms opening during an earthquake. The vein on his neck pulsed frantically.

The teacup was once again placed on a white platform in midair as the staircase disappeared. Lord Vistomus knelt to the prisoner and tilted his chin up so that he was forced to look the leader in the eyes. He clicked his mouth chidingly at the exhausted man and untied a filthy rag that pulled between his teeth. The man huffed and gasped heavily.

Niall then raised his left hand, which had been carrying a bat-winged spear—Tessio's spear.

"The weapon you wur requesting," Niall said and set the spear before the prisoner and Lord Vistomus. Tessio's skin rippled, and the tattoos on his hands twitched and tightened.

"This man was found in Segite, leading a southern resistance group on Hyperborea. He is a traitor to his race, and his disposal

CHAPTER TWO

will be a final amputation to his brand of dissent in Segite. Though this can't surprise you, Tessio."

Orange light bathed the ceremonial platform that had just become an execution altar.

"Show me you can lead in the face of tribulation," Lord Vistomus urged. His voice was so calm and powerful that it propelled Tessio forward. "Rid the Mitad of your brother."

Tessio claimed his spear. It was cold and strangely like a toy in his hands now. He turned the blade over in his hands, first reflecting his sharp features in the moonlight, then as he turned it, it showed him his brother, Cleon's, similar skin.

Ares found himself contemplating the situation. Tessio's brother was a traitor and an enemy…it should have been an easy decision. He had nearly done the same to Eos before Bellia stopped him, but would he have actually done it? He would have delivered pain and torment without hesitation. Would he have destroyed him entirely, though?

Tessio thought there was another possibility. A shimmer of hope was on his face as if he could ask his brother to join.

If Cleon had caught the faint sentiment, he quickly crushed it. "I…fought for freedom," he said with resolve. "I fought to free Corland of you, brother. For the Great Soul!"

Swoosh. Tessio's winged spear sliced the air as he whirled it into a striking pose from a distance.

The slight edge of humanity that Ares had sensed was gone. There was only calculated murderous intent about Tessio.

Clouds passed over the moon, and the orange-tinged night became colorless.

There came the soft blue glow of Tessio's spear as he poured his Soul Energy into it.

STRAY APART

Ares' feet shifted back.

Tessio whispered in the silence, "Then you chose your side poorly."

Ares didn't hear much else of what Lord Vistomus said on the platform. There was the sound of the spear piercing flesh like a wet cloth violently thrown against a wall. His mind became unfocused on the present. Instead, he saw Eos. He saw his failure to retrieve the glyphs replaying before him. It burned his lungs to breathe the night's ruined air.

"You will be a mirza of the Mitad, Tessio. You will serve the Master well," Lord Vistomus said.

The next thing Ares could recall, he was Soul Stepping down from the platform alongside Tessio, who now held the same rank as him; Tessio the mirza alongside him; Tessio whom he had once initiated into the Mitad—whom he had promoted to vizier.

When they set foot on the sand, Tessio cupped Ares' shoulders and pulled him into a maddened stare. "We will rise together. The loss of the glyphs will soon be forgotten by our new victories *together.*"

Ares knocked Tessio's hands off of his shoulders and whipped away angrily. Failure ate at him from the inside and soured his stomach as he returned to the desert-buried world of the past that had become the Mitad's network of underground bases in the North American Sector. He passed through halls that had once belonged to someone lavish and extravagant. This time there was only himself to blame, but Eos had played a part. Remembering his childhood suffering, his imprisonment, brought only more poison forth until Ares was brewing wretched pain in his chest.

The self-punishing trance was broken for an instant by a Renaissance era painting on the wall of the corridor. Inside a

CHAPTER TWO

golden frame, an exhausted-looking woman reached for a bowl of water with a ladle. A nurse held a sleeping child at the foot of the bed and a nobleman observed the scene carefully. Ares tore at the gaudy thing and heaved the frame from its mounting. His pale right hand punctured the canvas, leaving drops of blood from his palm over the scene.

He flung it into the wall.

Then he composed himself.

This would not stand! He had to redeem himself and find a way. He paced into Bellia's resting room and looked down at her as she woke from her sleep.

The bandages around her chest were stained, and she winced while turning her head. She gazed upon the handsome figure above her. His long black locks of hair suited him, she thought.

"I'll have those bandages changed immediately, Bellia."

"Thank you," she whispered.

Ares was always so sure...so steady, yet before an injured woman, he had to search for words. None could communicate his thoughts, but he had to try.

"I...I never meant for this, Bellia. I should have protected you."

"No," she said, "What more could you have done with such skilled opponents all around us. I'm just glad I could stop you before you lost control."

Ares' eyes darted about the room. He exhaled through his nose.

"It'll consume you. You know that," she said selflessly from her bed.

"It'll consume me whether I use the Mark or not...eventually."

STRAY APART

Bellia sighed with another wince, "But do you want to become like the Voro? Do you want to lose yourself for power? Is it worth it? I don't want to see you lost like that. You'll just have to learn to open the next gate on your own. I know you can do it, Ares."

Her reassurance was of little comfort to him.

He kneeled at her bedside.

Bellia brushed his black hair with the back of her hand. The pain of raising her arm was worth the comfort the gesture brought. She gasped, "What happened to your neck? It's burned. Can you smell that? It's fresh." She looked over the damaged skin. It would scar all the way up to his ear.

Ares looked away.

"A punishment for my failures. *There will be no more.* Lord Vistomus sees you as my weakness." His voice cracked. "I can't afford to be weak to him." Ares moved his mouth to speak the rest of the words, but the right ones wouldn't come. "Until I'm in better standings, we can't…" He couldn't finish the sentence while looking at the results of his failure.

Bellia's slender eyebrows drew together with a different kind of pain.

She watched the tortured soul stumble out of the room and leave her alone. She rested her hand protectively over her belly, and lost herself to the pain of her wound. Soon she was unconscious again.

CHAPTER THREE

FEAR UNDER THE STARS

The stars on Hyperborea were no different than those of Earth. They displayed a humbling vastness that made Eos feel small amidst the infinite space. He curled into a ball on the cool mountain floor where they had decided to rest for the night. The air had a chill to it, but it was not terribly cold, and they still had their winter clothes from Earth.

Eos struggled to fall asleep and instead toyed with the Mellizo Glyph. He held it up to the stars and turned it over, inspecting it for nothing in particular. There was a faint tingle in his arms like the glyph had magnetized his Soul Energy. It felt reassuring. The sensation eased his mind until his eyelids became heavy.

He put the Mellizo Glyph away.

The moment he did, a heaviness filled the air.

FEAR UNDER THE STARS

There was a ringing in his ears. Something was off about the night, and it hid behind the sweet dew filled mountain smell, making Eos shiver in his coat. He turned over to see Maxima and Aizo asleep.

Then he heard a noise.

Tatttaa Tattta Tatt Tatt.

Tatttaa Tattta Tatt Tatt.

The sound, like sticks banging together to a rhythm, could be heard not far away.

The clacking returned. The sounds made Eos very still, and he tried to sink into the ground instinctively. There was something on the other side of the ridge.

Carefully, as not to wake Aizo or Maxima until he was sure, he slipped away from their resting place. As quietly as he could, he crept to the nearby pass in the rocks. He breathed slowly with his heart beating in his chest so hard that he was sure anyone around the ridge could hear it.

Eos pressed himself against the cold stone at the edge of the pass.

Tatttaa Tattta Tatt Tatt.

Tatttaa Tattta Tatt Tatt.

The sound was louder now. He sucked in a deep breath, clenched his abdominals, and peaked around the rock corner.

He saw movements. Dark shapes wavered behind a boulder at the far end of the pass.

Chills ran down his back, and the sound of sticks clacking together grew louder.

Eos couldn't swallow his saliva. It was stuck along with the lump of fear in his throat, but he reminded himself: He was a powerful wielder; He had confronted Ares; He had opened the

CHAPTER THREE

first two gates of his soul and learned the technique called partial Severance. What could threaten him? Perhaps a corcinth, but the fearsome creatures surely didn't bang sticks together.

His breathing relaxed, and Eos took calculated, silent steps to the first set of boulders for cover.

He quickly jumped to the next set of rocks, then the next.

He was almost at the other end of the pass. Clacking sounds were growing so loud and frequent that they began to blend with their echo and travel through Eos' chest.

Tatttaa Tattta Tatt Tatt.

Crackle-booom.

A purple-red flash occurred on the other side of the concealment. It made a sound that Eos couldn't mistake. Soul Energy had been used briefly. The purple-red glow persisted slightly so that Eos' shadow hung in the afterglow. He peered around his cover enough to see the source of the now maddening clacking.

The night couldn't be dark enough to hide the horrible sight he saw.

Tens...no, there might have been over one hundred figures before him. All wore hideous mud masks that were held together with vines and leaves. Dark holes hid their eyes so that they looked like cavities in a humanoid shape.

Spiked sticks protruded from their masks, vines dangled from their face, and ragged clothing covered their semi-clothed bodies as they circled around a leader while striking spears together.

The masked man in the center held his hands above a small chunk of stone in a cult-like ritual.

FEAR UNDER THE STARS

A purple-red glow came from the stone at the center and bathed the circling tribe. They began stamping the end of their spears into the ground furiously.

Eos took it all in for a nightmarish second and whipped back around the corner into hiding.

A hand covered his mouth as he turned around.

He panicked and fell back, but the hand followed his fall and remained over his mouth.

Aizo crouched over him, supported by his uninjured leg with Maxima behind him. He removed his large hand from over Eos' face and whispered, "What did you see?"

"M…m…men in masks. With spears," he stammered back underneath the ceremonial noise.

Aizo's eyes were wide with disbelief.

"Monte barbarians," he mumbled to himself as if trying to understand. "What are they doing this far north? This is wrong. This is…quickly, how many were there?"

"Maybe a hundred. Maybe a…a…maybe a little less."

"Not good. That's too many. And a stone? Were they around a stone? What color was it? There are different tribes. Some are more violent than others. They fight over which stone to worship. *The color* is very important." Aizo urged with panic in his voice that made Eos lose confidence in their safety.

He shook as he responded hesitantly, "A kind of reddish color."

Aizo pressed back against the wall and slid down a few inches on his weak leg.

Maxima broke in, "Well, is that a peaceful tribe?"

CHAPTER THREE

A raised eyebrow preceded Aizo's response. "No. These are the most barbaric of the tribes. We must run. Too many for us, and in my state…" he hissed quietly.

The sound of spears stamping the ground grew all around them as if they were surrounded.

The three backed away, retreating from the mountain pass.

Tatttaa Tattta Tatt Tatt.

The sound was reverberating as if on top of them.

Eos looked up to see spears stamping the rocks in the direction of their retreat.

Dark, vacant holes for eyes stared them down through mud and vines. The spiked tips of the Monte barbarians' masks caught the reddish glow from behind them. There was a growl of bellowing words from the covered face, but they were undiscernible like the language came from deep in the barbarians' guts.

Aizo and the siblings backed away as the spears pointed at them.

"These barbarians should not be here. We will have to fight our way out, I'm afraid. Ready yourself—" but Aizo was cut short by arms wrapping around him.

Eos and Maxima watched as Aizo's weak leg collapsed, and he was drug into the circle of masked men. Then their arms were yanked behind them, and they too were led into the ring. Eos was shoved forward, his breathing tightened, and he felt as if he was watching it all happen from outside his body. He tried to think clearly as his shoulders bumped against the swarm of barbarians.

What should he do? How would they all get away?

He searched for Maxima through rags and vines and spears. She was being led to the center of the ring ahead of him. In front of her, Eos saw Aizo's limp leg being dragged. An orange trail of light glimmered on the dusty mountain floor behind the dragging leg.

Eos smiled. There was no need to panic. He closed his eyes, sucked in a confident breath, and began work on a Soul Sphere in his closed hand. He was thrown viciously into the center of the circle alongside Aizo and Maxima. The stamping spears stopped, and there was silence.

A barbarian held each of their arms behind their backs. Their knees were kicked from behind so that they fell into a kneel.

The deep, foreign language roared from the barbarian who led the ritual with the stone.

Aizo turned his head to Eos and Maxima but was struck by a spear for doing so. With his head down, he spoke lowly, "They don't understand our language. Give us a chance at getting out of this peacefully, but we'll soon be fighting them all, I think. I planted my Soul Energy in the dirt as I was being dragged. When I set it off, that is your signal to—" He was slammed in the head by a spear again.

The ritual leader ended his frantic yelling to the crowd. He turned and bent down to Aizo.

His mask had a mohawk of spikes protruding from it. They nearly pricked Aizo's face as he said in broken English, "Da Manus Gods huv give us sacrifice. Da animus stone is in favor." His stench filled, rotting breath made Aizo turn his head.

"Aizo, I don't think they're interested in letting us get out of this at all," Maxima said, worried.

The leader whirled his coat of vines to the center stone, an imperfect red rock was tinted with purple and sat on a raised table.

CHAPTER THREE

The leader chanted and produced the slightest amount of Soul Energy.

Eos felt reassured to see that the barbarian leader had almost no ability to wield. The energy was faint and trickled from his raised hands. The stone flickered brightly, amplified by it. Still, even if he was their only wielder, there were so many with spears.

Tatttaa Tattta Tatt Tatt.

The spears began again. This time more furiously.

Eos was yanked up first and thrown before the stone.

They tore his coat from his body and disrobed him before slamming his bare chest on the cold stone table.

"Aizo, *now* would be a good time," Eos urged. "A *very good* time." The leader produced a stone dagger and held it for the tribe to see. They clacked their spears together and cheered in blood-curdling cries.

Aizo drove his single strong leg into the ground and sprang up with a scream.

"TALUS BELLATOR!" he yelled so loud it was heard above the cries of bloodlust.

Silence.

The leader turned his mohawk of spikes upon Aizo and cocked his head.

"What dis name to you?" he questioned.

Aizo gave a fierce look. "We are protected by Talus Bellator. Return south to your territory."

Only heartbeats marked the silence of seconds.

"Gwhha haha," came a laugh from under the mask. He leaned in so close his spikes drew blood from Aizo's temple. "South der is worse dan him now." He raised his dagger above his head again, rallying his tribe into a frenzy.

FEAR UNDER THE STARS

Bwoooom!

An explosion of orange flashed in the crowd of bodies. Dozens of barbarians were thrown back by Aizo, releasing his buried energy from within the ground. They scattered momentarily, but it did not take them long to aim all their spears again at their captives.

Eos, Aizo, and Maxima stood back-to-back.

Aizo held fists full of dust and rock he had scooped up, and orange glowed in his palms. Maxima produced a sapphire Soul Sphere and skillfully pulled it apart so that she duplicated the weapon into her other hand in mere seconds. Eos bounded back from the rock where he was to be sacrificed and readied his Soul Sphere.

The three were back-to-back as spears came plunging toward them.

Aizo scattered his handfuls of debris out. The barbarians ran forward to kill but stepped on Aizo's trap. The minefield-like floor bloomed into a series of explosions that tossed the large men as if they weighed nothing.

Maxima threw one sphere in the opposite direction, stopping at least five more from advancing. Then she hurled the other at the figures charging towards Eos.

Eos was nearly ready with his sphere, but Aizo and Maxima's attacks had not held back the sheer number of barbarians. The first broke through at Aizo. He dodged to scoop up another handful of dirt, but his leg collapsed from under him and sent him tumbling.

Spears thrust at Maxima before she could produce another weapon. She stumbled back into Eos.

Aizo rolled in a panic. He was too weak to do it properly, but he had no choice. He cleared his mind and instantly opened another set of gates in his soul. The feeling of surging power that

CHAPTER THREE

should have been was dampened by his feeble state. He used his attack on the barbarians as he rolled on the ground to narrowly avoid being stabbed.

The air shimmered around Eos and Maxima. Orange static visibly emerged all around them. It crackled and jumped around in a vibrant storm of energy.

Bwoooom! Bwooom! Bw-bwooom!

The air became a field of mines that erupted around the attackers. Aizo's display of Severance dealt with half of the barbarians. Aizo cursed his circumstance. Had he not just escaped years of confinement, had he been at his peak combat ability, and not been in such an injured state—he would have wiped the entire tribe out in an instant. Years of confinement without the ability to hone his skills left him rusty. He could shield himself, but not Eos and Maxima as well.

Aizo slammed the ground angrily. He was exhausted, and his Soul Energy was depleted.

The barbarians were driven by illogical bloodlust after the captives. The remaining fifty or so men stepped over their tribesmen to advance on their victims.

There was nothing left for Aizo to do. He was unable to gather up enough energy for a quick attack.

Maxima was working another sphere to life, but she couldn't finish in time.

Eos, however, had been given the crucial seconds to complete his weapon. He wound back his blackened arm.

Crimson streaked the night.

Ten more barbarians were down.

The barrage of fearsome attacks gave them momentary pause, but there were still so many, and neither Eos, Maxima, nor Aizo could prepare another attack in time. Eos focused on creating another sphere as quickly as he could.

As the sphere formed, there was a shift in the night. The barbarians stopped.

The spears rose and pointed toward the captives. Fearful bellows chattered between them—their remaining numbers back-peddled.

Eos raised his cursed arm to the sky.

Crimson energy formed into a churning weapon that cast a pulsing light on him. His black hand was on display before them all. The dark markings crawled up his arm and whipped about like black flames under the red spotlight.

The barbarians began screaming incoherent words to each other.

Then they were fleeing, dragging their wounded away.

The leader grabbed their ritual stone and tore away from the mountain pass.

Just like that—they were gone, leaving Eos with a fully formed Soul Sphere held over his head.

He let it turn to wispy vapor and fall to the rocks at his feet.

Maxima didn't understand why the barbarians had fled. "Did they suddenly decide that they couldn't win?"

"We took out more than half of them. They realized that they couldn't have won," Eos said with certainty as he helped Aizo to his feet with Maxima.

Aizo gave a pained moan as he tried to walk properly. He corrected Eos, "I wouldn't have been able to stop another attack if they had tried. Maxima wasn't ready, nor was your Soul Sphere going to stop all of them. Maxima is right. They were scared of something. What makes me worry most is what their chief said:

CHAPTER THREE

There is someone worse than Talus in the south. If the map we have is accurate, I fear Talus may have a hold on the Anite Kingdom, but little else. There should be nothing they fear more than his name. Let's get back to our resting spot. We'll take turns keeping watch so that we can get what little sleep we're able."

Eos squinted back at where the reddish stone had been. "I'm not tired. I'll keep watch tonight," he said, reclaiming his coat and putting it over his shivering body. He watched his breath condense against the dark sky and thought.

He asked, "Why do they fear Talus?"

Aizo grunted, "There was a time, not so long ago, when the Monte Barbarians had tried to migrate into South Anite. They began raiding small towns and pillaging everything they could. Your father, myself, and Ramath made quick work of them. Sent them back into the mountains with fear in their eyes like you couldn't imagine. It was one of your father's first famed accomplishments that would lead to him becoming chosen for king. We were heroes of Anite after that...one could say we captured a bit of celebrity. The barbarians used to flee at the name or banner of Talus."

"Who's this Ramath you fought alongside?" asked Maxima.

Aizo smiled. The girl had a way of picking the finer points out of a story. "Our hostage and our brother. In the Winter Aisle of the mountain pass, is the Monte Kingdom. West of it, the Corleo Kingdom. Talus' father, King Bekrin Bellator, once had to push the Corleo military out of the Monte's territory when they got to be too power-hungry. The Corleo monarchy inherits the kingdom, unlike in Anite. King Bekrin took the only heir to the Corleo throne back with him and raised him alongside Talus as a son. Kept the Corleo right in line."

FEAR UNDER THE STARS

Maxima thought about Ramath's situation. "What a sad way to live…but effective."

They settled down into their rest spot.

"What about the stone the barbarians had? What was that?" Eos asked.

While he didn't have the careful analysis of Maxima, Eos' focus was surprising to Aizo. After an encounter like the one they had just had, he expected most people would ask about the barbarians that were about to use them as a human sacrifice. However, Eos had an obsession with knowledge of wielding and mysterious artifacts.

"There are two types of manus stones, which interact with Soul Energy, amgrite and condlucite. Amgrite stones amplify one's power briefly. If of high enough quality, it will appear much like a ruby and be called *animus* grade. Condlucite stones are glass-like and retain energy for long periods. The purest ones take on a blue color like a sapphire and are called *anima* grade. Most barbarian tribes of the Sepeleo mountain range worship the stones, a trait that stems from the Monte's ancient religion. These stone worshipers, like the ones we encountered, haven't evolved with their kinsmen in the mountain pass. They've remained primitive. The worst of them worship amgrite stones. The stone they had was borderline animus, which means they were a strong tribe that had defeated others to hold on to it—enough of this. Let's get some rest before tomorrow. We'll be crossing the Anite border in the morning."

No more was said of barbarian tribes, manus stones, hostage brothers, or anything else.

Eos sat watch through most of the night, kept awake by the wonders and dangers his first day in Hyperborea had brought. Aizo

CHAPTER THREE

relieved him of watch duty a few hours before light broke the next day.

Before the sun had broken over the horizon, the three were on their way.

An additional treatment from Maxima left Aizo strong enough to walk on his own.

Eos had a full night to let his thoughts simmer. "Aizo, the leader of the tribe last night...he was a Soul Wielder?"

Aizo became very serious. "No, he was not. Morax formed the Order of Soul Wielders; let's see..." he grumbled to himself. "Well, it's hard to translate time. There are two calendars on Hyperborea. Much more complicated star system...anyway, the texts say Morax brought about the Glyph Wielders...over 2,500 Earth years ago. Since the ancient history of Morax's time, the term Soul Wielder is used more loosely. Most would call someone like the barbarian leader simply *a wielder*. It is still generally accepted that you must train under an advanced teacher called an errant, or a master, called an inlume, and open at least the first gate yourself to be considered of the Order of Soul Wielders."

Eos tried to take in the information about two calendars and the origin of the Soul Wielders. "So...the barbarian wasn't trained...and isn't considered a Soul Wielder then?"

Aizo stopped. "It's so much more than that! You can ask anyone claiming to be a Soul Wielder who they trained under. I would answer Bekrin Bellator. You would answer Aizo Mudar of Anite. On Hyperborea, inlume masters are celebrated and famous."

"Then how many are there?" Maxima asked.

Aizo raised an eyebrow as they carried on their travels, leaving the Sepeleo mountains behind. "How many what? The clarification is important. On Corland, more than half of the population have their Essence completed, connecting their minds and souls. They can wield, mind you, but they aren't classically trained warriors nor *Soul Wielders*. Most use their small bit of skill to get by day to day in their trade; smithing stronger weapons and armor, heating water, lighting stones, and the like."

Eos cut in, "Well, then how many warriors are there?"

"If I had to guess, of all the kingdoms' armies put together…perhaps two hundred thousand can muster enough Soul Energy to light a manus stone sword or arrow. There are probably another thirty thousand who can make a Soul Sphere. Half of those can make a decent one. Those who can perform the first partial Severance number a couple hundred at best. They have studied under masters of the Soul Wielder Order or, in some cases, outside the Order. Most starry-eyed children can name the inlumes. Weren't more than thirty when I left. Their lineage is a subject studied more widely than arithmetic or history of Corland. Only the Great Soul knows what it's like now. I expect the Mitad has been training new warriors and slaying old masters who don't bend the knee to Saida and Vistomus."

The mystery and magical quality of it all had Eos like one of the starry-eyed children Aizo had mentioned. He was ready to learn of all the Soul Wielder inlumes and errants. Then a thought occurred to him. "Who trained Vistomus and Saida?"

Aizo did not answer for a while.

"Lunatics. Both of them. They spread rumors the original Soul Wielder Order trained them. Impossible to be trained by 2,500-year-old men, but it spreads fear in those who will succumb to it. No one knows. Perhaps they were trained by lesser-known and accounted for Krog masters. I… grow tired now. My injury pains me. Let's walk in quiet."

CHAPTER FOUR

AMBITIONS AND SCARS

They walked mostly silent for the better part of two days. Questions burned at the tips of Eos and Maxima's tongues, but Aizo was getting weaker. His face was pale, and he was too exhausted to Soul Step. Instead of traveling quickly, they frequently took breaks to rest and often aided Aizo in walking, but the weather beyond the mountains was kinder. The nipping remains of the Winter Aisle had melted into a mild climate. Two days went by before they were following a river toward a port town on the horizon.

"West Avem. If Anite has fared well, it will be largely unchanged." Aizo pressed on with no more wasted energy on words.

When they were close enough, a barrier wall of white rectangular buildings emerged. The chalk-colored structures had sloped walls and railings on every roof that turned the steep entrance of West Avem's bay into a bumpy milk-white marble reef with auburn trees protruding from all about.

When they were close enough to see the details of West Avem, Aizo stopped them.

"Maxima, I need fresh cloth," he said.

"If you wait a little longer, I'm sure we could get clean bandages in the city, right?" Maxima asked.

"They're not for me. They're for him." Aizo gestured at Eos.

"Me? What do I need them for?"

"To wrap up that hand. We don't want anyone seeing the curse mark on your arm. We need to attract as little attention from the masses as possible until we are in Anondorn."

Eos wrapped a strip of cloth over his blackened hand as he thought of the wall of wriggling ink that he had encountered in the Soul Void. He hid every last inch of his arm from sight.

Maxima frowned. "Aizo, the barbarians didn't speak the English language, did they?"

Their guardian shook his head in response. "They have kept isolated from surrounding cultures, and have kept their old words. I can see you are wondering how you'll communicate once in the city."

She nodded. "Right, will we be able to talk to anyone?"

Aizo stroked his chin beard. "Well, the writings from Morax's studies tell us that Earth and Hyperborea are intertwined in ways we can't fully understand. He called the language phenomenon *the relative common tongue*. Some interpret his writings that there is a common language that evolves similarly on both worlds. The spoken and written word is a very close approximation of English, but with local words and phrases being different. Other scholars, however, have interpreted the writings as the crossing of worlds creates a sort of translation between your language and the most common language you encounter. So that you may speak or write in your language, and we hear and read it in ours, and vice-versa. The result is the same either way. You'll need to learn words and phrases for things that don't exist on Earth, but you'll communicate everything else effectively."

"So, this Morax," Eos broke in. "I thought he founded the Soul Wielder Order. You're saying he also studied the two worlds."

"Morax transitioned the world out of the lost history and into the ancient. He initiated the study of a great many things besides wielding techniques."

With that, they walked to the city entrance.

"Guards are few out here on the west end of Anite. They watch the comings and goings of ships more than people. Keep quiet, and we should get through without any trouble." Aizo explained.

The three walked under an open portcullis and met a guard with more leather than metal protecting him. His spear lay against the wall, and in his hand, he held a quill.

"Welcome to West Avem. Names?" he inquired.

"Aizo Mudar."

The guard looked up from his parchment with hardened eyes. "I'm not as amused by that answer as you are. Clearly, you are not familiar with our city, but Aizo Mudar is a hero here who repelled the Monte barbarians. Now this time, answer with your names *and where you've traveled from*. I'll have no further mockery."

"Oh, I know a few things about repelling Monte barbarians," Aizo rattled to himself. "Worth a try." He sighed.

AMBITIONS AND SCARS

"Hardly…and *what are you wearing*?" Snorted the unamused guard as he cast his judgment over their earthly winter clothes. Eos was sure the man had never seen anything like them before.

Aizo appeased his suspicions. "We traded with foreigners for these. We'll be glad to get rid of them and find some proper robes in the city."

Fake names and a story of being travelers from the western coastal villages seeking trade got them through with little struggle. Soon, Eos and Maxima were waiting between chalk-colored buildings as Aizo used the bronze jital and silver dirhem coins to purchase food. They gorged themselves on a strange food called patine. Eos plopped a crispy, golden, grape-sized ball into his mouth. He was too hungry to worry about what it would taste like. The candied exterior cracked and burst in his mouth, much like a grape, revealing a mild flavor inside that Eos could only compare to the taste of almond. His and Maxima's hands were soon reaching into an empty cloth sack when Aizo came back carrying their new clothes. They changed in a back alley.

Eos held out his arms and examined the robe Aizo had brought. It was a light beige with a square curling pattern of jade trim. His sleeves were too long, but Aizo told him it hid his cursed arm well. He saw his sister was in the same light material, but hers was a dress with puffs of cloth on the shoulders and a gold pattern of swirls graced her upper body. They all put on leather boots. Eos found them considerably less comfortable than their Earth boots, but Aizo sighed as if they were made of clouds when he put them on.

They rounded a building, twisted through back alleys, past crowds of hurried sailors and merchants in beige and white, and found their way under the natural stone arch that opened to the

CHAPTER FOUR

bay of West Avem. Aizo had them dump their old clothes in the water.

In the shadow of the arch, Aizo produced a pair of cloth gloves. He handed them to Eos.

"It's warm enough in these long sleeves. I don't need those."

Aizo gave him a look that was much too serious. "They aren't to keep your hands warm."

Eos knew what he meant, and he was beginning to get annoyed. "I already wrapped it up before we got into the city. You can't be serious."

"I won't be asking again," Aizo said more firmly than Eos was used to from his wily teacher.

The gloves went on over the already wrapped hand. Eos couldn't help but feel Aizo was being too harsh. "Why do—" Aizo cut him off.

"I'll explain later. First, we need to see if an old scoundrel still works this port."

They walked through a port of sailors and workers, all wearing darker colors than those in the white walls of the town. Their faces were dirtier and hairier; their skin was worn by the salt and sun of their time at sea. They loaded crates onto boats that were more exotic than anything Eos had seen in books on Earth. The hulls were similar enough, but the vessels were sharper angled, had tails like fish, and sails like the wings of dragonflies. The boats looked like elegant wooden creatures, alive with the churning of the sea.

Aizo pointed to one as they walked through the bustle of dock workers. "Sea-striders have more sails than Earth's boats. The influence of multiple moons, depending on the calendar alignment, makes navigating waters more complex." They stopped in front of

AMBITIONS AND SCARS

a wooden shack that had a variety of fish in barrels outside it. The aroma of dead Hyperborean fish was far too similar to Earth's.

"Wait here quietly. Same as before. Draw no attention. I'll be back shortly," Aizo said.

"We're finally on Hyperborea, and all we've experienced of Anite is alleyways that you've made us wait in and the bag of patine we ate. Can't we come in with—" Eos didn't get to finish complaining.

"No, you may not come in with me. You'd rather experience Anondorn and your father and mother sooner, wouldn't you? If anyone figured out who we are, that would slow us down enough. Not to mention my injury. If the barbarians told us anything, it's to be…" Aizo glanced around. He leaned in and whispered, "*It's to be worried about how much influence the Mitad have in the outer cities.*"

Eos and Maxima didn't know what he meant by that and shared a strange look. They couldn't argue with speeding up their homecoming. Aizo was true to his word and collected the siblings just a few minutes later.

He explained, "My old acquaintance, Sergius Ora, used to work these docks. He also did some land transport to and from Anondorn. He may be able to give us safe and secretive passage, but it seems he's moved up in his business dealings." Aizo made a *thum thud thum thud* sound as he hobbled across the planks of the dock. They journeyed away from the water, onto stone paths. Further along the coastline, the docks and their accompanying wooden ramps, red and white fabric canopies, and sprawling warehouses ended. The sounds of creaking sea-striders and rope, splashing water, and men conducting business were absorbed into the white walls of the inner town. They passed under a bridge with a statue of a bird protruding from it, and it made Eos realize there was another tier of the sloping city above them. Aizo brought them to a hanging wooden sign that had *Ora Works* carved into it with the icon of sails set like a pair of wings.

"Oh, you have moved up in the world…" Aizo muttered to himself.

They walked under the sign and its archway and up a set of wide stairs. They emerged on the second level of West Avem. Eos and Maxima followed up another set of stairs that took them across a walkway. The walkway passed through window-like holes in a building. They continued like this until they were overlooking the ocean from a hundred feet up.

They stood before a building that was grander than most in the city, accented in gold trim. The doors were large and guarded, but these guards did not look the part of military men like those at the gate of the city. The two before them were looming, burly men dressed in dark fabrics, and had a look of unwholesomeness about them.

"I think you're lost. Turn around," one said as the trio approached.

Aizo gave a look of defiance. "I'm here to see Sergius Ora."

"Well, he ain't here to see you." The other retorted. He leaned in. "Skid off, yeah?"

A sigh showed Aizo's exasperation. "I'm here on behalf of Talus Bellator." He invoked the power of the name once more that day. It was enough to give the guards pause.

"Ha, and I'm Talus Bellator's long lost son," one jeered.

Eos stepped forward hotheadedly. Maxima put a hand on his shoulder before his temper flared.

Aizo pulled the robe off his shoulder and let his upper body go unclothed.

AMBITIONS AND SCARS

"What's this now? I said skid off, you crazy man. Put your clothes back—"

The other guard nudged him.

Aizo turned his back to the guards. Eos and Maxima saw for the first time what the guards saw: a large branding of an elsu, detailed with feathers, burned and scarred behind his right shoulder blade.

"I am here on behalf of Talus Bellator to see Sergius Ora," Aizo said with finality.

The guards nodded, and opened the door, and took them through the house of an incredibly rich man. Vases and rugs covered the floor. Paintings and imported goods hung from the walls. Gold glittered from almost every part of the house.

Before long, they were entering the private room of Sergius.

Eos observed that this room and each they had passed through were lit by white stones that shone like a lightbulb encased in a block of glass.

Sergius hunched over paperwork and stacks of coins. He dressed in vibrant colors of purple that encased the man so much that his fancy furled collar came up nearly over his chin. His greasy, receding hair fell over a gaunt face. The gold hoop of an earring shone from his left ear as he looked up at them with bulging eyes and tiny pupils. "My my...now, what would the high ruler of Anondorn want with a businessman like me? The name's Sergius Ora, but clearly, you already know that. And who might you three be?"

"We..." Aizo hesitated. "We are grateful for an audience with a busy man such as yourself, Sir Ora. We are agents of Talus Bellator seeking quick and secretive travel to the capital immediately."

CHAPTER FOUR

Sergius raised an eyebrow and smiled at the boldness so that the gold and silver in his teeth shone.

"With the coin to afford such demands, of course," Aizo finished. He placed two gold sol on the desk.

Sergius shook his head and clicked his tongue. "Times is hard. I'd think the royal budget could afford the proper six sol such a service would cost for *three travelers*."

Aizo nearly choked. "*Six?* Why that's a small fortune. You wouldn't have dreamed of so much when you were younger!"

"And what do you know of when I was younger? 'Sides, I'm older, not younger, and I don't dream of such sums. I bring six sol and many many more in each week. So, will you be payin' or leaving?"

Three more gold coins were set on the table. "That's all I have in pocket. The last one will come from the royal budget, as you say."

"Well, well…quite the sum. Throwing coin around like that would get you a knife in the back from less reputable men. Lucky for you, I'm Sergius Ora, and the price is right. I'll escort you myself." He faced the wall as he thumbed the gold coins.

"Then we have a deal, Sergius," Aizo said.

"That we do. Seems only fitting that I be the one to return Aizo Mudar to Anondorn after all."

Aizo chuckled. "You recognized me after all these years and still swindled a fortune out of me."

Sergius shrugged. "You didn't pay well when we were on the streets. 'Sides, Talus would pay the entire royal treasury for his children back, they say." He gave them a dangerous gleam. "My men will take you down to the dock. I'll meet you on my private speed-strider. We'll travel upriver and have you in Anondorn by

AMBITIONS AND SCARS

morning with no one the wiser that you've returned." He whistled in his guards and relayed the orders to them.

As they followed down to the Ora Works dock, Maxima asked, "Aizo, what was that on your back?" He responded, "Your grandfather gave it to me. A brand that welcomed me into the Bellator house. Made me as close to kin as I could be without sharing blood."

They stepped onto Sergius' speed-strider. It was painted gold at the stern and had blue sails that were as gaudy as the man himself. He climbed on board and threw something at Aizo without warning. Aizo caught a walking stick with a silver serpent head for a handle.

The wealthy merchant looked arrogantly upon them. "By the Great Soul man, you're walkin' like a homeless cripple. Now get under the deck before anyone else sees you. I can't be sure how many of these workers are clean and loyal anymore."

They were soon in the bilge of the ship, which Sergius had turned to a lavish recreation room. Maxima tended to Aizo's leg once more on a luxurious purple couch. Eos looked at the gold-trimmed mirrors and paintings that hung from the walls.

"Blood on the sofa will cost you an extra gold sol." Eos couldn't tell from the tone if Sergius' price increase was serious. "What do you think of my leisure strider, Boy?" Sergius eased himself down the stairs and pulled greasy strands of hair from his face.

Eos wasn't sure how to address the man giving them passage. "Err...it's very fancy, sir."

"You hear that, Aizo?" Sergius snickered. "The boy calls me, *sir*. Have you not told him that he's royalty and that I'm street scum

CHAPTER FOUR

risen higher than is my place in this life?" He continued to laugh and produced a decanter of alcohol from a cabinet.

"I've told him little of any of it," Aizo returned, seemingly distracted by his leg.

"Have a drink to celebrate your return! And, perhaps, to take your mind off that hideous wound. How did you manage that?" Sergius asked while circling the gold rim of his glass.

"Getting home was harder than you'd think. Mmm." Aizo grunted in a way that Eos recalled from their encounter in prison. "Much too difficult." Aizo nodded and grunted to himself.

Sergius seemed taken aback by the Aizo's manner of speech. "So, it seems. Well, perhaps a glass for the son and daughter of King Talus then?" He threw back the remains of his drink.

"No. I don't think so. We all need to finish the journey sober." Aizo nodded vacantly to himself as Maxima finished dressing his leg. He turned with a bit more focus. "Besides, their first drink on Corland, whether ale or hard drink, should be with their father, no?"

Eos couldn't help but notice that Sergius showed an abnormal displeasure at the rejection of his drink. He squinted at his guest and turned away. "Very well. I'll leave you to your thoughts. I'm needed above deck."

Aizo began to laugh softly with a crazed pitch. "Heh, when I was last in Anondorn, such...*frivolous* attire wasn't in style. Tell me, Sergius, have collars like that become the norm?" Aizo referred to the frilled collar around Sergius' neck that nearly covered his chin it came up so high, "or just a peculiar taste of yours? I'd never imagined to see you in such status even if you were given the opportunity."

AMBITIONS AND SCARS

Sergius spoke lowly. "There's much you couldn't imagine for as long as you've been gone. I seized opportunity by the throat as I always have."

Aizo repeatedly nodded in an act as if he lacked full mental capacity. "You have. You have."

"But that doesn't mean others don't go after your throat either." He stared at Aizo scornfully. "Ambitions can leave nasty scars. So, I wear a collar as not to upset any onlookers."

Aizo hopped up faster than he should have with his leg in its current state. Somehow, he stayed upright despite the undulations of the vessel. "On second thought. I could use something to ease the pain of this leg. Let's drink to wounds and scars that brought us together once more."

A smile crawled up to Sergius' gold earring. "Yes, let's. I warn you these are strong spirits."

Aizo hummed absent-mindedly, "I hope so." He reached for the decanter quickly. "I insist. Let me pour for you as you have agreed to provide us safe passage." Sergius gave the slightest nod. Aizo poured without looking at the glass as he patted his old acquaintance on the shoulder.

Eos blinked and shook his head. Maybe it was just the light, but the clear liquid had turned orange momentarily as it poured from the decanter. Eos shook himself awake and looked again. He was just tired; the drink was the same color it had always been.

Aizo handed the glass to Sergius, and the two drank to old times that Eos and Maxima hadn't the faintest knowledge of. Sergius poured a second glass and left it for Aizo. "Celebrate your return, friend. This bottle is my finest spirit on board. I expect you to finish it off for me."

CHAPTER FOUR

As Sergius climbed back up the stairs, Aizo called to him. "Sergius, I do hope you brought enough men just in case we run into trouble."

Sergius looked down from the shadow of the stairway. His eyes flickered with resentment towards Aizo. "Yes...in the event we meet any nosy sailors along the river, I've brought four of my best crewmen. *Surely the legendary wielder doesn't need any protection, hmm?*"

Aizo fell back onto the couch before he had meant to and took another swig from his glass. "This old wielder is..." Aizo slid into Maxima as the current tossed the vessel a bit. He continued with a bit of a slur, "is quite out of practice."

"Oh, let's hope not. Anondorn grows more threatened by the day." Sergius climbed above deck.

After the door closed, Maxima turned to Aizo. "I don't like this Sergius Ora."

Aizo grew quite sober and serious. "Nor should you." He tossed the liquid in his glass over his shoulder. "Blasted drink is strong enough to knock a corinth on its ass. Sergius was one of the less trustworthy men I worked with when I was young. No doubt, he did all sorts of foul things to get the riches he has now. I expect he'll try to get more gold out of us before Anondorn."

Eos spoke. "You asked him how much protection he had on purpose, didn't you?"

Aizo smiled with his eyes. "That's all we need to say for now. Get some sleep, both of you. I'll be awake in case there's any trouble." Aizo watched as the children fell asleep; Talus had trusted him to return them home. For over a decade, he had failed to protect them, but his task was nearly done. Tonight, the churning of the water made him feel invigorated. It screamed of dangers. The dangers they had encountered and those that were to come, but it was home turf. He felt sure, surer than he had in years. He basked in the soft light of the condlucite stones that hung from the ceiling. They shone so much clearer than lightbulbs did on earth. They sparkled in a way that only Soul Energy could. He stared at the burning stones for over an hour, recalling his years on Hyperborea.

Time was impossible to track between the buzz the spirits had caused in Aizo's head, the constant churn of the water, and the near silence otherwise. Aizo couldn't be certain how long, but much later, the condlucite stones flickered.

Zzztch. Zzzztch.

The stones crackled as they dimmed.

Eos and Maxima woke.

Zzzztt.

The lights went out entirely.

"Aizo, what's happening?" Eos asked with anticipation.

Aizo spoke quietly. "It seems Sergius brought a skilled lumenator aboard, and he has removed the lights."

The boat walls creaked.

Water splashed against the boat.

Eeeeeek. The boat creaked and groaned in the black of night.

Shhhk!

Aizo let out a scream of pain, and Eos heard his body fall to the ground.

The icy feel of metal came up against Eos' throat. He didn't dare squirm, or his throat would be slit.

Out of the corner of his eye, he saw the little bit of moonlight that reached below deck gleam against another knife. This one he saw against Maxima's throat. He seethed. Blood poured to his head in a rush that made his veins bulge against the blade pressed on him.

A red glow came from his hand, and he noticed blue already coming from Maxima's direction.

Warm liquid ran down to his chest as the knife dug in as a warning.

The room was dark again save the pale filtering of light from up the staircase. The blue and red were extinguished. Aizo's heavy panting let the siblings know he was still alive, if only for a while longer.

Violently, orange exploded into the condlucite stones and lit the room in a blinding flash before the light became colorless. Aizo was propped up on one arm but appeared unable to lift himself further. A dagger protruded from underneath his left collar bone, and blood soaked through his robe.

"It was too dark. I missed your heart," Sergius Ora said, revealing his gold and silver teeth.

The sight made Eos want to retch. His wielding master only stared up, shocked. He fought to breathe.

Sergius continued, "Out of practice indeed. I expected to stab your *solido*. Look at you."

Aizo rasped between panting and gurgling that Eos didn't want to contemplate, "I expected," *gurgle*, "extorsion. Hostages," *huff huff gurgle*, "maybe, but not…"

"But not that I'd try to kill you? Old ties would mean you could trust me with your wellbeing? Corland has new rules since you've been away. I love money, that's who I am. I love being alive more. Doesn't matter which end of a two-headed snake you grab, it'll bite you. So, I keep the snake happy. Not that they don't pay me well to move things for them."

AMBITIONS AND SCARS

Aizo inhaled deeply, enraged. "You have five seconds to stand down," he rasped lowly.

Sergius revealed a mouthful of metal and laughed. "Haghh Heghh. You threaten me like that?" He turned to his men.

Eos began counting in his head. *Five.*

"Tie them up for Emir Grimshaw," Sergius ordered.

Four.

Sergius addressed the man at the staircase, "They're handled. Go help Gaius turn the strider around."

Three.

Sergius picked up the decanter of spirits. It was untouched from before. He chided, "Aizo, you should have enjoyed my gift while you were still able."

Two.

Bwooor! There was a strange sound like a suffocated explosion from where Sergius stood. He folded over, clutching his abdomen as orange light roared from his belly. He slumped onto the tabletop and knocked the decanter to the floor. It shattered beneath him, and he was thrown off the table by the rocking of the strider. Blood ran from the corners of his mouth and soaked the belly of his purple robes so that they were nearly black. Sergius Ora lay dead in a puddle of alcohol and glass shards.

Aizo stood. He shook with rage and held a hand out to the knife at Maxima's neck.

"Knife," he huffed, but it was with more rage than struggle now. The conspirator hesitated, but Aizo convinced him. "Fine, you're next. *Three. Two...*" The knife was in Aizo's hand immediately. The cold metal pulled away from Eos without being urged further.

CHAPTER FOUR

Aizo bent over Sergius' body with the blade. He paused. "How long until we reach Anondorn?" He asked with the handle of a dagger sticking out of him like a planted flag.

The conspirator behind Maxima stuttered, "Uhhhhh. Three h…hours. If we turn back."

"Well, turn now. You have two hours, or you'll all be like him." Aizo took the knife in his hand and slit open Sergius' purple frilled collar. He tore the cloth back with a rip.

Eos' blood chilled, and goosebumps rose on his arms.

Tattooed around Sergius' neck was a two-headed snake. It wrapped around his neck entirely, and the two heads opened on either side of his adam's apple.

Aizo said with labored breath to Eos, "The barbarians in the Sepeleo mountains didn't fear death in battle. They feared this. *They feared your right hand.*"

Eos removed the glove and looked at his skin. He turned his hand over, shaking. This mark stained his identity and burdened him. Through the slits of his blackened fingers, he watched blood roll down Sergius' neck and over the open fangs of the black snake that choked him, the tattoo that bound him.

CHAPTER FIVE

MEMORIES AND SKIN

A rose-red velvet sofa adorned the middle of a lowly lit room. The room was part of the buried underground network of the Mitad's desert base. Amidst the faint organic buzz of the condlucite stones, Tessio stood and awaited the ceremony that promoted him to the rank of Mirza. He stared at the sofa in a trance, shirtless, and brandished his pale skin before the room. It glowed a tainted milky-white against the velvet and shadows.

Zolo watched uncomfortably. Tessio's ink-covered body displayed icons of religious art, fierce warnings of his strength and viciousness, erotic images, and homages that formed a map of hardships on his skin.

Ares leaned back against the wall with his arms folded. He smirked at Tessio, "Welcome to the mirza, my Mitad brother."

CHAPTER FIVE

Tessio removed his pants and left them at the foot of the sofa. He spread out against the seat, wearing nothing more than thin dark undergarments. "Should you have brought him?" He nodded his chin at Zolo.

"He has a decision to make," Ares said.

Tessio said nothing more. He produced a whiskey glass from behind his seat and held it boastfully with his elbow propped on the back of the sofa. The liquid in the glass swirled as he toyed with the drink.

Ares looked at the two-headed snake tattooed boldly on Tessio's left pectoral, making him one of the whole identity. His eyes moved from marking to marking. The *x* on each of his knuckles identified Tessio as a prisoner and laborer in his home kingdom, and The Human Essence triangle topped with a crown on his left forearm declared that he was a Soul Wielder worthy of being feared. There were rings tattooed on each finger in geometric patterns, among the myriad of other ink. He lingered at the empty space on Tessio's knees.

Images of the moonlit night atop the raised highway-alter flickered in Ares' thoughts. He was interrupted by flashes of Tessio running the spear through his own brother. Ares had done worse to many poor souls and enjoyed it nearly as much as Tessio...*nearly*.

Zolo watched from the opposite side of the room from the nearly nude man. The boy had placed a tracker, perhaps shot a few soldiers from a distance, but no more. He knew nothing of the violence that strangled Tessio and Ares...that held them like men with their heads forced underwater.

The brutal plunge of the winged spear stuck to Ares' eyelids.

Shlllpp. Tessio threw back the glass in one go and called out, "Amasis. I'm ready."

MEMORIES AND SKIN

A short man with buzzed hair and walrus mustache carried a case into the room. He showed no emotion and made no sound. He simply set his case down, ran his fingers over the corners tenderly, and prepared for his art. He opened his case and handled his tools with such meticulous care that one would think they were museum treasures.

Tessio lifted his legs and elevated them on the velvet ottoman.

Amasis produced a well of ink and metal stake. At the end of it, he attached a sharp instrument like a miniature scalpel. His wrinkled hands pulled two pieces of paper from the case. One contained a serpent twisted around a shard of stone on the left, and the other had a flame of Soul Energy with a serpent face inside.

The drawings suddenly sprang to life with a glow of yellow. The images burned on the paper Amasis held until the entire thing flashed violently and turned to ash. The old man closed his eyes and put the index and middle finger of each hand on either of Tessio's knee caps.

The yellow energy flashed back to life at Amasis' fingertips. When he opened his eyes, the tattoo patterns blazed brilliantly in Tessio's kneecaps. He pulled a pair of thin gloves over his hands and then dipped the miniature scalpel tool into the ink well.

He put a gloved hand on Tessio's bare leg and rested his tool in the crook of his thumb like a billiards player. Amasis stabbed the device into the first kneecap with masterful precision and speed. He stabbed again and again. Each time he plunged the ink into Tessio's skin, the knee turned darker. Droplets of blood beaded up against the excess ink and mixed. The glowing pattern of the serpent-wrapped gemstone faded slowly until only raw skin and the tattoo remained. Amasis set to work on the other knee, stabbing and stabbing and stabbing.

CHAPTER FIVE

Ares watched the marks of the rank of Mirza form until Amasis was finished with his work and cleaning his tool.

A voice at the doorway soothed the room, "You shall neither bend the knee nor bow to any authority other than the Mitad's emir and your masters. The manus stones and the Soul Energy serve us. Never believe otherwise." Lord Vistomus floated into the room on a cloud of shadow under his long cloak.

"I will serve you well, Master." Tessio bowed his head.

Lord Vistomus' voice went raspy and ghost-like as if speaking the words of another man, "Then it is time for you to receive my mark." He put a pointed nail to the blood that was beading up on Tessio's kneecap. There was a micro-flash of white Soul Energy at the tip of Lord Visotmus' nail before it plunged into the skin.

Tessio went rigid.

The tattoos on his knees began whipping around like black flames. His head snapped upward as his eyes rolled back in his head. The white of his eyes pierced the room for a few seconds before the black flame-like ink on his knees appeared between his eyelids. Two lifeless black holes stole the attention of all spectators in the room.

Zolo backed away from the red sofa.

A minute later, Tessio let out a high-pitched sigh. The black flames that licked at the inside of his skull receded. His pupils rolled down, and he looked up to Lord Vistomus like a changed man.

"How was your first taste?"

"…Invigorating…better than anything, Master," he said with a stuttered breath.

Lord Vistomus turned to Zolo. "The rebels against the North American regime is the surface reflection on a drop of wet paint on a canvas that contains my masterpiece. Ares has brought you far enough into our world that you must make a decision, Zolo. Will you become a part of the greater picture? The rebels act in accordance with the grander purpose of the Mitad. There is an entire world that you do not understand nor even know. There is no shame in remaining a rebel officer, but you will not know the truths, the glories, or the dangers of the greater reality."

Zolo's hands shook against his legs, but Lord Visomus Fulmen had saved his life…so the Mitad had as well, whatever they were. He resolved with a voice like he hadn't had water in days, "I wish to serve the greatest purpose for you that I can."

Ares put an arm around Zolo and whispered, "Good. Now you will share our world. Take a seat next to Tessio."

Zolo hesitated.

"Don't worry." Lord Vistomus eased his concern, "You will not receive the great gift that Tessio did. Initiation requires only the ink."

Zolo signaled his agreement with a nod and took a seat.

Tessio leaned in so close it made Zolo shiver. "Tradition says that you must bare all before the organization," he said and gestured to his nearly nude figure. Zolo looked to Ares, who signaled him to continue. Zolo did. He disrobed down to his undergarments.

Tessio threw his arm over the sofa back, arrogantly. "Stand and present yourself before the Master."

Zolo did as he was told.

"Now turn about so that he can see you have no marks of other allegiances." He eyed Zolo's unmarked body, pure of any blemishes at all. The feel of Tessio's eyes on him made his skin

CHAPTER FIVE

crawl as he thought of the impure black flames that had just filled that skull.

"Well, well..." Tessio stood. "It appears we will have a new member who is not only a manborum but an Earthling as well." He referenced Zolo's inability to Soul Wield and then put his robes back on before leaving the room.

Amasis pulled another piece of paper from his case. This one had the circular two-headed snake that was on the robe Ares, Tessio, and Lord Vistomus wore. Amasis waited for a command.

"Over his heart. So that he is reminded of his allegiance when tested," Lord Vistomus commanded Amasis. The paper burned in a flash of yellow and Amasis' fingers moved over his left ribs. Light sprang from Zolo's skin, and he couldn't help but let out a cry of surprise at the strangeness of it happening to him.

Stab. Stab. Amasis went to work, tainting Zolo's light, unmarked skin.

The pain was a raw and sharp kind, but one that Zolo could handle. He took his mark with gritted teeth but felt a part of himself changing as ink seeped beneath the surface.

When it was over, he was given a bandage to put over his ribs. The room hummed from the condlucite stones until Zolo could only think to bow his head and say, "Thank you for welcoming me into the Mitad."

"I will find good use for you. Remember who has your heart now, and you will do great things." Lord Vistomus affirmed from the swarming shadows of the room's edge. "That is a lesson even some mirza forget." He eyed Ares.

Amasis finished wiping down his tools and placed them back in the case, but Lord Vistomus stopped him. "Amasis, there is one more I want you to initiate tonight. There will be two from Earth." He called loudly, "You may join us."

What entered the room took Zolo's breath away. It stung more than Amasis' needle and agitated him into a rage. The first thing he saw was a bright white suit that swaggered into the room. A maroon tie bled from his collar down into his jacket.

Zolo stumbled back against the red velvet sofa and fell into it.

The lights in the room flickered as he was overcome with…with…a past he had nearly forgotten. In this sand buried room, in this pulsing instant of time, he was not the hardened desert rebel, he was not the self-taught medic who combed through forgotten books, and he was not Zolo.

He remembered what he repressed. He was Jace.

"Ma, get in the tent. Hide."

That's what he had said to her as soldiers swarmed over the newly formed camp called Sires.

Hands shoved him forward into a mass of prisoners as he looked back frantically to see if his tent had been passed over. He couldn't see through the bodies carrying him forward. He tried not to cry as he thought of his mom hiding for her life.

"Fifty for labor. Ten for the lab," cried out the leader of the soldiers. He wore all white amidst the dirt and rabble. All white except for the tie that he wore. Jace knew he could survive a week or two of the hard labor, but no one returned from the lab. They did terrible things to humans in there. The man in white made it so.

"No," curdled a female voice, and he knew. "Not my son. My son!" The sound pierced the prison camp above the noise of rounding up bodies.

Zolo ripped himself away from the men holding him. He threw a punch and then another.

CHAPTER FIVE

It was a blur he preferred to forget, but the burning of his ribs from the fresh tattoo reminded him of the burn in his heart.

He saw his mother being dragged out of the tent on her knees, begging for her son's life to be spared.

It was a flurry of limbs as he fought his way to her. Soldiers caught him, but he reached out enough to hold her hand…if only for a second. The man in white looked through his spectacles as they tore the mother and son apart. He slicked back his blonde hair with a gloved hand and smiled. His voice hissed like a snake, "She'll join the ten in the first truck." His eyes danced with playful enjoyment.

Zolo put his fingers over his bandaged heart, remembering the last touch of his mother as Kurt Fleischer entered the room.

Kurt Fleischer stopped, and his body went rigid. The blonde hairs on his neck raised. His hands tightened until his knuckles popped. He laughed in raspy disbelief, "It's beautiful. It doesn't get any better than this…"

Ares asked, "Who is this?"

"A man of Earth that I found. He had already performed the Mellizo Ritual," Lord Vistomus said.

Fleischer continued to laugh until it grew into sharp breaths.

Ares raised an eyebrow at the psychotic figure. "The Mellizo Ritual?"

Fleischer spoke in a hissing whine, "To think…my unfinished work was here. I remember you!" He pounced and flung himself towards the sofa. "You're the one that got away when the rebels tried to free some of our prisoners." His body came down on Zolo in a sheet of white, and his hand fell on Zolo's throat.

Even to Lord Vistomus, this was unexpected. He ordered in a booming steady voice, "Stop this instant."

MEMORIES AND SKIN

But Fleischer did not. He squeezed Zolo's throat so hard the veins bulged in his head. He raised his other hand and cried out, "I finish my work."

Zolo shook. His mother filled his thoughts as the maroon tie fell over him, and Fleischer crushed his trachea. He shook so violently that his body wanted to heave up his dinner. It tried to find an outlet for the pain and misery that he had buried away.

Ares strode forward, thoroughly annoyed with the events that were unfolding. "Enough of this disgrace before Lord Vistomus."

A punch landed on Zolo's face. He tasted blood. He didn't just want to fight back—he wanted to obliterate the man in white. He wanted him to cease existing.

He wanted to wipe him out.

Cleanse the world of his evil.

He…He…

Boooom!

A neon-orange stream of Soul Energy burst from Zolo's hands as he rejected Kurt Fleischer from the room. The man in white flew limply. He slammed into the wall so violently that a condlucite stone fell from it. The light landed near his head, casting a long shadow of the unconscious man across the room to the couch's foot.

Zolo stood and planted a foot on the edge of Fleischer's shadow as he prepared to erase the man.

Ares and Lord Vistomus were stunned. They had not expected such dissent during an initiation, let alone the violence.

Fleischer moaned and lifted his head.

Crackle-doooom!

CHAPTER FIVE

Lightning sprung from the ceiling and struck Fleischer's back. Lord Vistomus pursed his lips as if tasting something foul and bitter. "Such insolence will not do."

The strike of lightning recalled Zolo from his altered state. He turned his hands over in disbelief at what they had produced.

"Allow me to finish him." Ares formed the Soul Chains in his sleeves, but his mind was no longer on the slumped over man. *How had Zolo done that?*

"No," Lord Vistomus said. "I will need his bloodlust in the coming battle. Leave him, Ares." He turned to Amasis. "Tattoo the fool's tongue. See that it isn't a clean job." Amasis bowed and reopened his case obediently.

A single look from Lord Vistomus and Ares knew they were sharing the same thoughts: *Zolo was a boy of Earth, rescued from a prison camp. The opposite of a wielder's lineage. Neither had he given a drop of blood to the Mellizo Glyph to complete the ritual. So how?*

Zolo pushed his hands away from his body, repulsed and scared of what had happened.

"That shouldn't be possible," Ares murmured.

Lord Vistomus shook his head.

"And yet we've seen an… impossible awakening."

CHAPTER SIX

THE NIGHT OF WINGS

The tremendous rumbling of a fifty-wagon caravan reverberated underneath the blue sky outside the capital city of Anondorn. Like a giant's hand raking the green ground, the procession rolled on, announcing itself with the immense and proud sound of its sheer size.

Atop the lead caravan's roof, sat a man with brilliant white hair that, although thinning, was combed back to the nape of his neck in a majestic silver mane that crawled forward along his jawbone. His beard flowed like purified smoke from his face and surrounded the pipe at his lips.

The pipe was the purest anima stone that most were likely ever to see, shaped flat like a prism at the stem with a pointed-end near the chamber. The stone pipe glowed a piercing sapphire color

CHAPTER SIX

when he inhaled, lighting the leteb powder inside. The man, appearing late into his fifties, enjoyed the leteb buzz in his chest and warmth of the sun as he puffed a billow of smoke like a dragon sitting atop his trove of treasure. The pipe made his trail of smoke turn a soft blue when it flashed.

In the heart of Anondorn, Talus sat at his private table, reading through the morning reports.

There was an eager rap on his office door. Talus grunted for them to enter as he sipped his steaming morning black tea. An anxious young messenger boy stumbled in, knelt, and bowed his head as he reported in a stutter, "King Bellator, I am t-t-to inform you."

"I've never seen you before. You new?"

"Yes, s-s-sir."

Talus nodded from behind his large mug and the rising steam.

"A man named X-x-xaro is here. He has f-f-fifty wagons with him."

Talus nearly dropped his mug as he stood.

"Well, well. That's quite an increase in size from his usual. I wonder why?" Talus mumbled to himself as he made his way to the door. "Tell the staff to welcome him like we would the King of the Corleo or Monte Territories."

"Yes, s-s-sir." The boy tripped over himself to follow Talus, who had been too distracted to dismiss the boy from his kneeling position. "Shall I have rooms p-p-prepared for his entourage as well, s-s-sir?"

Talus stopped walking and looked out a southern window to see the massive body of fifty caravans traversing towards his castle like a living creature.

"Name?"

NIGHT OF WINGS

"They call m-m-me Tavy, my lord."

Talus shook his head. "You're new, but you best learn. Xaro Monte is one of the Ignoble Lords. You *have* heard of them?"

Startling recognition crossed the young face. "I have. Everyone has, my lord."

"Then, you heard what he did at the village of Daci?"

"They s-s-say he wiped it off the map." Tavy rambled, "There was a gang of thieves that stole from him there."

Talus nodded as he strode toward the stairs with steps twice that of most men. Tavy half-jogged to keep up. "That he did. Wiped out the thieves first, then their gang, and then their whole village. Most thought it was a rumor—a joke. Then an organized group from the small city of Ales tried the same a few years later. They got away with a single chest from his caravan. Ales has not existed for near twenty years. He brings only a handful of men with him to keep watch, and forbids them to leave the caravan." They reached the bottom of a spiraling staircase.

"S-s-so just a room for Lord X-x-xaro Monte?"

Talus smiled. "You're picking up quickly. Yes. Our finest room will do." He left the boy at a split in the hallway as his advisors, Scipio and Nerus, joined him. They began buzzing about the fair price for low-quality anima stone to light the kingdom and the shortage of weapon-grade stones that Xaro Monte was sure to price-gouge them over. They frantically discussed all this with Talus, who expertly navigated the conversation in the background of his personal thoughts.

Xaro Monte was not only an entire season early, but bringing twice the usual wagons through Anite. As one of the so-called Ignoble Lords, he commanded more power than most nobles and kings through his mining ventures and the resulting wealth…and he rivaled the masterful abilities of the

CHAPTER SIX

Soul Wielding Order's inlumes on top of that. Although he was friendly enough with Anite, this would need careful and precise handling.

Beneath the castle's white spired towers that lined the curtainwall like rows of canine teeth, Talus and his advisors waited. The rumble of the caravan train made no secret of Xaro Monte's arrival. The Ignoble Lord and his cargo muted the creaking and clacking of the gatehouse's portcullis opening.

Talus saw the luminous cloud of blue smoke from atop the lead wagon. When it stopped, Xaro Monte emerged from the haze. He stood at the precipice of his caravan with a heavy, fur-trimmed black coat hanging from his bare upper body. His arms were not in the sleeves; he wore it as one would a cape and displayed his severely scarred chest and abdomen to the world. He exhaled smoke a final time through his nostril and then leaped to the ground. The rope necklace of Animus jewels bounced at his clavicle.

The man landed powerfully beneath the portcullis.

"Talus!" He boomed. "Forgive my irregular visit. It is good to be in the kingdom of the elsu again."

"You are always welcome in Anite, Xaro. Though your visit is unexpected," Talus said. It was the truth, mostly. Xaro's stone supply was always welcome. His presence was not discouraged, but he did bring uncalculated risk by nature of being an Ignoble.

Xaro beamed proudly, but there was a hint of distress in his voice. "Circumstances in the Winter Aisle are changing. I have many reasons for breaking from my delivery schedule. Some business matters," he shrugged while holding his pipe out, "*Some private matters.*"

Talus nodded. "Let's go inside and discuss in my garden. Cool winds are blowing in. The warm season is nearing its end."

NIGHT OF WINGS

The shirtless man laughed. "I dress like this even at home...and home had seen its first snowfall before I left. But I welcome a good talk over pipe." He raised his now extinguished blue stone in the air.

Talus left behind even Scipio and Nerus as the wagons made their way inside the castle's outer wall. He led Xaro into his private garden in the castle's keep. The room was interior to the castle but open to the sky high above. The stone walls hade white marbled patterns of protruding rings and points like arrowheads, and at the center of each, there was a hole from which water poured. Intricate fountains came from the walls and floor and dumped into pools. The water was heated so that the room could serve as a bathhouse if one chose, or simply keep the moss, pale blue flowers, and twisting trees warm in the winter months. The splashing of the water masked all noise so that the garden room conversations were absolutely private. A serving girl brought in a mahogany pipe inlaid with gold for Talus, along with velvet pouches filled with flavored leteb powders.

Xaro waved his hand to reject leteb politely. "Astor Bruin supplies me with his highest quality blends and newest strains of his leteb berries." He pulled out his own old, embroidered pouch from underneath his oversized coat. "There's a new one he soaks with vanilla and some spice I haven't been able to place yet. Needless to say, I'm near addicted. Would you like to try?"

Talus hummed in acknowledgment as he packed his pipe. "I must confess, I've always been partial to the cacao blends myself." In actuality, he wasn't partial to any blend. Talus only smoked for business purposes and limited his vices to ale when he had a choice. He had no interest in Xaro's current fancy, but he noted that Astor Bruin, another ignoble lord, was friendlier with Xaro

CHAPTER SIX

Monte than he heard tell of. The Ignobles were autonomous, neither allied nor against kingdoms or each other...*usually*.

For a few minutes, there was only smoke and the soft splashing of the waterfalls and fountains.

Talus started, as he knew Xaro could go on like this for an hour. "I hope it is only the tides of business that have changed your schedule. Nothing too serious?"

Smoke poured from Xaro's nostrils and continued into his first words of importance. "I wish that were so. The Corleo kingdom brings me unease. I fear the Mitad has infiltrated their leadership. They haven't been permitted travel into their borders for well over six months. Worse, they keep pushing their border out. Now it is coming up against my mines."

"No communication from Ramath?" Talus asked sadly. His brow hung heavy over his eyes at the news, and he halted his smoking to stroke his auburn beard.

"Not a word." Xaro leaned back and dipped a finger in the nearest pool.

"By the Great Soul...this has gotten out of hand. Then you plan to take action against their encroachment?"

Xaro did not answer immediately. "I am old, Talus. The Winter Aisle is freezing for the year, and my mines will be closed. It's time for this weary body to take its first break in decades. I was thinking of waiting out the winter somewhere warmer."

Talus was taken aback. "Where did you have in mind?"

"Anondorn has come to mind...if I were welcome. Of course, I'd do a fair bit of traveling the countryside too." Xaro made his blue stone pipe surge with energy and glow, but he did not put it to his mouth. He waited for a response instead.

NIGHT OF WINGS

"You are welcome in Anondorn," Talus nodded, still stroking his strands of beard. "I would insist you make your bed the walls of this castle, both because there are no inns that could compare, but also for the sake of perception."

Xaro smirked a bit too gleefully for Talus' comfort. "Yes, we shall try to keep the Ignoble Lord from mingling with the common folk...though I am but common folk myself. I accept your gracious offer."

"Then, you plan to leave your mines behind?"

Xaro laughed so wildly that he broke into a cough, and said as he cleared his throat of the fit, "By the Soul Stones...Never! The mines are my empire and legacy. I have left a messenger to make continued efforts to break through to Ramath throughout the winter. They will know that, upon the thaw, if my business falls too close to their blockade lines...I will raze Corleo to the ground."

Talus dropped his pipe. "You can't mean that. You'd declare war by yourself? That's suicide, even for you. Even for me. We can't go on believing our own legends!"

"Talus," Xaro stopped him, "I'm old. I'll go down in a final fight if that's what it comes to. Fortunately, I think the Monte families will come to my aid."

There wasn't room for another word before Xaro changed the subject.

"Now, I hear you're in a shortage of weapons-grade stones."

Just like that, Xaro had completed his pre-business gossip. He was ready to discuss quantities and sums, and he did. He had tactfully surprised Talus and all of the Anite government with his arrival, made the land his home through winter, and now leveraged it to sell every last stone he brought with him.

CHAPTER SIX

They came to the end of the day after hours of discussion and scrutinizing over Xaro's inventory charts, which were gradated by quality—from cheap condlucite light sources, to middle-grade amgrite heating stones, and weapons-grade shards near animus and anima quality. The discussions would ensue the next day. After all, a quarter of the kingdom's budget was spent on products from Xaro's mines.

Talus concluded, "Xaro, this has been very productive. As always, I thank you for giving Anite the courtesy of the first choice from your inventory."

Xaro tucked away his pipe for the first time that day. The optimal sunlight had faded from the room as the afternoon wore on, and the garden fountains played a splashing background tune. "It's hardly a courtesy, Talus. I'm a businessman. You pay the highest price. As for hosting me, this winter…that is a courtesy for which I'm thankful for."

At least Talus had that bit of leverage to fall back on. It seemed Xaro had increased his prices for every inkling of threat that he felt from the Corleo territory. "Tomorrow, we can continue with the discussion of payment terms and the sort, but let's retire for the night and rejoin at dinner. I'll have a serving boy show you to your room."

Talus was too exhausted to digest what else was said. He found himself on the forward-facing balcony of the eighth floor of the central banquet keep, de-focusing from the world. He bent over the railing, resting on his forearms and looked out to his kingdom. The dipping sun bathed the domes, spires, and patchwork quilt of distant rooftops in a sublime orange mask.

NIGHT OF WINGS

Scipio waddled his squatty body to the edge of the balcony to join Talus in his nightly habit. "Will the Queen be joining you tonight, my lord?" He said in an uppity hum that vibrated his jowls.

"It's a rare night when she does."

Brushing back his locks of hair, Scipio said, "So, it is. If I may, my lord. She has been known to say you get too *nostalgic* when you have your evening balcony sessions."

Talus took in the sweet, crisp air of the night. The pastel overtones on Anite were rays of hope, he decided.

There was still hope.

Scipio changed the subject after his comment was ignored…no it was not even heard. "I do not know what Xaro Monte is after, but we must certainly keep a close watch on him. The man has run a ruthless business with no break for over thirty years. If he takes one now, you can be sure, hmmm, that he is using it strategically."

The mass of wagons stole Talus' attention. Every night he imagined—but no, he must stay grounded in reality. "Fifty caravans, Scipio. Fifty and—"

"Hmmm, yes, it is quite a lot more than his annual visits bring. In need of a large transaction, I'd say. No other reason for it. The prices are above the established market, however…"

His words warbled into an unfocused blur. Every night Talus would sit on the balcony to clear his head, but every night he'd fantasize about a single wagon coming through the gates. The one that never came. Tonight, his castle was full to the brim with wagons.

"It's strange…" Talus murmured to his elsu, Hermios. The bird perched on the railing near his propped forearm.

"Strange is the least of it, my lord. Hmmm. I'm glad you see, as I do, that there is more to this than meets the first pass. The

CHAPTER SIX

severe shortage of weapons-grade stone in his inventory is suspect, despite Nerus' disregard for the peculiarity."

Talus' mind was far away from the balcony. He stroked Hermios with his index finger. "Every night, I end up seeing one wagon pass through those gates."

Scipio was busy quibbling to himself. "I'd say he left his best quality behind—hmm? What? One, my lord?"

"Hundreds of them pass through the gates, but I only ever look for one."

"Oh…" Scipio cleared his throat awkwardly. "This again. Yes, well, only natural. I'll make sure not to tell of your fantasies, my lord. Would only bring about more gossip."

Talus whispered to himself, "Fantasies? Perhaps…"

Scipio good-heartedly tried to turn the conversation back. "I would appreciate hearing your thoughts on Xaro's visit. His prices are going to cripple the royal reserves. We must ask ourselves what we're willing to sacrifice, hmmm?"

The shimmer of sunset told Talus, his time on the balcony was ending. He had duties to attend to, but still…was it so wrong to fantasize about his children and best friend? "I'd give it all," he reflected solemnly.

Scipio let go of his papers, sending them all over the stone floor. "*All?* All, my lord?" He asked aghast as he bent over and waddled frantically to recollect all his dropped records. His large, green velvet-covered rear-end bumbled about in the air. "Surely not *all?*"

Talus thrust himself over the balcony, jutting is head out in disbelief. "Forget the damned business of stones, Scipio!" he said excitedly.

NIGHT OF WINGS

"Forget them, my lord? But you just said you'd pay it all for them. I don't believe you're thinking clearly. Perhaps—"

Talus sprang up to a crouched perch on the thick railing of the balcony.

The frantic grabbing for fallen papers was all the dexterity Scipio could manage. He cranked his head up to see the king of Anite perched like a bird on the eighth-floor railing and leaning towards a fall. The sight of Talus distracted him enough that his limbs tangled, and he was soon tumbling in the pile of papers.

With his head cranked back like a turned over bug struggling to right itself, Scipio witnessed the strangest sight he'd seen in years.

Talus exploded from the railing with a burst of Soul Energy at his feet. His body became a blot before the sunset.

Scipio rolled himself to the railing so that he could hoist himself back up. His puffy hands clambered up the spindle faster than he had moved in years, heaving himself up and over the edge so that his nose was hanging over the railing of the castle keep. He huffed and gasped for breath with red cheeks.

Talus was soaring towards the gate in a blur of speed and crimson energy. He Soul Stepped over the entire castle grounds in a few, mighty bounds. Then Scipio saw what Talus had—a single wagon was approaching the castle. The horses pulling it were of the street breeds and the driver looked incapable of laying a path of Soul Energy. The paint of the passenger cart was that of a lowly city ride, peeling and plain.

The caravan was entirely unroyal and unremarkable. Yet, it was one that Talus would remember for the rest of his days. Dusk was setting in as it stopped at the gate. The dimming light gave the

CHAPTER SIX

approach a dream-like quality. It was too surreal for Talus to comprehend.

He knew. He just knew. His Soul Energy frothed under his skin. *He could feel it—a decade of emotion coming to fruition.*

It had to be.

The event happened in chunks, the ones not blurred by adrenaline and the ones that slipped by in an indiscernible rush. He didn't comprehend or even remember landing, but he did recall bursting past the guards at the gate, bumping his brawny shoulders past theirs. The sight that came next was a tanned, dark-haired boy exiting the caravan, a stunningly elegant girl that was the spitting image of her mother followed, and a mostly bald master Soul Wielder hobbled out to complete the trio.

Talus shook with uncontrollable joy.

He didn't remember closing the distance to his son and daughter, but he stood before them so astonished that he nearly doubted the reality before him.

Eos and Maxima stood utterly still, unsure of the man before them.

Emotions overcame Talus so much so that his children began to realize who he was.

"That scar..." Talus put his thumb to his son's face and ran it over the dagger-shaped scar under Eos' left eye. He said with choked breath, "It grew with you."

Eos' eyes widened, and his lips tried to mouth a word, "Da..." but he was frozen in the fantastical aura of the moment.

Talus turned to Maxima and cupped her head with his massive hands. "You grew up too. So beautiful..." His voice strained. "And that hair...Even your mother would be jealous."

The air left Maxima in disbelief.

NIGHT OF WINGS

Eos and Maxima dove into Talus that instant. They embraced their father with the intensity of twelve lost years between them. The sun peaked through the darkening orange clouds a final time, and an electric warmth spread through them that halted time.

"I've been waiting…all my life." Eos heaved through watery eyes.

Maxima squeezed her hands as tightly as she could around Talus' clothes and let her tears fall onto his chest. "You're r-real." She sobbed in joy. "You're actually here."

"I've waited every day for you three to come back. I believed. I knew…you were still out there!" Talus said.

Maxima's knees went weak, but before she could fall, Talus embraced them. He squeezed them together in the last moments before the sky darkened to the twilight's calming hues.

Talus grinned with his inner teenager escaping at the sight of his lost friend. "You sure took your time, you old street *golan*," he teased.

Aizo gave a high-pitched laugh. "I may have run into a few delays during the mission, my king."

"I'd say so…but you're all alive, my closest friend."

Talus memorized the feel of every breath he took as he held his children and his lost friend after so long. Tears had begun pouring from his eyes, and he said with a quivering voice, "My family has returned." He repeated it again and again.

Talus let go after a long time and walked a few steps away towards the city. He screamed for the entire world to hear, "MY FAMILY HAS RETURNED!"

He thrust his fists to the sky as he made the declaration. He had not intended for it, but crimson Soul Energy flowed from his fists. It surged to the air in two mighty columns and exploded miles

CHAPTER SIX

above like a firework that blanketed a quarter of Anondorn. The energy exploded into a pair of crimson wings that hung in the hazy sky like a shimmering layer of dust that wouldn't fade. The emblem remained faintly imprinted in the air the next morning. It was a phenomenon of Soul Wielding that Anite would remember as the Night of Wings.

$$\infty \qquad \infty \qquad \infty$$

The doors to Talus' inner keep garden were closed. Eos, Maxima, and Aizo were immediately rushed into the room of soft splashing fountains and waterfalls. Scipio had made sure not a single castle dweller had seen them. Talus let the squatty man operate in his expertise. He was an astute economist and mathematician, but Talus needed Scipio for his masterful weaving of public relations.

Scipio left to consult with other advisors about how to break the news best. Lost for twelve years, the perception of their return was a delicate matter. Talus was grateful that someone else could handle such unimportant strategies. He had sent word to Terrava. Until she arrived, he sat in awe at his fortune. He had been right to hold on to hope.

Eos blurted out as soon as the doors shut behind him, "That was amazing—those wings! You must be the most powerful Soul Wielder on Hyperborea."

His childlike whimsy was matched only by Maxima's. "They covered most of the city! It was like one thousand times what I could even imagine doing," she said.

Talus burst out laughing. "I didn't even mean to do such an absurd thing." He put an arm around Aizo, and they laughed together.

"They witnessed me open my third gate," Aizo said, clutching his ribs in his seat from laughter, "and never said a word about it, but the Visrex of Wings shoots a little energy into the air…" He stopped, caught up by the twisting trees and water. "By the Great Soul, it's good to be home."

"Visrex of Wings?" Eos asked.

Aizo smiled. "There are, errr at least there were, four nobles so formidable in wielding and political power that they were said to be the orchestrators of Hyperborea's fate. On the Corland at the very least."

Talus rebutted, "Now, don't go turning me into some sort of mythical figure. Kairus is gone now, so there are only three anyway. If they think that was great, wait until they see their mother in action."

Maxima's eyes widened. "Is she as strong as you?"

A slow nod confirmed her notion. "At the very least…" He leaned in as if telling a secret. "Sometimes, she scares even me." He stood up very seriously and changed the subject. "Now…we must address one vital issue."

He let the statement hang in the air.

"Yes?" Eos and Maxima asked together.

"What in the world happened to Aizo's hair?" He burst out and gave his friend a hard slap on the back.

Aizo patted his head and looked up as if shocked. "What happened? Did it change…oh no…it's gone. My hair *is gone*." He patted his smooth head anxiously before giving a surprise jab to Talus' ribs. "You expect me to keep my hair while running from

CHAPTER SIX

the Mitad and trying to protect these two trouble makers? Impossible! Now, I want nothing more than to reminisce with the Bellators, but I fear my leg cannot wait. It has gone days with some makeshift treatments from Maxima, but it still has not been fully treated."

"I noticed the moment you stepped out of the caravan. The Sanofem's have been contacted and the lead healer is on her way."

The news gave Aizo a noticeable peace of mind. He sunk back in his chair as worry faded from his crinkled brow.

Whoosh! The doors of the room swung open faster than the massive, solid wood should have been able to. Eos saw a woman enter who he could only picture as an aged version of his sister. Her slender arms thrust out as she burst through the double doors. She sprinted forward in her dark blue dress, nearly tripping on it. She fell forward after a few paces, but not in a stumble. Instead, she propelled herself to the center of the garden with a graceful sequence of Soul Step that gave Eos and Maxima chills.

Terrava Bellator held her daughter's face in her hands and looked it over for five seconds in silent disbelief. Then she pulled Maxima's head into her embrace. She turned to Eos while still holding Maxima, traced the edge of his face with her fingertips, and pulled him into her arms as well.

Talus and Aizo watched Terrava act as she never had before, falling to her knees. Talus had not seen her cry since her children were lost. That was the only time he had ever seen a hint of vulnerable emotion from her. A single sapphire tear of Soul Energy shed from her eye. It splashed on the stone floor at her knees.

"My…my babies," she said in a quivering voice, and then she smiled a broken smile.

Talus helped her to a chair.

NIGHT OF WINGS

"Two miracles of Soul Energy in one night," Aizo said.

"I think what we both need to hear right now, is what happened," Talus said.

So, they recounted the twelve years of their severed legacy. Maxima led the account with interruptions of excitement from Eos and parallel events from Aizo's experience. They told nearly all of it to their mother and father. They left only one detail out. Eos was hyperaware of the fact that Aizo and Maxima left it untold. After hours of questions and recounting, the tale of their time on Earth came to an end.

"There is one other thing I haven't told you, Talus," Aizo said, almost as if he was guilty of something. "Eos, go ahead and show them."

Eos became very nervous. He didn't want to ruin the reunion already.

Aizo's stern look influenced him to remove the glove from his right arm. Then, he unfurled the wrapping down his forearm until it fell from his skin completely.

Eos' cursed right arm was on display for the room, the black ink like mark twisting and wriggling as if he had a tattoo that was alive.

Talus and Terrava both let out an audible gasp.

Whoosh!

The garden doors swung in once more.

Xaro Monte drifted into the room with his long coat fluttering behind him.

"Forgive me," he echoed through the room. "I got word of the joyous news, and I—"

His advance slowed, and he stopped short on his path.

CHAPTER SIX

"I—" He eyed Eos' uncovered arm. "The mark of the Mitad," he stated aghast. "Your son bears the mark of the Mitad!"

Eos tried to shrink from existence in the middle of the room. The reputation of his curse was just confirmed, before his parents no less, and now any chance of secrecy about the matter was a fool's dream.

CHAPTER SEVEN

BLIND FOUNDATION

Six stone swords pointed toward the center of the sacred Corleo foundation chamber from the top of great gray pillars. On each pillar was a knight who cast his sword downward on a pair of petrified corcinth horns centered in the circle. The horns were twisted, porous artifacts that protruded from the floor to stab five feet in the air.

Ramath stood beneath the sword tips of his ancestors and felt the weight of their legacy.

The room was silent and softly lit from behind the pillars. The room seemingly preserved the mountains' mossy smell, and it gave Ramath a feeling of ease. He put a rough palm on each of the petrified horns. The familiar feel was his alone. The horns were the responsibility of the king and meant only for his royal touch. He remembered the first time he laid his hands on the awe-inspiring

CHAPTER SEVEN

artifact. Lighting it for the first time at age nineteen had coronated him, as it had every king before him. Now, his hands lit the horns again. They did not glow in the energetic way they usually did. This renewal of his coronation. which he practiced in private on rare occasions, was weary and filled with a fondness for a previous time. His head fell against his hand.

Out of the corner of his eye, the swords' tips reminded him of the Corleo way—prosperity through strength. The blades pointed down on the horns as reminders that constant vigilance against great dangers was needed to maintain power and sovereignty.

Ramath's leather garments were modest for a king, but the earthy colors were trimmed with just enough gold and dark green to be regal. The dimness of the room muddied the colors together so that, before his ancestors, the powerful ruler felt unremarkable.

Through the gap between horns, Ramath saw an uninvited menace.

Standing between the pillars was one of the Mitad's Voro, the one that was called the Overseer. A silver-white helmet masked his true appearance. Each of the two draping pieces of metal covering the Overseer's cheeks was adorned with muted red eye patterns. The Mitad's symbol of the two-headed serpent adorned the helmet's forehead above a matt-black band with one long eye slit too narrow to properly see out of. It gave the feeling of a sort of all-sight from the height of the seven-foot-tall man.

"Emir Grimshaw would have respected the reverence we hold for this room," Ramath said with veiled aggression. "But you have no such eloquence in your methods, do you?"

A toothy smile spread like bleached stones floating in the Overseer's mouth. Porcelain pale skin showed from the center gap between the hypnotic eyes on his helmet cheeks. The pigment-free, scraggly chin-beard moved as he spoke with a slow and calm drawl, "Grimshaw has been reassigned. This has become *a special operation* not to be impeded by customs. This is a matter of urgency."

The blue glow that had faintly seeped from the cervices of the corcinth horns was gone. Ramath removed his hands and scratched at his arms anxiously. "What's this *matter* that required you to enter the Corleo foundation chamber?"

"My patrol found—" The Overseer was cut short.

Ramath rounded the horns and collected his three-pronged, golden royal scepter while muttering, "Emir Grimshaw also understood maintaining a degree of covertness. Your cursed creations are roaming the streets, filling the entire country with rumors."

The Overseer raised his voice to an unsettling level as his seven-foot frame cast a shadow over the room. The eye slit of his helmet and the red snake seemed to be gazing into Ramath's heart, and yet they also seemed to see all.

"They are roaming the streets, *and they are effective.* I have captured one of your devotees fleeing the borders for the Monte families." The Overseer's speech had an unrefined quality, but it slipped in and out from underneath a couth veil.

Ramath loosened his grip on the scepter as he picked at his arm again. "Explain yourself. I wouldn't, *couldn't* be betrayed by one from the court."

"And despite your foolish belief, you have been betrayed. Come out, Balaar." The Overseer commanded. A man in his late fifties walked into the circle from the shadow of the pillars. He had been stout when he was a young warrior, but his glory days were fading behind him. Rope tied his spotted hands, and his gray head fell at his chest in defeat.

CHAPTER SEVEN

Ramath clenched his scepter as if to crush it in anger. A feeling of corruption took hold of Ramath. A darkness rose in his mind that he could not hold back; it was not a feeling of his own, but one of a man being possessed. "Tell me you were not trying to run to the Montes, Balaar. Have I lost my loyal court member to those… *filthy stone worshippers?*" he spewed with rage.

The flash of light on a blade broke his mind's descent into darkness. Behind the Overseer, a low-grade manus stone sword leaned against the pillar. It hadn't been there when Ramath entered the chamber.

Balaar lifted his head to meet Ramath with tortured eyes. "You think I wanted to go to them? I surely did not, but someone has to save the kingdom from its mad king. Look at yourself." He gestured his tied hands to his King. The middle-aged man before him had dark bags under his eyes that seeped through his eyelids. It was a worn down, once handsome face. His shoulder-length waves of black hair were dulled, and his gauntness took prominence on his face. "You're a shell of our great leader…you're a shell to hide… *them*," Balaar said with disgust as he thrust his chin at the Overseer.

The seven-foot menace laughed at Ramath, "You see how they defy you?"

Ramath seethed. "Enough! You betrayed me for the manus stone worshiping dogs. Our ancestors would have slain you where you stand for leaving our *strength*…our *power* for those rock dwellers."

"They would never have given their strength away to the Mitad—" Balaar lifted his tied hands to the Overseer.

Ramath ended Balaar's speech. "How dare you speak to your King like this? The Mitad offers us strength in our time of waning power. If only you understood why I do these things, you would join me gladly. You don't deserve to be spared for such treason, but I'll let you live your days out in confinement for your past loyalty and valor for Corleo." Ramath held his scepter outreached towards Balaar.

Balaar stepped back twice and put his head back down.

"I had not planned to live if captured."

He lunged for the sword behind the Overseer and grasped it the best he could with wrists bound by rope.

The Overseer had his back turned to Balaar. His silver slit of vision seemed only on Ramath.

He could not see the manus blade raised behind him.

He caught no hint of a reaction in Ramath's face.

The first indication he could have noticed was the faint rose glow of the blade that swirled around his helm. If the pale, towering Mitad member of the special unit called the Voro, had realized the swing was coming, he showed no sign of it.

Balaar brought the sword down in a blow nearly as deadly as it would have been in his days of warrior youth.

Zaroommmm. The blade hummed as its glow spiked into a darker rose that bathed the Overseer.

Ramath's gut tightened. He held his breath.

In less time than Ramath could blink—

Vruummm!

The blade struck the Overseer's back.

There was a flood of Soul Energy spattering the room in a rejection made of neon sparks.

The Overseer had not flinched, but at the moment before the sword made contact, he had raised a veil of Soul Energy over his body. There was a cloudy shimmer of distorted white about him.

CHAPTER SEVEN

Balaar's sword sunk to the floor. It was a blade that had been made with average skill at best. Its manus stone quality was worse than average but it was the only weapon in the room, and he had been one of the best manus swordsmen of his day.

He cursed the Overseer for his existence and especially for raising his Solido before the sword had landed. He hadn't expected such a refined technique from the Mitad member, and had underestimated his opponent's Soul Wielding skill. It made his hands shake.

Another pink flash.

Vruumm!

The Overseer remained still.

Vrumm.

The third strike was much weaker. Balaar's second swing had not been enough to give the Overseer a reason to turn around. This blow would do no better. *Clank.*

The sword fell to the ground.

A static-filled white glow crawled onto the Overseer's shoulder. It was an arachnid-like creature with legs thicker than a spider's and more mechanical but made of purely Soul Energy. No larger than a pinky finger, the unnerving creature rattled its six legs until it perched near its master's neck.

"What have you brought into the kingdom, Ramath?" Balaar asked in creaking horror.

Ramath nearly wondered the same thing aloud.

The shoulder creature vibrated, making a synthetic rattling sound.

The Overseer spoke, "If I may humor you with a story?" He held is long fingers out for the shoulder creature to rattle onto with its six legs. He did not wait for permission. "I was born with no pigment in my skin—a skinny pale monstrosity among my peers. There were many Krogs and Mezclado where I wandered in the southern kingdoms. Dark skinned, all of them. I was an outcast who scrounged the waste piles for scraps. I shaved my head to hide my striking white hair from the community...and to avoid the beatings that came from being seen with that white hair." The creature crawled around his pale, albino hand. He turned his palm over so that it would not fall like one would with a bug. "To keep this story brief, I was beaten so bad that I was left to die at age nine. I had manifested my Soul Energy in my fear and nearly killed one of my assailants. They repaid me by leaving me for dead in the garbage without my eyes." The creature rattled and crawled up his forearm. The sound gave Ramath sickening goosebumps. "I was rescued by a journeying master Soul Wielder as fate would have it. I recovered a year later, alive in the world but nearly crippled and blind. I learned from that. Many things I learned." He hummed knowingly to himself. Neither Balaar nor Ramath dared speak. "Most of all, I learned from my master to control Soul Energy...and one day to see with it. Not like you do, of course. But in my own way, I see. I see with these. I believe the ones that roam the streets are called, well, what do you commoners call the ones that *roam the streets,* as you say Ramath?" He held the creature of pure Soul Energy at the end of his fingertip delicately.

Balaar opened his mouth and let out a sickened scoff. "Crawlers. We call the freaks: *crawlers.*"

"Yes," The Overseer hummed as he let the crawler make its way up to his shoulder again. "I was called a freak many times before they beat me." He then spoke seemingly to his creature, "They can't understand our uniqueness, can they? No. No, they can't. Once I was blind and forsaken, but now I can see. Now, I can see... everything." He turned to Balaar.

The Overseer flicked his gangly index finger, flinging the crawler through the air. It landed, with a rattling of its six legs, on Balaar.

Kratttle scree krattle scree krattle scree. It sputtered up his abdomen.

"Aghh! Ughh!" Balaar swatted at the crawler, but it evaded his strikes—a blur of light weaving itself around his attempts to remove it from his body.

Ramath groaned. "Don't do it. He is to be brought judgment by the court."

The Overseer shrugged. "The Mitad have overruled their judgment."

Balaar cried out and stumbled back behind the ring of pillars.

The crawler bubbled like cancer brought to a rapid boil before flashing into a tremendous explosion that consumed half of Balaar from the waist up.

Ramath crossed his arms and scratched at his sleeves furiously. His head shook violently as his once-loyal subject evaporated into a mist of liquified matter and Mitad energy. He roared and slammed down his scepter. "How dare you! In this sacred room? You have gone too far," his voice finished primally low. He closed his eyes and whispered fiercely, "Balaar, you betrayed me, but you were a fine warrior to the end."

The Overseer tilted his head. "You didn't warn me he was attacking. That's no less of a crime than if he attacked his own king. It matters not where a member of the Voro is attacked. We snuff out the poor decision immediately. I do not stand for such behavior, *nor should a leader of power such as yourself.*"

BLIND FOUNDATION

Ramath's blood boiled. "I didn't think I needed to warn one of the great *Voro*," he sarcastically spit the title at the Overseer.

The towering man responded in a cold tone, "I don't appreciate being tested."

Heavy breath filled the gap between the men as Ramath contemplated his move. He had to bear it. He must. He was too far in now. "Nor do I. You brought that sword in here so that he would feel cornered into acting as he did."

The door to the foundation chamber opened and closed with a creak before Ramath could say more. Both men turned to see who had joined them.

A bold voice echoed, "Father, I knew I'd find you down here, but didn't expect *him*." Durath Leorix strode into the light and glared from under a wild mane of hair. His maroon fur jacket swung from his shoulders like a cape.

"Durath...I was just telling our guest here about respect for the Corleo ways. He was in need of an education. Didn't know that this room was for royal family only."

The Overseer glanced between the formidable warriors. Father and son. The son was rumored to be twice the warrior of his father with a temperament that respected only the King. Durath was said to enter tournaments with the finest warriors and win with no regard for his life's status to the kingdom. The pale masked man ground his teeth with irritation, but found no words.

Durath nodded. "Well, now he knows." He lifted his hands as if to ask why the Overseer had not yet left the room.

"I'll leave you to clean up your mess and remove any sign that you ever plagued this room with your presence," Ramath said. The Overseer grumbled as if to respond, but Ramath cut him off, "Or else I will make a new ritual to bathe the pillars in Mitad blood starting with yours!" He stormed out of the room in a white rage that blinded him. His head throbbed at the disrespect of the Corleo founders. *The utter disrespect!*

His son followed him. "Father, he is growing too fearless in our castle. *They* are growing too fearless."

"Yes, Durath. They are. We threaten them with our combined power...can't let them separate us."

By the time he realized the throbbing had lessened, Ramath was resting in his enormous bed, examining his reflection in the gold of his scepter. He itched at his arms again. His skull had a splitting pain, and he was beginning to sweat through his outer robe.

Ramath tried to distract himself. He picked up his cantium tablet: a quarter-inch piece of porous stone. Each was handcrafted with the Soul Energy of the man called Headline Pulius Hurz. He earned the epithet *headline* when he invented the tablet thirty-five years ago. He was a Soul Wielding master, and the only one to ever live who could maintain a constant network of Soul Energy strings throughout Cor Land. They delivered the written news with an occasional image or two on the cantium tablets. Pulius Hurz controlled the string network, monopolized the headlines, and held more political power than most kings.

Ramath's forest green Soul Energy descended on the tablet. His energy was the ink that stained the preordained areas of the tablet. The great master, Hurz, did not provide the energy to populate every stone face on Hyperborea. That was his trick—he only programmed how other's energy would be arranged on that day; it was much less strenuous that way. The green light sifted into legible shapes and settled. The long date at the top read *"15.15.06.03.11"*.

BLIND FOUNDATION

"The Viator on the Brink of War Again," read the tablet headline.

Jitters seized Ramath. He had no interest in the squabbles of the Krogs in the Viator Kingdom.

Near the bottom of the tablet was a line that was slightly larger than the text that reported the Viator conflict: *"Comet of Nitocris Passes Hyperborea. Ill Omen for 30 Days."*.

Today his urges were too strong to be entertained by the headlines. He threw the stone onto his bed and stumbled to his dresser. His twitching fingers pulled open one of the smaller top drawers. As he struggled to remove the false bottom, he worried with paranoia. *The Mitad were gaining influence too quickly. His plan was on the brink of spiraling out of control. Ever since the Overseer had begun operating his factory in the north mountains, the Mitad had swarmed like a plague.* He reminded himself: *Prosperity through strength. It is the Corleo way. He would preserve the former might of his kingdom the only way he could. This was just a…a…a step in the grand plan. The son of the feared Donius Leorix would not be cornered. The descendant of the founders would play the delicate balance of dealing with the Mitad. Ramath Leorix would…*

The false bottom of the drawer came loose, and Ramath pulled a black velvet bag out. He ceased his scratching and untied the strings. He dumped the bag, and crystalline powder flowed out.

Ramath took a blade from the drawer and haphazardly chopped at the powder for a few seconds before diving in. His wide nose dipped into the pile of off-white granules. He breathed.

Soon, euphoria seized Ramath, and he fell back on the bed, free from the worries of playing the delicate balance required of a king branded by the Bellator wings dealing with devils.

Ramath Leorix would…would…

He sank into the bed's softness and became incapable of conscious thought. He stayed there, embraced by the comfortable

CHAPTER SEVEN

buzz the powder brought him, until he was asleep next to a black velvet bag decorated with an embroidered two-headed snake.

∞   ∞   ∞

Jezca cinched her blue fabric bag and tied it to her waist, making sure to turn the silver foil crest, a pair of reverent hands receiving a shining manus stone, to face her hip. She pulled the hood of her cloak as far as it would stretch over her face and put her head down—she didn't want to risk being hassled by the crowds at the Artimon market. All it would take is one of the laymen to see her face, and she would be crowded to no end.

Slip in. Get the information. Be back before any of the clergy notice I'm gone. That's the only way it could work without having to answer to High Priest Laud. She brushed the white-blonde hair over the right side of her face to cover herself and bit at her thumbnail. Archpriest Mellitus' chastising echoed in her head.

She bit her nails despite the reprimands that repeated in her head and hurried out of the dressing room. It had been empty, as usual, since there were only a total of ten other clergywomen in the Order of the Manus Priesthood's central temple. She turned in a circle, making sure no one was nearby, as she made her way down a hall full of iconography of manus stones, famous priests, and mountain peaks. The public cantium tablet in front of Mellitus' room caught her attention. The public news source was propped up on a bookstand and glowed with the Archpriest's dull residual energy twinkling.

The Soul Energy was dying out, confirming that Mellitus had left for his adoration ceremony as he routinely did every morning. He would be gone for another two hours.

BLIND FOUNDATION

She flicked her fingers nonchalantly from ten feet away, manifesting her pink and gray swirl of Soul Energy over the cantium tablet. It glowed; the words rejuvenated as she approached.

"*15.15.06.05.07,*" the dateline read. The headline screamed of trouble, "*Ignoble Liccidius Turns Down Public Meeting with Known Mitad Liaison. Will It Mean War in the Streets of Nebriath?*" Jezca knew it meant precisely that. Such a refusal would mean the Mitad would run interference on Liccidius' money runners. That could be a problem for the Manus Order as Liccidius was a benefactor to the priesthood. More importantly, at this moment, she cursed the date. Only twenty-eight days had passed since the short date *06.03.11*— the bad luck of Necrotis' Comet was still lingering. Two more days and the bad omen would have passed over, but bad luck was still likely as it stood. It was unfortunate the meeting had not been set just a few days later, but she wouldn't complain about getting to see Tavro sooner. Eager to learn of new leads, she chewed at her fingers as she pushed through the temple's door.

That's no habit for an Archpriest in training to have, young lady.

Jezca shook Mellitus' gripes from her head. Whatever had caused the urgent need for a meeting seemed important. She nearly fell forward in a choppy speed walk away from the temple and hurried down the high temple path. Then through the winding streets of monochromatic clay buildings built as outgrowths of the South Monte mountain range. The nearly empty streets became more populated as she entered the heart of the capital city of Petramon. Men and women pushed shoulder to shoulder to get into the Artimon market. There were many eyes that could potentially expose her for leaving the temple unaccompanied, and to such an unholy place no less. The market had been chosen

CHAPTER SEVEN

carefully. The evaluating, bidding, and acquiring goods and services distracted any curious eyes. The sea of bodies was cover for a lone priestess slipping through the crowd—as long as her face remained hidden.

Slip in. Get the information. Be back before any of the clergy notice I'm gone. Jezca reminded herself as the suffocation of sweat and shoving began to make her nervous. The hidden mountain society of Necogen had fewer people in its entirety than this single street. She had been allowed out in public a few times since she took up the cloak of priesthood. The screams for vendors' attentions, waving of money, clinking of coins, groans of livestock, and the stench that came from all of it distracted every instinct of awareness and calculation Necogen had taught her.

Finally, Jezca neared the designated jewelry station. She was just two rows from the stall front, but an oaf of a man was rooted in front of her, yelling his disapproval.

"Those were mine. Your bid count had ended!" His spittle rained on the young stall attendant with his displeasure.

"You were outbid, sir. You may offer a higher price if you wish to reclaim the lot—" The young, pale teen tried to stand firm on the decision. His words condensed in the chill morning air.

Jezca sidestepped the angry man's flailing arms.

He turned and looked down at the small cloak beneath him. "Wait your turn, street mouse. I'm not done with him yet." The man cleared his throat in a horrendous torrent of phlegm and spat near Jezca's feet.

She gritted her teeth. *She was a priestess now. She was a priestess, and this was a public place.* How she wished it was not. Then she could slit the man where he stood. *She was a priestess now.*

BLIND FOUNDATION

The oaf turned back to the stall attendant and barged forward to intimidate the goods into his possession. The watching mass jeered and shouted at the show being put on. She needed to get off the street quickly before she was spotted. The crowds moved with wild swaying and lashing of limbs. To them, the flick of Jezca's fingers by her waist was not a movement at all.

There was an instant, too brief for anyone not intent on the oaf's ankles to notice, where a pink layer formed around his right foot. The shimmering energy halted his back foot as he moved and then pulled his back leg out from under him.

His legs swung back, and he fell hard.

Jezca hopped over his fallen body and leaned in to speak to the young boy behind the counter.

"I'm here to pick up my order." She pulled her hood up just enough to reveal the right side of her face.

The stall boy's expression was a look of shocked admiration. He blushed.

"Of…of course. I was told you'd be coming for your…eh…your order. Please step behind the counter, and the owner will help you with that, my…my lady."

Jezca shot him an inelegant and furious glance.

"I mean, mam. The owner will help you in the stall, mam." He opened the counter and hurried her behind it. Jezca produced a few coins and put them in the boy's hand for the service.

"No payment, my lady," he said under the noise of the crowd. "It would be sinful to take payment from the future high priestess."

"It is sinful to let me go behind the order's back, and yet…"

"And yet your presence is payment enough. Not many can claim to have been this close to the most talented priestess in the

CHAPTER SEVEN

Manus Order's history." Then he finished with a blush, "Not to mention her beauty."

Her sudden rise to celebrity amongst the laypeople was unprecedented. No priest had ever enjoyed a level of following and gossip amongst the people quite like she had. To the escaped assassin of Necogen, it was all foreign.

"Yes, well…no payment it is," she responded as best she could to the boy's strange comments.

Her right eye remained hidden behind blonde hair, but for a moment, it appeared to the stall boy as if her hidden eye was glowing.

Jezca was shuffled through a door and behind the walls of the stall. She pulled back a curtain and sat down.

Tavro was already waiting at the table. He was a balding man with tough but noble features. His dark eyes gave no inclination of his emotional state, and his bearded face was unmoving.

"Priestess Jezca Monte. It is good to see you," he said formally.

"And you, Tavro."

"I apologize about the short notice, but it is rather urgent. Pieces are moving. The Mitad is accelerating their plans and I fear—" He cleared his throat as if it were only a refined part of his speech. "I fear the Priori will not soon meet again. We are scattered, and our public identities under intense pressure. I must leave the mountains we call home for some time."

Jezca felt her blood cool and stomach churn. "You're my only connection outside the temple. The only one who knows I was found by the priests and my only friend to turn to, even if only in hiding and on rare occasions. I hope you can keep safe in such a terrible time."

BLIND FOUNDATION

"I will do my best. There are few things I enjoy more than our talks together, Priestess. Unfortunately, we must be quick, and I must be off. I bring news of your brother and your search for your mother."

"Please." Jezca bawled up the cloth on her legs in her hands as she urged Tavro to continue. "What of Caldus?"

Tavro cleared his throat again, but the sound was a stalling tactic this time rather than a natural quirk. "Caldus has organized his bandits, the Red Corcinths, towards an agenda. He led them into an attack against the Mitad mine tunnels in neutral territory between the Monte and Corleo kingdoms.

Jezca gasped. "I heard the elders speaking of it when the King came for his prayers. They never mentioned Caldus by name."

"I suspect they wouldn't do that in front of you. None the less, Caldus has grown in power. Those rebellious enough to defy the Mitad at our doorstep are listening to him. He has found favor with them. They share his fears and respect his daggers. The Monte family, however, does not. They've ordered him to be stopped or killed."

Jezca covered her face with her hands. "No—they can't!"

"The Monte council is full of cowards who will not allow such defiance against the Mitad out of fear. Worse, I dread to admit there are a few that may have already pledged a secret allegiance. Either way, none will allow the provocation of the Mitad until Xaro has returned and made a decision to defend his mines that were captured. Not even the King."

"Where is their spine? They've lost their way so much that they would make my brother a tribute rather than fight back. *That idiot,*" she cursed Caldus for his boldness. If only he had accepted the priesthood.

CHAPTER SEVEN

"That is the truth of it, I'm afraid. There is nothing that I can do to sway their minds alone. Caldus has few allies in the council. I'm sorry, Priestess. His base of operations has eluded all searches. You can rest assured in his safety as long as that's true."

Jezca growled in exasperation, "Uggghh. Unless he is found by the Mitad first. He has crossed them now and collapsed their mines. Not to mention, he may get himself killed during his rebellions." She worried about Caldus, but she did not cry. Her fool of a brother would not get that, only anger, exasperation, and worry. That much she would do.

"I must deliver what I've found and be off." Tavro drew something out from under the table and set it before her.

"What is it?" Jezca gazed at the pile of yellowed parchment and a piece of leather. On it was an embossing pressed into the leather, but she couldn't make it out through the caked-on dirt and discoloration. She held her breath in anticipation. *Did she finally have the first clue?*

"It is a book or at least part of one. It was your mother's. Other members of the Priori of Karnak believe she wrote at least part of it. I have read some of the pages, but they reveal little to me. The majority of the book is missing." Tavro looked sad to deliver the news. "There is no knowledge of the missing pages. Perhaps you can make use of it in your search for what happened to her. There are strange references in it. Lands that I've never heard of much less seen and—"

There were five sharp knocks against the door.

The sound replaced Jezca's new sense of hope. She leapt from her chair. "The head priests must be looking for me! Why? They should be in adoration for another hour, at least. Shit."

BLIND FOUNDATION

Tavro pulled his hood up. "Then I must go too. I cannot be seen at this critical time. Take the book. Do not let anyone discover it exists. Perhaps only your eye can make something out of it."

Jezca nodded as they turned away from each other.

"Until next time, my priestess."

"Thank you, Tavro. You are a dear friend. Until next time. Be safe."

They left through opposite doors under the concealment of their cloaks. Tavro went behind the stall while Jezca merged with the crowd.

No sooner than she had begun fighting against the stream of bodies, they began to part before her. She looked around, bewildered. No one was facing her; their backs were all turned. She followed their parting to see two towering figures walking her way. They wore the blue and red garments of the Manus Order guards and wore swords at their hip.

A tunnel cleared between Jezca and the guards.

When their approach drew near, the market people fell to their knees and bowed their heads. "High Priest Laud has an urgent need of you at the temple. We are to take you back immediately." A Manus Order guard called out over the crowd.

The crowd became filled with gasps and chatter. "Priestess Jezca! Priestess Jezca is in the market! It's her." The words spread like a virus in all directions.

The guards rushed her in a sprint away from the crowd, so the spread of news stayed right behind them. When they finally stopped running at the temple doors, Jezca was sweating, despite winter's first winds. They only made the beads of sweat seem colder. She panted and clutched her side, out of breath. *Unacceptable. The previous Jezca would have had no problem with that light*

CHAPTER SEVEN

jog. She would have to begin training again. Her conditioning level was that of an inactive priestess, not the fine-tuned instrument she had once been.

Archpriest Mellitus waited impatiently inside. He paced around with his hands behind his back, purple-tinted jowls vibrating as he sighed. "How many times must I warn against your public appearances, Jezca? Yet you defy your elders again."

"Yes, Archpriest Mellitus," Jezca accepted with a mumble and put her head down. She realized Mellitus' mind was fretting something else. His chidings were streaming from subconscious habit.

"You must not mingle with the laypeople. You must...must...must..." He was lost in fretting, eyes darting from wall to wall. "Must be ready should the need for you arise. Come, we have a most unexpected guest. I don't know what to make of it. King Pallogos Monte allowed him in so must attend to him. High Priest Laud is seeing him in your absence."

No less than ten guards of the Manus Order blocked off the private adoration room.

"Who exactly is it that is visiting us?" Jezca wondered aloud as she passed between the columns of guards.

Mellitus muttered to himself, "He wants a reading. Specifically, from you. He'll speak about nothing else. He's mad...mad for even coming here." The old Archpriest's voice cracked with age.

The doors opened upon their approach.

Beyond the decorated double doors was a man dressed in earth-colored robes, marked with the crest of the Corcinth. The man stood haggard and jittery. He scratched at his arms nervously and scanned the room as if an assassin was hiding behind one of the rows of wooden benches.

BLIND FOUNDATION

A voice spoke with more age than any other Jezca could compare to. It was the voice of High Priest Laud. "King Ramath Leorix, I present you with Priestess Jezca Monte, adopted daughter into the Monte royal family and prodigy wielder of the Order of the Manus Priests."

Jezca was without words for a while. She had barely seen the King of Monte in person, let alone the King of Corleo. She had heard rumors of his disdain for the Monte people. They whispered of his slurs against *stone worshipers*. She expected to see her brother join the order before ever meeting the man before her. This must be a delicate diplomatic situation. She could not let her adoptive family down.

She bowed deeply. "King Leorix. How may I serve you?"

Ramath turned to High Priest Laud with a dry, quivering voice. "She's the one? She can use *the sight*?"

"She is the very one, King Ramath," High Priest Laud said with a clinking sound playing a greedy tune under his voice's rasp. He caressed a bulging bag of gold coins. Jezca noticed the fabric bore a symbol that looked the horned lion crest, but Laud hid the bag before she could be sure.

Ramath shook, his nostrils red, his eyes watering. Jezca could see the King was under an unmanageable amount of stress, and that was the least of his ailments, she guessed.

She nodded to him and gestured for him to follow.

They walked into a private room for counsel with priests. Jezca and Ramath sat across from each other on padded benches.

"Do it. Use the sight and tell me what they did to me." His words were strained and tumbled from a parched tongue. A line of uncontrollable tears suddenly streamed down his devastated face.

CHAPTER SEVEN

"They said it was just a mark of loyalty. It's not, though. It's more. It's...it's alive."

He pulled down his tall frilled collar to reveal a two-headed serpent wrapped around his throat in black ink.

"*What is this?*" King Ramath Leorix asked.

CHAPTER EIGHT

RUINS OF MORAX

The glowing wings of Soul Energy that had lit the night in Anondorn now faded. Golden rays of first light accented the gray-blue sky and outlined the clouds. Scipio bustled over to the carriage that Eos and Maxima sat in and opened the door for Talus, who tilted his broad shoulders as he awkwardly pulled himself through the small opening. Terrava slipped in beside her king in a fluid movement that made no sound.

Scipio hurriedly swung the door so that it was open only a few inches and looked around as if paranoid. There was only the sound of stable boys beginning work on the other side of the castle grounds. He spoke in a low voice and more quickly than Talus was accustomed to and barely paused for breath between sentences. "I will tell the assembly that we've located the royal children. That they have been located after being lost for years in the Burning

CHAPTER EIGHT

Lands. That both the King and Queen have gone to meet their returning children on the north shore at the Calid Sea. On the off chance that some may try to beat you to the north shore, they will have gone in the wrong direction. It will also buy me time to spread the news and manage relations—especially with the Cassion family. It will be a delicate situation. I will also have Xaro Monte watched at all times to ensure he doesn't talk about what he saw last night, and Aizo is already in the care of the Sanofem. Return on the fourth morning, and I shall have the entirety of Anondorn ready to receive you with a welcoming feast."

"You are a master of your craft, Scipio."

"Thank you, Talus my lord." The advisor shut the door, pleased with himself.

Eos looked at his parents with heavy eyes. They had spent the entire night recounting twelve years of Earth history, which apparently counted as more than seventeen years on the Corland calender. It was all too much to process after traveling through miles of mountains, encountering a barbarian tribe, and being nearly killed during their ride with Sergius Ora. Now his mother and father came in and out of focus as his eyelids fell; it was a happy dream-like vision. Maxima was already sleeping softly on his shoulder.

"Where are we going?" Eos asked. Talus, Terrava, and Scipio had made plans in hushed whispers as they rushed out of the castle.

Talus grinned. "Tradition is for a master Soul Wielder to take their disciples to the Ruins of Morax before they undergo their attempts to open the gates of their soul. That opportunity was taken from us, but we're going to make up for it now. We're going to teach you about Soul Energy, your history, and most importantly—train!"

RUINS OF MORAX

Eos grinned back at his father with childish whimsy. "Yes!" he murmured as excitedly as his exhausted mind would allow. "Training. I want to show you how much I've learned."

"Boys and their fighting." Terrava shook her head with amusement. "They never seem to tire of it."

There was a tingle of excitement in Eos' belly at the prospect of learning Soul Wielding from his father, but the joyous thought and the fascinating ruins ahead never turned to words as he fell asleep on Maxima.

The carriage pulled them along smoothly. The man that directed the carriage in the front simultaneously steered the horses and formed a smooth path of Soul Energy beneath each of the wheels so that the ride never had a bump. It was an entire day's ride from Anondorn to the Ruins of Morax, but the passengers were all four asleep for the first half of it.

It wasn't until Talus struck his knuckles against the caravan wall three times behind his head that the siblings woke. The huge hand may have moved only slightly, but they all felt the thuds through the wooden walls. The caravan's path-layer, as the craft was called, brought the group to a stop. Eos realized he had barely even felt the vehicle slow down.

Talus yawned and bellowed, "Figured we could stretch our legs and get a little food and drink in us."

As they emerged from the small door, they were greeted by a day of mild temperatures and surrounded by greenery—although Eos found the vegetation in Anite had more gold in it than he was accustomed to seeing. He then bent down to inspect the wheels that had carried them, then looked up at their path-layer, who was now stretching.

CHAPTER EIGHT

Terrava could see his curiosity about how they had traveled. "Path-layers wield Soul Energy beneath the wheels to keep the ride as smooth as possible. Not many could give us the flawless experience that Appocles did. Usually, it takes two at the head of the caravan, one to guide the horses and another to lay the path. Only the most skilled and practiced can do both so well."

"Why, thank you, my lady." Appocles bowed deeply.

After sharing a loaf of slightly sweet, dry bread and passing around a pair of water flasks, Talus produced a leather pouch the size of his head. "Your mother had the idea to bring these with us. It will be an introduction to basic living on the Corland that you missed, and you will need the lesson for your night at the Ruins of Morax."

Terrava lifted the bag from her husband's palm and pulled from it a small semitransparent stone slightly smaller than her fist. It was transparent like glass but full of streaks of opaque-white impurities. Despite the internal impurities, the edges were cleanly cut and polished so that the hunk of rock was a refined tetrahedron. "This is a condlucite stone, one of the two stones that interact with Soul Energy." She handed the one in her hand to Maxima and gave Eos another from the bag. "Condlucite stones have the property that allows them to retain Soul Energy long after it has been imbued into the stone. When of the highest quality, called anima, the stones are blue and retain the Soul Energy almost indefinitely. Anima stones don't produce light that is good to see by. These low-grade condlucites are refined into lighting stones, and they leak Soul Energy quickly but produce a white light that makes it easy to see. Take your stones and—"

There was a flash of light.

Pooomf! Tink Clink Clink Clink.

RUINS OF MORAX

Shards of condlucite sprayed in fine particles, hitting all four Bellators harmlessly and cascading to the ground. Eos' face went purple like a beet. The color spread down his neck, and his ears became hot.

"I-I-I just..." He looked at the fragments of the stone at their feet.

Talus suppressed a smirk while Terrava raised an eyebrow that seemed to say, "*You just... what?*"

"I just wanted to show you that I could do it. That I was..."

Talus pulled another stone from the bag. "Condlucite is fragile, and lighting it is somewhat delicate. It doesn't take much energy." He demonstrated with his lighting stone so that it gave a soft glow. "Get a little over-eager and..." He made his crack into pieces in his hand and let the crumbled stone fall. He pulled yet another stone from the bag. "Try again; we brought plenty."

Eos kept his head down dejectedly but remembered breaking into Lab 4 with Glenn back on Earth. He had controlled his Soul Energy to blow the door handle off and break in without being noticed. He hadn't been great at throttling his power back then either.

It didn't take long before Eos was producing stone light, though Maxima had effortlessly lit hers on the first try.

Talus turned his back to them and looked at the cluster of mountains on the horizon. "I don't know about you three, but I've been in a carriage long enough. Let's step the rest of the way to the mountains. They all agreed, and Eos was grateful not to be sitting for another hour with the embarrassment of shattering his lighting stone.

"Appocles, wait for us at the mountain entrance. We'll be back in two days." Talus grunted to their path layer. Then they were off.

CHAPTER EIGHT

Nothing felt so liberating as Soul Stepping alongside his father and mother.

Gold and green streaked by in Eos' peripheral as the Bellators Soul Stepped towards the mountain range ahead. The crisp air slid off his skin, reminding him how alive he was. The dark flowing hair of his mother and sister, and Talus' mane of auburn beard, warmed Eos' heart as he'd never felt before. He was with his family, about to participate in a ritual of his homeland, and had never felt more whole.

Maxima tried to match Terrava's graceful Soul Step, and for the most part, she succeeded. Their feet nearly matched in time, though Maxima was missing a component of certainty in her technique. Talus had none of his wife's grace but instead powered forward on planes of crimson Soul Energy that made his motion seem unstoppable. He moved with the momentum of a juggernaut. Eos did his best to keep up but found neither the grace and swiftness of his mother nor his father's raw power. Still, he did not lag too far behind their pace.

He smiled from ear to ear at the fun of just watching them and attempting to keep up.

It was almost a sad feeling when they slowed to approach the mountain. It was drowning in yellow grass and sage colored moss. When combined with the thousands of years of dirt and weathering, the white, chalky stone of the mountains peeked out from all the covering in patches that resembled scales.

"The Iussum Mountains. This is the home of the Order of Soul Wielders." Talus said with a touch of awe in his voice. "When you walk through the entrance, you'll see why."

RUINS OF MORAX

They all proceeded towards a small pass in the mountain wall's outer veil, but Maxima lingered behind. "Do...do you feel that? These mountains feel sort of...alive."

Terrava nodded. "Very good. They are not alive, but there is something in the mountains that you are feeling. You will soon find out what that is."

They walked through a narrow, winding path that made switchback patterns. It wound so that Eos was sure they spend only a quarter of the time progressing deeper into the mountain maze. "Can we step over the mountains?" Eos asked, trying to suggest a more efficient way. The moment the words left his lips, he knew it sounded impatient.

Terrava answered, "What we came to see isn't up there, and that feeling that the mountains are alive is difficult to track if you are not amongst the rocks."

Eventually, the overlapping ridges widened to an open area where the spines of different mountain groupings sloped down to meet the earth. Although the peaks threatened to scrape the heavens, the mouth of the pass contained four statues that were nearly as tall. Two robed, stone Soul Wielders lined each side of the clearing, facing inward. All four lifted one open hand to their waist level. In each hand was a sculpted flame to represent Soul Energy. None of them stood as tall as the foot of one statue. Eos marveled that they must be over one hundred feet high.

Terrava looked to Talus. "Shall I track the path while you begin? I know how much you love this story."

Talus looked pleased. "Please do. You know how badly I've always wanted to do this with our children." Terrava looked to the other end of the clearing, beyond the four statues, and wandered that direction. There was a glow of Soul Energy from her head, but she was facing away so that neither Eos nor Maxima could see what she had done.

"What I am about to tell you is known as the Legend of Morax," Talus began. "I have studied Earth as much as the texts available to the Order of Soul Wielders have allowed. One thing I noted is that time is kept differently between the two worlds. On Hyperborea, we track it in increments of sixteen. Sixteen days in a week, sixteen weeks in a year, sixteen years in a hexade, and sixteen hexades in an era. Eras are usually recorded based on world-changing events that make them distinct. We are in era Sixteen now. Era six and everything before it was not recorded, though many writings from era ten suggest the sixth era once had recorded history. That we regard as the Lost History. Era twelve is known as a primitive age where the early families of wielders, the Bellators, the Primane, the Monte, the Terrspar, and so on, warred amongst themselves over territories and resources, recreating and evolving beyond whatever they had forgotten during the Lost History."

Maxima interrupted, "If everything counts up to sixteen, what happens at the end of this era?"

"Aizo warned me you were too sharp for your own good and catch every detail," Talus said. "The long era calendar system was developed in incredibly ancient times. What the calendar creators intended to happen after this era is up for debate. Many think that since such world-changing events mark each era, this is the last. Hyperborea will come to an end after." Maxima's face went white. Talus continued, "Buuuut others will tell you that everyone will start the count over, and we won't have hardly noticed. I tend towards the latter theory." He smiled mischievously, knowing he had given his kids a brief scare.

RUINS OF MORAX

Terrava returned to their huddle between the statues. "I've found our path."

"We'll set off once they know who they're standing under," Talus said. Terrava seemed to agree. "Era fourteen is why we're in the Iussum Mountains now. The Corlanders discovered a new continent far to the west that they called Dacia. The natives on that continent were soon called Krogs. During their voyages to and from Dacia, many Krog people were brought back to Corland, and a mixed-race called the Mezclado came to exist. The Corlanders ended up enslaving most Krogs. Both looked down on the mixed-bloods. There was a new source of turmoil in Corland as the hexades went on. Soon war broke out, and enslavement of the Krogs was at the center of it all…at least that's what is written in the history books. The truth is more complex. The Mellizo Glyphs you returned home with are a pair, but it was not originally that way. One glyph resided on Corland. The other was found on Dacia during the voyages to the new continent. The fourteenth era's powerful families warred over the glyphs as much as the fate of the Krog people during this time. The bloodshed would have continued for longer than the eight years, had it not been for the most powerful Soul Wielder of the era. He was a Mezclado named Morax. He gathered wielders of like mind and put together a faction that overwhelmed the old families during their war. In doing so, he established peace and formed the Order of Soul Wielders. Together with his three disciples: Cintish the Corlander, Jaruus the Krog, and Straquil the Mezclado, he brought an era of peace to Corland. With it came a resurgence of knowledge and studies. We stand now beneath Morax, Cintish, Jaruus, and Straquil—the founders of the order of Soul Wielders. Thirty years after the Bellator and Primane families laid down their arms

CHAPTER EIGHT

alongside the Viator family of the Krogs, they had these four
statues made due to the lasting peace the order of Soul Wielders
brought."

Terrava cut in, "We still have more than a two-hour journey
ahead of us. We're standing under the statues made to honor the
order and its four founders, and most travel across kingdoms just
to see them. But there is much more in these mountains for those
who know where to look." She gave a cunning smile to her
children. "Follow me."

Talus motioned for them to go with their mother, and they all
set off again. Eos and Maxima found their heads being pulled back
to marvel at the unbelievable scale of the statues they were leaving
behind. Ahead, the mountain offered them four paths. Terrava
took the furthest left route without hesitation.

Maxima started into questions about Talus' tale of the
Corlanders, the Krogs, and the war fought for glyphs and freedom
for the Krogs. "You said the Bellators fought in this war?"

"I did."

"For which side then?" Maxima asked.

"There were more than two sides to the war. Our ancient
ancestor, Emperor Pertinax Bellator, fought for the freedom of the
Krogs, but against the Viator family. The Viator Krogs demanded
their own kingdom from pieces of the existing kingdoms. So, they
clashed. Krogs were split between Viator and Bellator, though
historians wrote that many more sided with the Viator. The
Primane wanted to keep the practices of enslavement in place for
both Krogs and low-class Corlanders. Throw in the subtext of the
Mellizo Glyphs, and the war was complicated and fought between
five factions."

RUINS OF MORAX

Maxima took a few seconds to absorb the information and reflect while chewing on her lip. Then she said, "So our family fought on the right side?"

Talus raised an eyebrow but looked proud. "The Bellators supported freedom. I believe that was right. However, there were other motivations at play for all sides."

They found themselves switching back and forth through winding paths, veering off on branches where the mountain split, and following an incomprehensible route that Eos doubted anyone could possibly remember by heart. Terrava was quiet and intently focused on leading them.

It was Eos' turn to ask a question. "What happened after the war?"

Talus sighed with a heavy disappointment. "The fall of the Order as it was originally constructed. The four founders opened a temple for the study of wielding and other higher learning. Society prospered for nearly three hexades...but corruption festered." They had to move quickly to keep up with Terrava, who was slipping around cracks in the mountain walls as if being pulled by an invisible thread. "The Mezclado founder, Straquil, was became taken by the idea reparations from the war. Jaruus grew more isolationist. Cintish favored anti-Krog laws as the post-war repercussions became less stable. Only the strength and unification brought by Morax could keep them all subdued. The official story becomes hazy after this. Some say it was Jaruus; other texts claim Cintish; most sources say it was Straquil who murdered Morax in his old age."

Maxima exclaimed, "They killed him?"

"They did. The wars brought about grudges and losses. Kings and lords whispered in the founders' ears and tried to sway their power. All that is known for sure is that Morax was killed, and his statue defaced."

"But the order still exists," Eos said, trying to make sense of it.

Talus nodded. "A strange thing happened—the texts and teachings lived on. The masters taught their students, and in turn, the students carried on the tradition and became masters. There has never since been a single leader of the order, but councils of inlumes have convened throughout the hexades of the eras. And it seems that wherever the true intent of the order gains influence, life improves for all."

"What is the true intent?" Eos asked.

Talus' eyes gleamed as he said, "We'll get to that."

Then, Terrava stopped. "We've come to the place." She said reverently. "Talus, let's give them time to find it for themselves."

Talus agreed.

Eos searched the chalky scales of rock and moss for what his mother had seen.

"There's nothing special here," he concluded. "It's just part of the mountain."

"No." Maxima corrected him, "Look there." She pointed to the top of the nearby ridge.

"Ah," Eos let out when he saw it. It was indistinct and completely camouflaged to anyone not told to look for something. Three swords, overgrown by eras of moss growth, were plunged into the ridge.

Talus confirmed Maxima's find. "The swords laid down by our ancestors as a peace offering to Morax. They mark the first temple of the Order of Soul Wielders, *Fanum Ortus*. This was Morax's private study. Come."

RUINS OF MORAX

The siblings followed Talus and Terrava to the top of the mountain ridge, bouncing up Soul Energy platforms. Shimmers of crimson and sapphire speckled the rocks as the four made their way up.

They stood together before the three ancient swords. Talus revealed, "The leftmost sword is that of our ancestor Pertinax. This," he knelt and set his hand on a manmade pedestal of rock that was further in from the edge of the cliff, "is the Record of the Order, also called the Turrim Cartus." The pedestal was a sequence of square cuts of stone that narrowed up from the base and expanded again from the middle until it was three feet high. It was carved from the same stone as the mountain, but dark veins of blue stone ran up the center of each side, meeting at the center of the pedestal's top surface in a dome.

Terrava put her hand on it too. The veins of blue stone became luminescent, and the siblings realized this was anima stone. Terrava spoke with the blue color washing over her face, "Every member of the order, alive and dead, has traces of their Soul Energy in this stone. It here that the master Soul Wielders, given the title *inlume*, mark their students as true members, called *anatus*. Every anatus takes their oath here. If one completes their training, they become an *errant* here. Once every hexade or so, one or two gifted wielders are witnessed by the order and become inlumes." She closed her eyes as if praying.

Blue light like spread over her forehead like a crown. Then, red light appeared over Talus'. As if tattooed with Soul Energy, marks floated above their eyes and rose from their skin. Three vertical lines adorned each of them, two falling from either side of the centerline. Horizontal lines formed crosses like the hilt of broken

CHAPTER EIGHT

swords on all three, and the edges twisted into a circlet of ornate weaving.

"Both your father and I bear the mark of the inlume," Terrava said, appearing as some sort of angel to the children.

Talus finished, "Before we leave, we want you to take the oath of the order...if you choose. There will be much to learn and experience."

The crowns of light had an awe-inducing effect, leaving Eos and Maxima mesmerized and almost believing they were ready to experience all Hyperborea had to offer. Yet, it also cast a light of responsibility and weight they didn't understand. The siblings were as eager as they were unsure of the implications that came with such a commitment. They stood on thousands of years of history with only a few hours of understanding. The decision loomed over them as the long shadow of three swords was stretched thin across the ridge.

CHAPTER NINE

CONSTRAINED REFLECTION

Layers of warm clothes bundled around Ares, and his breath clouded before his eyes, masking the room in an opaque layer every time he exhaled. The small arctic camp-building was full to the brim with crates of rifles, loot from their *trade* with General Braxton. Truckloads of rifles were shoved into the tiny tent-like structure. Now, it had enough men to carry each of the crates squeezed inside as well.

Lord Vistomus stood over the horde of Mitad underlings, crates, Ares, and the most crucial member of the operation—Bellia. Her wounds were still fresh, but Lord Vistomus had given her no time; *it was a matter of urgency for the organization to move the weapons.*

CHAPTER NINE

Ares had coached Bellia for the last fifteen hours without sleep to make sure she was ready. He had done it as a master would with a student, devoid of emotion and personal concern. There had been someone, a vizier or a rebel or an unranked Mitad member nearby the entire time. Ares was sure that hadn't been a coincidence.

Bellia couldn't so much as lift the arm that soldiers had shot during the Braxton trade. Instead, she had learned to remove the habit of associating wielding with the motions of her physical body. She was absolutely still. The only movements were clouds of breath slipping from beneath her pink lips in nervous stutters and the gentle thrashing of the blond tips of hair outside her hood when a gust blew through the open door.

The look in her eyes held a frightening beauty, but Ares made sure not to stare for more than a glance.

Everyone in the room stiffened. The air buzzed as if a synthesizer reverberated in a silent tune that shook bodies but never reached ears.

Craaaaackle-Zmmmmm.

The sound of Soul Energy tearing at the fabric of Earth rang out.

Violet tendrils squirmed like writhing limbs reaching out of a deep hole. The hole expanded as the strings of energy whipped about, revealing a portal to Hyperborea. It swelled at the tent's doorway but stopped before being a viable size for transporting the crates. Then it vibrated unstably.

Bellia clenched her jaw and frowned as beads of sweat formed on her face. Her teeth scraped against each other in resistance to her failing portal. The creation stabilized before expanding again.

CONSTRAINED REFLECTION

Two men lifted the first crate and shuffled quickly through the artificial passageway between worlds as soon as it was large enough to pass through. As they walked, the next box was raised. The Mitad made twenty through, and twenty pairs of men were gone to Hyperborea before the portal inevitably shook and folded in on itself.

Arctic air blew into the room once more. It chilled Bellia's wet skin. Her breath was heavy, and Ares could tell that she was struggling to remain standing.

"Again," Lord Vistomus commanded bluntly.

Bellia's eyes widened at the words. She reached deep in herself for the fortitude to carry on, remembering a time when she still had her father.

"Keep this with you. Remember me when you hold it. Let it help you find your way."

She reached into a pocket with her healthy arm and touched a toy carving of a sea turtle. Her finger passed over the ridges that her father had made. He had carved those *for her.* Each and every line had been for her—even the symbol of a tree with a flame in its branches that marked the turtle's belly.

Sweat poured, but the gateway opened once more. Only half as many crates made it through this time before Bellia began to shake uncontrollably. She heaved but clenched the turtle carving and managed not to fall.

"Again."

Ares had a thought to speak out, or even to comfort Bellia. The least he could do was give a few words of encouragement, but Lord Vistomus had forbidden any show of emotion. He could only watch.

The portal opened, and a few more crates made it through.

CHAPTER NINE

"Again."

The extreme test continued until Bellia's eyes were hollow and lifeless, and sweat drenched her hood.

When they had transported half of the crates off Earth, and all of the other Mitad members had disappeared through the portal, Lord Vistomus gave a final order. "Take us back."

Lord Vistomus passed through with parting words, "You did well, Bellia. Your ability grows."

Ares passed through a shaking ring of violet Soul Energy. He stepped out on the other side and found himself in the center chamber of the web of the Mitad's underground desert base. Bellia's talents were growing more accurate. Never before had she transported them to the inside of the hideout, let alone precisely where they had desired.

Thud.

Bellia collapsed to her knees behind him, barely making it through the portal before it closed. Lord Vistomus watched from the corner of his eye as he left the room.

Bellia put out a hand as Ares walked past her. Her feminine fingers gripped Ares' forearm and slid down to his hand as he brushed her gesture aside.

Lord Vistomus noted the coldness from a distance. He didn't smile, but his look was one of approval.

Bellia was left alone to carry herself to her room. Drips of sweat splashed the gray concrete floor.

That night, Ares dipped his quill in an inkpot, but he cursed to himself as a drop splashed unintentionally on his paper. He had never learned the skill of writing properly during his younger years in Anite. His handwriting was scratchy, and he still stained his pages with splotches.

CONSTRAINED REFLECTION

Bellia had not carried herself to her room, but instead, she had collapsed in Ares' doorway. Now, she was half awake on his sleeping mat, tracing the lines of his full back tattoo and whispering to him softly as he wrote letters. Lord Vistomus had tasked him with writing to Tenebrim's leader, Salvaluc, to organize for a coming operation on Saida's behalf. He dragged his quill against the paper in the low condlucite-stone light, scrawling the will of the Mitad.

Bellia murmured, "You've been so distant."

The light caress on his shirtless back was a welcomed comfort. It reassured him that Bellia could withstand the treatment he had given her. For the moment, they were alone. "You know why. Even now, you shouldn't be in here."

"But I am," her voice soothed.

Ares only appreciatively grunted as he scribbled the shape of a serpent with a head on either end. The mark completed the letter. While the ink was still wet, he let a thin stream of Soul Energy trickle from his finger into the snake mark. It shone with the brightness of a condlucite stone before drying with the deceivingly normal look of ink. This mark would come to life as proof of authenticity and as a warning to obey the words within.

The sensation of Bellia's nails running over his skin ceased. "Will this public act ever end? I don't see how it could," she thought to herself. Her voice was giving way to sleep, and a yawn interrupted her. "If this must continue, you'll have to do better when we're alone together."

"Mmmh," Ares replied as he sealed the letter.

"Tell me what your tattoo means. You've kept that from me long enough."

CHAPTER NINE

"Marks are either common to the Mitad or a personal secret," Ares returned.

Bellia's hand began tracing the mural of color on his back again, over the lines of a fierce bird seeming to fly underwater. She touched his skin, covered in white foam and wings. "But you'll tell me your secrets?" she teased as her touch ended on the red gem, plucked by the bird's claws at the bottom of the water.

Their eyes met, and Ares smiled mischievously. "Stealing my secrets, temptress?" He lay down next to her. "In Anite, the elsu is revered, much like the sea turtle in your homeland. The elsu gather at a great tree at the center of a lake that only the nobility can visit. I was taken to it…once. Its base was as wide as ten of us laying down, and its branches seemed like they could shade a village. My mother told me a legend while I was there. It was the tale of the matriarch elsu, Hasvela, who lived at the top of the tree. The birds are the fastest creatures alive now, but it wasn't always that way. Once they were normal birds, or so the story goes. Free to fly anywhere in the word, but the only place they weren't free to travel was under the water."

Bellia laughed weakly, "Well, a bird wouldn't be a bird if it could swim, would it?"

"Not true. You'd understand if you let me finish."

"Go on. I like this story." She stared into Ares' eyes, enthralled.

"It is said the tree grew so great and strong because its roots grew through a pure chunk of animus stone at the bottom of the lake. The great mother elsu one day flew high in the air and then dove into the lake. They say a miracle happened under the water and the mother elsu learned to beat its wings through the water as if it was air. What she couldn't do was breathe under the lake."

Bellia made a humming sound that urged him to continue.

CONSTRAINED REFLECTION

"The mother elsu saw the red shine of sunlight off of the animus stone at the bottom of the lake. She flew down further, drawn to it. As she ran out of air, she reached the stone and saw a piece had broken off, which she grabbed in her beak. But she was unable to breathe and out of air. It was then that she swallowed the stone. If you believe the story, she then gained the ability to Soul Wield with her feathers and guide the currents to make her faster than any living creature. This saved her as she burst out of the lake just in time."

"She lived?"

Ares nodded. "She became the mother of all elsu, and now they all wield Soul Energy when they fly...or so they say."

"And you believe it?"

Ares shrugged. "It's a story of bravery… and evolution into a stronger being."

Bellia tilted her head up with humored disbelief. "It's a tale of *arrogance and luck*."

"Perhaps." Ares sat up and began work on his last letter. "Lord Vistomus has called for a gathering of the cloaks. He summoned Emir Raggan and all twenty viziers on Earth to be there. Get your rest." Ares willed the Soul Energy from the condlucite stone and into his palm. He clenched his fist to extinguish the energy into glowing vapor. "Lord Vistomus will expect you to transport everyone."

∞   ∞   ∞

Twenty viziers and three Mirza stood in a mass of cloaks around a circular table that could seat all twenty-four members in the room. The table was of black stone, and in front of each walnut

CHAPTER NINE

chair was a folded piece of parchment. Arched mirrors covered the walls of the chamber, giving it an immense and contorted feeling. The reflections of gathered members filled the numerous mirrors so that it seemed the room went on forever and held an army of cloaks.

All the viziers, the Mitad leaders on the ground who performed general work for the organization, waited anxiously for orders. Ares, Tessio, and Bellia were the three mirza-ranked who carried out more skilled tasks and kept control of the vizier. They waited alongside their subordinates. Then there was the Emir. He was not waiting but instead thinking hard about something as he paced back and forth.

Emir Raggan was a short imposing figure, with the demeanor of a crazed bulldog. He stalked around the table with arms held out wide and a scowl on his stubble covered face.

"Right," he broke the silence with a quiet mumbling voice that seemed to give the room momentum as he rounded each chair and letter. "I've been called back from my trip to the orient. Things are a lot more orderly over there. Structured between the rabble and their masters. Not like this mess...but we'll fix that won' we? Take a seat in front of the letter with your name on it. It has the orders you are to carry out. You will read them. You will damn sure carry 'em out flawlessly, and you will not discuss 'em with anyone else beyond what is spoken aloud in this meeting."

There was a shuffle of feet and chairs that shimmered in a thousand reflections off the mirrored walls as everyone found their seat. Nearly all were seated when one haughty vizier joked to another, "Lord Vistomus isn't even here yet, and our new Emir is starting for him." The vizier next to him chuckled.

CONSTRAINED REFLECTION

Emir Raggan cocked his head and squinted his pale blue eyes. "No, no. Mmmm. Mmmmm." He covered his mouth as if distressed and grunted. He stalked over to the closest mirror, inspecting its arched lines and heavy stone frame as if judging it for quality. He removed his hand from over his mouth and lifted the mirror off the wall. Holding it up, the mirror drew the attention of everyone present. All eyes drifted with his mirror as he carried it around the table.

Smash!

Raggan brought the heavy mirror down over the head of the man who had spoken. The vizier's head split open and began immediately bleeding as he fell to the floor, seizing. Mirror shards rained down around the chair. Raggan patted his hands together, dusting off imaginary bits of shrapnel as the man shook and bled at his boots. "Now, I hate using Soul Energy if I don't have to. This way, is much more personal innit?" He looked down at the man emotionlessly and then took his place at the table. "He'll wake up, yeah? And he'll be more learned for it."

Ares smiled, appreciating Emir Raggan's style and command. *He handled that appropriately.* The smile quickly faded. Something was off in the room—hiding in the mirrored vastness.

Raggan continued, "Lord Vistomus will not be joining us. He is about doin' the Master's work. I will be leading all Mitad missions on Earth until he returns to us. Anyone with further questions about that may ask Vizier Lius o'er there on the floor."

Ares suddenly grew infuriated. In the shadows of the corner of the room, hidden by the reflections that stole everyone's attention, was an outsider.

"Lord Vistomus has run this operation much differently than it is run in the homeland. He asked me to shift things back into order now that the Mitad is settin' deeper roots. After the comin' missions are completed, we will begin the unification of the Mitad on two worlds. Half of the guns we've captured are on the Corland in Hyperborea, moving to Corleo territory. The other half have been left here. I will distribute 'em as I see fit o'er the next week."

Ares could barely pay attention to the words of the newly arrived Emir. The man in the corner of the room beamed at Ares as the light caught his round spectacles. The man gave a nod and stroked his bushy mustache.

"Emir Raggan, If I may speak?" Ares requested through gritted teeth.

"Ah, Ares. By all means, speak. I suggest doing so wisely, yeah?" Raggan said in a low mumbling slur and let out a dry laugh as he pointed to Vizier Lius.

Ares raised a gray pointed finger to the corner of the room. "May I inquire what an outsider, such as General Allenby, is doing at a Mitad council?" He recalled sending his Soul Chain through General Evetts, thus promoting the second in command, General Allenby, to head of the European Sector. An outsider at a gathering of cloaks broke traditions and irked Ares into a fit.

"Ah, a right question. I was told you were a sharp one. I've been looking forward to workin' with you. Unfortunately, Vistomus and Saida have other plans, as you'll see in your orders. So, you need not concern yourself with him." Raggan gestured back to Allenby. "For the rest of you, the takeover of the North American Sector will appear completely organic. They will think it was a well-timed rebellion from the inside, and the European Sector capitalized on that. I know I'm here to…reinstate structure, but matters of Earth will require a bit more…precise navigation, yeah? Occasionally that will break with tradition. General Allenby

CONSTRAINED REFLECTION

is here because he will be delivering the critical blow to the North American Sector when we strike."

Ares swallowed his rage. Emir Raggan had dismissed him so nonchalantly and removed him from the plans in a sentence. The fresh burn on Ares' neck from Lord Vistomus reminded him to control his emotions. He held the paper with his orders and crumpled it slightly with rigid fingers, anxious to learn of what Lord Vistomus had planned for him. His glance danced from pane of glass to pane of glass in the mirrors and settled on a single arched frame that contained only his reflection. He saw Tessio left of Emir Raggan in the pane next to it, and Bellia and the Vizier in the pane to the right, but this one…this one only showed him. He unfolded the parchment.

CHAPTER TEN

PENITUS OSTIUM

"When Saida gave you that scar, I had no idea it was a curse. Aizo did a remarkable job sealing it, but its nature is a mystery. With what you have told me so far, *we must* understand it as soon as possible," Talus said, sitting across from Eos.

The father and son sat with a waterfall falling in the distance, an hour's hike from the three swords of Fanum Ortus. It was a world hidden in moss and stone; the air was chilled at the altitude and smelled of rusty earth.

Eos finished unwrapping his right arm. He put his curse mark on display. "I want to know what the curse mark means. I've been close to an answer a few times…in the Soul Void…when I met Vistomus Fulmen…and I know that a similar type of mark took control of Ares. The more I learn about myself, the more it seems to haunt me. Sometimes, I don't think I can control it. What if Aizo's seal isn't enough?"

Talus leaned back with his thick muscular arms stretched behind him. "You remind me of my younger self. Rest assured; we'll find out how to manage it." He paused, thinking of the time they missed together while on separate worlds, and pondering how Terrava was handling the missing memories and lost time with Maxima. There was only the sound of water flowing and crashing.

Eos nodded with a trusting smile at his father.

"Was it difficult on Earth?"

"Everyone was afraid of us. We didn't belong there. Most of the time. There were a few people…a few moments."

Talus grimaced, pained by his son's struggle.

Eos beamed at Talus optimistically. "I'm here now. We can make up for lost time."

Stroking the great auburn braids of his beard, Talus pondered. "No. I don't think one can make up lost time, nor do I believe we need to. We'll build from scratch." He winked. "I know history and training would my favorite place to start."

Eos jumped at the words. "I'm going to train with you?"

Talus nodded in return.

A murmur of wonder slipped from Eos before he said, "There's so much I want to know."

A hearty chuckle followed from Talus. "To think, I waited twelve years to see you again knowing you were alive the whole time, and you return to me already having learned partial Severance! We have much to discuss, but first, show me."

"Show you what?"

"Severance. You can learn more about a person from the form their Soul Energy takes than from days of talking."

CHAPTER TEN

Eos protested as he had only used the technique for a few days of Aizo's training and once against Ares, but his father insisted.

Crimson tendrils of Soul Energy shimmered in Eos' hand.

"I don't know if I can do it well enough. It'll be nothing compared to what you can do—"

Talus cut him off, "Don't worry about what I can do. We're building a new foundation, remember?"

Eos breathed in deeply, relaxing his body and calming his mind. The sensation of static electricity brimmed under his skin as he focused on the first two gates of his soul. Like clearing a cluttered stream. Just as Aizo taught him.

Internal pathways opened, and his power surged forth.

A fiery bird spun to life from threads of Soul Energy—an elsu, the bird of the Anite Kingdom. Wisps turned into beating wings; tongues of red flame-like energy turned to shimmering feathers. The creation circled him once and settled into a hover at his shoulder.

Enormous hands clapped together as Talus laughed in disbelief. "Now that is something we can work with! By the Great Soul, you took after me. An elsu!"

The bird's natural churn of energy stuttered as Eos grew excited. He nearly lost the form entirely. "Your Severence is an elsu too?"

"Not like yours, but mine takes the form of the wings of an elsu. It's the Bellator family crest. We've been tied to the bird since Anite was founded, so it's hardly a surprise. Now send it over the stream." Talus gestured to the slow-moving body of water that moved out from the waterfall.

Eos obeyed, but the thrill of his father's affirmation filled his mind. Excitement fed excitement, and the creature of red light barely held its shape as the wings left streaks in the air. It burst forth with a *pop*. In an instant, it crossed the gap between them and the stream.

Then the wavering overcame the mass of Soul Energy. The elsu veered down, crashing violently into the shallow stream. *Booom!* The stream was displaced, and water foamed up twenty feet above the surface.

Talus' eyes were wide. He murmured, "I'll be hearing from Terrava about that. Right; focus and control. Not unlike what I needed at your age." Eos' face blushed, and he rubbed his cursed arm anxiously. Talus patted him on the back with hefty reassurance. "Not to worry, son. I honed the same skills here with my master. I warn you, though: the training isn't easy."

"I trained with Aizo over and over again until I went unconscious."

A deep belly laugh was Talus' response. He strode forward. "Well, this is different."

Eos followed to the base of the waterfall. Talus explained that Eos would practice focus by utilizing the breathing technique in the water. If he gained control, they would advance to wielding in the water.

Sitting with his legs crossed, Talus demonstrated meditating. He was a specimen of power that rested in perfect calm. Eos stripped down to his underwear and dipped a toe in the water. The moment the ice-cold water met his toes, the earthy scent of the mountains disappeared. His vision receded from attention. All he perceived in that instant was the freezing temperature of the water.

Before he could say a word, Talus perceived his thoughts and said, "Yes, it's unbearably cold, but you trained with Aizo. Surely you can handle it. It will focus your senses into a singular point.

CHAPTER TEN

When you overcome that primal urge to get warm, you refine your focus. Eventually, you'll learn to wield your Soul Energy calmly."

So, Eos took the plunge and submerged up to his chest. His skin perceived pain more than cold, and his brain urged him out of the stream.

Watching Eos fidget, Talus said, "That is only your primitive brain distracting you from reaching your potential and becoming an inlume."

The tease of that title and the urge to not disappoint his father was enough to keep Eos in the water.

"Breath is life. In and out. Slowly in and letting go," Talus repeated rhythmically, guiding Eos as his own master had taught him. "Slowly in and letting go. Focus on the sound of the waterfall. You are warm. You are too warm! Slowly in and letting go."

After many repetitions that were to Talus' satisfaction, Eos did indeed feel warm. Then he began trying to hold together Soul Spheres. Talus watched proudly as red spheres flickered in and out of existence, floating over the water with the pulsations of Eos' breath.

∞   ∞   ∞

The cold breeze whipped Maxima's raven hair across her face; it was identical in color to her mother's. The one thing she had only dreamed of with tragic hope was now real. She was alone with her mom. She worried about the right words to say next and went instinctually to bite down on her scarf, but it was no longer there. She caught her hair between her lips instead and squeezed.

Terrava looked at her daughter and noticed the hesitancy.

PENITUS OSTIUM

"What you did for Aizo…his leg during your journey back. That was a show of great talent. It wasn't the technique of the Sanofem healers exactly. No, something unique, but with their training, you could do great things."

Maxima smiled enough to let her hair fall back down to her shoulders and said, "I had a lot of practice."

Terrava's thin eyebrows raised curiously. "You did?"

"Eos started getting weak when he was using Soul Energy on Earth. The mark on his arm would end up hurting him." When she said this, her mother's eyes squinted with interest. Maxima continued, "I would heal him. My Soul Energy helped him somehow. On nights when we worked past his limitations, I lent him my energy. I figured something similar would help Aizo."

"It was a brilliant invention of soul technique. Would you like to learn how to hone that ability?"

Maxima's sapphire eyes lit up. "I would. Can you show me?" She thought for a few seconds. "Well, I want to learn anything I can…but what I want to do most is learn Severence like Eos has."

Booooom! The sound of energy exploding against water echoed through the mountain valleys.

Pointed red lips smirked with amusement. Terrava sighed. "Boys. I should have known Talus and Eos would blow something up immediately."

"I could have told you Eos would do something like that. He likes to jump into things, especially if it has to do with Soul Energy," Maxima said.

"I gathered that from his attempt to light the condlucite stone. Too much like his father. We'll have to work double-time together to keep them out of trouble. Now, if you're more interested in

CHAPTER TEN

Severance than the healing arts, then let's see what technique you can produce."

Maxima stumbled on her words. "I don't. I mean—it's probably not worth showing yet."

"Nonsense. If you really want to pursue Severance skills over the healing arts, there's no place for hesitancy. Show me what you've got, and we'll work from there."

There was a whistle of wind as Maxima closed her eyes. Blue light formed between her hands. Where there had been uncertainty and timidness, instinct took over. Her natural aptitude was on display, and the energy grew. Then it stretched and divided before snapping into two spheres.

"Now, isn't that something?" Terrava stood with her hands on her hips and a graceful grin. "With no formal training, you've already opened the first gate through intuition, and the second one is not far away. I can show you how to go further, and then we can work on that hesitancy."

"Please! Show me how to get past the second gate…but how do we work on hesitancy?" Maxima let her Soul Spheres evaporate away.

Terrava pointed to the gray cliff face above them. "You climb."

Maxima frowned and tilted her head in disbelief.

"Don't worry about that. Let's work on the second gate." Terrava smoothed her dress and cracked her knuckles. "The second deals with guilt. I need you to close your eyes and imagine the feeling of burden."

They began on the long meditative process of opening the gates of the Soul Reservoir. Maxima swam through the translucent vapors of her memories, grappling with the pleasant and painful ones.

PENITUS OSTIUM

"Do you have that feeling in your head? Speak it."

Maxima loosened her clenched jaw to say, "When we were little. General Braxton was hurting me…"

Terrava clenched her fists furiously but remembered not to interrupt the process.

"He lifted me up and was so much bigger. That's when Eos manifested his energy for the first time. He protected me. Saved me. Ever since that moment, I've felt like a burden to him. He always tried to carry more than his portion of the weight for my sake. I don't want to be a burden."

Eyes toughened by war, loss, and grief softened in that moment. Terrava reassured Maxima, "You have an immense talent within you. Don't just focus on the weight others carry, but also recognize your own achievements. Think of all the times you revived your brother after he became weak from the curse on his arm. You're strong and skilled, but you must recognize that for yourself."

The meditation continued, and then they transitioned into climbing the sharp cliff faces with Maxima's Soul Step as the only insurance if she fell. The day wore on into the indigo hues of dusk. Before darkness settled, Terrava and Maxima rejoined Talus and Eos at the three swords.

Their parents stood before the Turrim Cartus pedestal.

Talus began, "Usually, there would be more time before taking the oath, but you two have aged away from Hyperborea. You developed wielding techniques on your own, and I fear our next opportunity to perform the ceremony may not be soon."

Terrava continued, "The Order of Soul Wielders is a noble, respected, and feared society. We seek the preservation of cultures and continued progress towards peace and prosperity."

CHAPTER TEN

The crowns of light condensed over Talus and Terrava's head with crosses like broken swords at the center. The light formed a wreath of twisting threads that circled and joined near the outer crosses.

"We understand if you feel this is rushed," Talus said. "The decision is yours."

Eos did not need to consider the choice for long. He would do anything to join the same Order as his father. "My decision is yes. I'm ready."

"So am I," Maxima said.

Talus instructed them, "Very well. You will repeat after me, then place your hand on the Turrim Cartus, and contribute your Soul Energy to the Record of the Order."

They nodded, hanging on their parents' every word.

"Listen to the oath carefully so that you may contemplate it before committing to the Order," Terrava warned. "The words run through everything you will do as a Soul Wielder. Breaking your oath results in excommunication, so you must believe in your heart what you say and not stray from the path once you start on it."

Eos and Maxima glanced at each other, sharing an unspoken sibling thought. *Excommunication.* Joining the Order was more serious business than they had initially thought, but the moment their pupils met, they knew they both had always wanted this.

Talus spoke the words that would make them Soul Wielders:

"I believe in the Divine Soul, which all mankind may glimpse in their own reflection.

I believe in the right for all to make for themselves a free life.

I will use wisdom granted by the Divine Soul to guide my wielding towards this belief.

PENITUS OSTIUM

I will set aside the influences of nations and kingdoms when they are destructive to mankind.

I will transform chaos into order.

I will pursue the path of light.

I will uphold the Order of Soul Wielders so that they may defend all others."

They repeated after their father in their heads.

Terrava looked at them proudly. "You will soon be anatus of the Order of Soul Wielders: novices beginning the journey towards inlume. We will spend two nights here. The ceremony is always initiated by the new Soul Wielders spending a night meditating in Morax's private chambers. The experience often provides clarity and vision to your future journey. What you gain in Morax's ruins is for you alone. Then, when you have both taken part in this ritual, you will take the oath together."

The four descended from the site of the three swords and found an arched tunnel not far away. It was covered in moss and drew little attention from a distance. On either side of the entrance were life-like engravings of hooded Soul Wielders holding out Soul Spheres as if to light the way, and a tree's roots formed knotted vines that hung down, crawling over the arch to each Soul Wielder.

They passed through and found a locked double door at the end of the tunnel. Made of polished white marble, it had no handle or lock. Only the symbol of the Order of Soul Wielders was on it—three broken swords with the outer two staggered lower. These were at the peak of a twisting ring. Eos put a hand to the door and pushed, but it didn't budge.

"The secret to opening these doors is passed on from inlume to inlume," Talus said and raised his hand. He released Soul Energy

CHAPTER TEN

that floated up to the relief carvings above the door of three swords. The dull animus jewels in the hilts glowed, and the tumbling of a locking mechanism began to clunk. "I will leave the door open for the next two nights. Eos, you will stay tonight. Maxima, tomorrow. Go in with no expectations, but remember to meditate on the oath. Memorize it, ponder the meaning of each line, and maybe something of Morax's personal study will inspire your journey after you leave the Iussum mountains."

Maxima turned to Eos. "I'm glad you're going first. I wouldn't want to be the first to spend the night alone in there."

Terrava put her hand on his shoulder and said, "Remember, have an empty mind when you enter. It is a place full of history. You may read the books or ponder items in there, but they will only act as seeds of inspiration. We'll meet back at the Turrim Cartus at sunrise."

With that, Eos entered the shadows of the spiral staircase. Talus' dark red Soul Energy whipped past him suddenly and ran through the entirety of Morax's private study. Condlucite stones came to life and pushed the darkness back. Ornately engraved patterns and figures decorated the walls down the stairs.

The spiral descended multiple levels, but Eos felt curiously drawn to the second open door on his descent. There was a familiar tingle under his skin that both drew him and made him slightly uneasy.

The room was beautiful, though a bit underwhelming. Tapestries of wielders demonstrating techniques decorated the walls and alternated between bookshelves that receded into the mountain's stone. Eos picked a book from one of the many shelves and sat on the fraying, dull purple rug. He thumbed through it for the better part of an hour, reading what he interpreted to be the personal notes of one of Morax's students.

After losing interest, he determined he was better off trying to meditate like Talus had instructed him to. It was a mostly futile effort. His mind kept grasping for thoughts. His brother; the Mitad; his cursed arm; the amazing display of wings his father had created; being on Hyperborea; training in the cold waterfall with Talus. He remembered how he had focused on the cold and let his sense fade away with his breathing. *Slowly in and letting go.*

Chaos to order. The path of light.

The disembodied words of the oath echoed in his head for a long time until he grew too tired to stay awake any longer.

When he stirred enough to wake himself, he noticed a bookshelf of items instead of books. They were odd items that he mostly didn't recognize. There were tools that looked like they were for the study of planetary movements, vials and flasks, contraptions of metal that rotated and spun, and telescopes strapped together as if made for a creature with a dozen eyes. All of the mysterious devices eluded Eos' imagination. The fog of interrupted sleep left him staring at the shelf until the tingling sensation in his skin flared up. Eos tried to ignore it and go back to sleep, but something distracted him as he lay back down.

A whisper sang in the air so low that Eos questioned if he had heard it at all.

"Hello." The voice was childlike and haunting.

Eos turned about the room to see if his mind was creating sounds in the solitude.

"Hello. Can you see this place?"

This time the faint sound made the hairs of his neck raise. Eos' gaze fell on a dull, weathered mirror that was propped up on the

CHAPTER TEN

shelf of strange items. It was smaller than his head and made of dark iron. The top of the mirror was a great tree with a golden sun icon in the canopy, and at the bottom, the tree roots formed the border. In the roots was a silver snake, weaving about the tangled vines—approaching an icon of the crescent moon.

"Welcome," said the child's voice so that it echoed about the room.

The mirror was the source, and Eos drew near. There was something powerful about the mirror; something so powerful the mirror seemed only to be a mark of it. He reached to the dirty glass, irresistibly drawn in. The voice was no more, but the power thrummed like a reverberating string in the room.

Vertigo seized Eos and he stumbled into the mirror. It was dirty. He wiped the surface with his thumb. As the mirror's surface cleared, the vertigo was so intense that he fell, and the room shook around him.

He stood and gazed into the mirror.

In the reflection, he saw the room: its tapestries, its soul stone lights, its doorway to the spiral staircase—but he was not in it. His reflection was missing. It was as if this was a window, not a mirror.

Eos found himself standing on a tower of obsidian rock. Below was infinite darkness that undulated as a writhing mass. Spinning about the disorienting darkness, he found a path of obsidian towers that formed incredibly high, raised steppingstones. *How far above the ground was he?* The distance looked as if there was no end.

"You shouldn't be here," the child's voice said clearly. Then, Eos saw a white-cloaked boy some fifty steppingstones away. "How did you get in here?"

Eos carefully put his weight on the next black-rock structure ahead of him on the path to the boy.

PENITUS OSTIUM

"I just touched...it called out...where am I?" Eos asked.

"Where you couldn't possibly be."

Eos took more confident steps forward as his vertigo faded, and the writhing mass of ink below distracted him less. "Is this my Soul Void?" he reasoned aloud. "It couldn't be...not mine...no...a Soul Void...but not mine. It looks very different." He breathed in the scent of an ocean-like salty dampness mixed with rot.

"No, not yours at all," the child confirmed. "Where did you come from?"

"I was in Morax's study. Then, I was suddenly here."

The black mass below splashed up in an arm like a wave at the hooded child, but he seemed to push it back without looking by holding out his white-clothed arm. The squirming form beat against an invisible barrier before falling, and the boy spoke again, "You will disrupt the delicate balance. They will push you out. I don't know how you got in here, but each Soul Void takes a unique form for that person and time. You have breached this one."

Eos tilted his head and stopped a few rocks short of the boy's white disruption amidst the void. The boy wore a mask with no color—save a few triangular streaks on the cheeks—just like the figure Eos had seen in his Soul Void during training with Aizo.

"Who are you?" Eos asked.

"Who do you think I am?"

"You visited me before...during my training?"

The boy seemed amused. "Perhaps. That I don't recall. This is only an instance of me. A once that was but is now a portal and a monument to power. A fragment, you could say."

CHAPTER TEN

A splash of the ink-like substance clawed onto the rock where Eos stood but was dragged back into the abyss. He shifted away and shivered. "Why am I here?"

"You must have encountered another fragment somehow."

Instinctually, Eos raised his cursed arm. The strands of the black curse matched the void.

The young boy motioned him closer. "That is…quite the mark." He hummed to himself as Eos stepped closer. "I understand now. It was completed."

Eos grasped his forearm as anger rose in him. He knew now that this was no chance encounter, nor a harmless one. "What *is this curse?* You know. Tell me." The salty wind blew his jet-black hair across his face as he confronted the boy.

"I only understand its nature. It is something I sought, but I am likely an ancient power to you. Where you visit me from…I have not experienced. As I said, the mirror is like a preserved relic. Powerful, but forgotten. Neglected. What you have in your right arm—" his voice became deep and possessed, "is power. Raw power. It is a gift."

"A gift?" Eos asked, outraged. "How could you call it that? It's trying to take over my soul." He held it out to be seen closer and stepped on the same rock platform as the boy.

Black waves surged onto the rock.

They stabbed like spears at Eos and the white cloak.

The boy raised both hands this time. Eos could hear him grunt as he strained.

The ink strands beat against his invisible barrier, fighting the boy's will.

They slammed against the rocks, thrashing wildly.

After their attempts failed, the waves plummeted below again.

PENITUS OSTIUM

"You shouldn't be here. The balance is going to break. It will collapse."

Eos did not relent. "Then tell me what this is and what I can do to get rid of it."

The air fell still. The smell of rot wafted up the rocks.

"Rid yourself of it? No. You can never do that. Let it consume you if you must, but you *must use it*. It is a gift. The gift paired with your potential…it is a combination that has not been seen since… Use it at all costs. You will need it, but I cannot tell for what ends."

The sound of the darkness squirming below signaled that another wave was coming.

"How do I use it?" Eos asked, frustrated. The impending attack from below was rushing the conversation.

The boy looked below on each side and tensed his hand muscles, trying to hold something below the rocks from rising. "It is time for you to leave. The mirror. It is an ancient tool. Find someone who understands what it is. You must make a bridge to your Soul Void. Find someone who will teach you to use your mark of power."

Eos closed his cursed hand. As he did, a flame of blue Soul Energy sparked to life in the space between Eos and the masked boy.

From behind the mask came a grimace of pain. "What have you done?" he cried out.

"That wasn't me. My energy is red—"

"You've brought a contamination in with you!"

Blue energy crackled between them. The boy's focus broke, and his body went rigid.

"You must leave now!" He thrust forward an open palm at Eos.

CHAPTER TEN

The palm never met Eos. A misty glow of pale light sent him flying back. It tore him from the stone platform and launched him above the infinite darkness below.

The black mass rose again, but this time in a wall that the boy could not hold at bay.

It pursued Eos as he was ripped from this strange place.

The ink chased him through the air.

It spat in smaller strands that reached like venom magnetized to him. Horrible, twisted faces seemed to emerge from the wall, moaning. They came for him with formless arms of the ink. The stench of the room emanated from them.

Slam!

Eos' back hit the mirror so hard he became nauseated.

Then the stench of rot was gone. The obsidian stones were no longer below him, and he lay on his back in Morax's ruins. It was a few moments before he was able to breathe again, but then he sat up. The room was the same—as if nothing had happened. The feeling of power emanating from the mirror was dormant.

CHAPTER ELEVEN

MAPS AND MIRRORS

W hen Eos left Morax's ruins, sweet morning dew and blinding natural light greeted him. He didn't have an urge to return immediately because of the night's events. So, he wandered for a few hours while contemplating. Then, he found his family waiting in the afternoon. They had retrieved their tent and supplies from Appocles, the path layer, and made camp no more than ten minutes beyond the Turrim Cartus pedestal.

Talus was quick to embrace his son. The auburn braids of his beard bristled across Eos' face. "I hope your night was an appropriate welcome to Hyperborea and the Order of Soul Wielders. I still remember my initiation night. A magical time," he said in a deep, enthusiastic voice.

CHAPTER ELEVEN

Eos rubbed the exposed curse on his arm. He cherished his father's embrace, but what happened the previous night with the mirror left him uneasy. He separated from Talus and said nervously, "Actually, it was, well, something strange happened."

"A lot of your experiences here are going to seem strange. On Earth, I found life to be the same," Talus said.

"No, not like that. Last night, I think I found something. Something no one else has before."

Talus' eyes widened, and he leaned in with interest. "Did you really? What did you find?"

Terrava tapped Talus' chest with the back of her hand.

"It's hard to describe, but I think I met—"

Terrava stopped Eos. "Remember that your experience and what you learn on your initiation night is supposed to be your own. The tradition is that it is not shared. The same goes for you, Maxima." She shot her husband a warning look.

"That's right." Talus grimaced as he said it. He looked back and forth between Eos and his wife with pursed lips to resist his curiosity. "We don't usually talk about our experiences inside."

Maxima stifled a laugh at her brother and father's mutual excitement. Her raven hair flowed behind her as she followed her mother, and they departed for the ruins' entrance.

Talus hung back, and Eos waited with him.

They shot mischievous glances at each other until they both knew they were out of earshot.

"Well, let's hear it. What did you find in there?"

Eos smirked. "Isn't that supposed to be a secret?"

"Yes, yes, but this sounded too important to not consult a master inlume about."

MAPS AND MIRRORS

As Eos ran his fingers over the moss and dewdrops of the mountain, the humor fell from his face. He spoke softly, "There was a mirror that was calling out to me, and then somehow...I was inside it. Like the Soul Void that Aizo taught me to enter once during training, but it didn't feel like my own. It was dark, and there was someone else in there. I don't know who, but he tried to talk to me."

The auburn beard was still. Talus' expression was somber. His eyes moved from side to side as he thought, and he put his hand over his mouth before finally whispering, "It can't be. What did this person in the mirror say?"

"He said that I shouldn't be there. It wasn't supposed to be possible. He told me I should learn to use this curse." Eos held up his arm.

In a low murmur, his father said words foreign to Eos, "*Penitus ostium.*"

"What does that mean?"

"A penitus ostium is an item—a tool one can use to enter their Soul Void. Anything in Fanum Ortus should be ancient and from Morax's time period unless someone planted it there for you recently. They are extremely difficult to make and only usable by the owner. What you did *should not be possible.*" He was quiet for a minute as his experienced mind worked. "Perhaps, this was some sort of preservation in a relic. It could be like a trapped memory. Regardless, the fact that the person mentioned your curse mark is worrying. This matter requires a more nuanced understanding of Soul Energy than what I possess."

Eos shifted and ran his hands through his hair. "Should I tell Mom?"

CHAPTER ELEVEN

"No. I'll discuss it with her when the time is right. It's best if we get down there to see your sister off. Let's hope she does not repeat your adventure with the mirror."

Terrava illuminated Morax's chambers in a chain reaction of sapphire diffusing into white.

Just before she passed the threshold, Eos put a hand on her shoulder and leaned in. He hesitated but hurriedly whispered, "Watch out for the mirror that looks like a tree."

Maxima's eyebrows drew together, trying to interpret the cryptic comment. She could make no sense of it and so entered for her night of initiation to become an anatus of the Order of Soul Wielders. Down the stairs she went, spiraling past carvings of heroes, tapestries of family trees and crests, and railings with decorative spire knobs. She stopped in front of the second door on her way down and lingered. A new feeling broiled under her skin. It was not pleasant—as if warning her that something was nearby. Her Soul Energy prickled her arms, and she turned away quickly. It was moments like these when she wished she had her scarf from Earth to hide under. She descended the stairs further and decided on the third door.

The room was a deep library, capped with four reddish marble pillars at the far end that supported a domed alcove. More books filled the walls than Maxima had collectively seen in her entire life. She put her index fingers to her lips and smiled uncontrollably as she spun around the room, admiring the different colors and textures of leather-bound rows.

There was a lightness in her step as she danced from shelf to shelf. An hour later, she found herself at a table with two volumes in front of her. The first was maroon, and the words *Saniartem: The Healing Techniques of Oribas* were pressed into the cover. She was particularly fascinated by a chapter that detailed a technique in which Soul Energy infused the blood to increase nutrient delivery through the body and improve physical performance. Though, from what she could interpret from the old language and handwriting, it was a perilous idea and led to many deaths. The other book was called *Philosophi and Disciplines of Magnan.* He was the top military leader, a title called *hariban*, in Pertinax Bellator's army during the Fourteenth Era. The thick tome contained philosophy on exercise, mathematics, military tactics, and spiritual practices regarding the *Great Soul.* It also detailed many methods for honing a Soul Wielder's skills.

Maxima flipped and flipped, absorbing pages like they could quench her thirst for the time lost on Earth. Eventually, she decided to take notes of some of the interesting passages. In her roaming, she found a shelf of unmarked parchment bound in thin skins. Nearby, at another table, was a quill and inkpot containing a dark indigo pigment. She had no experience with such tools and bled ink over a dozen pages before learning to steady her hand enough to put down legible words. She copied down some of Magnan's methods and Oribas' healing notes. She caught herself dozing off multiple times until she ran a line of ink down her arm. The accident prompted her to stand in the pulsing glow of the lighting-stones and walk around. She wanted to sleep but knew that would be wasted time. Every bit of knowledge should be extracted from her time in Fanum Ortus.

In the middle of the domed alcove, Maxima saw a cloth-covered display. Something in her tired mind commanded her toward it. Between the four pillars of red marble, she hovered over the ivy-colored cloth with an embroidered symbol of the Order of Soul Wielders: three crosses, the outer two were lower than the

CHAPTER ELEVEN

center cross, at the crown of a golden ring. So many paintings surrounded the centerpiece that the walls were entirely covered. Gold frames contained scenery from at least thirty different locations. Some were foreign lands that could only exist on Hyperborea, like the oil rendering of the Sacrum Crypt's glowing lake where they had collected the Anite map. The lake-side civilization was in significantly better condition when the painting had been made. Still, others were so familiar she could swear they were from Earth. In particular, there was one that looked like an image she had seen in a book—a red wooden gate in the ocean with a thin, curved ceramic roof. The painting captured the sunset over the mountains between the gate's supports. All the locations seemed to be united in their ancient task: watching over the Order's three embroidered crosses.

When she pulled back the cloth, it revealed a glass case containing a map. It was suspended by two arms that allowed the case to rotate freely on a gear system. The paper was crusted yellow-brown, but the map was beautifully drawn in black ink that had not faded. The continent of Corland was laid out in detail: The northern kingdom of Anite which sat under the Burning Lands and the Calid sea, the Winter Aisle divided by the Scindo—a narrow canyon that separated the Sepeleo and Iussum Mountain ranges, the allied nations in the Vale of Aleric, and a trail of other countries that tailed into the southern sea. She scanned every border's jagged edges, the twisting rivers, sprawling mountains, and memorized the islands such as Lenape with keen eyes. She mouthed the names of cities and nations with the hope of one day visiting them.

Then Maxima took particular notice of runes under dozens of locations, pressed in a metallic silver foil. Her mind processed the curious inscriptions. She had seen them before, but she couldn't place where. She chewed her lip, frustrated that her sharp memory was failing her. The puzzle led her to subconsciously lacing her fingers together and flexing them out to pop her knuckles.

The runes were placed purposefully, that much she knew.

An hour later, Maxima was furiously scribbling in her notebook on a table she had dragged over to the glass map case. Turning the handwheels carefully, she made sure the runes caught the soul stone light just right to recreate the symbols in her notebook perfectly.

The time was a blur to her, but eventually, Maxima decided to close her geography notes and step out of Fanum Ortus for fresh air. It was only a few steps up the spiral staircase when the skin-crawling feeling returned. Her Soul Energy jittered unnaturally insider her, and she had the urge to run outside as fast as she could. It was the memory of climbing the unforgiving cliff rock under Terrava's guidance that gave her pause. She remembered why her mother had pushed her to ascend past hesitations. There was something inside the room that was worth investigating—even if it made her uneasy.

Inside, she found tapestries of wielders and shelves of books. Her first circle through the room stopped on a shelf of items. There was an apparatus with a two-armed top on a metal track, a set of vials in some sort of chemistry set up, a large golden magnifying glass on a stand, astrology tools, and metal globes of various sizes. However, what caught Maxima's eye was propped in the corner of the middle shelf. It was a tool of some sort, made of concentric rings subdivided into small sections with runes. These centered on a relic carved with the circle and crosses of the Order of Soul Wielders.

CHAPTER ELEVEN

The map symbols were fresh in her mind, and Maxima pulled out her notebook to compare. Sure enough, the runes of this artifact were, at least partially, a match. She found a quill and began sketching her findings.

It was not long before the feeling of unease grew. There came a moment when she felt like her skin was being shocked, and she set down her notes. The sensation was not coming from the artifacts in front of her but something else in the room. She closed her eyes and focused, wanting more than anything for the feeling to stop, but willed her attention to the source.

Maxima sauntered toward it with her eyes nearly shut. When she felt certain the source of the awful feeling was near, she opened them.

Eos' words replayed in her head. *Watch out for the mirror that looks like a tree.* Her face reflected off a mirror framed in a tree with silver roots. It vibrated—not in a real way. She was sure it was physically motionless...and yet it shook so angrily that she could feel it resonate in her skull. It *hated* that she was there. That much was sure.

As Maxima raised a finger towards it, the violent humming shrieked louder until her finger bones grew red hot. They were ready to explode. She remembered fearfully gripping the slippery sloped rocks at the command of her mother. She had been afraid then, but she kept reaching.

When her finger was only an inch away, the heat in her pointer finger reached a fervor. A spark of blue came out without being willed to do so. It stretched the distance and struck the mirror face. Then, it disappeared inside. Stolen away.

MAPS AND MIRRORS

The blue flame of Soul Energy floated in the reflection but did not exist outside the mirror. The phenomenon only lasted a minute. *Shatter!* The glass exploded out of the frame.

Jagged shards cut at Maxima's cheeks and sliced her hand. She turned her face away in time to avoid the worst of it.

That was enough excitement. The night was not over, but it had been a sensory overload. Now, she was bleeding from multiple lacerations. She was sure that was not supposed to be part of the ritual night.

The air outside was thick with humidity, and starlight poked holes in the sky. It would be a few minutes back to her family's camp, and the feeling that something wasn't right had not left entirely. She hurried away from the entrance and into a narrow canyon.

Something moved in the shadows behind her.

She sensed another presence.

There was the sound of air whipping around.

Maxima shifted her weight back and turned her body preemptively. She had anticipated correctly.

A painful line slashed across her tricep, and a warm sting came with it. She whirled around to see the gleam of a blade.

The starlight showed her the knife's owner. His eyes were narrow, teeth jagged, and hair like dull matted clay. The young man made a soft *tsk-tsk* sound as if disappointed.

"Who are you?" Maxima asked in a shocked reaction as she grasped her arm.

The slender figure shrugged. "No use in hiding now." Dark violet energy lit his palm. "The name's Dero, and I'm the most talented unranked Mitad member."

CHAPTER ELEVEN

"Wh-what do you want?" Maxima bought time as she recovered from the initial panic. Blood seeped between her fingers.

"I'm going to gift your head to Emir Grimshaw." Dero smiled. He flicked his knife hand out.

A surge of adrenaline pumped through Maxima's veins. She slammed back into the wall to dodge the attack. By the time she caught her lost breath, she could see Dero's palm was growing brighter with Soul Energy. It was clear what she must do.

Sapphire light appeared between Maxima's fingertips in response.

Dero had the advantage, and he pressed it. His knife would buy him the moments the violet glow needed, and the narrow mountain pass left Maxima with little room to maneuver.

He lunged.

Maxima felt the cold metal clip her left shoulder.

She let out a cry of pain.

The next slash came.

Maxima slammed her open hand into Dero's wrist. She felt it collapse in and heard the knife clink to the floor. Dero cursed.

Sapphire and violet fought the shadows, but the purple light was stronger.

With pale hands, Dero cast his sphere forward.

"No. Please," Maxima pleaded softly to herself.

She shuffled back as the Soul Sphere released from Dero's hand.

It came at her, leaving no room to dodge. She back peddled, and her heel met a large stone on the floor. The rock sent her tumbling, and she struck the ground. Air left her and her ears pounded, but her vision focused as the Soul Sphere skimmed above her fallen body. The heat from it burned her face.

MAPS AND MIRRORS

She was saved, but only momentarily.

Dero cursed her in words she didn't recognize.

It didn't matter. There was only a blue glow casting long shadows at Dero's feet. Maxima was ready. She got to her feet in a thrust forward, releasing her sapphire orb.

Dero's nose curled as he realized what was about to happen.

Maxima's Soul Sphere split into two smaller weapons in mid-air. She gestured with two fingers extended near her waist.

Dero pressed himself to one side of the rock-face to dodge. The narrow beady eyes widened when they saw the inevitable collision.

The right sphere passed by him, but the left one…

Boom!

It found its target. Rocks fell down the walls, and dust rolled into a cloud of Maxima's wrath.

Weak violet light shimmered in the cloud.

Maxima breathed heavily, tired from lack of sleep, exhausted from the sudden struggle, but she didn't lose focus.

The settling debris revealed Dero, smiling maniacally from the protection of his Solido. The layer of defensive energy formed weakly around him, shuttering like a spasming muscle. His face and body were semi-burned, and he bled from numerous wounds.

"I told you, *the most talented.*" He struggled to raise an arm but had another attack nearly ready.

Maxima couldn't believe he was still standing. Nothing had prepared her to fight like this. She had fought Ares once to assist her brother, but she was no trained warrior.

Dero brought his arm back in preparation for a final attack.

Maxima closed her eyes. She had learned a few things attacking the rebels near the desert bridge on Earth, struggling against Ares, and training the day before with her mother. Her index and middle finger stayed rigidly pointed. Then, she curled them towards her in a gesture to return.

"You're done," Dero said. He positioned for victory.

Sapphire light rushed at him from behind. Maxima recalled the second sphere she had projected. It had not been lost but directed in a boomerang-like arc.

The ball of blue flame crashed into Dero's back, and he flew forward in a bloody heap.

Maxima didn't wait this time to see if he survived—she ran back towards camp.

It was only a few seconds before she ran into her family. They had all been on their way towards the noise.

Talus hugged his bloodied and frightened daughter with one arm. The other, he held up to light the path and ready to fight. The multicolored display of Eos, Talus, and Terrava's Soul Energies lit the pass as if it were day.

Far at the other end behind pillars of rocks, Dero's limping mass scurried into the shadows of the Iussum mountains.

Talus bellowed, "Shall we pursue?"

"No," Terrava decided quickly. "If they are in the mountains and after any one of us, it's best not to risk being ambushed. Let's return to Appocles and tend to Maxima."

Eos went to his sister. "Maxima, you're bleeding all over."

"They're all shallow. It just hurts a little," she said honestly as the rush of chemicals in her brain masked most of the sensations.

"I think we will need to break tradition and discuss what happened here the last two nights," Talus said as he whisked his children away into a sprint.

MAPS AND MIRRORS

Terrava grunted. "Shall we send an elsu messenger ahead to call it?"

"Yes," Talus agreed. "The wounded corcinth they saw on the mountain, the barbarians too far north, Sergius Ora's betrayal, and now this...the Mitad is moving into Anite. We must call the conclave."

∞   ∞   ∞

Walking was excruciating. That wretched girl's blast had been devastating. Dero was sure the girl had broken most of his ribs. Burns covered all of his back. Every step required a high degree of concentration, and his desperate run from the fight had slowed to a hobble.

But he made it. Only a quarter-mile outside of the Iussum mountains, he collapsed at a small, grass-covered rock formation. Drops of water splashed periodically on his bare shoulders. Dero was in such a poor state that the drips made him feel as if he was swimming in waters of relief.

The sky turned dull, and the inconsistent rain continued, drawing out the mountain's metallic odor. He faded in and out of sleep.

It was not the distant roll of thunder that awoke him. No, it was the dark presence—the sense that he was suddenly surrounded by judgment.

Dero grunted as he sat up. A woman stood over him.

She was slender with jet-black hair that fell in waves over the curves of her bare shoulders. Her irises were a cold amber, dark eye shadow sunk in her otherwise sultry eyes, and she wore a black dahlia flower in her hair.

CHAPTER ELEVEN

When she spoke, the silver piercing under her articulately drawn-on burgundy lips moved. Her voice was like liquid silk. "Unranked soldier, what is your name?"

He knew that he was staring up at death beautifully and sensually incarnated in a long, tight Mitad-crested dress. "D-d-dero Rud—"

"Ah, yes. Last names won't be necessary. Who gave you the order to move on Soul Wielder territory and attack royal families?"

"I only th-thou-thought that it would please Emir Grimshaw to have the head of one of the Bellator children to give to Lord Saida," Dero stammered.

"Do you know why I've come for you?"

Dero tried to swallow, but his throat closed in fear. "I've heard about you," he murmured in disbelief. "Lady Sugra of the Voro. The Negotiator."

Lady Sugra smiled, "Very astute observation. *Do you know why I've come for you?*"

"I did it for Emir Grimshaw. Please?" Dero knew the Negotiator's reputation.

"A waste of your raw talent, really. I'm here to carry out the execution of one unranked Mitad soldier for the crime of acting without orders from a superior officer. Against a royal family, no less. That could start a war. You may have provoked Talus into moving prematurely."

"No. Please don't. I…I'll make it right. Anything."

The Negotiator narrowed her eyes and summoned a burgundy-black Soul Energy that matched her lipstick. It curled like smoke in the air. Then, her eyes became lifeless black marbles.

Dero screamed weakly as the strands of light crawled up his legs. He stood to run, but his body was too broken. The burgundy energy snapped in a flash and formed a box around him on all sides.

The Soul Energy box lifted into the air as Lady Sugra held her flat hand vertically before her. Dero's cries and pathetic screams couldn't be heard outside the coffin of darkness. She paused. A window in the Soul Coffin formed momentarily so that Dero could comprehend the last words he would ever hear.

"You have been found guilty by the Mitad of high crimes."

The window closed, and energy sealed the box again. The Negotiator curled her rigid fingers into a claw. As she did, the coffin shrunk to half its original size, crushing its contents.

The Negotiator let her Soul Energy linger in the air as she unpinned the black dahlia from her hair and set it on the ground. The black-purple petals thrashed in the wind, and raindrops wilted it under a gray sky.

∞   ∞   ∞

Appocles' path created a gentle bumping of the cart's wheels that made a rhythmic sound that filled the pondering silence inside the caravan.

Terrava thought aloud, "I don't like this mirror. It could have been placed there as a trap, but someone within the order must have done it. And not many know about the detailed working of a penitus ostium. We could have consulted Kairus if he were still alive. These days, who would know? Perhaps my inlume master, Saier Fey?"

"It will take a long time to find master Fey. She only appears for inlume gatherings now," Talus rationalized.

CHAPTER ELEVEN

"It called out to both of us. That must be intentional," Eos added.

Kawwww.

There was the call from a bird of prey outside the caravan. Eos and Maxima exchanged curious glances.

Talus unlatched the window near him and opened it, letting in the sunrise fog. Then, he put out an arm. An elsu burst in. It lurched onto Talus' arm with a scroll dangling from his foot.

Terrava untied the scroll from Hermios' leg as Talus held the messenger bird steady. Her thin hands unrolled the letter with hesitancy, and she presented it before her husband to read.

The King tried to pass Soul Energy over the letter to decode it, but he was unsurprised when there was no reaction. The hurriedly scrawled words indicated that the message was sent in a rush. He read it aloud:

Dear King of Anite,

This is the last letter I will be able to send.

Their influence grows. I have taken the mark, but remain loyal. This Mitad mark is more than it seems. It's almost as if it is alive. I don't know how much longer I will remain in control of it.

It will appear as if I have betrayed you, but in the darkest moments, remember the times we collected emerald moss from the Sacrum Crypt. I remain as loyal and work towards the same ends today.

Your rock-head in the Winter Aisle,

MAPS AND MIRRORS

Ramath Leorix

The going away rhythm of Appocles' carriage continued as the family members took in the message. Terrava put her arm around her husband's to console his stern expression.

Eos thought of the mysteries he had seen over the past few days, and his mind remained fixed on the Turrim Cartus. *The Record of the Order.* He was supposed to be part of that record. So was Maxima. Now they were riding away from it. He lamented, "I guess becoming anatus of the Order will have to wait."

Talus did not look away from the letter as he replied, "We will complete the ceremony another time. We must hold a conclave to address the many omens that are before us. Something has been bubbling in the North for too long, and I fear it has overflowed into our borders."

Laying his head against the carriage wall, Eos listened to the wind hiss threateningly outside.

CHAPTER TWELVE

CAUGHT ON A STRING OF LIGHT

Tremlay Monte clutched his gaunt cheekbones as the ache under his eye sockets crawled to the back of his skull. He had not slept in two days. Slowly, he dragged his hands and knees down the slight decline to the end of the stone prison cell.

With shaky hands, he dropped a pebble into the chasm and began counting. Twenty was the count he had averaged before he could hear a distant *plink* of the pebble striking below. The Corleo prison, Meteora, was infamous for its rooms that offered every prisoner a choice—rot away slowly or discover how far it was to the base of the mountain. Though some found third way, rolling down the sloped cell in their sleep.

Dirt-caked leather was all that kept Tremlay thinking rationally. He had labored over his decision endlessly, holding the half-spine and tattered journal pages of Grace Lapithos. The Priori of Karnak had cut him off from their order. Rightfully so. The action prevented him from ever learning of the other half of the journal.

The assassins of Necogen had been efficient in finding him. They were the Mitad's tool of choice, and he understood why. They had somehow located their bounty and extracted him from the hidden royal chambers under Petramon.

The half-book teetered at the edge of the drop-off. *It was too important to let fall into the Mitad's hands, but it was too vital to the cause to be lost down the prison-pit.* He tapped the journal. Each time his finger lifted, the book shifted further over the edge, and each time his finger came down on the leather again, it settled on the stone floor. *Better in the hands of the Mitad, but still recoverable?*

The cell door opened with a grinding of rusted hinges.

To Temlay's horror, it was not a human being that entered first. A static-white glow crawled into the room—arachnid-like and mechanical. Its six legs vibrated as the creature made of Soul Energy rattled into the room. The Overseer followed his crawler inside.

Ares joined the Overseer, followed by an angry-looking man. His hair was parted and swept back to curls around his grey-toned neck. Crooked eyebrows contorted on a wrinkled brow, a brown mustache and goatee scowled in two parts from a long gash of a scar, and piercing red-amethyst eyes stared Tremlay down as if ready to tear his heart out.

Tremlay clutched the journal to his chest and heaved a sick laugh. His parched words cut sharply. "I heard about the crawlers. Rumors. Some said the things had made it to the western Monte territory near the mines. I see the rumors were true." He mumbled to himself, "Voro."

CHAPTER TWELVE

The Overseer grinned a crooked, bleached smile. "Tremlay, the book if you please," he said in a subtle drawl of the southern kingdoms.

The long slit in the Overseer's helmet stole Tremlay's gaze. He couldn't look away as he tore his rigid fingers from the journal and stretched his arm out to dangle the precious thing over the hole. "What have I done to deserve such a visit. Ares, fallen son of Anite?" Ares scowled at the words. "A wretched albino of the Voro, and, oh my. If I could be so bold as to assume from that scar and your demeanor, I'm graced by the presence of the great politician gone Mitad leader, Saida himself."

Saida spat on the floor in Tremlay's direction.

The Overseer continued, "The book and the location of Grace Lapithos."

"Isn't this the part where we negotiate how you get the book and I get out of here alive?" Termlay dangled the book.

"No," grumbled Saida. "This is the part where you give me the book, and then I kill you."

Nervous fingers loosened, and Tremlay let the journal slip through his grasp before clenching it again at the last moment before it fell down the chasm.

The Overseer's scraggly white chin-beard sagged as his lips mouthed the word *no*. Then he hissed, "There are three of us here who could kill you an infinite number of ways. Put the book down, and we'll talk about how you get out of this."

Saida rolled his eyes. "I did the politician act and negotiating for too many years. Enough of that garbage." He strode up to Tremlay and grinned sadistically.

Tremlay thrust his arm out further over the chasm.

CAUGHT ON A STRING OF LIGHT

Saida knelt and stroked his prisoner's face softly. "Right. You think I buy that, Tremlay? You want the book in the hands of your Priori of Karnak more than you want to keep it from us. You worship the true knowledge, you little slimy silver-spoon scum."

Tremlay shivered uncontrollably.

Saida let the gesture of his hand end behind his prisoner's head. He yanked the young man's hair viscously, ripping his head back over the hole. "Let me be blunt. You will tell us where Grace is, and it will buy you a less torturous death. If you volunteer extra information, I may not leave him in here to toy with you like his personal blood bag in need of draining." He nodded to the Overseer with amusement.

"If...if I knew where she was. I would tell you. I want to go home to my family. I really d-d-do." Tremlay heaved. "No one knows where Grace is, or she would be extracted by now. She's been missing for years."

Saida turned and slapped Tremlay across the face savagely. Blood trickled from the corner of lips.

"Please. If I knew...they wouldn't have given me half the answer. I just want to go home. I was supposed to deliver the journal to a senior member of the Priori." Tears welled up in his eyes. "I wasn't going to have it long. It wasn't supposed to be me."

Slap!

The half binding of leather and pages slipped from Tremlay's hands. He gasped and sputtered.

Light flashed from the tip of Saida's fingers. Murky violet energy threaded from it in an instant.

Everyone in the room looked over the edge in disbelief...except Saida.

CHAPTER TWELVE

The Mitad leader stared Tremlay down. "You see, I didn't care if you dropped the book by accident. You never had an inkling of power from the moment you were caught." He curled his pointed fingernail inward. The stream of faint energy whipped up like a taut string and retracted from over the edge. Wrapped in the line of mauve light was the journal. "It has been mine since you were put in this cell. It's unfortunate, though. I spent too long as a politician, navigating contrived little games. I know when someone is lying to me." The journal fell to the ground.

"I don't! I really don't know an-an-anything."

Saida raised a crooked eyebrow. "Oh, I'm aware." He turned walked out of the room. Before stepping through the door, he said, "I am generous. I won't let you suffer long."

"I'm the nephew of King Pallogos. You wouldn't incite a war after you already took what you wanted?" Tremlay uttered in confusion.

Without turning around, Saida said with a flick of the wrist over his shoulder, "King Pallogos has many nephews. Send him down the pit."

The Overseer's crawler moved with a furious *kratttle scree krattle scree krattle scree* of arachnid legs. It launched into Tremlay and took him over the black drop-off.

"Ares, grab my new book off the floor," Saida said as he left the room.

Bending over, Ares rifled through the pages on the ground. His mind fixated on the contents he saw. He recognized a great many things in a few glimpses. His mind began to churn—

An echoing explosion rumbled from below. The crawler had hit the bottom with its victim.

CAUGHT ON A STRING OF LIGHT

∞   ∞   ∞

Outside the prison, the pillared balcony provided a breathtaking view, offering a distant panorama of the Corleo capital, Aritrea. Golden groundcover combed back in forth in the breeze under patches of teal pine trees. The mountain basin was a chest of treasure left open that had enticed the Loerix family to settle and guard it for over four eras.

The Overseer had been quick to attend to another prisoner, leaving Ares and Saida looking out at the incomprehensibly vast golden-brown valley below.

"It's a shame the prisoners don't get a window. This is one of my favorite views in the Corland." Saida laughed. "Who am I kidding, down the pit for the prisoners. I want this view all to myself." He chewed on his lip a while and scrunched his nose while thinking.

Ares used the moment to speak. "In Emir Raggan's orders—"

"Close your yap. I'm not done thinking. I should have sent you off torturing prisoners with pale helmet-boy and his little bugs." He leaned over the sandstone railing and whistled to himself at the drop below.

Gritting his teeth, Ares summoned his patience as Saida paced and brooded. The air had a crispness that left no question that winter was rolling into the mountain isle.

Finally, he said, "Yes, you've been transferred over to me. I wrote the orders, and you're going east to ready an invasion force. Figured that would make you happy, right? Getting to take a stab at daddy's kingdom."

Ares glared, "Such a simple task is—"

CHAPTER TWELVE

"Did I tell you to speak? I don't care one iota if you think the task is below you. You're going to do it, and you're going to learn some diplomacy in the process. My old master would never assist me now, however, we need his blessing to sneak through to Anite's eastern border." Saida moved in so that he was inches from Ares. "If you do this right—*big if*—your failures on Earth will be forgotten, and you'll be on the path of promotion to Emir. Personally, I don't think you can do it. You're a hothead, you're impulsive, and you never know when to stop running your whiney mouth."

Ares would have normally been enraged by the insults, but instead, he squinted and stared Saida in the eyes. "You didn't make this call, did you?"

"If I made this call, you wouldn't be the one going."

"I want to meet him," Ares said.

"Meet who?"

"The Master."

Saida nodded to himself, irritated. He pointed at Ares, "You're not ready, and you're not worthy."

Ares thrust his chin out. "Does a son need to be worthy to meet his real father?"

"Yeah…in this case, yeah." Saida slapped both of Ares' shoulders and snickered. "Okay. You know what? You think you're a real special case? Only Vistomus, myself, and the Voro know the Master, but you have daddy issues. So, that makes you *so* special." He tilted his head clicked his tongue. "Let's see. Show me what you can do when you open your fourth gate!"

Ares raised a fist but slowly dropped his shaking arm. This was his chance, but he couldn't. Not on his own, at least. Saida knew it as well as he did. It was a test of his willingness.

CAUGHT ON A STRING OF LIGHT

"That's right. You're not ready. Do your assignment, take the promotion to Emir, and stop jumping ahead." Saida turned away. "I'll have more details for you in a week."

There would only be this one chance. Ares couldn't let it slip away, but it meant using *that*. It meant losing himself. He thought of the tattoo on his back. The elsu swam under the water without knowing how to breathe. It just took the plunge.

A black mark like the one that marked Eos' arm crawled up Ares' neck. It moved up his cheeks and darkened the whites of his eyes. He could feel his will slipping. It was like losing himself and giving over to something else. The sensation of Soul Energy manifesting fluttered through his whole body. Then it became more violent; painful. It burned his skin.

Then he gave in.

Crackle.

Black Soul Energy poured out of his hand.

Ares' soul came forth into a living form. A serpentine body twisted out from his forearm with a snapping hybrid-head. It was like a dragon with a wolf's snout; pale gray eyes glowed from the marbled black energy. The creation churned with toxic color, and the beast's eyes were the only sign of Ares' real Soul Energy. Two long whiskers undulated from either side of its face, almost taunting Saida.

"Well, you at least had the wherewithal to do what it takes like a man. That's enough now."

Ares was not in conscious control, and the dragon bared its fangs with curled lips. It drifted effortlessly forward.

Saida sighed, exasperated. "You have talent. I'll give you that, but you're on the path to becoming one of the Voro if you keep it up. Don't think I don't know you're aiming for my spot. The mark

CHAPTER TWELVE

is supposed to assist you, not be your permanent crutch." He shrugged to himself and muttered, "You'd make a strong member of the Voro. Perhaps this is for the best."

The ink-colored dragon drifted further forward and snapped its jaws violently.

"Listen, you little cretin. I was hunting down inlumes of the Soul Wielding Order before you were crying to your mommy for milk. If you don't put that possessed toy away, I'll break it."

Ares' neck veins bulged. The mark wrapped around most of his face now. He breathed heavily and said with a strained voice, "I want to meet him."

Saida brought his fist in front of his face and stared Ares down from over his knuckles. Then he cracked his neck, flicked his fingers open, and faded-purple strings of energy sprung from the tips.

Ares' creature darted forward at Saida.

The mauve strings met it.

Saida contorted his fingers like playing an instrument as he controlled the strings. They glittered in the sunlight before slicing through Ares' energy like sharp wires moving through soft fruit—tearing the black beast into pieces with a clashing that chirped like a high-pitch engine roar. The harsh scream of Soul Energies left a burnt plastic smell in the air.

Five strings caught the intact pieces of Ares black creature and held them, hovering in the air. Saida let them hang, suspending time as Ares was paralyzed and breathing heavily.

"You have much to learn."

He then waved a finger in the direction of the valley and flung the pieces of the dragon over the railing. They evaporated into the air. But Saida wasn't done.

CAUGHT ON A STRING OF LIGHT

Strings darted through the space between the two men, seizing Ares by his limbs. He was thrust back and slammed into the pillar at the mountain's edge with his arms spread out and his feet off the ground.

"An impressive power, but it is nothing more than an amusement to me."

Ares heaved for air. The destruction of his possessed technique had taxed him beyond what any physical activity could. He tilted his head down weakly and let the words fall from his lips, "I want...to meet him."

A mustached smile was the response. Saida closed his eyes as if consulting someone in a private conversation.

Heavy breathing filled the lingering moment.

When he opened his eyes, Saida spoke with a gravel-filled voice, "The Master has an offer. You may meet him, but first, there is a young woman he needs you to get rid of. The opportunity will come soon."

The strings lowered Ares until he was nearly touching the floor again. Saida whispered a name in his ear.

Ares' eyes bulged.

The strings withdrew, and Ares fell to his hands and knees.

Pitying laughter echoed off the vaulted ceilings as Saida strutted away.

It was night when Ares returned to the city stench of Aritrea. Inside the Corleo castle, Zolo received him in his room. Ares was exhausted and mentally shaken. So much so that he didn't think of perceptions when he leaned on Zolo's shoulders to hobble back to his bed.

"Master Ares, you don't look well."

CHAPTER TWELVE

Ares sat in the dull brick room and contemplated the choice before him while groaning at the pain in his bones. The Mark of the Chosen had taken its toll. His mind began weaving a plan.

There was his task in readying the Mitad's military move. The constraint of not being seen showing public affection for Bellia. The responsibility of guiding Zolo. The request for an assassination he had just received...and then there were the pages he had quickly skimmed in the Meteora prison cell.

"Zolo," Ares said with a voice like he hadn't drunk in days. "There is something I need, but I can't get it myself. I need you to steal a book. Well, half of a book."

CHAPTER THIRTEEN

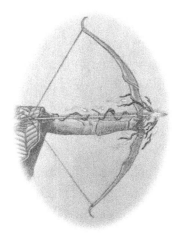

CONCLAVE

Silvery spires stabbed the clouds as Eos stared up in wonder from the balcony of the Anondorn castle's third story. Maxima shivered beside him—from the temperature and her nerves. She laced her fingers together with clasped hands as she paced. Eos' light beige dress-cloak fluttered in the wind with decorative woven patterns of gold rippling along his skin. Maxima wore a dress of the same fabric but with raised leaf designs entwining her whole body. The Bellator crest of the elsu adorned both of their chests. Scipio had told the two siblings that winter came up from the mountains early this year but that it wouldn't get much colder than it was now in the northern kingdoms.

"This is what I've always wanted. What I've been waiting and dreaming of for years. So, why am I scared?" Eos asked himself.

CHAPTER THIRTEEN

Maxima knew him well. "Because you don't want to make a mistake. You're afraid it won't be perfect."

"You're not afraid that you'll mess something up? I already did with this curse mark." Eos held up his blackened hand and swore against it silently. "What if it doesn't go like I hoped?"

"That would be realistic," Maxima said.

Eos watched his breathe condense for a while.

"Do you remember, Maxima, when we were at the silo, and I lost the gold sol coin?"

His sister nodded, looking out over the balcony at little shapes of busy people preparing for a feast. They streamed into the castle with guests, carts of supplies, and other essentials.

"Back then, I was frustrated that nothing I did seemed to get me closer to my goal. The coin was all I had, but even losing it had no real effect. Now every small move has so much more weight, don't you think?"

Pulling back the loose hanging sleeves of her dress, Maxima tenderly ran her fingers over the countless scratches and scabs on her arms from her fight against the Mitad soldier named Dero. Her face had been covered in makeup pastes and powders to hide the signs of her battle. She knew what Eos said was true and whispered, "The stakes have changed."

Two thin pillars twisted on either side of the balcony doorway. The door rose into a pointed arch at the top. A quick knock came, and Scipio poked his head through the door.

"It's time."

Eos and Maxima followed down the corridor towards their return home banquet. Scipio had been preparing ever since they left for Fanum Ortus. The significance of the moment caused a buzzing inside the siblings. Every banner, tapestry, and painting

CONCLAVE

they passed reinforced the monumental moment—they were being welcomed home by the Anite kingdom.

Then, Scipio pushed through the first-floor banquet hall doors. A harp introduced them on their slow march, and then drums rose into a fervor, and flutes, horns, and fiddles joined in to fill the enormous hall with the joyous announcement. They must have passed fifty tables before reaching the front of the hall where the royal court members were seated before a long crimson and silver tablecloth that overlooked the whole festivity from a raised platform.

As they had been told, Eos and Maxima bowed before their parents and turned to the crowd of hundreds. There was a loud outbreak of cheers and celebration. Then, Talus stood, and the room went silent. The instruments diminished into a hush.

"Today, what was lost has been restored. The hauntings that lingered from the Pacem Derex rebellion are vanquished. My long-lost children have returned," Talus spoke in a thundering voice that commanded the attention of the entire room. His braided beard swayed as he turned from side to side in his address. "I couldn't be happier as a father that my children have come back to Terrava and I after all these years. I couldn't be more grateful that the Great Soul has brought them home, and I can't express how proud I am that Eos and Maxima overcame their trials abroad in the Burning Lands to restore the Bellator bloodline. Their return means more than a simple homecoming. It is the correction of the misguided actions of Pacem Derex fifteen years ago and the rebuke to the Mitad's vile attempts to destroy them. Most importantly, the fact that they stand in these halls once more means that the Bellator family, dedicated to Anite prosperity since our ancestral forefather

CHAPTER THIRTEEN

Pertinax, will continue to serve and protect the people of the Anite kingdom for generations to come."

The hall broke out in an approving roar as chalices were raised. Eos couldn't help but notice the frontmost table on the left was decidedly more reserved in their mild clapping.

After being seated, a never-ending procession of entertainment, food, and drink began. Singers and musicians performed in group and solo. Racks of meat and mead filled the tables. Fire jugglers, dancers, and actors performed, and sweets and bread rained on the tables. Eos, sitting at Talus' right side, favored the roasted meat in gravy, while Maxima, sitting at Terrava's left, showed a preference for a treat that was like a chocolate-filled puff of pastry.

Between chewing, slurping, laughing, and clapping, Talus gave Eos the rundown of their guests.

"The right front table seats the four inlumes that reside in our borders: Spintha, Enodor, Agathon, and Prax. Beside them are errants of the Order of Soul Wielders and hariban: our military leaders."

Eos looked over the four elderly soul wielders with captivation. He did his best to memorize their faces—three men and one woman, Spintha.

"The left table," Talus nodded subtly to the ones who were more reserved in their celebration, "is the family of our political rivals, the Cassions. Julian sits at the head of the table. Not everyone is happy with your arrival. His two eldest sons, Arioth and Benedir, are positioning to take my place in a hexade or so. Julian has come close to putting together a delegation that would overcome me in the election but never succeeded." Talus noticed Eos still glancing over at the table of inlumes. "Memorize the

CONCLAVE

Cassion family faces well, for they will be watching for any misstep you or Maxima make."

Terrava pointed to a table of women. "Those are the Sanofem, the sacred healing sect of our people." The women were astounding in facial beauty, but their pale green veils hid much of it. They moved with careful poise and delicacy.

"Those are the political delegates and legates who govern the Anite principalities."

Maxima took in a table of well-to-do characters, all appearing to try and outdo the others in every gesture and word.

The parents pointed out more tables: the Caerule family of Terrava's brother, Talus' cousins, and Monte and Corleo descendants who represented their nation abroad.

After the second course of desserts, Julian Cassion approached the head table and bowed deeply before the King. "My Lord, Benedir has prepared a performance for Eos and Maxima if you are willing to grant him the honor."

"We are honored by your son's gesture. Please." Talus spread his hands out over the table approvingly.

Benedir was a slight young man, thin in the face and with a scraggly half-grown beard, but his jaw was strong, and his noble features and chestnut locks of hair hinted at status. He bore the mark of a tree with talons as his sigil. Eos couldn't help but sense an air of arrogance coming from Benedir.

The performance was a mixture of dance, martial arts, and wielding. Eos had to admit: his rival was talented. Benedir bowed with a sweeping hand. A Soul Sphere of white mist developed as he did so. He drew his arms up and straight out in a slow drama as the sphere dissolved into ropes weaving around his torso. They spun and danced around his body as he performed martial arts

CHAPTER THIRTEEN

patterns of strikes. The show went on for a few minutes, concluding with a move that Eos couldn't help be awed by. Benedir formed his white sphere, rolled it in a wave from one arm to the other, flicked it into the air, leaped in an aerial cartwheel, and finally catching it with his arm outstretched just as he started. The Soul Energy fell and hit the ground, but in a finale, it splashed up in a shimmering pillar around Benedir, cloaking him in a wall all around. Then he bowed to Talus, his own father, and the crowd.

"A wonderful show, Benedir," Talus said. "Enodor is teaching you well, and your progress exceeds anything I've seen this hexade."

"Thank you, my lord. I strive to become an Errant at my next evaluation before the Order."

To Eos' anxiety, Talus urged him to go to the Cassion table to commend the performance that had been on his behalf.

Eos did as he was told. He nervously approached the table.

Julian stood, and the rest of the table followed. "Eos, it is our fortune that you visit the Cassion table." The man looked like a graying, wrinkled mirror image of his eldest son.

Trying not to mumble, Eos said, "The performance was extraordinary. I...er...how could I not speak with Benedir myself when he put on such a show in my honor?" He tried to remember the formalities that Scipio had coached him on for nearly a day.

Benedir smirked, "Yes. Well, master Enodor does say I have the best soul forms of anyone he's ever trained. Perhaps you could show us a similar form you learned in the Burning Lands? I'm sure their ways are cruder, but it should be...enlightening nonetheless."

Eos was not sure how to respond to such a bold statement. He barely knew how to create a decent Soul Sphere and had achieved partial Severence only a few times. He knew nothing of soul forms, putting on performances, or doing anything of the sort that Benedir had. Not to mention he had never been to the Burning Lands.

"Yes. I will ah…I'll have to show you what I learned while I was away."

"Let's not push our newly returned wielder," Julian said while shooting Benedir a warning glance, but Eos could see that underneath the formality, he was quite pleased with the words.

Continuing despite the warning, Benedir stroked his thinly grown beard and said, "Eos, please tell us what it feels like to be back from the dead. Did you develop a love for the commoners and savages of the Burning Lands like your father has for our kingdom's little people?"

Eos frowned, taken aback yet again. "I learned many things while I was gone. One is that those you call little people often surprise the ones who look down on them."

"That is quite enough!" Julian clasped Benedir's shoulder aggressively and forced him into his seat. "Forgive his insolence. He's simply overly excited by your return and the performance."

Benedir snickered in his seat.

After Eos returned to his chair, Scipio rose from the table.

"If everyone has had enough to eat and drink, please follow King Talus Bellator to the courtyard for our main events of the night. For those of you that have a larger appetite for mead, please fill your cups again before heading out. I'm sure legate Wessio will demonstrate for us how to manage two chalices while spectating the games," Scipio raised his glass to legate Wessio. He brought two up in good cheer to return the gesture.

The Bellator family left the castle, followed by the crowd of excited attendees.

CHAPTER THIRTEEN

Soldiers stood on the teal grass, browning as winter set in. Six were armed with swords while another dozen carried bows. They stood at attention in steel helms with wings flaring back from either side of their heads. Scipio announced that an archery demonstration by the elite kyrja unit would take place, followed by five soul sword duels between some of the vangar guard members.

The family and their court of advisors climbed wooden stairs and took their seats in a raised spectating box overlooking the courtyard. The crowds gathered below in lower boxes or standing behind wooden rails on the grass.

The kyrja moved into a star formation and faced down humanoid wooden targets. They snapped their bows to the ready on their commander's order, drew from their gilded quivers, and knocked special arrows. The arrowheads were no ordinary metal but were folded with manus stone. The archers pointed two fingers in line with their readied projectiles and ran their fingers down from the manus stone to the end of the shaft, causing a flurry of red sparks as if they had put the arrow to a grindstone.

"Draw!"

The bowstrings, like fine threads of silver, became taught.

"Aim!"

They did not aim first at their targets but at the sky instead.

"Release!"

The archer at the head of the formation fired straight into the sky. A streamer of red energy zipped towards the clouds, led by a glowing red manus stone. Immediately after the first arrow left the bow, the next archer behind him released his. Bowstrings snapped in quick succession, and arrows whistled a *thrumming* hymn in the sky. Neon red lines pulsed above the crowd.

CONCLAVE

The second arrow found the first. It erupted into an explosion—a light show in the clouds. With a perfect rhythm, each projectile flew up into the same spot.

Zing. Zing. Boom. Zing. Zing. Boom.

Every kryja demonstrated their perfect mastery of their discipline by shooting down the preceding arrow in a shower of Soul Energy.

The spectators roared in approval.

Then they dropped their bows to a lower angle and knocked their arrows again.

The lead soldier fired again, this time in the direction of the targets but not directly at them.

The red flash sparked through the space between soldiers and targets. However, the angle was far to the left of the leftmost target. The arrow suddenly curled, glowing brighter. Eos could tell that the kryja soldier was guiding the energy he had planted in it. The projectile bent around, striking the first target from the side. The collision tore through the wooden figure entirely and pierced all twelve in succession until it erupted into a volcanic detonation on the rightmost dummy.

A flurry of arrows followed, winding through the air in an impossible arc, striking the leftmost figure, and bursting into flames on the next in line that was still standing. This barrage continued until all the mannequins were stumps. The show concluded with twelve flashes in the sky as the kryja created a fog of red.

Wild cheers showered the archers as they marched from the field.

Then the duels began.

CHAPTER THIRTEEN

Swords forged with condlucite stone rang out against sword and armor. Some warriors carried shields while others fought with two-handed swords. Sparks of metal and Soul Energy showered the field.

Gondul was a giant in haunting black armor who showed clear domination over a warrior named Eir. He battered his shield with blows, driving him back again and again. Each impact was devastating and vicious, denting armor and causing blazes of light. Eir back peddled, barely covering himself with his shield and unable to raise his sword in anything other than defense.

A small vangar warrior named Karo performed similarly against Hildor but defended more carefully with his sword until the opportune moment to counterstrike. He laid his blade into the right ribcage of Hildor's armor with such a powerful stroke that when the Soul Energy erupted from the sword edge, it sent the man off of his feet.

The final duel of the first round was Rotir against Skult. The guard members were evenly matched, clashing weapons rapidly and alternating who advanced on the other. In the end, Skult delt a strike that tore Rotir's weapon from his hand. Rotir took a knee of defeat.

Talus leaned toward Eos and said, "Although the fights are violent, the guard members don't intend to harm each other. They have real duties to perform after this show. The armor is well made of the strongest metal in Anite, and they pull their attacks back enough to only look impressive. The vangar are the best soul-sword wielders in the entirety of Corland. If they chose, they could release enough Soul Energy in one blow to make their opponents nothing but a melted puddle of armor."

CONCLAVE

The tournament continued with a bye for the massive Gondul. He watched from the shadows of his helm's eye slit as Karo and Skult fought valiantly. The two swayed in a show of footwork and swordsmanship that left Eos and Maxima breathless at the edge of their seat. Each *clang* of the blades and flare of light drew the crowd more on edge. After wearing down the heavier Skult, Karo set to work finishing his slower opponent.

Talus commended the guard members on their impressive fights. "A great demonstration by all." He clapped with large hands that echoed over the field. "Gondul and Karo will fight the final round for this token," he said and produced a small statue of a golden elsu. "And as a special treat for our guests, we will allow ranged blade attacks, but be warned I'll have no lasting injuries to my best swordsman or close calls with the guests. So, moderate those attacks appropriately."

Every step Gondul took seemed to sink into the ground as he moved his mass onto the battlefield. Karo moved with sure, light steps to meet his opponent.

Talus put two fingers between his lips and blew a shrieking whistle that signaled the duel to begin. It unfolded as Eos expected. Karo danced with agile moves around Gondul, who swung heavy strikes that seemed like they would split the small man in two if they had connected. The black suit of armor didn't seem to tire, however. Karo landed an excellent blow to Gondul's left leg, but the brute carried on, clashing his blade. The weapons glowed from blue to an almost white hue as the amount of energy required to counter the other increased. Concussions swam out as the fervor increased.

Teasing, Karo said, "Those heavy feet could crush me. If they could ever catch me." He danced into the range of the black blade.

CHAPTER THIRTEEN

Finally, a well-calculated move from Karo deflected an overhead attack. Gondul's momentum brought his arm around as Karo spun off the deflection. He landed a mighty hit on the giant's chest.

Gondul stumbled.

A concave indention was left behind, but the attack had also distanced Gondul from Karo. Gondul took away the small man's advantage as he rose, clutching his chest but keeping his opponent at sword's distance

Karo was unable to regain his positioning inside Gondul's defenses.

Gondul swung his black blade as the panting Karo stayed outside his reach.

This time, Gondul's blade glowed before reaching its full arc.

Karo's pupils dilated as he saw what was coming at him.

A stream of light broke from the sword.

It left the metal and ripped through the gap between the swordsman.

The crowd went silent.

The devastation of the victory swing left everyone wondering if Gondul had gone too far. Karo was tossed yards away, rolling violently when he came back to the ground.

Eos watched Karo's stillness. After a hushed minute, he rolled over to his back and exposed the crumpled form of his armor. He removed his bronze-colored helmet with blood running from the corner of his mouth, but he was able to stand. The defeated vangar soldier stumbled and took a knee before the king's box.

Talus addressed the fighters, "Well fought both of you. Karo, I have noted your skill for tasks to come. Gondul, this statue will commemorate your victory on the day of my children's return!"

CONCLAVE

Eos looked to Maxima. They both breathed a sigh of relief that Karo had survived and then smiled in wide-eyed wonder at the magnificence of Hyperborean skills. It was the most impressive entertainment either of them could have imagined, and it was all for their homecoming.

Despite this, Eos dreaded what was to come. The festivities were certainly a celebration, but also a disguise. Talus planned to gather what he had called *the conclave* on the next morning. The party had served the dual purpose of calling all the members of the conclave into Anondorn on short notice. Eos' future and the specter of his curse mark were certain to underlie the gathering of Anite's most powerful players.

$$\infty \qquad \infty \qquad \infty$$

The stone-covered bridges, oak archways, domes, and twisting spires of the Anondorn castle were left behind at first light. Talus and Terrava led Aizo, Eos, and Maxima away from the city.

Aizo walked better after days of healing with the Sanofem, but he still had an awkward shift when he put weight on his injured leg. He grinned as they entered a forest of white-veined leaves on foot. The setting winter caused many of the pale leaves to have already fallen on the ground, and they waded through dulling foliage between trunks covered in amber bark. Knowing what was to come prevented Aizo from being overly excited when he said, "The Forest of Hasvela. How many years has it been since I have seen such beauty? I don't deserve this gift."

"Nonsense, Aizo." Terrava put an arm on the man's back. "You returned my children home safely. You deserve to retire to these woods any day you choose."

CHAPTER THIRTEEN

Maxima remained silent, knowing they were on some sort of sacred grounds. She could feel the reverence in the air.

Eos was quiet in uneasy anticipation.

The path to the conclave pavilion took over an hour to walk. It was a distance that they could have accomplished quicker using Soul Step, but Terrava informed them that wielding was prohibited in the Forest of Hasvela. There was a hush to the woods that filled everyone with a sense of inner peace.

Whoosh.

A gust of air slapped Eos and Maxima as a streak of glowing feathers cut through the trees above them. Eos shifted into a ready stance, scanning the canopy of pale leaves and amber branches for the source.

Talus bellowed a hearty laugh. "No need to be on guard. That was an elsu, and this is their home."

When they broke past the tree line, they came upon the heart of Hasvela's forest. It was a turquoise lake that was bouncing the morning sun off its surface. The refractions were of a warm orange hue as they gleamed with the tree bark's color at the center of the waters. A tree that dwarfed the surrounding forest grew from the center of the lake. Taller than five trees and wider than ten, it was a towering castle on its own.

Terrava explained, "That is the Ashva tree. Its roots grow into the manus stone core at the lake bottom, and it is the home of the mother of all elsu. This is where the first wielders learned, generations before Pertinax and the Glyph Wars. The Great Soul flows strong beneath this lake, and it is a place where kings come to pray for guidance."

"It is also," Talus interrupted, "where leaders and the king's council meet for private decisions that can only be discussed on

CONCLAVE

sacred ground. That conclave pavilion is where some of Corland history's greatest decisions have been made. It's where we decided how to deal with the Pacem Derex rebellion, where my father, Bekrin, determined how to deal with barbarian invasions and Corleo attacks on the Montes, and now…I fear it is fitting that I must decide how to deal with the Loerix family in Corleo like my father before me. This time, the Mitad is my burden as well."

They made their way down to the foot of the lake where the pavilion was. The structure was a porcelain-like circular set of pillars, capped with an intricate dome. It was open to the outside air but obscured by fine silk curtains hanging nearly a hundred feet from the ceiling between each pillar. This pattern continued all the way around the building except for the arched glass windows that ran floor-to-roof overlooking the water and Ashva tree.

Maxima followed Terrava inside, but Talus nudged Eos to remain behind for a moment. "We will not expose your curse mark directly. Keep it hidden as we've discussed, but I will insist that you are part of my plan and solution due to your entanglement with the Mitad on Earth. I will say that the Mitad has used an ancient type of wielding on you that a specialist must examine in the Monte kingdom. Your mother and I agreed that you will join me for our journey to the Winter Aisle."

"Who is this specialist, and what can they do to help?" Eos asked.

"In truth, she is not the sole reason we are going. Though, I do wonder what her powers will reveal about this mark. I will explain more when the time is right. Come now; it's time for the conclave. Practice wisdom and patience inside. Keep your words to yourself unless necessary. There will be many clashing personalities that we must navigate. Until you know them all well, it is better to observe only."

Before they could enter, an older man barged out. The doors slammed shut behind his silver ponytail and bearded scowl. His face was scarred and hardened, and his yellow eyes communicated their stubbornness before his words could. "Talus, you are my king and my commander, but hurramit—I will not sit idly by with a Krog in the conclave. I want him out!"

Talus beaded his eyebrows together. "Scavok, you're like a father to me, but I do not have time for this."

Scavok looked like a battle-worn wolf as he glared relentlessly in heavy leather and metal armor. "You have all the time in the world, but the children I found in the rubble of Pacem…the ones I found in their slave houses, they didn't have any more time. The things those Krogs were doing to helpless innocents." Scavok grimaced. "I will not willingly sit in a meeting of such high esteem with one of them."

"Then do it against your will. Time is short, and this is the most important conclave I have ever called together. You can't blame the actions of a rebellion on an entire race, and we have need of Dreibo Nebris. No one else will be able to make my plans proceed smoothly." Talus locked eyes with Scavok. He embraced him on both shoulders and said, "Now I'll hear no more of this today. It is the joyous celebration of my son's return."

Reluctantly, Scavok nodded, and they all entered the Ashva pavilion.

Eos took a seat next to Maxima and only a few spaces away from the four inlumes of Anite. He couldn't help but notice that Julian Cassion had brought his son, Benedir.

Talus stood at the head of an onyx crescent table.

CONCLAVE

He commanded the room with each step. The two dozen members in the conclave swayed their gaze with his approach. "When the founders of Anite made their first trip to the Burning Lands beyond Corland, they brought back this slab of rock across the ocean as a sign of their achievement. When my father, Bekrin, repurposed it from a decorative piece in the castle to this important table, he soon after held a conclave to deal with invading barbarians. I fear we face similar circumstances now. My children return from a foreign land, and we have dire matters to act on."

Julian spoke first, "Then it is simple mountain barbarians? That should be no problem to deal with again."

Stroking his beard, Talus shook his head slowly. "There are many interlocking factors that make this the most complex issue of my time leading Anite. I'll ask that Aizo start explaining with his observations during his return through the Sepeleo mountains." Talus took a seat in a chair that faced the table, where the crescent would have completed a circle had it been a whole piece.

Aizo stood. His face was tired, but there was still a powerful spirit under the weight he carried. "It is only practical that I cover the key events. Upon our return to Corland, there were a series of unsettling interactions. First, we journeyed through the north Sepeleo mountains, where we encountered a pride of corcinths far beyond their territory, led by a badly wounded leader. If this wasn't a bad enough omen, a barbarian tribe captured us further north. When I invoked the Bellator family name, they only told us that they feared much worse these days. Something is pushing the mountain dwellers out of the Corleo territory."

The conclave rumbled with commentary.

Agathon, the elderly inlume, interrupted. "If the barbarians and corcinth are moving into Anite territory, this bodes of a

CHAPTER THIRTEEN

powerful force in the Corleo kingdom." The room went quiet to listen to the sagely bald man. "Do we have any indication of who this force could be, and have we had any response from Ramath Leorix? A silent king is further bad news."

"I will address Ramath's silence soon," Talus said.

Julian asked, "If there is a powerful foe in the mountains, what could it be that threatens Anite? Surely it must be sanctioned by Ramath?"

Aizo reclaimed the conversation, "The answer was given to us shortly after escaping the barbarians. A powerful river merchant named Sergius Ora gave us safe passage on his personal strider from West Avem to Anondorn—only the trip turned out to be anything but safe. We were attacked for a second time on our journey. Betrayed by someone I once knew well on that ride to Anondorn. Sergius Ora revealed that he was on the take from the Mitad's Emir Grimshaw."

The room went silent.

Julian's face went pale.

The room echoed with sudden outcries. *An emir having sway in West Avem—impossible! You must be mistaken. So far into Anite? How could this be?* The voices fought over each other.

Once again, Talus commanded the room with a bold whistle and said sternly, "The story gets worse. Terrava and I took Eos and Maxima to Fanum Ortus for a few days to prepare the stage for their return announcement. There, Maxima was attacked by a Mitad soldier who claimed to be working for Emir Grimshaw. She was nearly killed, had it not for her sharp wits and quick wielding talent."

Julian Cassion stuttered, "S-s-surely the Mitad would not be ready to move into our territory. It's an act of war!"

CONCLAVE

"War?" Talus asked. "And whom should we attack? They are a terrorist group in the borders of every major nation now."

Inlume Agathon questioned aloud, "The question is: has Ramath succumbed to their growing strength?"

Talus nodded as Aizo took his seat, "Exactly the right question." He stood and unrolled Ramath's scroll. "The one and only letter from Ramath in the last year arrived on our journey from Fanum Ortus back to Anondorn." He read it aloud. "As you can hear for yourselves, Ramath claims to remain loyal, and I trust him, but he is clearly under pressure from the Mitad. I fear he cannot withstand their influence much longer."

"How can you trust a man who we kept as a loyalty hostage for so many years?" asked a face that Eos didn't recognize.

It was simple for Talus, "He is a brother to me. He's saved my life before. I know him well, and betrayal is not in him."

Terrava came in to support her husband as many voices began questioning the notion of Ramath's loyalty. "I too have posed this question to my husband, but he is certain. No one knows Ramath better than Talus. There is little more to be said."

Talus added, "And it is my proposition that we verify."

"How?" asked Julian nervously.

"My son, Eos, experienced an ancient kind of wielding that has afflicted him during his time away. It is something beyond the Sanofem's abilities, beyond Aizo's knowledge, and I can only think of one person to help him…"

The Cassions perked up interestedly at the news.

Spintha spoke for the first time. Her voice was soft and steady, matching her gray-streaked dark hair. "You plan to see the manus stone priestess?"

Talus nodded his head in affirmation.

CHAPTER THIRTEEN

"Then you journey to the Winter Aisles?" Spintha concluded wisely.

"Spintha, I wonder if you learned to read my mind when you trained me. I intend to put together a small party—as small as possible. Every group member will serve a purpose and allow us to enter the winter aisle in secret. We will visit Priestess Jezca Monte and see what she can tell us of Eos' affliction. At the same time, we will find a way into the Corleo kingdom to contact Ramath in private and investigate the disturbance in the Sepeleo mountains."

A deep, monotone voice responded, "Then you will require my service, my lord?" The man was incredibly tall and lean. His ashen-toned skin and amethyst eyes set him apart from the members of the room. Spiraling tribal tattoos that ran down the sides of his shaved skull and his stature assured that he disturbed everyone's attention when he stood.

"You play a key role in this plan, Dreibo," Talus confirmed.

Disgruntled grumbles were made throughout the pavilion with no intention of being discreet. It was obvious that Dreibo polarized opinions in the room.

Dreibo Nebris placed a hand over his heart and bowed. "It will be my honor to go ahead and prepare a stealthy passage into the kingdom."

Julian Cassion stood in a hasty movement and shrugged uncomfortably. "King Talus, it would be only right that the Cassion family be present for such a critical diplomatic mission." He glanced around the room to try threatening support of the idea. "Both to serve our royal family in their time of need and to provide a balance of...perceptions about Ramath." A moment of pause in the room led him to add, "Not to mention, I have been wanting

CONCLAVE

some sort of rite of passage to try young Benedir as he works towards Errant."

Talus' eyes closed as he thought. His words were carefully chosen, "I appreciate this gesture, Julian. However, there will be plenty of *balanced perceptions* traveling already. We need to limit the number of our party." He knew that Julian was trying to garner political favor by participating, and that was only the most innocent of reasons he could have for volunteering.

"My lord, Eos' will be in need of someone his age to accompany him. It would be good to have Benedir with him as a training partner."

The legate from East Avem agreed, "I approve of this idea. One more will not harm the venture."

Political alliances were at work.

The Garuda legate sealed the decision with his words, "Talus, we all admire you as our king, but an extra set of eyes as you verify your childhood friend's loyalty will be good, and a boy Eos' age will be what he needs to adjust to his return home."

Backed into a corner of political maneuvering, Talus relented. "Very well. We welcome Benedir on this journey. I will also require hariban Scavok's skills to scout out the source of the barbarian and corcinth disturbance."

Scavok only scowled, eyed Drebio, and nodded his consent.

"Then it will be myself, Eos, Dreibo, Scavok, and young Benedir who go to the winter aisle."

Maxima could not help but speak. "Father, if Eos is going on this journey, I want to be with him."

"No," Terrava cautioned. "Your father and I have plans for you in Anondorn. This is not the time for you to sneak into foreign kingdoms."

CHAPTER THIRTEEN

Eos got out of his chair. Talus eyed him warningly, but that didn't stop Eos from speaking his mind. "I wouldn't want to go anywhere without Maxima. She knows things about my affliction that will be important."

Tension pulled between the Bellators.

Spintha calmly decided the matter, "Talus, may I recommend that you do not separate Eos and Maxima so soon after their return. I sense a bond that is better kept close in them. I believe she will be invaluable in your journey."

Talus stroked his beard, annoyed. He knew his old master was never wrong about such matters. "Six members we will be then."

Maxima hopped excitedly in her seat before remembering that gratitude was the proper disposition in this formal situation. "Thank you, Father."

"We will wait out the harshness of winter. I pray it will not give enough time for the Mitad to make further advances in Corleo. Then, we shall make our expedition."

Julian had further interests to pursue. "My King, I think it is of value for the conclave to know—what is the nature of this affliction on Eos? Perhaps one of may be of assistance." He smiled slyly, stroking his platinum hair.

Talus strode to the glass window and looked out at the incredible Ashva tree that sprung from the lake. Its white-veined leaves stole his thoughts momentarily. "His affliction is best left as a family matter for now. This conclave is concluded," he said without looking back at his counsel.

"You know best," Julian conceded but eyed Benedir with a plotting grin.

Eos pulled at the glove on his cursed arm nervously.

CONCLAVE

Talus was lost in the noise of his mind as he looked over the turquoise lake. It reflected morning sunlight into the room. He thought: *This would be an adventure to decide many things. The fate of Corland hangs in the balance. And this curse.* Talus could feel dread in his bones. *The curse is worse than any of us know. Now, Maxima will be involved in the dangers…*

Worries weighed on him as the Ashva tree rustled in the breeze like a giant was breathing over the forest.

CHAPTER FOURTEEN

RAID ON THE CRAWLERS

Patchwork patterns of tin sheets and brittle wood sewed together the shacks that made up the Mircite Valley in the western reaches of the Monte Kingdom. It was appropriately disjointed as it lay on the border of two contentious countries, but it was the boot heel of both. The mine workers that filled the sooty streets dressed in plain colors, and Caldus was no exception. He hugged the furred fringes of his overtunic against his neck as he trudged through the year's first dusting of snow in the Winter Aisle.

The only distinction between every filthy worker on the Mircite roads and Caldus was the bronze pin that held his cloak in place. The bronze piece had a small set of curled horns, crudely fashioned at the end. On his trek home, he occasionally crossed paths with a dirt-covered face that had the same pin. He would give them a slight nod, which they would return.

Smokestacks rose from every shack to direct away the pollution of the year-round fires required to keep the valley's conditions livable. Caldus had worked hard to acquire a third-story dwelling. It had taken many long days in the mines, nearly every day since he had fled from the Manus Temple, to scrape together enough to live above the lower shacks. The wooden support slats that held it over the alley creaked with a disturbing weariness, and the walls were no better than any other building, but it was a home above the common grime. The air was more tolerable, and that was important for Philo.

Caldus carried his legs, heavy from a day's work in the mines, up the three flights of stairs carved into the mountain. He fell on the slatted floor in exhaustion but did not rest for more than a few breaths. Philo slept on the mat at the other side of the single-room home, near the embers of the dead fire.

Grabbing a ladle of clean water from their small supply barrel's bottom, he filled a cup for his adoptive father. When Caldus attempted to roll him over, Philo's breathing was shaky, and he was sweating profusely.

"No," Caldus whispered to himself. "Dad. Wake up." He gently shook Philo awake. A confused grumble was the only response, but the old man's eyes opened.

"Drink."

Philo shook his head.

"Dad, you need your strength."

"You...need it more. For the mines," Philo said.

Caldus closed his pale blue eyes. "I'm getting more safe water tomorrow. Supplies are coming into the valley. Now, drink."

CHAPTER FOURTEEN

Finally, Philo conceded and took the cup to his lips. The drinking was interrupted by a rattling cough and groan.

Caldus slammed his fist into his leg. "Why did you drink from the stream water? You know it's not safe."

"There wasn't…" he wheezed, "enough for both of us."

"There is always enough. We ration." Caldus knew his words were not true. The price of clean water had been going up weekly, and his extra work in the mine was not keeping up. Philo was getting slower. His contribution was less and less, but Caldus owed him everything.

"You took me in off the streets when no one else would. Taught me to work. You should never have to risk the stream water."

There was a long pause. Philo admitted weakly, "I had been cutting…my ration with stream water for a few weeks. It was bound to happen."

Caldus' lip curled up. *Why? Stubborn old man.*

"I'm going to get you medicine tonight."

Philo's eyes opened more than Caldus had seen since he had taken permanently to the mat. "How?"

"Don't worry, Dad. I found a source."

"You better not be mixing up with the *Red Corcinths*. I hear things. I know about those rebels—" a coughing fit interrupted him. "They will get you killed."

"I know. I found a safe way and saved up enough money."

Philo eyed him warily but said no more. He had no more energy to argue.

Poking the embers, Caldus stirred up a fire and threw more tinder under the cooking pot. He prepared a simple stew and ate quietly, leaving a bowl for whenever Philo woke again. That was everything. The water barrel was empty. His money bag lay in the same state—the month's payment on their home had drained it. Tonight, everything was on the line.

Sitting in a cross-legged meditation, he prepared for what lay ahead. In the morning, there would be more water and medicine.

It was almost dark in the valley. The chirping of the stone-frogs filled the air with low bellowing croaks. It was time for Caldus' night work.

There were many panels where the shack met the wall of the mountain, but one was ajar outside the abode. Caldus lifted it away and reached behind, pulling a cold ceramic piece off a nail in the hidden space. He slid the red and white corcinth mask over his face and tied it securely to his head. The disguise had large fangs and curled horns that would have made a ginning mockery of the fierce beast if it did not create a simultaneously creepy effect.

The back alleyways of the slum were full of waste, but that was the only way for rebels to travel. *Tap tap tap.* He would rap his knuckles slightly on the back of tin sheets every few blocks. When he did, another red mask would join him. Each one was a crude imitation of Caldus'. They had made theirs by hand, but his was a specially stolen collectible from a wealthy mine manager. The story was infamous around the slum, and the manager still had a bounty out for its return. The red masks stepped through piles of unburned trash together.

An hour later, he led half a dozen of the Red Corcinths into a private room. Another member closed the backdoor quickly behind them. "Good," said a female voice. "That makes ten of us. Caldus, here is the map that Talker made."

CHAPTER FOURTEEN

Talker had squinted eyes and wore a bandana on his head. He nodded, his thinly grown mustache bobbing up and down as he spread out his hand-drawn creation.

Everyone removed their masks for the plan review session.

"Thank you, Alia. And thank you, Talker."

The short, mute man nodded vigorously.

Alia winked at Caldus on the side that no one else in the room could see. She brushed back her dark brown hair and said, "Take it away, boss. We have a big score tonight."

Caldus began, "This is a new mine shaft, and it's in the Corleo territory. That means we can expect to see crawlers in the area. Hopefully, we don't meet any, but if we do—you know the protocol. Lead them away from the group. Finish them quickly from a distance or our cover is blown, and if that fails—lose them. The same goes for any Mitad workers we may run into. Talker, how many guards did you find earlier?"

Talker held up two fingers.

"Alright, it'll be like they left it for us to take. Simple enough. Find the water and the silver they collected for the month. Bring it back here. Alia, Talker, and I will go further ahead for their stash of medicine. There are multiple routes to the mine entrance that we've planned out." Caldus traced red lines with his finger. "We go separately in pairs to reduce our risk of being spotted."

They strategized for another hour before setting off in the black of night. Alia hung closely behind him as they set into the ridge for cover, moving carefully over loose rocks.

Alia broke the silence in a low voice, "Caldus, tonight is important for the water, but you do know that there is no guarantee the medicine is being held there. Talker only thinks he saw them carry it in. He may not have actually seen medicine, or somebody could have moved it."

Silence.

"Caldus, I just don't want you to get caught up in there if we don't find it. I know how important it is to you."

They stopped their midnight journey. Caldus looked at Alia's dark skin in the moonlight. He let his eyes linger on her delicate features, hardened by days in the mines. Despite spending as much time in the tunnels as he did, she always managed to smell like the blue lilac found just south of Mircite. "I'm not coming back empty-handed. If that means I search alone, then so be it, but it's Philo's best chance."

"You have other options."

"*No*, I don't," he warned in an irritated tone.

"Philo means a lot to me too. I'm just asking you to try every option. You could attempt to contact her. The rumors say she's powerful, even at healing."

"It's been years. That line is cut off. I'm not crossing to Petramon for them to turn me away at the temple door. I spent enough time with those charlatans to know that I wouldn't get past the front gate."

"Jezca is your sister!"

"That was a long time ago." Caldus whipped his winter cape around him and stormed off into the night.

Two hours later, the Red Corinths assembled at the cave on the border between the Monte and Corleo kingdoms. The mine entrance was more than twice the height of Caldus and constructed with an etched *M* overhead. He knew it must belong to the Ignoble Lord, Xaro Monte. However, Xaro had left for the winter, and the Mitad had decided to move in.

CHAPTER FOURTEEN

They followed the mine cart rails into the tunnel with the quiet footsteps of practiced street thieves. After they had left the entrance a few minutes behind them, there was no lack of light in the musty-smelling hole. Lighting stones speckled the walls in a periodic chain. This arrangement was typical practice for the Mitad. They avoided having their supply depots raided by keeping the mine dark from an outside view but lit it further in, where they would not be discovered.

Ten long shadows wavered behind the first storage room in the damp mine. It was a circular cavern that branched into three other paths. Inside, the sound of dice rolling and two men bantering over cards echoed down the entrance path. Caldus halted his group. He motioned for half of them to move behind a stack of water barrels near the table and led the other half towards the two guards.

One cloaked man kicked his foot on the table as he tipped his chair back and thumbed his hand of cards. "You aren't going to want to do that unless you want me to take all your money tonight."

"Sure, try and bluff your empty hand." The guard at the far end rolled a six-sided die decorated in symbols. "Ha, no way that I'm losing with a roll like that."

The other man grunted. "Whose night is it to check on the big tunnel, Kilsig's or Rohl's?"

"I don't keep track of that. Whoever shows up, it doesn't matter to me as long as I stay far back from those things inside. All I know is that Ozen hasn't left the factory for weeks, so it sure ain't him."

RAID ON THE CRAWLERS

Caldus scanned the room. There were three large stacks of barrels throughout the cavern but nothing else—no sign of the medicine boxes that Talker had seen three nights before.

Slipping deftly through the shadows, Caldus moved behind the man tipping his chair. Like weaving a thread, his feet moved in smooth, silent steps until he was in a position to bring his blade around the chair. He held it against the man's throat.

The guard seized up. His friend across the table jumped and blurted, "What in the—" But Alia's blade appeared from the darkness and mirrored Caldus.

"Who're you, people? Wait…" His eyes widened at the horrifying grins of the crews' red masks. "Red Corcinths." He cursed.

Caldus growled threateningly, "Where is the medicine?"

The man that Alia held laughed. "Wouldn't you like to know? Mirza Yann Kilsig would be happy to show you if you'd like to die."

"You have ten seconds to wipe that grin off your face and give us the location of the medicine."

The man did not comply. He cleared his bearded throat and scoffed as the metal pressed into his jugular. Caldus nodded to Alia. "Show him we're serious."

Alia slid the blade. The man gurgled as he dropped to the floor.

Caldus threw his captive's chair back. It crashed to the ground, and the frightened guard rolled, clutching his head after it slammed into the rock floor.

"Ten seconds for you."

The living guard's eyes darted, searching for options. He pulled a forked piece of metal from his robe pocket and struck it against

CHAPTER FOURTEEN

a metal bracket on the table. It rang in a high pitch frequency as he bolted for the entrance tunnel.

Talker and two others revealed themselves from behind the stack of water barrels. They surrounded him as he tried to flee. The metal tool in his hand fell to the floor as he realized there was no escape.

Alia came close to the guard so that her horned mask was just inches from his face. "Feel like talking?"

The guard squealed and did not hesitate to divulge the information.

"The factory. Please don't kill me. The medicine was taken to the factory yesterday."

Caldus was agitated. "What is *the factory*? We didn't see anyone go in or out of here. Lying will only get you killed."

"The factory! It's deeper in the mountains. You can follow the mountain runoff streams to it. The t-t-tunnel is quicker. It's only an hour through it."

Pacing back and forth, Caldus considered the words. "Well, if you're telling the truth, then we take the tunnel to this factory."

"Yes, but…the mirzas and the crawlers will kill you. You won't get near the factory."

There was a moment of quiet.

The guard smirked sadly and said, "You're going to kill me, but they're coming. You won't see tomorrow either."

At Caldus' command, Talker stabbed his blade into the guard's abdomen multiple times.

"Let's get the water loaded," Caldus ordered. "And grab the bags of silver. They're behind the table."

Fifteen minutes later, they had filled the cart with barrels. It would be a slow haul through the night to get it back to the Mircite

RAID ON THE CRAWLERS

Valley with two pulling and three pushing from behind. Only Caldus and Alia were left in the nearly empty cavern as Talker joined the others outside the mine.

"I think we should find the factory. It's our only shot, and the medicine will save everyone who's sick in the valley," Caldus said with certainty.

Alia sighed, "Caldus, do you really want to face a mirza? That's certain death."

Caldus removed his mask and winked. "Since when do we get caught?"

A rattling of limbs and inhumane screeches came from deep in the mine.

"What was that?"

Talker re-entered the mine but froze when he heard the sound. They all knew what it meant. Chills ran through their bodies.

Crawlers were coming.

"Talker, go! We'll distract them to give you a head start," Caldus yelled as he sheathed his steel blades and reached into his tunic. He pulled out Amon's daggers—the jeweled hilt and ruby-red blades gleamed in the twinkling lights. The skull that decorated the handle stared at him with sunken eye sockets.

Alia muttered nervously, "That sounds like a lot. I'm not sure Caldus." She pulled out two dull red stones from a bag tied to her belt.

"We don't have a choice. We're the only ones who can wield. The water won't make it to Mircite if we can't hold them."

The clattering of limbs grew louder, echoing down the halls in a horrific approaching rumble.

Caldus stared into Alia's eyes, appreciating their earthy brown tone one more time before they both fought for their lives. He held

CHAPTER FOURTEEN

his reverse grip on the daggers with sweaty palms. He had run into a crawler a few times before in the mountains but never had he heard a sound like this.

The first crawler broke through the veil of darkness, glowing a blue-white that crackled, filled with static-electric noise. It was a ghostly arachnoid monstrosity.

Whispering to himself in a meditative state, he produced Soul Energy. He had never been able to manifest it exteriorly, but that didn't matter. Amon's daggers countered his inability to wield and channeled it. The blades glowed a blood-red as they slashed through the space between him and the crawler.

A crimson wave of energy shot out of the dagger's edge.

It cut the air in a sharp whistle and collided with the crawler.

The creatures were like bombs, ready to go off when they made contact with anything perceived hostile. The long-range attack from the blades met the pale creation in a high pitch ring followed by a violent explosion. Rubble showered from the ceiling, and the crawler disappeared into a fiery vapor.

Another crawler emerged from the rising dust cloud. It screeched as if alive and angry. Alia summoned her Soul Energy, but only enough to activate her specially prepared amgrite stones. They were dull, low-quality shards, but she had filled them to their capacity with energy ahead of time. Each magma-tinted piece of rock gleamed in her hand. She hurled the first amgrite-bomb to meet the approaching creature at the entrance of its tunnel. The stone didn't hold much energy, but it was enough to trigger the crawler.

Another explosion shook the cavern.

RAID ON THE CRAWLERS

Caldus and Alia moved away from the falling rock. White glows, and the sound of dozens of limbs grew close from behind a wall of dust.

Alia coughed as she said, "There are a lot more coming. Can you feel them?"

As dust hovered in the air, dull lights began pouring into the haze. The crawlers tumbled over each other in a spider-like mass. They moved with a hivemind until over a hundred spilled into the room—cutting off the exit.

A look was all that the two needed, to agree on their only option. Run.

They threw themselves to the only open tunnel available. Alia tossed amgrite shards blindly behind her as they made their escape. Echoes of rupturing crawlers and rattling limbs pinged through the cave system, chasing them endlessly. Each time a wave of energy from Caldus' dagger or an amgrite stone caught the head of the crawler horde, a few would explode and fill the area with a burnt rubber smell.

Speed was their only advantage. The wave of creatures wasn't able to keep up with their running speed, but after minutes of stumbling blindly through the dark, Caldus and Alia's endurance was waning. Their lungs pained them, but not enough to overcome their fear yet.

So, they ran. Sprinting and sending attacks backward as they distanced themselves from the horde. Sparse light-stones lit some paths; others were utterly dark. In these, they were as good as blind, tripping multiple times and using the sound of each other's voice to avoid getting separated.

"I don't think I can keep going," Alia panted.

CHAPTER FOURTEEN

"We're going to get out. We just have to make our way through the tunnels. It can't be much further," Caldus assured. They had put distance between them and their pursuers. The ominous glow was out of sight, and the sounds were dampened. However, Caldus worried that they could be getting lost deeper in the cave. He made sure to keep his concern to himself. "We just keep taking paths with light-stones. Those will eventually take us out of here." *He hoped.*

At least an hour had passed. Their pace became a jog, but the far-away sound of the crawlers had not closed in. Eventually, Caldus slowed to a walk in a well-lit room. He led them slowly to the other side with his dagger grip never loosening.

The floor smoothed, and the path widened until it was easily twenty people across. Both Caldus and Alia came to a complete stop.

Before them was a split path, the left continued on the same, but the right dwarfed anything Caldus had ever seen. It looked as if made for an army of corcinths to pass through. The circular opening expanded until it was ten times wider than any path they had seen so far. It was no simple undertaking to make a tunnel like that, Caldus knew. His work in the mines had taught him how much reinforcement was required for something of that scale. He could make out pillars and overhead beams supporting the structure into the darkness. The light-stones down that path were not lit, and neither of them desired to change that. There was a presence coming from the heart of the mountain. Something waited in the dark. It was like the horde that chased them but multiplied many times and concentrated.

RAID ON THE CRAWLERS

Caldus and Alia shook under the scale of the tunnel and the feeling emanating from it. They quickly moved down the left path and began to run again.

"What was that?" Alia asked.

"I've never seen anything like it, and I'm sure that direction is deeper into the north range. The question is, was that made by Xaro over the years or recently by the Mitad?" Caldus spoke through labored breath. They both knew that Xaro had never attempted such a project in all their years working for his mines, but also that it would take far longer to construct than Xaro had been gone.

It was not long before the sound of their pursuers was faintly audible again.

They shared a tired look of dread before Caldus felt a rush of boldness, "Alia, once we get the medicine and Philo recovers...I'm taking him away from the valley. I want him to live the rest of his life in peace."

"Where would you go? What about the Red Corcinths?"

"South. I've heard there is work in the Terspar plains and plenty of land. The Red Corcinths will carry on. I've already begun making preparations."

Alia's lips pursed as she thought of a possibility she didn't enjoy.

"You want me to lead them without you?" she asked sadly.

"No, Alia. I want you to join us. Come to the Terspar plains with me."

Her mouth relaxed into a slight smile. She didn't need to think long about leaving the dirty Mircite valley with her longtime companion. Caldus stepped closer to her and took her hands in his. "Please come with me."

CHAPTER FOURTEEN

Alia nodded vigorously, speechless, but the moment was cut short as the first crawler of the pack rounded the corner down the tunnel. She panicked, throwing an amgrite stone down to buy them a few extra seconds.

They were lost in the mountain, pursued by numerous creatures, terrified by what lay inside the massive mine shaft, but they had a hope to cling on. If it wasn't for the vision of golden fields and clean air, neither would have been able to keep running.

Heavy legs moved on the fuel of hope and fear.

They began to believe that they would find the medicine and return to town.

The mass of soul energy beasts fell away...and then finally, they saw the light. It wasn't the artificial glow of light-stones. It was natural and accompanied by the smell of fresh moisture splashing from the river, chilled by mountain winds.

Then, they were outside the mines. Caldus squinted through the auburn twilight at a wide switchback trail overlooking the raging water from hundreds of feet above. A large group of factories blew plumes of smoke into the gray cloud cover from the edge of the river just a few miles away. *What was the Mitad making this deep in the mountains?*

"We found it." Caldus smiled in disbelief. They had been on the run for hours, and this was the success his aching legs needed to justify their pain.

His mood instantly fell into a dismal disgust. The factories were pouring a sludge out of their river-side pipes. He didn't know what it was, but he could see purple, oily slew was flowing freely into the water. The concentration was so strong that the water near the building was dyed. The symptoms faded as the water moved down the mountain. *The water that was making everyone sick—these factories*

RAID ON THE CRAWLERS

were causing it. The Mitad were dumping their waste! But waste from what? Caldus shook with frustration, looking at the toxic source of the water shortage, the cause of so many deaths in the valley. *The source of Philo's illness was also holding the medicine he needed.*

Alia saw it too with an audible gasp as they stood close together, staring.

The back of her hand brushed Caldus', and for a few seconds, their fingers locked together.

The solitude was short-lived.

Heavy steps of gray leather boots announced someone else reaching the top of the trail. A man dressed in a brass-buttoned black jacket and black pants sauntered toward them. He stopped a way out and looked them up and down from beneath his black flat-brimmed hat as if deciding how much he didn't like the sight of Caldus and Alia. The golden crossed sabers on his hat bobbed up and down as he stroked his dark mutton chop beard.

He tipped his hat to them, pausing with his outer hand exposed to them.

"How do ya do?" he asked in a gruff voice that made a mockery of the formal greeting.

Caldus could clearly make out a two-headed snake tattooed on the face of both his boney hands.

The two stepped back in a rush of fear when they realized a Mitad officer approached them, but behind them was a cave full of crawlers and a cliff drop-off.

"Now, I imagine with those red masks that you two are a couple of trouble makers. I also imagine you ran into a few of the Overseer's pets if you got this close to my tunnel." He paused. "We can't be having that. No, we can't." He whistled softly to himself and rested his hands on the saber handles at both sides of his waist.

CHAPTER FOURTEEN

Alia reached into her bag, and Caldus clenched Amon's daggers.

"Who are you?" Caldus growled.

The man in black grinned a crooked smile. "The name's Yann Kilsig. I'm what ya call a mirza in the Mitad's Voro division. So, ya two better think carefully about what kind of threatening action yer taking. Looking like you have a mighty death wish."

There was a cry from the wind as the three had a standoff.

Yann Kilsig was in no rush.

Voro. Caldus had heard the name. It was a special operations division that he caught whispers of when operating as a Red Corcinth. They were ghosts and deadly ghosts at that. No one he had spoken to knew what they did in any detail, but very few who crossed paths with the Voro lived. From what he understood, the Voro leaders themselves were the equivalent of the emir rank.

"What might ya two be doing in my tunnel? Besides looking for a shorter end to yer miserable valley rat lives." Yann laughed arrogantly.

Caldus knew there was no proper answer to his question that didn't end in a battle to the death. "Mirza. You work for the man who makes those *monsters* that were chasing us?"

"Aw, I see ya didn't enjoy your time with the crawlers." He threw his head back and laughed some more. "That's right; I work for the Overseer, Jaco Hetfel. That's his factory. These are his mines. Yer trespassing."

Alia tilted her head to the side and interjected, "We'll just be going then."

"Doesn't work like that."

Metal clinked in a shrill grinding sound as Yann drew one saber from his side.

RAID ON THE CRAWLERS

Pulling an amgrite stone from her pouch, Alia moved first. She let her soul energy flow into the rock for a second before she lobbed it towards the mirza.

The explosive weapon flew at Yann Kilsig.

It only ever got halfway to him. He swung his saber across his body and up in a mighty stroke. The blade flashed with a golden light. A wave of energy ripped from the metal and met the amgrite stone midair. The explosion shook the switchback trail. Light flashed, blinding all three momentarily.

Caldus understood the ability. Yann could project from his bladed weapon just like Caldus. It wasn't a pure weapon like his dagger but instead high-quality steel folded in the forge with manus stone.

Yann Kilsig glared with deadly aggravation in his brown eyes. "Stupid choice." He pointed his blade at Alia and gave it a flick with his wrist. The movement was tiny but precise. A singular point of gold concentrated from the sword's tip and blasted in a beam towards Alia.

Watching in horror, Caldus saw the golden beam slice into Alia's chest.

It struck her with more blunt force than explosive power.

Blood immediately sprung from her skin, but by the time the breath left her, she was taken off her feet. He watched her hover over the dirt path and then soar over the cliff edge.

There was a soft scream of surprise, but it wasn't the loud outcry against death that he had imagined would accompany such an event. It was quick, like a quiver from an instrument during a pause before the next note. Then the song should have carried on, and the previous sound was gone.

In this song, no following note was played.

CHAPTER FOURTEEN

It ended abruptly.

Alia was floating above the ravine. The next second, she was gone, and the fleeting dream of the Terspar plains plummeted with her.

The lump in his throat prevented Caldus from screaming out. His head shook back and forth in disbelief. *Alia was gone.* He had to unclench his jaw and remember to breathe as pressure swelled in his head. His urge was to lash out—to strike Yann Kilsig, but he knew that he was outclassed. The gap between their skills was a death sentence, and his mind was still stumbling over itself to process.

Alia was dead.

Dead.

Yann's mustache curled up on one side as he beamed at Caldus. "Now, why don't ya play a little nicer than she did?" He waved the tip of his sword brazenly with his words. "Ah! This is my lucky day. Ya lead those Red Corcinths, don't you?"

Caldus could barely focus enough to hear the words. He shook his head, knowing that his position would only compromise him further. His blades went back into their sheathes under his tunic.

The leather boots drew closer. "Ya know they put out a handsome reward for ya—alive, unfortunately." Yann squinted. "They say yer related to that priestess girl. That's the only reason my blade isn't through yer skull. And I want the gold."

"You're taking me to the Voro?"

"'Course not. Then I wouldn't get paid. Don't worry. I won't kill ya yet. Ya belong to the Monte royal family now. So, ya have at least two days more to live before they kill ya." Yann gave a throaty laugh.

RAID ON THE CRAWLERS

Caldus grimaced. He knew what he had to do—Yann wouldn't kill him, and he must keep the Amon's daggers. With swift hands, he reached into his tunic again and drew two plain blades—*decoy weapons*.

A mad dash forward caught Yann off guard. It was the split second Caldus needed to close the distance and get inside Yann's defensive range.

Slit.

Yann's black sleeve tore, and Caldus drew blood from the mirza's shoulder. His broad nose wrinkled at the pain, but he didn't hesitate to swing his saber around as he slid away from most of the attack. With a twist of his wrist, Yann brought the hilt of his blade around. *Thunk.*

The gold handle struck Caldus in the side of the head.

He had known it was coming and wanted it that way. He just hoped the decoy daggers were all that Yann Kilsig would confiscate. Vision blurred, and the sharp pain in his head seemed to pull his consciousness away from his body as he collapsed.

It hurt unbelievably bad, but it didn't matter. The pain of his thoughts was greater. *Alia was dead. They would never go to Terspar together.*

A heavy boot rested on Caldus' chest. Yann slid his saber back into its sheath and put pressure on the shoulder graze.

"Slippery little devil, but the Red Corcinths turned out to be a couple of playing kids." He cleared his throat and spit. Then, Yann picked Caldus' limp body up and threw him over his shoulder.

"Little pest could have at least walked himself back. *Tsk.*" Yann pulled the brim of his hat down as he walked in the sunrise.

CHAPTER FIFTEEN

INCOMPLETE PAGES

Stone chairs for men of the mountain. The Monte families had always resisted comforts when on official business in Petramurus castle. It was the way of their people. King Pallogos Monte held the weekly evening council, but this one was riddled with more problems than usual. So many issues, he wondered if the manus gods were angry with him. He squeezed the bridge of his nose, further wrinkling his aged skin like cracking rice paper. His brother—Peladan, Plumos Bellator, advisors Tavro and Bohm, a handful of legates, and numerous politicians surrounded him.

A special guest was attending the counsel today, legate Roki of the Mircite valley. He thumbed his mustache as he rambled out his concerns. His thinning hair bobbed nervously with his head as he said, "The Mircite Valley water supply is contaminated without a doubt. The water is killing our people and disrupting the mining operations. This problem has grown out of control."

King Pallogos croaked wearily, "And I have increased the clean water supply delivered to the Valley. What has your investigation revealed about the source of this problem? We cannot continue to drain increasing resources into Mircite with diminishing returns from the mines."

"My lord," Roki whined, "There is smoke rising from the mountains on the Corleo side. When we try to investigate, we are met with...*those creatures.*"

There was a hush in the room. King Pallogos stroked his long gray beard. "Crawlers? So, the rumors have truth to them?"

"Indeed, my lord."

"Then we must report this finding to King Leorix immediately and have answers. The Mitad have infested his territory. He is either paralyzed with fear or is aiding them. Regardless, it is a bane to the Montes and must be dealt with," the King pondered with grunts of exhaustion.

"That is not all," Roki continued. "They have encroached on Xaro's western mines." There were aghast murmurs, but no one dared broach the topic. "Finally, as King Pallogos now knows, I have delivered the rebel leader of the Red Corcinths, a young man named Caldus, into the hands of the royal guard. This troublemaker has been interfering with mining operations and royal affairs for far too long. Most are aware of his infamous wannabe heroic antics. I look forward to his punishment."

The room erupted into an echo of cheer.

The King's spotted hand went up to silence the room. "We must decide how to handle him carefully. Once his identity was

CHAPTER FIFTEEN

revealed last week, we became aware that he is the blood brother of Jezca Monte."

The legate of Petramon interrupted, "Then execution is off the table?"

"Undoubtedly," King Pallogos decided. "For the moment. He will remain in prison until we determine how to handle the delicate matter."

An auburn-haired man, lanky but composed, spoke up. "And what of this matter with King Leorix visiting the Manus Temple? They call our people stone worshipping dogs, yet he seeks the high priests? Does it not seem that all are tied together?"

With fingertips tapping together, King Leorix agreed. "Yes, Plumos. Too many strange coincidences for it to not be. He convened, at my approval, with the Priestess Jezca Monte in the private confessory chambers. Their order is sworn to reveal nothing of what goes on behind those closed doors. Perhaps...we can leverage the imprisonment of her brother?" he wondered aloud.

The meeting continued. Minor problems followed that paled next to the worries on the King's mind from the Mircite Valley and the Manus Priesthood. *Too many secrets. Too many disturbances.*

The hours of political banter ended with a final concern. The King's younger brother approached and then knelt before King Pallogos. "My King...my brother...Tremlay has been missing for over two weeks now. Scouring Petramon and the outskirts has turned up nothing. I beg that we probe into Corleo territory."

Nodding, the King croaked, "Peladan, for my brother and missing nephew, there is nothing I would hold back. I will assign members of the stealth unit to you until he is found."

INCOMPLETE PAGES

Everyone raised from their stone chairs and proceeded out on the blue-tiled floor, patterned with the iconography of the Monte men of renown. Plumos Bellator remained behind before his king.

"King Pallogos," he whispered in private, "Dreibo Nebris has come to Petramon. He told me that my uncle, King Talus, is making a secret journey to visit you. The matter of Ramath is dire even to Anite. He has much news and many requests. Dreibo desires an audience as soon as possible."

Shaken by the announcement, King Pallogos stood and fixed his gaze on his favorite bit of tile: the blue brushstrokes that showed the high priest placing a crown on his ancestor. "Heavy is the crown," he bellowed. "Nonsense. Heavy is the weight of other crowns who require mine. I can manage the affairs of my nation well. However, there is an increasing number of crowns in the Winter Aisle poking each other. Talus Bellator is an old friend. I shall meet with Dreibo tomorrow and accommodate anything Talus should need." *Curse Ramath Leorix. That fool is going to provoke a war.*

Outside the chamber, Tavro leaned in to speak quietly with Peladan, "Knowledge is power."

Peladan smirked and tapped his pointed nose. "Power must be preserved and knowledge retained." With the mantra answered, the two members knew they were about to share important words.

Tavro was solemn. "The disappearance of your son is terrible news and a frightful omen."

"Aye. I haven't slept for many nights. Both his life and his possession are on my mind. If either were to fall into the Mitad's hands…I cannot imagine it. The Priori would have failed to preserve the knowledge."

CHAPTER FIFTEEN

"I have placed my half of Grace Lapithos' journal in safe custody. I have no fear for it. The half that we trusted to Tremlay...I worry it may be lost," Tavro said.

"Do not say such things—we must hold hope for his life."

"I said nothing of his life. That outcome I can't see. However, I can sense a disturbance. The knowledge is in their hands now. Of your son, his soul is out of range for my skill to sense."

Peladan cursed too loud for their secret conversation. "Necogen assassins must have intercepted him. The Mitad have been using them exclusively to hunt us."

Tavro grunted in unhappy agreement.

"Does anyone else have the contents of the journal? We will never decipher it ourselves, but perhaps it can lead us to Grace's location." Peladan clawed for hope.

"You know the elders forbade copies. The Priori cannot have that information copied or lost. It is the true knowledge. I read half of it. Though I can't understand it all, I know it contains what the elders have sought. Karnak's truths are in there, in some form." Tavro said this, but he knew it was a lie. *A copy was made.* Tavro had never forgotten a single dot of ink he had ever read. *A mind's copy.*

Tavro embraced Peladan in consolation for his lost son. Then the two departed opposite ways down the sapphire marbling of the halls. Two halves of the lost knowledge, two missing members of the Priori, and two siblings escaped from Necogen that now shifted the powers in Petramon. He thought, *The Great Soul sure has a way of working in patterns. I must seek a meeting with one of the elders.*

∞   ∞   ∞

INCOMPLETE PAGES

"Pain is a fundamental reality. You see, when I become agitated, you will be forced to take a position. One side or the other." Saida held out two open hands before bringing them up to trace his mustache. He inhaled with exasperation, debating how to handle the situation. "You, Zolo, are the most unique case I've seen on Earth or Hyperborea—but that won't stop me from watching your blood drain out right here and now."

Zolo quivered. He was locked in place. Saida's slicked-back hair and mustache loomed over him like a predator ready to pounce. Uncontrolled anger seethed from the Mitad leader as he towered over his green painted desk, fit for a king and crested with silver. Parchment, wooden boxes, and haphazardly gathered bottles of betel powder next to his pipe littered the surface. Maps were pasted over the walls—a quick adaption to his newly settled residence in Aritrea. He had taken over Ramath's secondary study room.

Ares' arm twitched as he subconsciously decided to intervene. No sooner than the thought formed, Saida shut him down.

"No! Nothing from you. If I hear one word come out of your mouth hole, prepare to be silent for the rest of eternity. Now, I admit that the journal wasn't in the vault yet," Saida pointed to a metal enclosure built into the wall behind his desk and shook his head regretfully, "but entering into my office is one curious way to ask for death. I don't want excess blood in here. It'll put me off of my planning. I'm having a hard enough time focusing in this temporary, makeshift slum. So, I offer you a choice."

The lump in Zolo's throat prevented him from swallowing, but he managed to blurt out, "I-I didn't know it was your office, sir. I only saw a book. I haven't s-s-seen a book since I arrived here."

CHAPTER FIFTEEN

"So, you fancy yourself a scholar?" Saida raised a brow and looked to Ares for confirmation.

Ares jumped at the chance to defend Zolo. "He would be found at the libraries on Earth through all hours of the night."

An uninterested grunt was Saida's response. He thought to himself before saying, "Regardless. That is one of the most important books on Hyperborea right now. Only enemies of the Mitad are after it. This is *my office*. You went into my office uninvited, read what only the enemy is after…I can't have that. I'll make your choice easy."

The two open hands returned over the desk. "One side or the other. Loyalty," he said as a mauve ring of Soul Energy sparked over his palm. "Or…" he tilted his head at his at the empty palm.

"I didn't know. Sir, I—"

"No excuses. Take your lesson, and we can overlook this. Vistomus Fulmen sent you with high recommendations for your mind's capabilities, so I trust you can think through your choice here. Just a finger."

Ares ground his teeth together.

Zolo examined his hand worriedly. He turned it over and extended it hesitantly toward the ring of Soul Energy. *Please, master Ares. Please. Stop this.*

No intervention came.

"Just the little one will do."

His pinky finger had barely entered the open ring before it seized down around the first digit. The energy was hotter than Zolo could fathom, like sticking his hand into the sun. It was over quickly. Charred skin filled the air as the tip of Zolo's little finger fell onto the desk. The pain was overwhelming. For an instant, he thought his heart would stop altogether at the searing sensation. It took everything he had not to fall over. By the time he made eye contact with the Mitad leader, he wasn't sure how long he had been paralyzed over the green painted desk.

"You did well. Never give me a reason to distrust you again," Saida said and brushed the removed bit into the wastebin with a snarled lip.

"Yes…master Saida."

Shortly after, Zolo stumbled into Ares' private chambers in shock. He took Zolo by the shoulders and said, "Look at me. Hey, look at me. That was not supposed to happen."

Zolo's green eyes darted away skittishly.

"I need you to trust me. *I will not let something like that happen again.* What you did was a great help today in securing our freedom in the future. Saida did not lie. That book is one of the most important on Hyperborea. I need you to show me. How far did you get?"

An emotionally wounded eye looked up at Ares. Zolo said softly, "I had it for hours before he found me." He lifted his tunic and pulled a stack of folded papers from his waist. "I copied down the entire thing…all that was there at least. It was only part of the book."

"All of it?" Ares said with excitement. "Good. You will be rewarded." *The boy had outdone himself yet again.*

"Master Ares? Are you crossing Saida?"

There was a pause as Ares tossed the waves of his raven hair out of his face. "To get what I want…for that, I need knowledge and power. That book is the means. Saida is just in the way. He's dangerous, but I have no loyalty to him outside what is required by the Mitad." He could feel the poisonous hatred bubbling up in him as he envisioned his goals.

CHAPTER FIFTEEN

"I thought he was the leader of the Mitad?"

A cold laugh answered. "Vistomus pulls strings on Earth—Saida on Hyperborea. I'm after the one who pulls their strings. For the meantime, I want you to take this." Ares placed in his palm a piece of anima stone. "I know you understand how these work from the book I gave you on Earth. This is one of the purest shards I've ever come across. If you are ever in danger again, light it. I'll come to you as quickly as I can."

Zolo examined its glimmer. "Is that an ability that I could achieve one day: to sense something like that?"

"No. To sense at a great distance is something only a few inlumes of the Soul Wielding Order can achieve. The distance I can sense at…the one who pulls the strings did something to me. He made me sensitive to Soul Energy. Guard that stone. It's only a small repayment for your sacrifice. More will come."

There was a tingle in the missing space where his fingertip used to be. Zolo supposed it was a kindness to have only removed so little. He recalled stealing the Mellizo Glyph from Vistomus Fulmen. He deserved worse. "Master Ares, you owe me nothing. I'm at your service." He thought for a moment and grimaced. "Actually, I would appreciate some pain killer."

Ares smirked. "None of that here, but there is some alcohol on that shelf." He unfolded the copy of Grace Lapithos' journal and became lost in the knowledge that only the select few, highest positioned and well informed on Corland, sought after…and killed for.

∞   ∞   ∞

INCOMPLETE PAGES

Terrava sauntered to her maidservant with Maxima following behind. It had been four months since the conclave, and Maxima had learned much of the ways of Anondorn. The etiquette, the food, the customs, the way of speaking, the public baths—never for the Queen's daughter though, the art of writing with a quill, the nuances of religions and states, the functions of manus stones in society. Every step behind her mother was one she tried to learn from.

"Is my bath ready, Paracur Loana?" Terrava asked.

Maxima had not yet gotten used to the word. It meant bedmaker in the tongue of an ancient family of Anondorn. They served the royal house for eras. Loana was the matriarch and therefore personal attendant of Terrava.

The maidservant bowed her head. "Yes, my lady."

They passed through a white marble tunnel with a bird wing arch. The cream-colored stone transitioned to a cerulean blue floor, veined with sandy gold. Maxima was awed at the luxurious bath. Her own bath chamber was more extravagant than anything she had experience on Earth, but this was fit for a queen. Fountains with running horses adorned the corner of each room. They spit fresh water streams into the pool, but the crashing sound of water was not from the horses. A miniature waterfall fell gently from the ceiling at the other end of the room. Its stream caught on shelves of the vibrant blue rock that made up the floor.

A pleased smile observed Maxima's wonder. Terrava explained to her daughter, "All of the castle is birds and white stone— Bellator and Anite through to the bone. This room was Talus' gift to me. It is a piece of home. I was Terrava Caerule of Caracta once. I came from waterfalls before I was taken under Bellator wings.

CHAPTER FIFTEEN

This floor is made from the shores of Caracta's sacred waterfall caverns."

"It's so beautiful. This room feels…familiar."

An amused hum left Terrava's lips as she lit a myriad of manus stones. They twinkled a low light between hundreds of candles that shimmered off the pool. "You have Caerule blood in you. We're a loyal and fiercely stubborn bunch. This," she pointed above her to a painting of a handsomely regal man, "is my lord father, Iberius, in his younger days."

The scent of rosemary oils filled the air with sweetness.

"Mother, thank you for showing me this special place."

"Tonight is a special night. I have much to tell you. More to ask of you. Something to give." Terrava opened a small jewelry cabinet etched with feathers, the only sign of Anondorn in the whole room, and withdrew a small object. "This room is mine alone. Not a soul enters it except Paracur Loana to light the candles. Even your father has never entered here after it was built. The walls are soundproof. It is my room for *secrets*," she whispered the last word so that it was almost hidden under the sound of bubbling water.

"Secrets?"

"My secrets shall become yours. The frost of the Winter Aisle has left, and I will lose you again for a time." Terrava clutched her hand to her chest with a thin loop of silver chain hanging from her fingers. She turned away and then proceeded to slide her dress off.

Maxima wished at that moment that she would age like her mother. The woman had skin like someone in the peak of youth and a figure like a hardened warrior smoothed by feminine graces. It was not for modesty that her mother had turned away. As the silks fell below her waist, she revealed a tattoo all the way down the small of her back that started at her mid-spine. The black ink formed a tree whose branches held a flame, and it sprung from the base of her spine.

Terrava descended the steps into the bath, dragging her fingers over the surface. "Once I was Terrava Caerule—a rebellious child. I got into more mischief than was good for me. Mostly because my dear mother didn't want me to." She laughed. "Join me. The water is quite warm. I think we should start with the gift."

Maxima joined her mother with careful movements that matched the feeling the room impressed on her but with a slightly embarrassed demeanor at her nakedness. She clutched her bicep with one hand as she joined her mother in the water.

"No need to be timid. If you had grown up here, you would have shared secrets about boys and gossip about kings in bath chambers with your friends. Besides, this is the only room where we can speak so freely."

The words relaxed Maxima enough.

The steam from the bath rose and mixed with the waterfall as they waded in further. Terrava held up her clutched hand. When she opened it, a pendant fell just above the water level and swung. It was a silver elsu, but its wings were distinct. A single feather on each wing was made of sapphire stone, so brilliant that the shards appeared to suck in all the room's light and refract it infinitely inside.

"What is that, Mother?"

"This was given to me by Rebus Bellator, your uncle." There was a pause while Terrava closed her eyes. It was a moment full of melancholy longing. "The wings contain the two finest grade shards of anima stone in the entire kingdom. They could hold the Soul Energy of an individual for a lifetime, and a trained member

CHAPTER FIFTEEN

of the Order could still recognize the identity of the soul at the end of his life."

With elegant movement, Terrava's hand flicked over the gemstones. A flame of Soul Energy drew out of it and followed her fingers away until it drifted up with the steam. She breathed in heavily and brought her eyebrows together. "That was mine. I sealed it there more than twenty-five years ago. I want you to replace it with your Soul Energy."

Maxima hesitated. There was a deep significance to the action that she didn't comprehend.

"Please."

She obeyed her mother. The anima shard sparkled as if an entire cosmos were inside it.

"Thank you, Maxima. I know how badly you wanted to become an anatus of the Order of Soul Wielders. I've noticed how many times you've asked to return to Fanum Ortus, but it is not safe. Scavok Alter has had his best men in the area and will not clear it as a safe place. I can't have you in such danger again."

"I understand. The Mitad is looking for a chance to get to me."

Terrava sighed. "Why they came for you specifically, we can't say. Your victory against the Mitad soldier at Fanum Ortus is one of the things I am most proud of. I will have Scavok take me to the Turrim Cartus, and I will place you in the Record of the Order."

The blue light glimmered off Maxima's eyes, and she exclaimed, "Oh! That would be the best gift, Mother."

The Queen was pleased by the reaction.

Maxima thought aloud, "Will you also put Eos' Soul Energy in the other shard?"

INCOMPLETE PAGES

Terrava shook her head. "That is a decision for Talus to make, and he feels it should wait until after they understand the curse mark that is on him. Talus decides for Eos. I decide for you. Besides, the shard is already holding someone else's Soul Energy."

A nod signaled that Maxima understood. "Is that why you looked so sad? Is it Rebus?"

The comment cracked a smile on Terrava's somber face. "Too perceptive. Aizo said you were clever. Yes, Rebus and I put our Soul Energy into this pendant."

"Then you two…"

"We were to be married. We were young, idealistic, and reckless. The way of a woman in this world is difficult, my daughter. We were mixed up in an organization that led us places we couldn't fathom."

Astutely, Maxima said, "The back tattoo."

An amused hum was the only response Terrava could muster at her daughter's wise observations. "Yes. The back tattoo. We thought we were some sort of archeologists seeking a legend and knowledge of the lost era. He was killed for it before our wedding. Being a good man and better than I deserve, your father knew that I would struggle to marry off a second time. He took me as his bride in memory of his brother and made me swear off my past associations."

There was a saddened curl on Maxima's lips.

"Make no mistake," Terrava's voice shook. "I love your father more than anyone in this world. I would die for him. Rebus was a daydream many years ago in my youth. A book that had its pages torn out before it could be written."

Maxima nodded.

CHAPTER FIFTEEN

The two women made their way to the waterfall. They had an unspoken understanding and began to wash before the tiers of blue-gold shelves.

Terrava broke the silence much later, "There is another reason we're here. I have a task for you since you insist on venturing into the Monte kingdom. The same night that Rebus was killed, one of my best friends in this world barely got away. Her name was Grace Lapithos. I saw her again a few times, but then…she went missing. I swore off the way of the Priori for Talus. However, old ways are hard to kill. My past has come to tell me that I couldn't stay out of that life entirely. I would never ask you to lie to your father, but unless he asks, do not disclose what you seek in the Monte kingdom on my behalf. Can you do that?"

It took a moment of careful contemplation before Maxima agreed. "Yes. I'll do whatever you ask."

"Thank you. It has recently come to my knowledge that she has a son who lives and unknowingly carries information about her location. His name is Caldus Lapithos. This is what you are to do…"

CHAPTER SIXTEEN

DEPTH OF BOND

The pink mist of morning light swimming through fog colored Ramath's face and highlighted the sunken bags under his eyes. The chief engineer for the Aritrea Mining Company, Palino, watched with caution. The King hadn't slept through the night, nor had he allowed Palino. However, from the gauntness that tugged at Ramath's cheeks, he likely hadn't eaten or rested in days.

His thoughts were scattered between multiple stressors. Mines and his son weighed on him.

Why hasn't Durath returned home?

The answer was known in his mind, but he dared not entertain it.

Ramath paced over a miniature representing the tunnel support structure, his coffee-brown hair falling over his face. "Say

CHAPTER SIXTEEN

that I wanted to collapse this mine—the biggest tunnel ever attempted—how could I do it in the simplest way?"

They had been over the theory of mechanical tunnel support for hours. Palino grew weary of the exercise as he answered, "My King, we have discussed this in every intricacy. One would need to know the inner workings of *my mind* and be inside the company's blueprints to make such an attack. The mine is guarded. It would take a feat of mental and military genius to pull off something like that."

Stroking his disheveled beard, Ramath sighed. He put his fingers to his temples and massaged them. His voice was taut with anxiety as he explained, "I have enemies too numerous to count. Their resources and wit are beyond your understanding. I don't want you to tell me how challenging it would be. *How would it be done?*"

Palino gulped as the Lion of Corleo towered over him. The man's raw aggression was palpable.

"It could be done, sire. Were this enemy to possess the knowledge required, they could strike the critical support structures. With a mine this large, no single blow would take it down. However, there are points of accumulated stress. Key weight-bearing members." He unrolled one of the many scrolls that littered the planning table. This one contained the whole of the north Sepeleo mountain range. With a red-dipped quill, he marked various locations along the mine plan with an *x*. "There are roughly ten points throughout that would cause a critical collapse and blockage. If any three of these were destroyed simultaneously, it would trigger a cascading collapse that would bring the whole place down. No doubt, the initiator of such an attack would also die in the mines."

DEPTH OF BOND

"No doubt," the King whispered to himself as he tapped his scepter. "Any fool willing to try it would have to be a zealot ready to die."

The massive presence of Ramath Leorix was suddenly diminished as footsteps approached. The towering pale figure of the Overseer entered and chided with his slow drawl, "Ramath, you're still at this madness?"

Ramath ignored the Overseer. "Show me all ten locations, especially the ones closest to the Anite side. And how would one identify these weak points? I plan to reinforce them with guards."

The engineer retraced the tunnel path in red. His stroke followed a jagged twist through the Sepeleo mountains, from the Mircite valley to the foot of Anite's West Avem. "These last three," he circled the locations, "will be particularly vulnerable should Talus realize our venture. They will have the least amount of time to be reinforced and are under considerably more load than the rest of the tunnel. It is a risk, but the alternative paths would require miles of deviation and an additional month of work."

The Overseer swayed to the table in his long dark cloak. His lips pulled tight over the bleached stone teeth as he said, "An additional month is unacceptable. There is no cause for concern. My...*crawlers*...as you refer to them, will be abundant in the tunnels—"

"No," Ramath growled. "Crawlers at the entrance only. Nothing past the first primary support beam here." He put his thick finger down on the red *x* in Mircite. "The explosion those things cause would bring the whole din-carruck place down. When I need mindless violence, you will be alerted. This is a matter of delicacy."

CHAPTER SIXTEEN

Sharp seething came from under the helmet. "Why has your interest in the plan increased, Ramath? You were reluctant to topple your old friend initially."

There was a charged moment where the two only stared each other down. Palino backed away. If either of these two powder kegs went off, he wanted to be out of the room.

"*Old friend?*" Ramath let out a dry laugh. "My reluctance is to let your kind into my kingdom. I make no effort to hide that I don't like the Mitad mucking about my castle. I was just six years old when I was plucked from my family like a pretty stone from a mine. The Bellators held me hostage against my father for fifteen years. *Fifteen years!*" he screamed the last words with a voice cracking from emotion. "Talus is one of the wisest men in all of Corland and misses no detail of what goes on within his borders and nearby them. His master assassin, Scavok Alter, has men combing every inch of the boundary because the Mitad can't make a stealthy move if their cause depended on it. Not to mention, the Red Corcinths went trouncing through the mine—where your little monsters were—and it took Yann Kilsig to actually accomplish anything!"

He turned to model on the table, walking to the Anite side. "So, forgive me if I am worried that our plan is vulnerable." He flicked the outermost wooden leg of the tiny miniature with bearish force. The entire assembly of wooden pieces came crashing down.

Ramath left the two men in shock as he stormed out of the room. His mind remembered what the girl had told him—those cursed words spoken by Jezca Monte. The notion bothered him so much that he let the thought of his bedside drawer wash the wretched words away. A mind-numbing morning awaited him in his bed-chamber, and perhaps, he might be able to close his eyes without the snake around his throat squeezing that last simple pleasure from him. It wouldn't be enough this time. The mental anguish couldn't completely be numbed. Durath Leorix, King's Son, hadn't been seen in the kingdom for weeks.

The Mitad have taken my son.

∞   ∞   ∞

The private study chamber was decorated by porcelain elsu that perched along the walls with watchful white eyes. Eos was reviewing a book on the culture of the Winter Aisle and a map that detailed their path. They would skirt around Pacem Derex on the west side, through the edge of the mountains. Then they would cut through a trade route that would be unused until spring thawed the path thoroughly. From there, Dreibo would guide them across the Aisle to Petramon.

Talus stood at the far end of the study, examining one of the Mellizo Glyphs under the colorful tint of a stained-glass window. "How I wondered if I would ever see one of these again."

"We didn't bring them back easily. The Mitad desperately wanted them."

"Yes. Free travel between worlds isn't their goal anymore, now that they have this Bellia woman. The amplification of power, though…in the hands of an Emir or Saida. That would be a dangerous thing."

"We have them in our control."

"For today. We must always be vigilant as the Mitad move closer."

CHAPTER SIXTEEN

Returning to his book, Eos nodded with a murmur. Lost in his own thoughts of the journey ahead, Eos asked, "What are the Montes like, Father?"

Talus gave a dry grumble. "They will be kind enough at first. Greedy actors lead the Monte family. They will be formal as long as they see an advantage to it. My father saved them from barbarians, the same that I saved Anite from. But they dislike our god and our values. They hold the stones above all else. They spread the stones hoping that they spread piousness, and we accept them for their utility. They are a technology to us. To many of the Monte Kingdom, they are an expression of worship. Anite buys their goods and offers protection from future threats through alliance." Thinking to himself, he tugged on his braided beard. "I fear that new power dynamics may strain loyalty in the region. Surely, they have not given way to the Mitad, but they may have infiltrators, and some will play both sides for profit. We will trust no one."

It was curious. Eos wondered, "Doesn't Plumos guarantee some degree of loyalty?"

"These days, my nephew's marriage into the Monte family prevents outright betrayal, but nothing more." Talus chided himself at the prospect of their encounters. "Their priests will like us even less. Yet, we must call upon the priestess, Jezca."

"To examine my curse?"

His father nodded with a sigh. "She has *the sight*, as they say in the Winter Aisle. The priests have played visionaries for their entire existence, but even the head priests revere her abilities. We must at least try to consult her."

"Part of me hopes the powers aren't real."

DEPTH OF BOND

"You're right to fear your curse. However, hiding from it will only add to the suffering." The stained glass darkened his auburn hair and made a light mosaic on his face as he turned the glyph over in his palms nostalgically.

"Father, do you believe Ramath is still loyal?"

Remember the first time we collected emerald moss from the Sacrum Crypt. The words of Ramath's letter couldn't be from anyone else, and they couldn't be insincere. "I know he is still loyal inside. What I can't say is if the Mitad has seized his power completely." He thought back to simpler times. Times when they were just boys coming of age. Aizo, Ramath, and he were brothers—closer than he had been with Rebus. Their worries were only a humorous joke from today's perspective, and their optimism seemed eternal.

Talus laughed as he remembered their first trip to the emerald pools. It was Aizo who had discovered the Sacrum Crypt. He had led them to it and the emerald pools in the days of their youth…

"This is why Aizo can't attract women," young Talus teased in a pubescent tone. "He lacks your looks, Ramath. He doesn't have my charm. And he would rather spend his time wandering in the mountains when Ellena couldn't have been any clearer that she wanted you to take her to the summer festival."

Aizo jabbed Talus in the ribs playfully. "Glowing ponds! Ruins that look to be from the Lost Eras. If I were as distracted as you, none of us would know about this place."

Talus shoved his friend.

Ramath rubbed his brow, exhausted of their rowdy antics.

"I'm not so preoccupied that I'm exploring ruins when I promised to see Ellena," the Bellator heir laughed.

CHAPTER SIXTEEN

That was enough to set off Aizo. He hadn't needed an excuse. The two boys wrestled as a second language. Aizo swept up Talus' left leg and took him to the ground.

"Hey, hey, hey! We're trying to get to these glowing ponds, aren't we?" Ramath reminded them, but it was too late. They were already rolling around and throwing punches. He continued walking towards their destination, hoping his friends would not want to be left behind. However, after he reached a ridge that was difficult to traverse, he looked back to see Aizo in a headlock.

There was a flash of orange Soul Energy.

"Not fair! There's no wielding in wrestling."

Red light filled Ramath's peripheral vision as he tried not to give the two any additional attention.

The sound of clashing Soul Energy echoed off the mountain walls.

Orange. Red. Flares of both colors jumped against the stone.

"Let's declare a truce. No more wielding, and we finish when one of us taps," Talus said.

"You'd like that because you'd lose if we keep this up."

Ramath interjected, "Stop! You need to see this."

"No, I'm trying to give you a fighting chance, Aizo."

"*Children*—Look!" Ramath demeaned them to get their attention.

"Ramath, we are trying to settle…oh." Aizo's untamed hair whipped in the sweet summer air as he stared with a slack-jaw. "That's a…a…"

Talus finished for him in a hushed voice, "Corcinth. Though, I've never seen one in person."

A blue-gray mane and ferocious horns loomed over them from atop the nearest ridge. The golden eyes of the spirit-like beast gleamed at them disapprovingly. The tail swung against the ground as if threatening them.

Ramath whispered through closed teeth, "See what you've done? We couldn't just get to these pools in peace. No. Never quiet with you two."

Aizo and Talus locked eyes, thinking the same thought, and they grinned devilishly.

Talus goaded, "I bet you I can catch it first."

"No—" Ramath begged, knowing the rumored danger of such a mythical creature.

Aizo disagreed, "I'll be riding it before you get that close."

The two were off in a sprint of Soul Step. Talus shoved Aizo mid-stride and sent him tumbling. The sturdy young teen rolled back up without missing a step, and they were scaling up the ridge without hesitation. The corcinth was gone from view, but Ramath knew it was better if they didn't catch it. He also knew he needed to keep up in case the two got close enough to provoke the creature. His Soul Step was better than anyone his age, and he was not far behind them when they went over the top of the crest of rock.

The corcinth's tail flicked around a corner, and they followed recklessly laughing and taunting each other along the way. Talus ducked a push from Aizo, but all three came to a stop as they reached ruins that were unlike any architecture they had ever seen. Mostly-sunken bridges and buildings peaked from moss overgrowth. The towers that leaned from the ground and water were domed sand-colored stone. Pillars and rounded roofs filled their vision. Every window was shaped like a key hole, and entrances were rounded. Balconies protruded from cylindrical structures with small buildings floating at the end of each.

CHAPTER SIXTEEN

"I told you." Aizo laughed and snorted proudly. "Sacrum Crypt. Definitely from the Lost Eras."

Ramath had to give credit where it was due. "You really did find one. This is something special. Neither my forefathers nor yours have written about this place as anything more than a myth."

"Well, boys," Aizo said in a high-pitched voice as he got excited, "You can thank me now."

Rooooooaaaaar!

The corcinth shook the sunken city gate and jutting watch towers. The mountains trembled before the mighty sound, and the three boys shivered. The fear tingled their limbs, but Talus was never one to let his friends think he was scared.

"By the look on your faces, it looks like I'll be the first of us to touch the corcinth." Talus bolted toward the crooked city gate.

Ramath had a feeling this would not end well. He chased after his brothers-in-bond: up slanting bridges, around circular buildings, and through fourth-story windows that sat at ground level now. There was no slowing the momentum of competition between them. Even Ramath was eager to see the corcinth again, but it seemed they were chasing after a ghost. It alluded their pursuit through the ruins with little more than a momentary threatening glance to be caught as it looked over its massive shoulders at them in an alleyway.

Finally, the three turned a corner and found a massive spiral staircase that turned around a building covered in brown-red moss that looked like furry rust. The corcinth huffed through flared nostrils that were nearly the size of the boys' heads.

"I think this is as close as we get," Ramath concluded.

The corcinth pawed at the ground and showed its teeth.

DEPTH OF BOND

Talus said lowly, "Nonsense. That is a clear indication from a corcinth that he is ready to be ridden." Even he didn't sound like he believed his verbal swaggering.

Aizo gulped. "That may be an indication that we're about to die."

The horns of the majestic blue lion glowed a pure white like stars did in the fabric of night.

Ramath led the retreat back behind the nearest wall, followed by Aizo, but Talus didn't follow.

Soul Energy formed between the corcinth's horns. A sphere manifested that looked like oil on the surface of water, rainbowed in sheen over the pure white. Then, a blast shot out from the spot between the horns.

The Corleo brother turned and grabbed Talus by the fur of his cloak, yanking him behind cover. The action was not a second too late.

A beam of energy tore through the sunken city and eviscerated the wall behind where Talus was standing. Pale faces sunk behind the shelter.

The boys sprinted from the city on adrenaline and instinct.

The boasting of adolescence soon returned when they were outside the boundary Sacrum Crypt. They lay panting on the rock floor. Talus declared victory. "Since no one was able to ride him...I won by being the closest," he said between heaves for breath.

Ramath was aghast. "If I hadn't saved you—"

"My Solido would have protected me. There was nothing to worry about."

"Protected you? From a Crypt Keeper? That would have torn through you. There would have been more hole than body left behind!"

CHAPTER SIXTEEN

They all laughed tensely from the near-death experience.

Aizo got to his feet first. "That was the best thing we've done yet."

"You mean most foolish."

"Is there any difference, Ramath? Now, we came for glowing lakes, not chasing corcinths. Let's go," Aizo declared.

Ramath gritted his teeth in frustration that his prior attempts to direct the party toward their destination were ignored in favor of a deadly chase, but he ended up smirking. He loved these two fools for all their reckless adventure. An hour later, they were approaching emerald pools.

"If East Avem has another riot," Talus said, "we will put it down *before* Rebus gets word. Father can't think that my older brother has to bail us out of tricky situations."

Aizo shrugged. "We were losing a bit of control on the situation."

"But next time?" Talus implored.

"Yes. Next time we will have it wrapped up before Rebus gets there to save the day."

The three stopped to peer into the glowing abyss. Green light shone from the lake like stars through liquid glass. It was a sight to behold even for the King's Son.

"After I found it, I discovered the source is a kind of seaweed. It grows on an underwater city. I can't dive deep enough to get to it, but I figured you two could swim better than me to get a good look. The Sanofem examined the small amount I could gather. They believe it has healing properties and even increases Soul Energy circulation. They called it *viri-arbo*. It's some rare plant that is lore in the oldest manuscripts of the royal archives. There hasn't been any seen or used in one thousand years." Aizo saw a blur of motion as he finished.

Talus was sprinting toward the water while ripping his shirt and tunic off mid-stride. He leaped into the air, leaving his clothes in a trail behind him, and splashed into the lake.

Ramath sighed.

The water's refracting light and incredible depth made it difficult to see well, but Talus kicked, making his way deeper. After plunging more than twenty feet, he saw the first patch of glowing reeds. The semi-translucent plant wavered in the water and created a gradient from emerald to dark blue. Talus looked past it—deeper. He saw what Aizo had spoken of. Another fifty feet below was a vast temple-looking structure, collapsed almost entirely onto its side so that it veered over a massive trench. The bell-shaped building had an upside-down keyhole entrance large enough to fit caravans through. Despite his lungs beginning to burn, he went deeper, swimming until he nearly reached the fallen sanctuary. He could see sun iconography carved around it and pillars that must have decorated a courtyard. Now, they were stacks of rubble sliding off into the darkness of the lake floor. His lungs could take no more, and he kicked violently back to the surface, grabbing two handfuls of the viri-arbo on his way up.

When he broke the surface, Ramath was leaping over his head. "I'll be back with twice that much," he hollered as he entered the water.

After hours of exploration, they had sizeable stacks of the viri-arbo drying on the shore.

Azio grinned at the other two. His teeth glowed like green-tinted lighting stones as he chewed on their harvest.

"You're eating a king's fortune, Aizo," Ramath warned.

CHAPTER SIXTEEN

It did no good. Talus was giggling with a glow from his mouth too.

Ramath shrugged and joined them, contorting his face into a hideous mockery. With mouths of bioluminescent light, the three brothers were making faces and laughing so hard their sides ached.

"Shall we pack our treasure and head back?" Aizo asked later.

Talus thought for a moment before saying, "I want to get one more look at the city down there. Then we can return home."

Ramath nodded, half asleep under the sun.

This time, Talus made it to the foot of the main temple. At the rock shelf, he could see the icons telling pictorial lore of a lost people. *How old was this civilization? It defied anything in the history books.* He swam on, despite feeling his oxygen limit approaching, and placed a hand on a moss-covered column. The thing was cracked and broken by time and water…and something else. The sinking didn't look…natural. He couldn't place why.

The mass of stone shifted and then broke! Rocks slid over his arm, trapping it before he could pull his limb back.

Talus pulled frantically. No progress.

He placed his feet against the pile and struggled.

Bubbles escaped his mouth. Lungs burned.

He contemplated using Soul Energy, but he might blow up his arm. Only as a final resort.

Vision blurred.

On shore, Aizo nudged Ramath awake. "Talus has been down there too long. Can either of you hold your breath that long?"

Ramath sat up. "Maybe about this long. Not much more. It has been a while."

They both looked into the water, but Talus was too deep to find with their eyes.

DEPTH OF BOND

Crimson flashed below. So deep, only faint distortions made it to the surface. Bubbles of air gurgled from the Soul Energy source. The boys locked panicked eyes. Ramath went headfirst into the water without thinking. Soul Energy poured from his feet—propelling him like a missile toward the traces of red that broke through emerald.

Ramath scanned the lake frantically. Nothing. Nothing. There!

He spotted Talus sending flares toward the surface and adapted his path. His feet kicked in a modified form of Soul Step. It was just quick enough. He reached his adoptive brother as the last spurts of air left his mouth.

Ramath yanked on the rocks around Talus' arms. The one attribute he always had over Talus was brute strength. It was his Leorix genetics to be a hulking mass of muscle. He fought with the collapsed pile. It was everything he could do to budge one rock—but it gave way. As the stones shifted, he managed to pull Talus' arm free. He threw it over his shoulder and shot towards the surface!

Talus was unconscious when they met air. He lay still on the shore as Aizo heaved against his chest with both arms.

Water spurted from his lips. Coughing broke the deathly stillness.

Ramath had been just in time. He fell back with an exhausted sigh.

After heaving out all the lake water, Talus looked silently at Ramath with grateful eyes. Words formed on his lips, but he didn't know what to say yet.

Turning, Ramath exposed his back to Talus and showed him the same branding that Aizo had: the Bellator crest on his back. He

CHAPTER SIXTEEN

had asked for the mark and was duty-bound to his brother. Talus nodded.

The brothers gathered their haul of viri-arbo, knowing the bond between them had become even more unbreakable.

The memory pained Talus. He rubbed his temples to focus on the present day. Nostalgic daydreams seemed to haunt him more and more.

"Father…" Eos prodded hesitantly.

"Yes?"

"Do you think…I mean…Would it be okay if…Can I carry the Mellizo Glyph on our journey?"

Talus' eyes crinkled proudly. "You brought it back home. It is your right. Make sure it is never seen. *Keep it secret. It must not fall into the wrong hands.*" He let the artifact and its chain sift from his hand into Eos' palms.

The door of the study room swung open.

Aizo hobbled in and pretended to examine something on the wall with his hands in his pockets. He mumbled to himself loudly, "Those Sanofem. So strict. They do wonders, but no fun with them. No no. Talus, I brought something important. It requires your immediate attention."

"What is it? Whatever you need—" Talus was interrupted by the sight of Aizo's face when he turned toward them.

Emerald glow beamed from Aizo's teeth as he chuckled deeply. From his pockets as he produced dried viri-arbo. "Sneaking this past the Sanofem was not easy. Let me tell you."

Soon, all three of them had green-lit mouths.

The moment was one Eos would always remember with his father and his first teacher. As he nearly choked on the bitterness

DEPTH OF BOND

of the plant and the absurdity of his father's face, he tucked the Mellizo glyph into his shirt.

He would show his father that he could be trusted with such responsibility, and remembered the words.

Keep it secret. It must not fall into the wrong hands.

CHAPTER SEVENTEEN

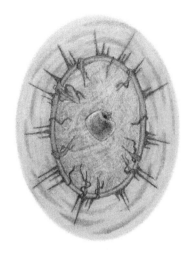

WHISPER'S MOTIVE

Tavro rushed through the mountain halls of Petramurus, the Monte castle stronghold. He moved in the secrecy of the narrow corridor called the *king's whisper*. It was a private passage to King Pallogos' royal advisory chamber that only he and Bohm had keys to access. When he entered under the green and gold banner of pious hands holding a stone above crossed swords, he found the old King ordering a haul of silver into the royal vaults. The voice quivered with age as King Constantine Pallogos directed his servants. Then he stopped.

"If my old ears don't deceive, I believe that is the sound of my whisper coming into the room. Out. All of you." King Pallogos commanded.

As soon as he crossed before the throne, Tavro fell to a knee. "My lord, the news has reached me that you intend to cast Caldus into an adere pit. This is not what Bohm and I have advised. I must beg you to reconsider the impacts of such an action," Tavro fretted. The plan left a burning feeling in his stomach—both for Jezaca's loss and Caldus' misfortune. The adere pits were remnants of the ancient manus practice—deep holes where rejected manus stones were discarded. Now, they were deep holes where the worst prisoners would never see daylight again.

"The king hears his whispers, but at times he must act on his own. There are considerations that you do not understand."

"Please, my lord, enlighten my lack of knowledge. It appears to me that this will enrage the future high priestess."

King Pallogos raised a shaky withered finger. "Only if she ever finds out. Thus, he shall disappear into the place where the gods reject their creations. You see, High Priest Laud has visited me. He would like that the Caldus problem ceases to exist. I already expunged the record of his time in prison. The priesthood paid well to make it so."

The intricate web of power dynamics that the royal family and clergy wove was something that the Tavro held no sway in. He knew immediately that his counsel would fall on ears deafened by politics and money.

"Then it shall be," Tavro concluded. He rose from his bow, and the King's Whisper left the chamber. After he locked the door behind him, he broke into a sprint. *There wasn't much time.*

Layers of damp, cold stone below Petramurus, Caldus lay handcuffed in a prison cell. He had been still for hours, staring into the corners where the dim light couldn't reach. Alia's face hung in the shadows like a mirage from the other side. "We were going to go to Terspar…together," he mumbled and chewed his lip angrily.

CHAPTER SEVENTEEN

He had cried. No one was there to see. He had no pride to protect at the moment.

His life since the Necogen escape had been one of few comforts and fewer hopes.

Now his favorite one was gone.

Erased. By a Mitad mirza. *Yann Kilsig.*

Scabs on his ankles bit painfully from miles of walking with the sheathes of Amon's daggers cutting into him. He was grateful that they kept him awake. Otherwise, he would have been asleep when his cell door opened. The way he saw it, he should have been in the cell days longer as the bureaucrats decided what to do with him. They couldn't let him go free because he had led numerous raids that were a nuisance to the kingdom. They wouldn't kill him for fear of ruining their future alliance with the clergy of the Manus Priesthood. It was limbo. As long as both sides knew he was captured…unless…

Two smooth gray suits of armor stood at the door. Their crested helms looked down on him. The monte armor was simple and geometric. Like pressed stone adorning the men.

"Up," ne commanded.

Caldus remained still, staring at where he had last imagined Alia's soft brown eyes before the voice had caused the vision to evaporate.

"Up!"

His non-compliance was met with a boot in his ribs. That jolted him into standing.

"Where are you taking me?" Caldus asked as they led him led down the prison block.

Silence.

WHISPER'S MOTIVE

He responded by halting his march. The guards lifted him by the arms enough to drag him along.

"It's much too early to be moving me. Execution or release?" Caldus asked teasingly. He saw they passed the stairs that led up to the castle. *What did that mean? If he wasn't going back up, then where?* He began to feel panic but reassured himself. Calm. The opening scabs on his ankles reminded him that he had options. "I can't imagine they pay you enough to be *this* silent. The least you could do is tell a man what fate awaits him."

The less disciplined of the two guards replied. "Not another word out of you."

Caldus frowned and said dramatically, "Execution then? I was really hoping it wouldn't come to that."

The lack of reaction told him otherwise. "Oh, I'm a free man then?" He knew that couldn't be the case. His attention locked onto a descending stairwell at the far end of the room. This sentence was something else.

"Free?" The guard laughed. "You won't be seeing light again where we're taking you."

Those words combined with a gleam and splash of red against the monochrome room made Caldus decide. The guard station ahead had a key ring and his Red Corcinth mask. Regardless of what happened, between the daggers in his boot and what lay on the desk—it was everything he needed.

With a quick jerk, he freed his arms enough for the guards to drop him.

Rolling purposefully, he brought his cuffed hands to his boot and freed one dagger from its sheathe.

As he sprang to his feet, he faced his captors with the manus blade ready.

CHAPTER SEVENTEEN

A double grip on one dagger wasn't ideal, but it was the only option until he unlocked his hands.

They were unprepared for resistance.

Caldus channeled his Soul Energy into the animus blade.

Spin.

Red light.

Metal clash.

The first guard watched his partner's hardened armor get sliced through the chest like it was soft cheese. There must have been a gaping wound beneath the glowing metal slit. He drew his short sword in time to distance the prisoner from himself.

Dancing from foot to foot anxiously, Caldus approached.

The guard swung on him.

His weight shifted to evade the attack, but they backed him into the guard station table. *The space was too cramped with his hands tied.* Another slash came across his body.

Caldus ducked it and rolled, coming out of it to his feet on the other side of the guard's swing. He capitalized on the exposed position.

Amon's dagger ripped up the ribcage of the armor and tore through the armpit.

When he pulled the glowing blade out, his foe was already falling to the floor. He tried once, then twice to rise, but the pooling blood in his armor was already spreading on the floor.

He hadn't lost his edge. That was fortunate. It had been a few months since he had been in a real fight. Though, he credited Amon's daggers with the victory. The relic weapons were his blessing. He was opposite his sister in many ways—and none more so than wielding. His Soul Energy had never left his body. Years of attempts, even tutelage under a few knowledgeable craftsmen-wielders, had not helped.

But the daggers. The precious animus stone blades were the perfect solution for his problem. They were an extension of his body that could focus his potent energy into an attack.

Caldus thanked whatever higher force had urged him to steal them from Necogen the night he and his sister had escaped. He juggled the keyring quickly until he tested the one that released his hands. Then, he slipped on his red mask and drew his second blade. It would be a bloody sprint through the castle until he found a way out.

Up the spiral staircase he went, seeking free air with every muscle twitch. *Alia was dead. Gone. Curse Yann Kilsig. The saber wielding-man in the black hat would pay. He must get back to Philo as quickly as he could. Tomorrow morning was the latest he could tolerate returning to the Mircite valley.*

A tough featured man with dark eyes and a thick, neatly kept beard walked towards him when Caldus reached the top of the staircase. He was nobility; that much was clear from his fine cloak and the royal signet on his right hand.

Agile hands flipped Amon's daggers into a reverse grip as Caldus lunged toward the unarmed man. There was only freedom on his mind. He had to get out.

"Woah! Woaaah!" The man tried to calm his aggressor like a wild horse as a dagger nearly caught his arm. The ceramic red face of a corinth stared fiercely into his eyes. "I'm here on Jezca's behalf. My name is Tavro." He bleated quickly, hoping to spare his life.

Huffing, Caldus glared from the recesses of his mask.

CHAPTER SEVENTEEN

"I was on my way down to your cell to try and get there before the guards. Clearly, you didn't need my help."

After a few wild breaths, Caldus said, "Why would my sister send you?"

"Well, she doesn't know you're captured yet—but she tries to keep tabs on you often. She worries about you."

"Hmmph."

"She does."

"Tell my sister that if she wants to really help people, there are sick and poor and dying in Mircite. Mining is killing them. Her *precious stones* are killing them. She prays to the cause of their subjugation."

Tavro didn't know how to respond. He hadn't expected such a strained relationship.

Caldus continued, "If she wants to do good, meet me in Mircite at the entrance to Xaro's twelfth mine at sunrise. I'll wait there each morning. Then she can see the Mitad's operation—see with eyes unclouded."

"The Mitad? No…"

"They poison our water. Kill our people."

"Impossible. The King wouldn't allow that."

"A mirza turned me over to the royal guards."

Tavro was again without words for a while. Caldus turned to leave, but Tavro managed to speak his conviction, "King Pallogos would never work with *them*."

"No, but he doesn't work against them. He fears them, and that makes him compliant."

The conviction, pain, and seething rage in Caldus' voice made Tavro sure the words held some truth. The Mitad must be operating near the valley. King Pallogos must have willingly received the young man from their officers. "Even if she wanted to, the priesthood doesn't let Jezca leave the temple anymore."

"That wouldn't stop my sister."

Tavro smirked uncontrollably. Nothing could be truer. "Aye. You know your sister well. She'll meet you when I can get word to her. Besides, she has news for you."

"News of what?"

"Your mother."

Caldus froze. He hadn't felt that kind of hope that tingled his spine and shattered his concentration in years. Yet, he refused to be the victim of such fantasies.

"Right. Xaro's twelfth mine at sunrise. Now, how do I get out of this castle?"

∞   ∞   ∞

The soft pulse of light-stones cast shadows in Ares' quarters. Only half the stones were lit, and it created a dimness that shadowed his features. He listened to the croaking and chirping of insects outside between Bellia's heavy breaths.

Ares' spun an apple in one hand as he looked at the pile on his work table. Another dozen red pieces of fruit remained. "This time, try to make the portal open just the instant before it hits the wall. We need it to be unnoticeable to someone who didn't know to look for it."

Picking a random block of stone behind his bed, Ares threw the apple at it. He gave it some speed but held back a great deal. It had to be achievable. Speed would come. There was a pulse of violet energy against the wall. A ring of tendrils formed for a moment so quick, an untrained eye would miss with a blink. The

CHAPTER SEVENTEEN

fruit struck the wall just to the right of the portal. By the time it began to fall, the portal was gone, and the stone was dark again.

Bellia sighed, exasperated. "Why does it have to be so brief?"

"For my plan to work, we need to pull this off without a room full of people seeing, and it will have to be in the middle of a sequence of events."

"You make it sound like we're pulling off a heist."

Ares grunted. "Something like that."

"Can we at least find a way to slow the apple down?"

"No. It'll be coming much faster."

"What will?" Bellia grew tired of the hiddenness behind every word.

"When I have all the information and a plan, I will tell you every detail."

Bellia conceded in her gentle way with a slight nod of her pointed chin. Her elfish features smiled at Ares. She let him work his plans in silence, and he was grateful that she extended such trust. The practice continued.

Apples flew. Portals flashed.

Occasionally the apple disappeared through the wall. When this happened, Ares would give a pleased grunt, and they would go again.

She was gifted and picking up quickly. However, what he had in mind would be moving incredibly fast. The apple was only play in comparison, and if they failed... *death*.

The pile of apples dwindled over the course of an hour.

Ares picked up the last one and leaned back on the desk with nonchalant calmness. He was in his evening tunic, but she wore her Mitad cloak. In fact, she had not removed it in recent memory. His gaze lingered.

WHISPER'S MOTIVE

"Let's finish," Bellia said.

The last apple flew at the wall, but Ares threw it wildly on purpose.

Bellia leaned her body out, trying to adjust her portal mid-thought as she created it.

The way the cloak pulled against her body...like a mound hidden until the wind bent tall grass just so.

There was a dull thunk and then the apple fell to the bed.

"What is that?" Ares pointed at her.

Bellia shifted back knowingly. "What?"

"Your cloak there."

Silence.

Ares moved towards her carfully with his hand extended. He rested it on her belly. Just as he expected, there was a raised tightness to her abdomen. There was a sense of someone else in the room. The presence was faint, but he realized that his overly sensitive abilities had felt it since Bellia had entered the room.

A pale hand caressed his face. Amythest eyes looked deeply into his. There were words unspoken—and they were words of apology. Of excitement. Of new life. Of love. But lips only moved without speaking. "You..." Ares sputtered. "You're...with child?"

She nodded with a slight smile.

Stillness.

Shock.

He had plans still. His lifelong plottings were just beginning to bear results. He needed to loosen the grip Saida and Fulmen had on him, and he needed to acquire more power! Not...this. Not this. How could he shoulder such responsibility? Could he be what he had never had for himself?

CHAPTER SEVENTEEN

Ares faltered towards the bed and sat down with eyes that darted with processing thoughts. For the first time he could remember since he was a child—he felt fear!

Bellia joined beside him and put her reassuring hand on his leg. "It's like the story of the great elsu that you have on your back. Hasvela learned to guide the currents with her feathers. You said it was an opportunity for bravery and to evolve into something stronger."

The bruised and dented apple lay by his side. Ares picked it up and examined the smashed apple quietly. It was no longer perfect, but still, he took a bite.

CHAPTER EIGHTEEN

UNCROWNED

The silhouettes of her children and husband were all Terrava could see as they journeyed away from her. Azio put a consoling arm around her when he noticed her dismay. Her rigid shoulders relaxed a bit at the gesture. The ink-black morning was not the sky Aizo favored separating under, but he had given Eos as many lessons as he could over the past four months. The boy and his sister were as ready as they would ever be this year.

The journey would be covert. The risk was minimal. Still, the last hints of frozen air sucked away the sweet scent of Anite mornings, and Terrava worried.

The Queen shot Aizo a glance. He removed his arm at once. They were under the eyes of Xaro Monte, and such familiarity was uncustomary for the King's Regent. Terrava must lead her

CHAPTER EIGHTEEN

kingdom until her husband returned. She had done it before and was more than capable, but the sight of her children disappearing into the darkness left her unsettled, especially under the eyes of one of the ignoble lords.

Xaro Monte puffed his anima stone pipe. His smoky beard glistened in the blue light. "My lady, it is a tough thing to see, but there is no reason to fret when the Visrex of Wings and his master of assassins are guiding the secret travel party. There will be much to occupy your mind here at home."

Terrava made no eye contact with Xaro Monte. She did not like the man nor his presence in castle Alasedis. She glided by him and said, "I worry not for my husband. Talus could bring down all of Petramon before anything harmed my family."

It was necessary for the six shadowy profiles to depart before first light. Secrecy was the primary objective, and no one in Anite should know that Talus led Dreibo Nebris, Scavok Alter, Benedir Cassion, Eos, and Maxima out of the Anite border until they were already long since on their way. Only King Pallogos and select members of his court would know they were coming.

Talus strode forth with giant footsteps. Even the Anite court did not know that they had initiated their plan. Everyone who had witnessed the conclave was *anticipating* the departure, but Terrava would deliver the news that she was regent in Talus' place that afternoon.

They walked with heavy leather travel packs strapped to their back and secured around their chest and waist. Tents, food, and supplies were distributed amongst the six. They marched slowly through the blue-green grass and leafless trees of Anondorn. As they planned, the first interval of Soul Step began outside the city gates.

UNCROWNED

Soul Step was awkward and burdened by their travel gear. Eos had practiced with Aizo but now wished he had spent a few more hours on the technique while carrying weights. Dreibo glided effortlessly, Talus sailed ahead of the three youths, but Scavok showed a mastery of movement that ascended beyond any of them. He moved effortlessly with fluid bursts of Soul Energy sprouting like rails from his feet in a glacial-blue color. The speed with which he moved seemed to dance around all of the travelers.

This was the master of assassins. Hariban Scavok Alter.

The packs weighed on them, but Eos was determined to show minimal pain in front of Benedir, who was better conditioned to such exercise. When he thought he could take it no more, Talus saved his aching lungs, legs, and back.

"Scavok," Talus called ahead, "I believe we may need to pace ourselves. Our young companions are not seasoned to this kind of travel."

"Mmm. I'll scout ahead, then. I forgot myself, apologies."

Benedir wanted to be sure that Talus wouldn't count him among those needing a rest. "King Bellator, while it may be wise to rest *for some of us*," he glanced haughtily at Eos and Maxima, "I assure you that this young companion has been preparing for his trial to become an Errant. This was hardly a challenge."

Talus smiled kindly. "So it is, Benedir. We shall see if you keep that enthusiasm after an entire day of these intervals."

Maxima's jaw clenched at the thought of an entire day of this rigor. No, *days* of this.

"Our first major landmark will be Pacem Derex," Talus said.

Eos recalled Aizo's story of the revolt that occurred when he was an infant. "That's where it happened, right? The revolt?" Eos

CHAPTER EIGHTEEN

touched the scar under his eye subconsciously. "That's where Ares…"

The memory of Saida making the small cut on Eos' face flashed before Talus. The wretched night replayed in his mind. The smoke of battle. The physical and mental wounds.

"Your brother played his part, but he was young and manipulated. Saida twisted his mind in ways I cannot imagine. We lost so much that day."

The wind whistled to fill the lull in the conversation.

Eos knew one thing for sure. "He hasn't gotten any better."

Talus would have responded, but Benedir interrupted.

"Wait—You've met Ares Bellator? No. And you lived to talk about it?"

A chill went down Eos' spine. He knew he had made a mistake and let his emotions give away information that conflicted with the cover story they told in Anite. "I…er…there was…"

"Eos and Maxima had an encounter with Ares in the Burning Lands," Talus interjected. "The Mitad followed them even into the far north sands."

Maxima put the finishing touches on the fiction. "It isn't something we like to talk about."

Benedir nodded almost respectfully with all eyes fixed on him, but there was devious curiosity on his curled lips.

Talus finished his original statement, "Pacem Derex is now infested with encampments of every sort—Krog and Corland bandits, Mezclado gangs, and likely Mitad spies. We cannot dare be seen inside those gates. Even with our hoods over our faces, a party our size would be found out quickly. So, we will go around through a pass the Pacem Fingers that Dreibo has mapped out for us with King Pallogos."

Dreibo added, "It is a winding path that will slow us without the ability to Soul Step; however, it will preserve our secrecy until we reach the Monte kingdom."

They made camp at the beginnings of the fingers, where the Sepeleo mountains dwindled into the valley corridor. Their lightweight tents were tucked behind the first ridge of the blue-toned stone face. Talus planned in his tent with Scavok, detailing the seamless execution of what he had prepared in his mind but not yet shared aloud. Maxima walked with Dreibo, discussing something that Eos could not make out from his distance.

"Benedir, would you mind showing me a piece of the soul form you performed?" Eos asked as a friendly gesture.

"Yes, well, I suppose that I could give you a few pointers on the nuances of soul forms, but it is *surely nothing* compared to facing your brother, Ares." Benedir stroked his patchy blonde beard.

"Quite the opposite," Eos didn't take the bait to disclose anything further about Ares. "I've never seen a soul form besides yours. The idea is foreign to me."

Benedir glanced away and curled his nose up. "They're a basic form of practice here for those wishing to enter the Order. Let's start with the simplest: the soul arm-weave." He demonstrated a rope of energy twisting around his outreached right arm like a springing snake, compressing at his shoulder, winding back down his forearm, and resting in a turning circular band around his wrist. "Simple enough. Let's see what you've got, Bellator."

Eos didn't like the way he had addressed him by his family name, and he was certain this technique was more advanced in order to make him look foolish. When his crimson light appeared, the shape of the rope warbled and shook, barely stable. It wound up his arm inconsistently and shuttered awkwardly at his shoulder.

CHAPTER EIGHTEEN

The precise control that Benedir demonstrated was nothing short of extraordinary to Eos.

"Sloppy. Your technique needs work, but I suppose it was only your first time."

They practiced for the next hour. Benedir would correct his form and then move on to a new piece of soul form just before Eos could grasp the last—always looking amateur in his attempts.

As the orange sunset announced the day's end to the travelers, the array of reds fell on the chain at Eos' neck. Benedir noted the bulge under Eos' shirt.

"What's that you're wearing on your neck?"

Eos froze again. Just like his slip in mentioning Ares, this felt like a critical moment where he was about to disclose what his father had wanted secret. "Only a family token," he said.

"May I see it?"

Hesitation. Benedir made a note of the delayed response.

Eos' mind processed quickly. It was better to act less suspiciously.

To the Cassion son, it would only be a relic.

He pulled it out from under his tunic. The bone-like material carved with runes dangled against the sun, falling over the ridge.

"And what is it? It's very strange for a family relic."

Benedir was shrewd. It would be better to tell half-truths than complete lies, Eos decided.

"This is an old piece that my father gave me. It has…family meaning. There is a bit of anima stone inside that can amplify wielding for protection in an emergency." As he said it, Eos felt the silent *thrum* of vibrational energy from the Mellizo Glyph. It called to him in a language without words. The feeling of it at his chest was calming, but he could sense that Benedir felt nothing of the glyph's unique cry.

A slight raise of the eyebrows and a murmur was Benedir's response to the words: anima stone. "May I see it? A precious trinket to be carrying on this journey."

"Sorry, I'd rather you didn't."

"Just for a moment. I'd like to…feel what an anima reserve is like. I've heard of such—"

"I promised my father that I would not take it off."

Benedir squinted. "Have it your way. I wouldn't want to go against the King's will. Perhaps you should utilize that relic to do your soul form properly." He turned and went inside the tent.

The following day's slow traverse through the winding maze of the Pacem Derex bypass was monotonous. When they set up camp the next night, Eos' brain was blank. His mind only remembered the aching, so constant and enduring that it overwrote any conversations that may have been had that day. The six sat around the campfire, eating a tasteless oatmeal-like grain. Benedir ate quickly and purposefully.

"My lord," Benedir stood, "I would like your leave to go for a private walk. I'd like to clear my head before we sleep tonight."

Talus nodded with exhaustion in his movement. "Stay close. Many things in these mountains could threaten you."

"Yes, King Bellator."

Maxima sat, writing in one of her two thin leather-bound notebooks. She carefully and precisely moved her quill to waste no ink.

Eos gestured to the green notebook that was closed by her side. "Can I take a look?"

CHAPTER EIGHTEEN

A soft hum gave him permission. Eos thumbed through the pages.

"That's a record of wielding techniques that I have collected from the Alasedis library and my night in Fanum Ortus. Although, a few of them have some of my experimental ideas added," Maxima said.

Stopping on a page with multiple colors of ink, Eos read the black-ink title: *Blood Ascension*. The details of a dangerous technique involving the infusion of Soul Energy into the bloodstream to give one superhuman physical characteristics were laid out in the same color. However, a red-brown color scratched out entire sentences, added lines, and filled the margins. *Maxima...was...gifted*, Eos thought. *Perhaps genius*. Eos barely comprehended the nuances of wielding that were crawling around corners and modifications filling in-between lines of text.

"This Blood Ascension, have you tried it?"

Maxima finished writing her thoughts before responding. She laced her fingers together and popped her knuckles as she said, "No. I'm still working out the details. In its original conception, an attempt would take a decade off your life span, if not kill you immediately after. There's cellular damage to arteries that I'm still trying to prevent. I believe I solved it in my notes, but I need to think it through more to be sure."

Scavok, Dreibo, and Talus were slack-jawed.

"Maxima," Dreibo interrupted with a sophisticated tone, "Where did you find this technique originally?"

"*Philosophi and Disciplines of Magnan*," she replied absentmindedly as she chewed on her lip, solving whatever problem she was writing about.

"You…are…improving upon the techniques of Magnan the Great?" Dreibo asked in disbelief.

"Yes, I believe the understanding of cellular walls and arterial function were unrefined in his time. By including the modern understanding, it may be performed in a less damaging way. Perhaps only shaving a few years off of one's life span. I wouldn't recommend it, though."

The men looked at each other as if a quickening had gone through them.

Eos laughed with only a partial understanding of the significance of Maxima's invention. "Well, you're not even an anatus yet, and you're improving on inlumes' work." He had memorized nearly every inlume in the history of the order. His notebook, left in his Alasedis bed-chamber, contained the details of their accomplishments and renown. "They may take you straight to errant."

Maxima smiled at her brother. "Oh, I doubt that. But, *I am already an anatus.*" She closed her eyes as a wreath of sapphire light spun tendrils around her head, condensing into a break at her forehead that held a single sword-like cross of Soul Energy. It was the crown of an initiate in the Order of Soul Wielders.

Eos dropped the notebook, stunned. "How? That-I mean-we weren't able to-I'm not even…" He darted his eyes between his sister and father.

"Mother carried my energy to Turrim Cartus in an anima stone since we were forbidden to return."

A smallness overcame Eos. He felt a gap form between himself and his sister. She was ahead of him. She was part of the Order. A thing he longed for.

CHAPTER EIGHTEEN

Dreibo was quick to intervene. "Maxima, I would like to discuss this Blood Ascension technique and your modifications to it! This is profound work that you've done. Please, walk with me, and we shall talk about it."

Maxima saw the hurt in her brother's face. It was an expression she hadn't seen since Eos lost the gold sol coin in the North American Sector desert. When he thought he had lost the only token of his family. She agreed and left the fire circle. Scavok Alter had disappeared sometime during the conversation, Eos realized. He was alone with his father.

"Why? Couldn't you have done the same for me?"

Talus sighed. "I could have. What would it have changed?"

"I wanted so badly..." he hesitated with a strained voice. "I wanted to be part of the same order as you."

"And you will be! There is no rush and no gain from a title quickly added."

"Is Maxima more ready than I am?"

"That could be, but it was a decision between her inlume master and her. It is a decision that Terrava and her made in private. I had no say in the thing." Talus put an arm around his son's shoulder and embraced him. "We will do the ceremony in its own time and with no pressing journey weighing on us."

Eos nodded.

Talus added, "Besides, there is still a matter I'm considering. It is a decision to be made with *your* inlume master."

"That's you!"

"Mmm. Perhaps. There is also the matter of your curse mark. We should understand it fully before you proceed down this path—"

UNCROWNED

Eos gasped. "You mean my curse mark is preventing me from becoming an anatus?"

"That's not what I meant. Only that our focus should be—"

"I'd like to go to bed, Father." Eos rose.

Talus struggled for the proper words. He realized parenting was not the simple task he believed it would be. There were no words to comfort Eos properly, and he couldn't imagine what kind of memories the curse mark brought forth from his time on Earth.

Eos staggered, emotionally drained. His curse mark as holding him back once again. There was a distance forming between his sister and him. Now, his father and him. He was not the same.

Sleep found him as he stared at his right arm and envisioned himself with the anatus wreath.

The journey's third day combined an awkwardness from the night before with exhaustion cementing into all of their bodies. The packs felt heavier, the turns of the pass seemed steeper, and their minds all sensed the nearing of the Monte kingdom—and with it an unknown confrontation. By nightfall, they would be through the fingers of the mountain range and sleeping in beds that Dreibo had previously arranged for them.

It was mid-day, just before they had planned to pause for lunch, that they felt a reverberation in the mountain. There was shaking as if a herd of beasts was approaching, and a static sound filled the air like a radio humming without finding a channel.

Something approached.

Talus looked to Scavok.

The master assassin shook his head, "There was nothing that could cause this when I scouted earlier. That's something large. I would have seen it."

CHAPTER EIGHTEEN

The Anite King knew Scavok was correct. This advancing threat had manifested in an undetectable way.

The shaking magnified. Their attentions were all drawn up to the top of the ridge, one hundred feet above.

A figure stepped to the edge.

The sun was to his back, making the man more shadow than person. A brass-buttoned leather trench coat with collar bathed the man in black. His bald head shone above a coarse chin beard. He looked down on them in stillness with his arm extended over a staff. Silver talons winged out from the handle just below his gloved hand.

Scavok muttered, "That's a mirza. Rohl Ford. I've had reports from my spies about him."

"Mitad here? Impossible. No one knows we took this route," Talus said in disbelief.

Scavok turned accusingly to Dreibo. "No one else could have given away our location. I told you so many times Talus—"

"No!" Dreibo denied it. "I would never. King Pallogos would sooner betray King Bellator than I would." His head shook in confusion as his voice fell. "Maybe someone in King Pallogos' court...or...."

"We have no time for this," Talus said. "The Montes may have betrayed us, but it's just as likely that it was a member of our own conclave. Perhaps both. Stay together and be on guard. A single mirza poses no threat to us together."

The sound *Kratttle scree krattle scree krattle scree* overwhelmed their ears. It was a mass of Soul Energy squealing behind Rohl Ford. Crawlers suddenly lined the cliff.

Rohl's upper lip disappeared as he cast a toothy smile. "My master, Jaco Hetfel, known to those of the Winter Aisle as the

Overseer, sends his regards…and his puppets." He raised his taloned staff and struck it against the ground. A bolt of purple-black energy shot from the end of it and shook the cliff.

A slab of the rock face broke free.

A slow—then sudden cracking sheared the mass down upon the group.

Eos and Benedir sprinted right to avoid the rockfall.

Chunks of stone rained down. Any one of them was enough to kill a man. Talus only hesitated for the briefest of moments before casting up a red burst of Soul Energy that spread into wings over them. The technique took the brunt of the debris, but it couldn't stop the main slab from separating Eos and Benedir from the group.

The army of crawlers flowed down the cliff like glowing spiders toward Talus' side. Dozens rushed toward them, a wave of abominations.

"Maxima and Dreibo, behind me!" the King growled. "Scavok, what do you know about these creatures?"

"Little, but if they are the so-called *crawlers* of the Voro, then they will explode on contact. Suicidal mindless creations of Soul Energy."

Talus nodded. "Keep your distance. Strike as many now before they get close to us. Then we run to keep our distance. Scavok, when they descend on us, go over the blockage and retrieve Eos and Benedir. I suspect they're only after one of us as their target."

Maxima readied dual sapphire spheres, Talus formed crimson feathers from his fingertips, and Scavok drew short sword, *Safisay*. Ice-blue slashes projected out with each swing.

Soul Energy clashed with the Overseer's crawlers.

CHAPTER EIGHTEEN

White bubbling explosions bloomed on the wall of the mountain as the creatures were struck, but there were more than one hundred of them. There were too many and too spread out for the barrage of attacks to stop. The things crawled down to the floor of the pass in a blur of legs and speed.

On the other side of the fallen slab, Eos looked up to see Rohl dropping down on a staircase of light that shimmered where his feet stepped. The dark trench coat fluttered behind him as he neared.

Benedir had a look of panic.

"That is a mirza. If he is anywhere as strong as Ares was, we're in trouble," Eos said.

The arrogant look that Eos was accustomed to replaced Benedir's fear. He smirked and spat overconfidently, "Then I'll be a hero when I get home."

"No. You don't understand what they're capable of," Eos warned.

Rohl planted his feet on the floor of the pass. "Please. Take your best shot, kid." He threw his arms out and laughed, his cane shaking in the air with amusement.

Benedir wound ropes of Soul Energy around both arms. He immediately lashed out an extended arm and projected one of the ropes at Rohl.

It was unbelievably fast.

The attack struck just after the mirza tapped his staff on the floor once more.

A shield of thin, translucent-purple energy veiled Rohl.

Vmmmm.

Energies clashed.

The Soul Energy deflected off the shield.

Rohl mocked the boy. "Really? Is that all, little Cassion?"

Benedir turned to Eos with veins pulsing in his forehead. "I'm going to need to borrow that family relic."

"Absolutely not!" Eos put waved off Benedir's approach.

"I'm not asking." Benedir lunged at Eos, seized the chain, and ripped the links from around his neck, striking Eos in the chest violently in the process.

Eos fell back, shocked that his companion would do such a thing. He knew Benedir was conceited but didn't think he was so malevolent as to steal the Mellizo Glyph. He felt the artifact part from him. The hum of the glyph became momentarily angry and more intense.

Keep it secret. It must not fall into the wrong hands.

Half a dozen ropes sprouted around Benedir's forearm and joined the weaving motion. "Oh, this is *powerful.*" He charged forth recklessly at Rohl.

When he reached the Mirza, he extended his arm in an open-fisted strike.

Rohl did not shift his stance.

The vines of light shot forward.

The cane whipped up, breaking Benedir's forearm and shifting the attack off to the left.

Benedir stumbled. His eyes widened, and he tried to catch his breath to scream, but Rohl moved quicker. The Mirza shifted his feet, lifted his staff, and struck Benedir with a jab to his chest. Eos heard ribs crack as energy poured from the end of the weapon.

The young man's body flew limply into the slab.

It fell to the ground.

All was still. Lifeless.

CHAPTER EIGHTEEN

Rohl bent down over the brash boy's body and plucked the Mellizo Glyph from his hand. He lifted the body and threw it over his shoulder.

"Powerful indeed. I believe," he tilted his head to Eos, "that Saida will be wanting to see you soon."

Eos was on the ground in shock when Scavok found him. They looked up together as Rohl bounded over the top of the cliff and vanished with Benedir's body.

Scavok scowled, "Is he...?"

Eos shook his head to silently confirm that Benedir Cassion was no longer with the living.

Just like that, the journey had changed. The party was now five. The Mitad had known of their plan and struck.

And Eos' had lost the Mellizo Glyph his father had entrusted him with.

He had failed.

Keep it secret. It must not fall into the wrong hands.

Keep it...

The mountain walls seemed to be closing in on him as Eos was helped off of the ground by his father's master assassin.

CHAPTER NINETEEN

GRAVES AND CAGES

B lue lilacs filled Caldus' hands before light peeked over the Sepeleo mountains. The smell reminded him of Alia as he set the petals before a makeshift memorial of a stone in a pillar-like form. It was engraved with the hand-carved characters of her name and a lilac shape. Caldus took a pouch of shards, barely larger than grains of sand, and poured out half of them. The anima grains twinkled, not even filling his palm. It was the memorial offering of the impoverished. No grave plot nor chunk of high-quality condlucite stone could be afforded in the typical Monte fashion.

With watery eyes, Caldus sprinkled the offering into a pile before the headstone and lilacs. Being unable to manifest his Soul Energy externally, he was forced to place his fingers into the ground up stone.

CHAPTER NINETEEN

The grains emitted a fluttering of blue sparks. Then, before the glow died, he fell to his knees and pressed the condlucite into the soil.

What came next was a struggle. For Caldus to believe in a universal guiding power was as difficult for him as when he had been with Jezca at the Necogen shrines. His faith had not grown by what he saw of the world...and yet today, he needed it.

"Sakhralah. Tawah alru maek," he murmured with a combined ancestral memory and fragmented education of the ancient tongue. It was the death rite—one he didn't believe in. The words asked the manus god of Soul Energy to unite the deceased with the great flow of souls. There was a powerful truth in the phrase. It was almost genetic that the words brought comfort, yet his mind did not embrace them. Still, he needed to believe. The rite had more words, but those four were all he knew. "I dreamed of finding a peaceful life with you in Terspar. I will seek that life after. But, first, *Yann Kilsig must pay for the life he took*," Caldus seethed.

Then he laid the equipment of a miner below the soil and covered it before a second headstone. This one was carved with *Philo Faber*. He repeated the foreign words that asked for Philo's spirit to join with...something greater. Then he cried. The combined deaths were too much to hold back tears. Philo had died while he was in Monte prison. His voice was choked as he said, "Thank you. You were the only father I ever had. I survived after fleeing the priesthood's grip because you took me in. When you needed me...I wasn't able to provide medicine." This too was a result of Yann Kilsig's work. The resolve for revenge doubled. "I will rid this valley of those factories and purge us of the Mitad!"

Those were the only words he could get out, but he thought to himself: *These will be the last tears I shed for many years.*

GRAVES AND CAGES

Caldus stood. He would mourn his losses internally, perhaps for the rest of his life. However, he had to be at the entrance of Xaro's closed mine. Tavro's messenger had told him that Jezca would visit today. He crossed the valley to see his sister for the first time in many years, filled with uncertainty.

He waited at the abandoned entrance and tapped his fingers against the corcinth mask on his hip constantly. Jezca should have arrived already. Was the message wrong? Did she not make it? The thought of leaving crossed his mind. Caldus didn't know why. It wasn't sunrise yet, but he was anxious. Something in him wasn't sure that seeing his sister was the correct choice.

When Jezca appeared over the hill, the sun was seeping into the valley. It highlighted the golden-brown hair of her brother. He looked handsome and taller than she remembered. *If only Mother could see him.* She removed her hood as she approached.

Jezca's tiny figure came gracefully towards the mine; her blonde hair was tied back into a braid. She halted far out, and the siblings stared silently. The right eye was stunning—both beautiful beyond compare and slightly upsetting as if a powerful magician was seeing into you. A pink anima stone marbled with violet-red clouds looked out from the right eye socket. It sat above elfishly high cheekbones. There was no need to make the thing look more like human flesh. Anyone who saw her would know immediately that this was the whispered about priestess. If they had not heard the legend, they would understand that this was a fabled stone, and its owner would become of equal renown.

"Brother…" Jezca said softly and then ran to embrace him.

Caldus stood awkwardly, neither resisting nor returning the embrace.

"Come on, Caldus. I'm your sister. No need to be so stiff."

CHAPTER NINETEEN

"Sorry, Jezca. It's just…it's been years."

"And very little has changed," Jezca smirked. "Except maybe you're taller. Still swinging stolen daggers and stirring up trouble. Your exploits are being gossiped about even in the Manus Temple. I won't be able to help you if you keep this up. My political sway is not—"

"It's already too late for that. If Tavro didn't tell you, I escaped the Petramurus prison on my way down to an adere pit. Tavro assisted my escape."

Jezca gasped. "He didn't say anything. They wouldn't dare send you to an adere pit! If the priesthood heard that…"

"*The priesthood paid to make it so!* It's so like you, Jezca, to believe in the righteousness of the Manus Priesthood. They'd sooner have me disappeared than have you find out they were dealing with me."

"That can't be true. Sure, you have raided a few royal supply caravans, but that is too extreme for King Pallogos. They would be angering their future high priestess," Jezca said in disbelief.

"Do you know who turned me over?"

Jezca had no guess. Her manus eye began to sparkle with light.

"No! Never on me!" Caldus warned. "If you ever use your *sight* on me again, it will be the last time you do. *Your* trusted royal family was paid off by *your* precious priests after receiving me from the hands of a Mitad mirza," Caldus said through gritted teeth.

"I'm sorry, Brother. I promised I would never use my abilities on you, but…surely…that can't be." Jezca was stunned. "That would mean they're working with the Mitad. Neither the Monte's nor the priests are desperate enough to do that."

"And yet they did. After murdering my best friend in front of me and poisoning my father with their Mircite Valley project!"

Thin fingers covered Jezca's mouth. "Philo is dead?"

GRAVES AND CAGES

Caldus nodded solemnly.

"Oh god, Caldus. I'm sorry. I'm so sorry."

"Now you see them for what they are. Whether out of fear, convenience, or worse, they conspired with the Mitad to solve their Red Corcinth rebel problem. So leave the priesthood and join me to do some real good. Undo some of the violence they have done to me."

She shook her head, her braid racing as she did. "Violence isn't the way, Caldus. I can't leave. You know that. I can do more good healing the sick, spreading the word, and rising rank up the priesthood. You could too. Your talent is wasted on daggers. If you gave up your ways and came back to the priesthood, they would surely forgive your transgressions. The other eye is still—"

"*I never want to hear such an absurd idea again!* I would sooner go back to Necogen than the Manus Priesthood. At least the assassins kill without feigning moral superiority. Listen to me, Jezca. The Mitad is in the Monte Kingdom. They are here. They are building."

It nearly made her cry to hear her brother reject the offer of a clean record. However, she knew his stubbornness could not be swayed. "How can you be sure the Mitad—listen to me entertain such an idea—the Mitad in the Valley?"

"I'll show you. I'm taking you there now."

"I have to be back soon. I'm supposed to be fasting in private retreat today and tomorrow."

Caldus scowled and said sharply, "Do you want to see the proof besides Alia and Philo's gravestones?"

A short head nod confirmed her agreement.

"Follow me, then. We can be there quickly if you still remember how to Soul Step. I seem to recall you could do it with

me on your back at one time. Though we did take a nasty fall."
Caldus raised an eyebrow to tease his sister.

She nearly laughed. Nearly. "There is another reason I came.
Half of a journal was recovered and given to me."

Hesitating to ask, for it might give hope that he had long since
killed, Caldus waited.

"It belongs to Grace Lapithos. Mom's journal. She was
working on something. But, whatever it was, the Mitad and others
wanted it to stay hidden."

Caldus choked. "Mom left behind a journal?" There was a
moment to digest the news. He had wanted that curiosity to remain
buried. It would seem fate had other ideas. "Let's talk as we move.
We have a hike ahead of us."

They set off to discuss the lost journal of an assassin, a spy,
and a researcher who was also their mother.

They set off to witness the three smoke-churning factories that
hid in the mountain.

∞   ∞   ∞

A ghoulish green smoke billowed from the chimney of the
southernmost riverside factory. All three buildings were covered in
a dingy film of soot, but the north two facilities generated typical
gray plumes. The toxic green made Zolo uneasy as if he should
have been holding his breath.

Ares put a hand on Zolo's back and gently urged him to follow
Saida, who was dressed in the formal attire of a collared maroon
shirt under a black robe that split at his waist. The Mitad leader
powered forward in trimmed boots and black-winged shoulders.

GRAVES AND CAGES

Zolo tenderly rubbed his shortened pinky as he followed behind Saida's swept-back curls. The sight of the factories didn't sit right. In the little time he had spent on Hyperborea, Zolo could tell that these were out of place. They were not a natural feature of this world.

Saida stopped and turned to Zolo. "Ares told me about your *smart* little idea with the manus stone tracker on Earth that led us to Eos and Maxima. He also explained how much you read. I was never partial to words myself, but…" He shrugged and made a dismissing face. "Our organization needs thinking like that. *I need it here.* We're making military maneuvers soon, and I need ammunition. As much as I can get. So, I had these facilities built. The northern two are already in production."

Zolo frowned. "That looks like something from—"

"From Earth. Yes. Yes. No need to point out the obvious. I'd keep a halfwit with me if I need someone to observe things that I already knew. I stole top engineers from Earth who could get the endeavor started years ago." He saw a concerned look on Zolo's face. "Don't worry. I feed them twice a day if they behave."

"Master Saida, how am I supposed to help with manufacturing bullets?"

A single dark brown eyebrow rose with amusement. "With bullets? No. I didn't say a thing about that, did I? I want you in the south factory."

All three of them watched the rolling clouds of sickly pollution rise and a steady current of sludgy waste flowing out into the river. It gave the river valley an acrid smell that burned the nostrils slightly.

Saida continued. "I'll introduce you to our head of the project, Mirza Borne Ozen. I expect you to help him get our most

CHAPTER NINETEEN

ambitious research project to produce a higher yield. Right now, we're producing less than one percent as useable product."

Even Ares was too curious to resist asking, "What is the product?"

Saida gave a half laugh and continued toward the factory.

Inside the filthy facility, Borne Ozen received them. The Mirza was pale with long black hair that fell below his shoulders. He wore circular black glasses that completely wrapped like goggles around his eye sockets. His appearance was that of a strung-out mad scientist, and his speech was a rapid stutter-mumbling that Zolo could hardly make out. Ozen slurred loudly, "Master. It's so good to-to-to have ya visit again. We've made much progress since ya left. The experiment is-is-is going splendid."

Saida looked around while stroking his beard. "Yes. I'd say it must be, or else he'd have destroyed this whole place, and you'd be dead."

Ozen laughed with heaves, "Hahuh hahuh. Right, ya are Master. He-he-he's 'bout given up hope."

"This is Lord Vistomus' young apprentice from Earth, Zolo. Ozen, please show him what you're working on, and we'll stop by to see the first implementation in person. Ares, I believe you will be particularly amused to see what we've accomplished here.

Passing through a room of metallurgy-like machines and processes, Zolo began to sweat. The heat was so intense, it was like an invisible barrier in the room. Molten materials poured from massive crucibles the size of small pools, ran in streams, and showered sparks.

The streams of lava reflected in the black lenses of Borne Ozen's goggles. "Here, we concentrate the anima and animus stones. It is-is-is a similar process to refining any condlucite or amgrite, but we use only the purest materials. The concentration process is repeated and-and-and repeated. Then the supersaturated ore material is moved to the refining process. The solvent is quite potent, so don't breathe too deeply in-in-in the next room."

They only peaked into a maze of glass tubes and putrid chemical scents, but they all observed red and blue streams distilling in glass apparatuses the size of their heads and purified in massive teardrop separation funnels.

Finally, they entered the third step of the process. This part required an entire half of the building.

Ozen explained, "The joining of the two stones into the metus stone hybrid requires that we overcome incredible repelling forces and collide the two Soul Energy conducting materials in a very particular way. The temperature must be extremely high, and the Soul Energy input required by me is so draining to the point that I am hindered by my own recovery time. Even then, the equilibrium state is rarely reached." He presented a metallic doughnut-shaped structure that was a story tall and had the diameter of nearly half the building. The looming ring brought a sense of coldness in the skin as if the shingled metal plates that gave it form were drawing some tribute of life force from everyone in the room. "We still don't perfectly understand the fields, but the toroidal structure was the key to completing the first metus stone, or as I like to call it, *soul-negate.*"

The scientist produced a fingernail-sized shard of black diamond-like substance. However, this material appeared to suck all light into it like a black hole. It had both an underlying hue of dead light and a polished gleam to the surface.

Ozen dropped it in Ares' hand.

CHAPTER NINETEEN

Ares tensed his entire arm as soon as it fell into contact with him. The sense of something dying crawled over him. It was as if he was turning into crumpled paper...as if cells were drying out and cracking at the molecular level. He knew this was not possible nor happening in reality. He remembered his training and focused internally to search his mind for what was occurring.

All he felt was spiritual death. Cut off from the source. Separated from what brought transcendence.

Final sleep that made bodily demise seem like a gift.

The screeching of obliteration.

The crying out of finality from within.

He dropped the horrifying material in an effort to return to normal.

Ozen caught it with a gloved hand.

"The soul-negate produces a special field. The overall effect is to cancel all Soul Energy it encounters. The natural flow of life force energy in the universe ceases where this stone's field touches. It renders a wielder...powerless."

Ares and Zolo froze. The words paralyzed them with existential dread.

Zolo had only been able to wield Soul Energy for a few months, but the effect of the metus stone instantly seemed like a violation of everything natural.

There had to be proof, Ares thought. He held his hand out for a second time and nodded to Borne Ozen. When the horrible thing touched his palm again, he called forth his chains of Soul Energy through the morbid shrieks that filled his mind. He searched.

Searching.

Searching.

GRAVES AND CAGES

Static. Like his soul was tuned to a dead channel. There was nothing to call forth. He quickly returned the soul-negate.

Saida grinned and said, "Pure hell, isn't it?"

"Like all meaning has gone away," Ares confirmed.

Saida nodded his head towards a door. "Come see the first demonstration."

In a removed corner of the facility was a dim chamber with a small cage that barely allowed a person to stand. Inside it was a cowering figure, huddled over with his head down.

Ares recognized the man immediately. "Is that…Durath Leorix?"

Saida stood within reach of the cage with his thumbs in the waistband of his dress pants. He looked through the bars of the prison as if observing a piece of trash in the street.

"It is, indeed. King's Son of the Corleo empire," Saida confirmed.

Ares knew this was the most formidable wielder in the entire Corleo territory. Durath had proven his wielding merit and become renowned in the Winter Aisle for downing every opponent in tournaments with ease. Moreover, he had led military defenses from the front lines for his father. It made no sense. "How? What have you done to him? Drugged?" he asked in disbelief.

"Hardly. He's neither strong enough to bend the steel from Earth nor able to wield with the array of metus stone we integrated into his new home."

Durath looked up with eyes sunken deep within black bags. They were the eyes of a man who had been tortured endlessly, and yet…they radiated murderous intent.

"When did you do this?"

CHAPTER NINETEEN

Saida patted the cage. "Last week. Ramath has been getting out of hand. His true motives can't be trusted, his drug use is spinning out of control, and I need to transform him from a wild card into a sure bet."

Borne Ozen's goggles reflected Saida's mustached grin as the long-haired mirza waved the shard of spiritual death at Ares proudly.

CHAPTER TWENTY

CRACK IN THE EYE

The thin wax paper barrier between Archpriest Mellitus and Jezca Monte let in a soft yellow light that speckled the young woman's face through the decorative metal lattice of the confessory window.

"Is that all of your sins, my child?" The Archpriest bellowed from heavy jowls.

"Yes, Father Mellitus. However…there is another thing I wish to speak with you about."

"Is the confessory the proper place?"

"I need to know, Father. If my brother, Caldus, has been seen yet."

CHAPTER TWENTY

There was a low rumble of discontent through the paper window. "Your brother is a wanted man. He fled our protection and now raids royal supply carts. We have not heard of his whereabouts recently, but if he is spotted, the royal guard will have him arrested."

Jezca restrained herself and tempered her voice in response to the lie she heard, "Perhaps he raids only to help the needy, Father. Is it not our duty to serve the poor?"

"Serve them, we must. Break the law, we shall not."

Lying, we shall not! The shadow of Jezca's head nodded from the other side of the confessory box. "Yes, Father. As you say. If he is caught…would he still have protection at the temple?"

Jezca could see the outline of the priest stroking his chin. "The High Lady of the temple saw the same potential in him as she saw in you. It would not do to waste the gifts of the manus gods. If he repented his way when we offered the chance, then he could return." Mellitus' voice rose to a falsely sweet tone, "After all, his eye still waits in the temple vaults. No more of this talk of your brother. It only distracts from your studies, and we are in confession."

Lie after lie. What could be the true motive? There was no offer to return and repent—though Caldus would surely reject it.

"One last thing, Father. Please." A grunt told her that she could continue. "I have heard that there is a sickness in the Mircite Valley. The water there is not safe to drink. Might we raise an initiative to assist the poor souls suffering there?"

Instead of the expected concerned response, Archpriest Mellitus grew defensive. "Where did you hear such things?"

"During my healing sessions with the public. One called out to me to tell me about their sorrow."

CRACK IN THE EYE

"You cannot take the word of every beggar that comes in need without verification."

"Father!" Jezca said in disbelief at the cruelness of his words.

"Jezca, there are practicalities you must learn if you are to become the *Tawas Kajina*."

Brushing the white-blonde hair from her eyes, Jezca replied. "I serve the manus gods. Their children are all of our people. I am concerned for their well-being and only want to serve the gods properly." *Mellitus knew what was going on in the valley! Why else would he want to cast disbelief on the idea?*

"Priestess, your kind heart is well noted. Our priesthood is the right arm of the gods. Our leadership's concerns are the gods' concerns. Protecting criminals and investigating tall tales is not the way of the faith. Right now, your disobedience is causing me to question if your prayers and disciplines are properly directed."

For the first time, Jezca was truly angry with one of her mentors. However, she repressed the urge to defend the labeling of her brother as a criminal. "No!"

"No?"

She recovered from her outburst, "I-I-I mean that the anima walls of the Eye of the Gods would sooner crumble than I would be disobedient to the faith."

"Good. I will look into the issue and raise funds to support the Mircite Valley if there is truly a problem. Now we must prepare. King Talus Bellator will be here tomorrow. Let's absolve you of your sins and discuss the arrangements in the main hall."

Jezca barely heard the words of the ancient language that were professed over her as she pondered why Mellitus had behaved so defensively.

The walls of the Eye crumbling…what a foolish thing to say.

CHAPTER TWENTY

∞   ∞   ∞

Eos sat in an inner-chamber of the Manus Temple and recalled the visceral brutality with which Mirza Rohl Ford had struck Benedir with his staff. He heard again the dull thud of a lifeless body hitting the fallen rock wall. The feeling of the mellizo glyph being ripped from his neck hadn't left him. Cold chains becoming taught. Painfully snapping against his neck. The vibrational pulse of the glyph leaving his person.

King Pallogos Monte was in a heated conversation with Talus, too far down the chamber's hall for Eos to make out a word. He could tell they were whispering intensely about topics that clearly made both leaders uncomfortable and on edge.

Talus said lowly, "I know you would not betray me, Pallogos. *But I am urging*—examine your inner circle. The Mitad killed the son of Julian Cassion!" He tilted his head in frustration. "When I share that news, and I will have to share it soon, Julian will make it a personal attack on me. Anite politics will devolve into speculation. Is the Mitad in control of Monte territory? Did I want my rival's heir to disappear to secure my son's future? Did King Monte betray us?"

Pallogos stroked his dull beard, the color of dead straw, with both hands and sighed. "I have thought it through over and over again. Even in my inner circle, only a handful could have known. I'd trust that handful with my own life. And Dreibo—"

"Dreibo is innocent of wrongdoing. That, I'm sure."

"As am I. Those rumors will have to be dispelled. I will assist you in a narrative. It will look just as poorly for me to have *a mirza*, by the stones I can barely bring myself to say it, in the eastern edge of my kingdom. I have my elite units scouting the Pacem Fingers. We will erase any trace of the Mitad from our territory."

"I hope you will," Talus said, unsure that such a thing was as simple as King Pallogos made it sound. "They're like chasing smoke, though. Enough. What of my brother? Have you heard from Ramath?"

"Your...brother...has been absolutely silent. Save for one instance."

"There's been contact?"

"More." Pallogos leaned in to whisper, "He was received in the very room we will enter tonight."

Talus' eyes squinted in disbelief. "Here in the Manus Temple?"

The Monte king nodded slowly. "The priesthood met with him under the Eye of the Manus Gods. In the heart chamber of the temple. The priests and their vows. They've held silent on the reason for his visit. Ramath refused to meet with me and was gone as quickly as he arrived."

Talus shook his head. "I've heard Ramath curse the manus worshipers more times than I've seen him drinking. For him to come here..."

"Yessss. It is troubling," Pallogos cooed.

"This is your kingdom! Don't tell me that your spies don't know what he said here."

"Even I cannot spy under the Eye of the Gods. I dare not violate the religious laws," Pallogos said, aghast.

Though he was tempted to begin a tirade against such absurd ideas, Talus held his tongue. "Ramath Leorix visits the Manus Temple for the first time in his life after not being heard from for nearly a year, and we know nothing."

CHAPTER TWENTY

"The priests and their foolish laws. Even I can't bypass that. He came to meet with priestess Jezca, and that is all we know—which is why you are here as well. Quite the popular young woman these days."

Talus nodded. "We will see. Her skills will speak for themselves, if they can. Now, what of our safe passage? Have you made arrangements?"

"You truly intend to enter Corleo uninvited? You think Ramath will welcome his long-separated brother with open arms?" Pallogos hissed.

Talus stared fiercely. The silent giant's demeanor was enough to pressure Pallogos to reveal his arrangements.

"There are two ways. One is south. I trust it not. You will have to evade the gaze of the mountain assassin clan, and you'd be under the public view of the priesthood and their territory."

"May this priesthood and their politics…" Talus again held his tongue. He could not offend the King, who also worshiped the manus gods. "Scavok Alter will begin examining the south pass tonight. What of the second option?"

"The preferred alternative requires crossing to the north. My hariban have mapped out a few options through the Mircite Valley mountain ranges. They've all been unused for hexades, but that provides you more secrecy."

Eos watched from down the hall as his father and the Monte King planned and battled with words. Meanwhile, he relived the horror of Mirza Rohl Ford. As he shook off remembering the experience yet again, he realized that his father stood over him.

Talus introduced Eos, "King Pallogos, please meet my son: Eos Bellator returned from the Burning Lands. Alive again to the Anite kingdom and at service to Corland."

CRACK IN THE EYE

Eos fell to a knee as he had been taught.

King Pallogos' voice was deep and slow, "Rise, King's Son. I require no bowing tonight. I am overjoyed that you are once again among your people and alive to Corland."

After formalities finished, Eos and Maxima were led to an entryway. Double doors were gilded with eight panels each of gold plates that illustrated some mythical narrative. It was a lavish illustration of the tales of the manus faith. Above it was a marble slab with ancient writing, much like Eos knew from the Mellizo Glyph. And on top of that was a porcelain statue of the Manus Priesthood emblem: praying hands beneath a gemstone.

They passed through the doors like crossing a threshold meant for others. People of piety and devotion to the stones. Not the Bellators. They were out of place here. Then, they were in the heart of the temple, *the Eye of the Gods*. It was immediately clear why they called it such a name. The room was a dome of polished anima stone all the way from floor to ceiling. It was a sapphire lens that glimpsed into their soul and absorbed everything in its scale. The room could only have been made from a natural formation, for there was no imperfection in the walls. Two segments of pews striped the floor to the left and right, leading up to the altar. Three arched openings were centered on the altar table. The outer two contained reverent praying hand sculptures holding chunks of animus stone worth a king's fortune. The center had a tablet of ancient writing that towered over anyone before the altar.

High Priest Laud was a decrepit husk of a man. His golden flowing vestments hung over a withering frame, liver-spotted skin, and sunken purple eyes. He was led down the center of the temple's heart by a young woman who glided over the floor as she supported the elder's clunky, wooden walk.

CHAPTER TWENTY

Laud proceeded with a jutted chin while supporting himself on the arm of this woman, and Eos saw that every inch of the man was wrinkled or sagging from the weight of time. Eos could take in such features for no more than an instant as his attention fell on the High Priest's right eye. His right eye was missing, and in its place was a perfect sphere of blood-red jewel—a manus stone. It made Eos let out a tiny gasp but remembered that he had been forewarned: *high-ranking manus priests have an eye of manus stone to mark their status and increase their supposed prescient abilities.*

The white-blonde hair of the short woman guiding Laud fell to cover much of the right side of her face. She had a fierceness in her umber eye, a youthful complexion on her skin, and an out-of-place timidity when the High Priest leaned into her.

She bowed her head, "I present to you the High Priest of the Manus Temple."

A ghostly rasp said, "Thank you, Jezca. That will do."

Jezca turned to leave from earshot of the nobles' conversations with a swish of her priestly violet cloak. Her striking hair brushed over the intricate gold trim of her garments, but the High Priest shot his hand out and caught her arm.

"Stay. You should meet the King of Anondorn. You will have to work with him someday, perhaps...after me, *future Tawas Kajina,*" he referenced the title of high lady of the priesthood in the ancient tongue. "Then, you will use your *sight* on this boy."

With a quick pivot, Jezca faced Eos and Talus. Her hair swept enough to reveal her right eye was also missing. In its place was as stone far deeper and more brilliant than the High Priest's. It was a pink-red that magnetized all to it.

CRACK IN THE EYE

Eos let out another small gasp. The High Priest's jewel eye lent a particular viciousness to his decrepit face, but hers only added something… entirely different…and beautiful.

Talus bent down to a knee, a movement that Eos followed by the sheer momentum of this father's large frame. While still bowing his head and with a fist on the floor, Talus said, "Thank you for honoring us with your presence, High Priest."

The High Priest glared down over the dark bags under his eyes, "No need to prostrate yourself before an old man whose life and beliefs you do not believe in yourself."

Talus rose and commanded all eyes with him. "I need not share every belief to respect yours and your honorable position. Please, let us make an offering before we talk further."

Laud nodded ever so slightly and let a weak breath of approval.

Eos remembered how Talus had prepared him. Only priests could make adequate offerings to the manus gods via the anima chunks on the altar. The laity, those outside the priesthood, must offer their Soul Energy at the small shrines before the alter.

The shrines lined the front of the altar and grew organically from the floor in gently curved bases. Atop each was an open-faced box with a roof. Flecks of the highest purity animus stones glittered a scarlet hue from within. Eos bowed before the shrines with Talus. Then, they held their hands out in a receiving position and let wisps of Soul Energy meet the tiny shards.

The small offerings made a striking contrast in the sapphire room as ruby glimmers bounced around the chamber. Then, the dome reacted. As if an entire galaxy was laminated above the anima ceiling, twinkles of starlight began to dance with an almost musical quality. White points of light speckled the dome-like stars singing a voiceless song.

CHAPTER TWENTY

When the brief event ended, Laud said shakily, "A great offering from a great king." There was a slyness under his smile as he said it. "I have not seen the Eye of the Gods react like that in many years. The boy's offering was quite impressive as well. I commend your training of him, Talus."

Eos' heart leaped inside. It was the first thing that had made his father smile since he had lost the Mellizo Glyph.

"Thank you, Father Laud. My vassal is quite skilled—"

The creaky voice teased, "More than a mere vassal, I think."

Talus was taken aback. He had not revealed anything about Eos, nor had he intended to.

Laud continued, "We are honored to be visited by the King's son...and daughter...if I may presume." He tapped under his jeweled eye. "I can see all, Talus."

King Pallogos chimed in, "That you can, Father. We meant no secrecy. It is only that they have just arrived back on the Corland. Your perception and sight are a gift to behold."

Laud nodded and made a groan of annoyance. "They are only a gift from the manus gods. By their will, not mine. I believe," he coughed feebly, "that Eos is to have the sight performed over him, yes?"

Eos locked gazes with Jezca and said with nervous resolve that the thing must be done, "Yes."

"Please follow Lady Jezca to the alter," Laud ordered.

Following behind the small sauntering priestess, Eos approached the altar and bowed before it, following Jezca's lead. She spoke in an ancient tongue that held magic in its pronunciation. It was archaic and melodic. She chanted under her breath so that the only words he heard were: "Ahfir khatayu. Yawiy uyati."

CRACK IN THE EYE

She then gestured for him to join her on the altar between the two penitent pairs of hands. Her fair fingers rose to Eos' temples on either side of his head. "May I perform the sight on you?"

"Lady Jezca…" Eos hesitated. He knew what Jezca would find would not be what he wanted.

So that only they could hear, she murmured, "Please. Just Jezca. And I've been ordered to perform it regardless, but your agreement is preferred."

There was dread in Eos' voice as he displayed his right forearm and replied, "It must be done." The palms of his hands began to sweat. His curse was exposed to the world. The secret was now more public than when Xaro had intruded.

Vibratory resonance tore through his temples. It was invasive. Bone shaking. Fear inducing. But not painful. He could feel pink energy working through his skin as the beautiful priestess' stone eye shimmered with activated power.

Eos shut out the world in favor of his eyelids. It was all he could do to hold on to consciousness. Pink waves hummed like pond ripples in his mind.

"This…is similar to something I've seen before," Jezca said and moved her left fingers down to Eos' forearm. "There's foreign Soul Energy in you. It's old…and hostile. There is something holding it at bay, but the energy wants to spread. And there is *something else*." She hesitated on that statement, shaking her head. Then she projected her voice for the room to hear, "I need to go deeper to get a better picture. It will be painful."

"Do it," Eos grunted. He had to know, and there was no better chance.

The sonic assault on his brain intensified. The pink ripples began to jump erratically. He lost his sense of smell and hearing as

CHAPTER TWENTY

the energy chipped at the base of his skull. He couldn't hear himself, but he knew he was crying out.

Suddenly, he didn't need to open his eyes to see.

A world manifested before him.

Chalky stone mountain walls appeared, and golden grass was at his feet. Teal moss textured the world around him. He knew exactly where he was—and wasn't. The dimension was visually overlayed with the Iussum mountains near Fantum Ortus. However, the sensation of the realm was a perfect match to the place he had gone during training with Aizo. He was in his Soul Void.

Cautiously, he walked through the maze of ridges. A map of the place was planted in his mind in a way he couldn't explain. Instinctively, he knew where every turn was taking him. The rustic scents of the mountains and the cool air heightened his alertness. The rules of his last trip to the Soul Void ran through his head. *No wielding. At least, not directly. Moving towards the goal did not get him any closer—if this time was the same.*

Like being pulled by a string, he arrived at the door to Fanum Ortus, beneath the Turrim Cartus. However, the entrance was not there. Where it should have been was only mountain face.

"Oh no no no. You didn't think you could just enter the private study of the Order of Soul Wielders, did you?" a voice said from behind him with an arrogant coolness. "Your sister may see the entrance, but you? No."

Without needing to turn, Eos could sense the man in the white mask behind him. The striking image remained with him from his last encounter: a contoured oval with one wide, triangular strokes across the left side of the face that covered the cheek, mouth, and nose in a blood-like paint. Two smaller strokes ran alongside the main one. Eos recalled one of his worst memories. Falling. Infinite falling in the Soul Void. The man had taunted him during his fall.

"You lack many things but particularly the mindset to take it for yourself." The masked man pointed above with pale gray hands.

Eos saw a massive emanation of the crown of Soul Energy that marked an anatus. It hovered near where the Turrim Cartus would have been in this reconstruction of Fanum Ortus. He growled, "Then I'll take it. I'm ready." With a bowed head, he prepared as he had done previously in the Soul Void. He summoned the anatus crown with an outreached arm.

It didn't move.

He strained harder.

Nothing.

The masked man sneered, "You couldn't wield last time because of how you entered this place. You were depleted and irritating the seal on your energy. Wielding here is possible, but you are still not worthy. Not ready." The words froze Eos. "The King of Anite trusted you with the Mellizo Glyph—your own father— and you failed at such a simple task! You may as well have remained on Earth. You betrayed his trust and made things worse."

Heat rose in Eos' neck. His veins flared, and his eyes watered with frustration. Dozens of rebuttals came to mind, but his tensed throat could only get out a strained bark, "I will be a Soul Wielder of the Order!" He stepped up the mountain pass on planes of his Soul Energy, bounding towards the crown.

Thud.

The masked man appeared before him and stuck him with an open palm. It sent him tumbling ten feet down. The air left him as he struck the stone floor.

CHAPTER TWENTY

"You are not worthy! First, show that you deserve such a thing. Show me how strong you are. *Show me.*"

Standing shakily, Eos manifested a Soul Sphere angrily. He lunged at the man in his Soul Void. Had he been calm and aware, he would have noticed the walls of the mountain began to tremble.

Jezca did not remove her fingers from Eos' temples and curse-marked arm.

The boy's body began to shake violently, but she pushed forward. The nature of the curse was unraveling to her, but slowly. Too slowly.

Eos' body went limp.

His feet were slack as his figure shimmered in crimson like a possessed form of Solido had encompassed him. Then, he floated off the ground, head dangling back. His eyes rolled to whites, and then...flame-colored energy burst out of his eye holes in beams! His curse mark flashed red-white.

"Evil things. On the manus gods, this violates the sanctity of—" High Priest Laud was interrupted as trembles in the chamber forced him to catch himself on a pew. He let out a devastated moan.

The crimson beams struck the roof of the temple's heart.

White star shapes blinked on the anima stone in a frantic cadence. They seemed to warn of impending damage. *Blink. Blink-blink. Blink.* The glows pulsed faster until the ceiling seemed to be white-hot.

Eos was two feet off the ground.

Jezca stood on the tips of her toes to remain in contact with him. She shook her head and thought in a panic of how to calm the situation.

CRACK IN THE EYE

Inside the void, the masked man's grip strangled Eos' throat. He lifted the young man from the ground by his neck and pinned him against the wall. He was bleeding from multiple lacerations and his ribs felt like more of them were broken than not. Staring into the amethyst eyes, Eos saw that this was indeed the same person he had encountered in the mirror at the real Fanum Ortus. What had the young boy said?

This is only an instance of me. A once that was but is now a portal and a monument to power. A fragment, you could say.

With a closing windpipe, Eos wheezed, "Are y-y-you, a f-f-fragment too?"

The man dropped Eos, and he slid to the ground.

"Where did you hear that? You may call me that, but it does not matter now. All that matters is that you prove yourself, and you chose to do so through a pathetic show. The distance between us is like an ant looking at the moon. Show me how strong you really are. *True power!*"

"H-h-how?" Eos gurgled.

"Use the curse that was given to you. Embrace the power it offers. It is a gift of the highest kind."

Eos looked up, unsure of how to proceed.

"Allow me to show you," the man said and reached to him.

Stretching out his cursed arm to the man, he took his hand. He wanted no more of the beating. No more failure and heartache. Just relief from the curse. That is all he wanted.

Inside the temple chamber, the outpouring of Soul Energy magnified.

The ceiling trembled until a crack formed above.

It was minor but an imperfection in the Eye of the Gods, nonetheless.

CHAPTER TWENTY

Jezca knew what she had to do. She had to go deeper. Too deep. She wasn't supposed to. She had vowed never to perform such a powerful invasion with the sight—but this was a situation so dire, she could see no other way out.

A flow of memories spilled into her brain. It was like a flood moving in reverse, surging against entropy and splitting her skull. Jezca screamed as memories filled her. Memories that were not hers.

Cruel testing in a laboratory. A gun pointed at a child. Shrieks. Desperation. Fear. Watching Maxima be sealed in a tank. Dueling with a man in white. Confrontation with a half-brother.

The overwhelming inflow of data burned her skin, but she didn't stop. Eos had ceased shaking.

Maxima was at Eos' side. She had ignored the cries that she could not approach the altar. She laid her hands on her brother alongside Jezca.

After a few moments of uncertainty…the energy ceased to flow from Eos. The shimmer around his body faded. He floated back to the ground into his sister's arms.

A pebble of anima stone broke from the ceiling and fell onto Jezca's head. She barely noticed the pelting as she collapsed to her knees, exhausted.

In a dull mumble, Jezca said, "I believe I understand it. Not entirely…but enough."

Eos opened his eyes and stared into Jezca's. They shared a prescient awareness and connection. She had violated his mind to reel him back to the living world. The cost was something entirely unnatural.

CRACK IN THE EYE

Jezca focused on the fallen chunk of the Eye of the Gods. A piece of the heavenly realm had crumbled, broken, and collapsed down on her.

CHAPTER TWENTY-ONE

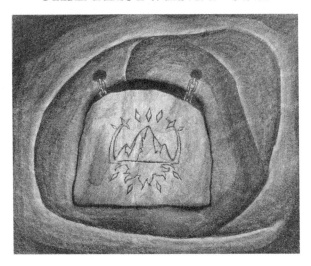

LIGHT FROM ABOVE

The pink and orange waves of sandstone canyons wrapped around Ares like nature's tapestry documenting the slow eternal passing of time in vibrant rock. As he climbed down into the crevices of the Tenebrim borders, he saw evidence of the people. Occasional markings or divots were carved into the walls. The splendor of the color faded as he descended. Light became sparse. From above, Tenebrim was a patchwork quilt of farmland spotting the available flat surface that didn't drop off into sheered crevices of colorful rock. Once in the cracks, it was a world where darkness enveloped everything—a hidden world that must be navigated carefully.

Ares had learned the way when Saida had taken him there as a young teenager. He felt along the wall for indented instructions that told him how to proceed. The glow of a light-stone eased his mind but did little to help guide him more than a few feet ahead. The canyon dwellers knew the importance of using the wall impressions for navigation, and he had learned from them a long time ago.

The darkness left him with a lack of sensation that forced him to reflect on his own thought. A lot was weighing on him: the coming invasion plans, the implications of the soul negating metus stone, the journal entries of Grace Lapithos, but only one notion percolated to the surface with every step. *I am going to be a father.*

The thought struck terror in him. It numbed his awareness to the point that he barely noticed hours later when the stronghold door opened for him. The stone wall, marked with the people's emblem of the sun under the mountain, broke free from the canyon. A series of chains allowed the enormous piece to ease down like a drawbridge.

Am I ready? Can I live this life and raise a child? Do I want to? No, there is no choice. I know what it is like to be without a father. But Saida will find out. There is no way to hide this. I must protect Bellia and the child.

"Please. Follow me. We have been expecting you," the soft voice of a servant in all brown clothes urged. The vast array of light-stones strung along the cave-society in a web that would have typically awed him. He still felt the off-balancing effects of a world under the light of Soul Energy alone. The sensation was subtle but disorienting. He bumped shoulders with pale people who hadn't seen the surface sun in years. By the time he slowed his mind enough to notice the lights and people, he was already in the private crevices of the Tenebrim leader.

"Salvaluc will call for you when he's ready," the servant bowed and left.

CHAPTER TWENTY-ONE

Richly dyed fabrics hung from the walls, a wealthy symbol among the subterranean community. Behind a particularly deep violet cloth, Ares knew that the old inlume, Salvaluc, was meditating in a sun chamber. The pale people of this canyon world revered their leader. He was a legend of the Order of Soul Wielders, had improved the farming and sanitary techniques of Tenebrim, and single-handedly held off an invasion in the days of old. The people worshiped him as a prophet-like figure; however, their only true worship was the *great soul in the sky*. Sunlight was everything to these people, and they would work large portions of their day to be exposed to a few moments of it.

His real name had been forgotten in the building of his mythos, but Salvaluc was one of the most renowned Soul Wielders on Hyperborea. And yet…Ares didn't have time to play the guest humbled before a cult leader. There were pressing issues to be attended to, and this simple messenger's task was beneath him. He pulled aside the violet tapestry and passed by murals of suns morphing into energy that showered the people.

Salvaluc was a silver mustached man with bushy eyebrows and short prickly hair. He sat in a thin mahogany-colored monk robe under a square patch of natural light. The source was a sky tunnel: a specialized set of magnifying lenses that reached the surface; they were expensive, rare, and sacred among the Tenebrim people.

It was impossible for an inlume not to notice Ares enter the room, but Salvaluc did not give the slightest reaction to the intrusion. He only bathed in the sun.

"Great inlume, Salvaluc, you received my letters, I presume."

The old man opened weary eyes and said in a heavily accented voice, "We commune with the Great Soul through the light. We sit in silence under the sun to gain wisdom and discipline. This is the art of soul mediation. However, the Mitad is so much greater than nature—they are a force to make nature *bow before their might*. How could I refuse such an eloquent intrusion? What use is communing with divine source when in the presence of the great mirza, Ares." Salvaluc's words dripped with annoyance and sarcasm.

Ares recalled Saida's words. *You're going to learn some diplomacy…*

"So, you did receive the letter," Ares said, feigning not to hear the hostile sarcasm of the inlume.

Salvaluc squeezed his eyebrows together. "Your master would like me to allow his army of terrorists to pass through my people's canyons and through the tiny border we share with east Anite. And he wants me not to slaughter every last one of these terrorists."

"Something like that."

"Saida is aware of my rank in the Soul Wielder Order?"

Ares nodded subtly. Too strong of a motion would give Salvaluc cause for aggression. Lack of acknowledgment would only prompt an end to the negotiation. It was a delicate balance with an old master who made no effort to hide his disdain for the Mitad.

Salvaluc hummed thoughtfully. "Then you realize that I must rectify this decision against the code of the Order?"

Ares stuck his arm into the light of the sky tunnel. The tips of his fingers were illuminated as he passed the threshold. He turned his hand in the sun, thoughtfully. "I see no issue. Your people will cause trouble for us, no doubt, with your elaborate tunnels, hidden world, and fighting tactics—"

"More than twenty outlook posts saw you and restrained themselves during your journey down here," Salvaluc threatened.

CHAPTER TWENTY-ONE

"No doubt. I did not come in stealth. Regardless of how many you command here, the Mitad would eventually crush them and move through your lands."

The inlume was silent with his eyes shut for a while. He chose his next words carefully, "You're not afraid that I will warn Talus and lead to your slaughter?"

A sly smile crept from Ares' lips. "We're counting on it that you do."

"Complexity on complexity. It seems I must navigate your game. Tell me this, son of the Mitad: Why is someone of your stature here to negotiate? If the task was a simple message delivery, any underling could do. If negotiations were required in-depth, Emir Grimshaw would have come himself. So why you?"

Ares stepped into the light, partially covering Salvaluc in his shadow. "I suppose Saida is trying to teach me a lesson, and I have a history here when I was younger. I believe he also wants you to feel the stab in the back he delt you...those years ago."

"This is true. You were among us for some time." Salvaluc stood and looked eye to eye with Ares. The man's gray irises pierced him with a knowing. "However, I believe *you* wanted to be here for other reasons. I sense much apprehension."

Rubbing his face with an anxious hand, Ares laid out his intentions plainly. "I have come into some knowledge. Deep. Ancient. You might say that *a tree has been lit afire in my mind.*"

Silver eyebrows raised suspiciously.

Ares continued, "I have learned that *knowledge is power.*"

"Power must be preserved, and knowledge retained," Salvaluc said with slow, annunciated words that smoothed out most of his accent. "Allowing the Mitad to pass...this I can do for the preservation of my people's life blood. I will alert the Bellators, as you have assumed. This other matter…it is not Mitad business?"

"Personal."

A nod answered.

Ares pushed the issue, "Will you help me? I'm looking for something, and you know where it is."

A pale finger gestured for Ares to follow. Salvaluc led him through a green embroidered tapestry and a maze of sandstone passageways. Artificial light and silence allowed Ares' mind to wander once more. *Did I make the correct move? Salvaluc answered with the code and appears to know what I want…but it could be a trap. The Priori would sooner kill than give up the knowledge.*

The minutes wore on. Footsteps dulled against pink-gray floors.

I'm going to be a father.

They entered a circular chamber, spotted with small sky tunnels that beamed checkers of light down like pixelated rain. In it, women of the spiritual path were attending to young children on mats. The room was filled with young, frail lives. Their walk weaved through rows of boys.

"Food. Shelter. Light. Here in Tenebrim, we live against these constraints. The top land is precious for growing food. The hidden world provides shelter. Amongst this balance, my people trade their excess resources for time under the sky lights. All journey to the surface world at their coming of age, but doing so regularly is too costly in time and resources to sustain us as a people. So, we pilgrimage up on a cycle. However, for some boys, this is not enough. They have been born with genetic inefficiencies. Their life is failing."

CHAPTER TWENTY-ONE

They stopped at a mat with a boy whose biceps were not much thicker than his wrists.

Ares knew much of the value system from his time in Tenebrim. He had heard of the shadow illness but never seen the victims—it did not unnerve him.

"What is this matter to me?"

Salvaluc made a chiding noise, "I sense much in you, Ares, child of the Great Soul. True knowledge is not for the Mitad. It is my duty as an inlume to bring order to chaos. It is a necessity as a member of the Priori that I keep *the knowledge* secret. You know too much. But I have seen in my meditations…my communing with the Great Soul. You have a path that I am not meant to snuff out."

"Then you will help me?"

"If you can learn what I have to teach."

"And that is?"

"Ego dissolution. This boy's name is Cavo. He will die soon. His death is not a problem affecting you as an ego, but his soul is part of the universal flow. His life is our responsibility as human beings."

Ares scanned the fragile body, searching for the value that Salvaluc saw. He was weak, near death, and looked hopeless. "What am I to do?"

"Carry him to the surface. There, he will live and become a farmer for our people."

Ares scowled. "Anyone could do that."

"Yet, you must."

There was an annoying number of simple tasks being assigned recently. Deliver a message. Carry a boy on my back. These are tasks of a novice. I am not that! As he thought, the boy's intermittent breathing shook him to his previous ponderings.

LIGHT FROM ABOVE

I am going to be a father.

Minutes later, the slender limbs were being tied around Ares' back.

As the securing of his passenger was completed, Ares asked, "After I do this, you will teach me what I need to know to find it?"

Salvaluc looked mildly pleased and turned. Walking away, he replied, "I am teaching you right now."

So, it will be like this...

But externally, Ares grumbled, "I don't work for free, old man."

An amused laugh echoed back to Ares. He shifted his weight to balance the boy attached to him and walked through the luminous mist of sky tunnel distillations.

∞   ∞   ∞

Terrava stood at the head of the onyx table in the Ashva pavilion. With her husband gone, she was the leader of Anite...a role she had no desire to fill, especially at a time like this. Yet, she was the most capable. Her poise and grace brought calm to the immense seriousness in the room. This gathering was not a traditional conclave—it was an emergency preparatory meeting. The four inlumes, five haribans near enough to join, Aizo Mudar, and Xaro Monte sat before her.

She observed them. The haribans were restless. The inlumes were anticipating with aged tranquility. Aizo tapped his foot and stirred. But Xaro Monte eagerly smiled as he puffed on his betel pipe made of anima stone.

"The Tenebrim leader, Salvaluc, has sent us a warning," Terrava said and held out a scroll that contained the message. "As

CHAPTER TWENTY-ONE

I alluded when I summoned you all…the Mitad is moving through the canyons toward Anite."

Spintha spoke on behalf of her elder Soul Wielders, "Why would a fellow inlume of the Order allow such a thing? It betrays our oath and begs for excommunication."

"Hardly," Aizo said in a high-pitched tone as he thought. He ran his hands through the wild hair that grew only on the sides of his head. "It spares the blood of his people and allows us to prepare an adequate military response. We can maximize damage to the Mitad and minimize our losses."

Xaro spoke through a cloud of smoke, "Can we trust him? Why would the Mitad make a move against us now?"

Enodor had no doubt. "Salvaluc can be trusted above any inlume. His word is as good as the Order itself."

"Forgive me," Xaro laughed, "The word of the Order means little to me."

Terrava snapped her fingers to end the conflict before it started. "Xaro, you are not part of the conclave but allowed here only because you are one of the Ignoble. Your assistance could be critical in our victory. I'll have no squabble."

Xaro's gray mane bowed low. He spoke mechanically. "Yes. Forgive me, my lady."

Hariban Sulla interjected, "How many are they marching?"

The room anticipated the next words so intensely that the rustling of the trees outside the pavilion could be heard like a deafening scream.

"Salvaluc estimates…over ten thousand."

"Hmmm," Sulla grumbled. "Perplexing. Surely that is a small force for them, but far too many to sacrifice in a territorial testing."

LIGHT FROM ABOVE

Terrava agreed. "Yes. There is some trick behind it, but we can only respond based on what we know. What response do you recommend, High Hariban."

Sulla rubbed his bald head and thought. "A pincer between the Iussum mountains and the canyon from East and West is the best strategy, but the force we use to knock them back…that is the question. We could send the majority of our military might to crush them. My instincts advocate for that; however, it would leave other parts of the nation undefended."

Xaro set down his pipe and released smoke from his nose that hung around his beard. "What concern is there of another attack? Anite is secured by the ocean and the Sepeleo mountains everywhere but the southeast border. The answer seems simple: strike the trouble makers down with everything you have and ensure they never think of such a bold advance again."

The discussions continued for hours, but plans were settled before sunset. As the dusk fell, Terrava stood among the albino-veined trees at the edge of the water. She paced the forest at its edge. Scenarios played in her mind. Responsibility drained her of emotions, yet she found the motherly instinct to settle her wandering thoughts on Talus, Eos, and Maxima. *How could all three of them be gone at such a dangerous moment?*

Aizo found her and sat at the water, within earshot. Terrava's pacing eventually meandered near him.

"Full force to the southern border—a wise move. I see no flaw in it with myself, Xaro, and you here in the capital to defend against disaster," he said.

"Unless…"

CHAPTER TWENTY-ONE

"No. The haribans are already moving. We can't doubt that crushing the Mitad before they start encroaching is the best choice."

Terrava sighed. "They infest the Winter Aisle. They infect Tenebrim. Something else is at play, but I can't figure out what. Normally, I would be able to see through such a move, but my thoughts—"

Aizo finished for her, "Are where a mother's thoughts should be. You had the inlumes and haribans to search for ulterior motives and tactics for you."

The sun went behind the Ashva tree, so the amber bark shimmered like a tower made of gold foil, and the leaves glowed a semi-transparent honey color. It was a peaceful view, but it was at the lake's center, and Terrava was on the shore. It was a distant view, and the sun would go down soon. She knew a war was coming.

CHAPTER TWENTY-TWO

DANCE WITH DAGGERS

The world blasted through the slits of Eos' eyelids to reveal Maxima tending to him as his pupils adjusted to the light. The same sight had greeted Eos numerous times in the generator facility back on Earth when he had awakened from the unconscious state.

Eos knew that Maxima had been using some form of healer wielding, dripping her Soul Energy into his reservoir to tame his curse mark and regenerate his stamina. He knew that it worked, but not how—though he now recognized it was related to the techniques of the Sanofem in Anite.

"How…long?" Eos asked.

"Four days. Father thought we'd lost you. We're in the Mircite Valley now," Maxima answered with her cool hand on his sweating forehead. She hesitated to ask but had to. "What happened in the

Manus Temple, Eos? That wasn't like what I've seen on Earth. It was more intense…more violent."

The vision of Jezca flickered in his imagination. Blond hair like platinum. Feminine lips. The animus stone eye that seared into his skull. Memories of training as an assassin in the mountains, escaping in a near death fall, and being found by the priesthood while on the run. Eos tensed up. *Those were not his memories.* Then he remembered everything. The destruction of the Eye of the Gods and the conflict in the Soul Void came back to him. He had fought the masked man in the Soul Void and was losing badly. He would have been killed. Then he had been offered a path out by using the curse mark and breaking the seal.

"I…I went into the Soul Void again. Jezca's abilities were digging too deep. It triggered something that I don't understand. But I know that I went back there," Eos said. Then he muttered lowly, "For a moment, I gave up control."

Maxima returned to her sisterly instincts. "I'd say so! You put a crack in the ceiling of the most important room in the Manus Temple."

"Were they angry?"

His sister smirked. "Hard to tell. High Priest Laud was furious. Outraged. But also in awe. He said something about the gods speaking to their servants. I didn't understand it. I think there was as much fear as anger. A lot happened since then. Priestess Jezca is going to meet us here to interpret what she saw when she looked inside you."

Eos shivered, remembering the memory swap that imprinted their existences on each other. He smiled goofily. Seeing the Priestess again excited him, but then the smile faded. It also

DANCE WITH DAGGERS

frightened him. *What if she learned something dark about me? What if she delivers news that I couldn't take?* He shook away the thoughts.

"And what about Dad?"

"Scavok and Father are investigating paths through the Sepeleo into Corleo territory. He wants us to remain here and stay away from any more trouble."

Eos scowled. "He wants us to just sit on the sideline and let him finish what we all came here for?"

Maxima eyed her brother with a chastising glare. "This isn't Earth, Eos. It's more dangerous. We came here to learn about your curse mark. Jezca will be the completion of that mission. Ramath is Father's mission. You need to take this more seriously!"

"I am taking this seriously. I want to help."

Maxima reminded Eos, "You're in no condition to help. Benedir died! We can't have anyone else getting hurt. The Mitad is all over this area, and I've been doing some investigations while Father's been away. Things aren't stable in the Winter Aisle."

Eos fell quiet, and Rohl Ford's deadly strike replayed. The stakes were different now.

Benedir was gone.

"I have a decision to make soon," Eos mumbled to himself. "I don't know what I will decide when that time comes."

"About what you saw in the Soul Void?"

Eos nodded slowly. He attempted to stand, but his body felt hollow and disjointed.

"No, you don't. Maxima shoved him back onto his sleeping mat. "Rest. I'll be back before morning. If Scavok comes to check on us, tell him that I couldn't sleep and went for a walk."

"Where are you going?"

CHAPTER TWENTY-TWO

Maxima only smiled gently. "Rest." She pushed a jar of water to him and walked across the creaky floorboards of a cabin-like room. It was all wood, except for the far wall that appeared to be made of the Sepeleo mountains.

As his sister's raven hair trailed out of the doorframe, Eos tripped to his feet. He ignored the sensation that his limbs were made of gum and hurled himself to a window. He saw a shantytown built into the mountain valley. Wooden structures with slanted roofs were stacked and crammed atop one another as if they had been spilled and left where they fell. He found himself looking down at a staircase built into the rock. It flowed down two levels of housing in an uneven sprawl, and Maxima was descending it.

Eos rushed for his boots at the edge of his mat and danced to get them on as he moved towards the room's exit. He stutter-sprinted through a hallway inside the mountain walls and then out onto the staircase. Pressing himself against the wall as he moved, he chased his sister. Her back was constantly turning around the corner of a shack or vanishing down staircases so that he almost lost her trail as he tried to remain unnoticed.

He froze. *Am I exposed? No.*

A relieved sigh escaped as Eos observed cloth tied around his cursed arm. It was coming loose but was good enough for now. He ducked behind a stack of crates and piled trash as his sister slowed up ahead. A figure masked in red ceramic in the likeness of a horned creature met her in the alley—*a corcinth mask*. Eos moved as close as he could without being seen.

More masked figures joined the group, but theirs were not as well made as the leader's.

DANCE WITH DAGGERS

"Are you sure you're ready, Maxima? You've been plenty of help so far. You don't have to do this," The leader spoke muted words from behind his red disguise.

"I'm doing this. I've seen the people poisoned by the river water. I've seen the poor suffering here. I can't sit by idly." There was steel in Maxima's voice that he had heard very few times in his life.

The leader gestured for her to move past him with his head. "Follow Talker. He'll keep you with the rear group that'll take the supplies back once the path is cleared."

Maxima followed a group through the piles of trash and shambles.

Eos shifted his weight to see where they were going, bracing himself against a mound of rubbish as tall as he was.

Shift. Creak. Crash!

The pile's weight pushed against the crates, and it all shifted. The swaying tower spilled into the meeting space.

Red Corcinths swarmed him immediately. Then, before he could think, they were lifting him before the leader.

"What's this we've found among the trash?" Caldus taunted.

Eos' cloth hung dangerously loose around his forearm. He tried to remember his training and think calmly. Aizo would have told him, *clarity will see you through this situation.* Or something wise like that. But Aizo wasn't here. It was only Eos in a dark alleyway surrounded by a dozen menacing masks. Corcinth eyes followed his struggling movements through the hazy moonlight.

"Well, do you speak for yourself, or are we to make our judgment for you?"

Eos strained his neck to look into the distance, but Maxima had disappeared. He chose his words carefully. "I'm just passing

CHAPTER TWENTY-TWO

by. I don't know who you are, but I just want to be on my way peacefully."

"If you don't know of the Red Corcinths, then you're a liar or an outsider of this valley. We do promote *peace*," there was a tease in Caldus' voice as he said it. "So, please stop with the lies. They don't lead to peaceful resolutions."

A dim crimson glow sparked at Eos' fingertips. Too subtle to notice, but preparing for action.

"I am a visitor to Mircite. Just passing by. What else do you need to know?"

Caldus drew one of Amon's daggers. The skull hilt smiled a toothy silver death at Eos. "Let's start with a name, *outsider*."

Eos closed his fingers around a marble-sized sphere of Soul Energy.

The light was too noticeable in the darkness.

One of the many Red Corcinths blurted, "Soul Energy! He's a wielder."

Immediately, his arms were wrenched forcefully behind him, nearly pulling them out of socket. Eos ripped his arms free a few times, losing the Soul Sphere, but the numerous bodies around him won.

He felt skin-to-skin contact against his forearm—his forearm!

The cloth covering blew across the ground to Caldus' feet.

His right arm was stretched out by two men so that his curse mark was laid bare. It pulsed and moved against Eos' will, wriggling near his elbow and exposing the nature of the black ink-like pattern.

"If you're a visitor...you look like a Mitad visitor to me!" Caldus said venomously. He walked his dagger up to Eos' cheek.

DANCE WITH DAGGERS

"Allow me to show you what we think of the Mitad." The chill of the knife blade's flat edge moved down his throat.

Eos couldn't move. All he could think to do was create a distraction.

Droplets of his energy fell from his fingertips. They hit the ground like firecrackers—loud, bright, and harmless. It was enough to break free of his captors in their instant of lost concentration.

Diving to the other side of Caldus, Eos freed himself of the Red Corcinth's restraints.

There were enough members of the group behind him to prevent his escape, and so he moved his feet carefully, ready to evade the threat of knives.

Three approached from behind.

Caldus stopped them, "No. I'll handle him. Stay back." He shifted forward at the boy with the curse-marked arm.

"My name is Eos."

"Well, Eos, is there a reason I shouldn't leave your body with the trash you were hiding in?"

Caldus flipped one dagger into a reverse grip.

"I was following the girl you were talking to. She's my sister."

A smug grin spread under the mask, and it could be heard in Caldus' voice. "If that were true…then you have a very beautiful sister," he said with teasing intention. "But I don't believe you—"
He lunged with the standard gripped knife in his left hand.

Eos rolled off to the side of the stab, but Caldus anticipated it and followed up with a slash from his reverse gripped dagger. Eos had to drop to the ground and scrambled on his back to avoid the deadly strike.

CHAPTER TWENTY-TWO

Forming a Soul Sphere wasn't an option. He tried, but Caldus kept the pressured attacks.

Caldus advanced on Eos relentlessly, but he held his attacks back from lethal strikes as if to tease some kind of evidence.

"For a Mitad wielder, you're not a very good one."

Eos grimaced. "You're right about that. I can't be good at something that I'm not."

"You have the mark of one of their senior ranking officials. You're either mirza... or higher. Your attempts to play innocent are beyond foolish. We know what rank receives those marks."

Stab. Slash. Stab.

Eos narrowly avoided the latest flurry of attacks.

This time, Caldus let him pace backward and create distance.

The distorted voice said from behind red ceramic, "Fine. I'll force it out of you."

One of his animus daggers lit up. The jagged edges of stone shone with Soul Energy.

Eos recognized it immediately and began forming a sphere in response. *What is he doing?* He recalled something that saved his life: Gondul swinging his sword at Karo during the vangar dueling tournament. Soul Energy had left the black knight's giant blade, and the same happened now. A pink light sliced through the air.

The moment it emerged from the dagger, Eos cast out his Soul Sphere instinctively.

Znnng. The concussion of the two energies clashing rattled the flimsy shacks on either side of them and sent a few planks of wood clattering to the ground. The Red Corcinth members looked around nervously. This could attract too much attention.

Caldus nodded as if getting what he was seeking.

DANCE WITH DAGGERS

Eos thought tactfully and said, "Fine, I'll prove to you who I am. No more of this."

"Let's see it then," Caldus provoked.

Eos cleared his mind. Like he had done at the waterfall with Talus.

Inner peace. Breathing in and letting go.

The gates opened within him.

An elsu of Soul Energy beat its wings and rose from his hand. It circled his head before floating over his shoulder. The eyes and beak locked on Caldus.

"I am Eos Bellator. Son of Talus. Brother of Maxima."

Caldus' shoulders went slack. His mouth hung slightly open as he stared at the elsu that blazed before him. "Hurramit," he swore quietly as one of his blades clattered to the ground.

Hours later, Eos was helping Maxima push a cart full of water barrels. Caldus had refused to let them join in on the raiding portion of the mission once he had learned that they were Bellators. Small bursts of Soul Step were accelerating the process and helping keep the Red Corcinths far ahead of any Monte soldiers that would be searching for the lost shipment.

In between intervals of Soul Step, Maxima hissed at her brother, "You followed me? I can't believe you. You're supposed to be recovering. It's just like you to not listen and to not take care of yourself!"

Eos growled a quiet annoyance and said, "Right, like I'm going to not find out what you're doing and instead sit alone in a room, bored."

"You're going to hurt yourself, wielding again so soon."

In truth, Eos felt fine. After the clash with Caldus, he had completely overcome the shaky state of his body through the

CHAPTER TWENTY-TWO

adrenaline of battle. He squinted at his sister and whispered, "Is there something going on between you two?" Caldus' teasing words repeated in his head.

Maxima blushed. "What do you mean?"

Eos tilted his head, not buying her misunderstanding.

"What? *No!* I just met him. We bumped into each other in the market. I was asking him why there are so many sick people in the valley...and it led to this." Maxima purposefully neglected to mention that Terrava had told her how to find Caldus Lapithos.

"Are there a lot of sick people here?" Eos asked.

Maxima's head fell, saddened. "The Mitad is doing something in the mountains that is poisoning the water supply. Anyone who drinks the water...dies without medicine."

Eos clenched his jaw and ground his teeth together. He remembered Tessio slaying Major Clark, Ares holding Maxima hostage, their clash over the glyphs on Earth, Sergius Ora attempting to kill them, the attack on Maxima at Fanum Ortus, and the ambush by Rohl Ford. Then, he thought of the suffering people of the valley that lived in the sprawl of shacks he had walked through. They were the reason that Caldus was raiding royal supply deliveries for clean drinking water.

"Let's stop them," Eos resolved.

Maxima shook her head and rolled her eyes. "This isn't Earth, Eos. The Mitad is everywhere here. Their numbers, their wielders, their influence...it's nothing like on Earth. Caldus told me that there are multiple mirzas involved. That's like stopping a dozen of Ares. We could barely stop him together on Earth."

"We're stronger now."

DANCE WITH DAGGERS

"This is different!" Maxima sighed, exasperated. "And now, we'll have to explain to Scavok why we weren't there when he gets back."

Eos shrugged.

They pushed the water delivery to the edge of town without the assistance of Soul Energy to be more covert. Caldus' associate took the cart, and the job was done.

In the dusk, Caldus led them through a makeshift hospital, ran by his friend who received the barrels of drinking water. It was a junction of shacks that had been joined. The ill and dying lay curled on sleeping mats. Their bodies were dehydrated husks of human beings. The siblings walked through lives, grasping in pain, but resigned to die. Shallow moans stirred the air, and the waste-sweat hybrid scent stalled anyone who entered the room for the first time.

"Is there any way to save them?" Maxima asked, trying to breathe shallowly to evade the odor.

Caldus' eyes were glassed over. There was some kind of deep jaded sorrow turned to rage that boiled beneath his distant look. He said softly, "There is medicine. A bit trickles in from the capital, but the Mitad have more. Much more. But it's out of reach. They will all die. We can only provide some comfort in the meantime."

Eos shook at the scene of death. Hot anger was building. "Where? Where is the medicine? I've dealt with the Mitad before."

Caldus liked the way Eos had asked it. It was the sound of someone who had lost someone close. There was a numb, single-minded readiness to change things. It meant conviction. "Meet me here in two days. I'll take you to the factories where they keep it."

CHAPTER TWENTY-TWO

Maxima nodded her head in agreement. "Two days then. Come on, Eos. We have to get back before Scavok sends people looking for us. Tomorrow Jezca will be here to finish what we started."

Eos froze, reliving the memory swap.

"Jezca Monte is coming? Here?" Caldus asked.

"Yes. She has business with Eos and our father."

Caldus' head bounced as his eyes darted in thought. He hummed pensively, "Good. Bring her too. I have something to show you all. Bigger than the factories...*much bigger.*"

CHAPTER TWENTY-THREE

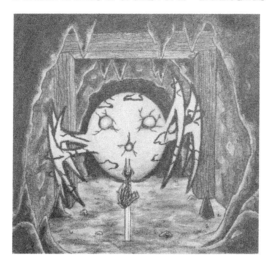

TUNNEL VISION

The rose-pink stone eye of Priestess Jezca flashed with white light. Eos sat across from her in the third level of the Mircite dwellings they stayed in to avoid attention. The brilliance of the eye mesmerized Eos. He looked longingly at her features: the platinum hair, the noble pointed chin, the powerful yet gentle demeanor she carried. Yet, all this could not mesmerize him enough to overcome the dread when he noticed her beginning to wield her Soul Energy. It was an almost psychic type of wielding—Eos knew that she could manifest the power inside of his brain from a distance if she chose to. Though he didn't have the deep understanding of the master wielders, he knew this ability was something that an inlume would be in awe of.

Eos flinched. He tried to delay the event. "Priestess…"

"Please, call me Jezca."

CHAPTER TWENTY-THREE

"Oh. Yes. Well, Priestess…" Eos said but caught the annoyed glance of Jezca. "I'm not sure that I want to repeat what happened last time."

"Do I have to ask again that you call me Jezca?" She leaned in and said lowly, "I think we know each other too well for those formalities now."

Eos swallowed nervously.

Archpriest Mellitus stood next to Scavok Alter and watched with brooding hawkish eyes. "At least the boy has the propriety to know your place in society. Now, remember it for yourself and proceed, Lady Jezca," he said.

Jezca said soothingly, "Don't worry. I won't perform that technique on you ever again. I just need one more look inside. It'll be less intrusive, and I won't do it without your permission."

Eos agreed.

Her fingers touched his temples. They were strangely calming. Warm like the heat coming off of a campfire that pushed away the chill of night. A pink fog of Soul Energy came from her fingertips. Then Eos was faced with the memories once more. Not his own. But hers.

Minutes later, they stood on a balcony overlooking the valley of shacks. Talus was not present for this encounter with the Priestess, and Eos had asked to learn about her findings in private.

"The curse is ancient. It is like a fragment of another person that resides inside you, waiting for the chance to take control. The seal that your mentor, Aizo, created holds it at bay, but it waits for the chance to seize control of your mind."

Eos acknowledged the findings with a hum. This much he had assumed from his encounters.

TUNNEL VISION

"What scares me is the similarity it had to someone else that I saw recently. My sight was able to read more from him because he didn't have his mark sealed. In an unsealed state, the curse is available for the user to leverage for increased power. One could draw from the source for more ability—"

Eos thought of the Mellizo Glyphs. "This source, is it Saida?"

Jezca shook her head, her hair dancing to reveal the animus eye momentarily. "It's something that he is only the mediator for. I can't tell who or what the source is, but the one who gave it to you is only the transmitter. I couldn't speak to it, so to say, but I could understand some of its intent. It's like a parasite that will offer you power in return for a chance to consume your free will. It wants your mind."

Leaning over the railing, Eos looked off distractedly at the bustle of the mining town below. He allowed the movement to distract him enough not to panic. *Ramath. That was the other person she saw. He had taken the mark as well.* The revelation shocked him more than he expected.

"There is more. I sensed that it is also waiting for your death. Like a harvest. I can't say what it will do or wants, but that is the intent I could interpret." After a pause that was only filled by stone-frogs croaking and Mircite bustling below, Jezca said, "That's everything I could see."

"Well, not everything," Eos said.

"The memory exchange?"

"Yeah. That."

"I don't know what to tell you. It is a phenomenon that even I had not experienced before. I'd never pushed that far into someone's consciousness. There was a rebound...and now we know each other. There is nothing to hide."

CHAPTER TWENTY-THREE

Eos shuddered. "I know your hopes and dreams. I felt your fears and anxieties. All that without ever asking you what they were."

"And I know yours. We are bonded now in a way no one else would understand."

Eos touched the scar under his eye with a weary hand.

"Your life, Jezca...it has been difficult."

"Just like yours. We're the same in that way. We walked different paths from what a childhood should be. Yours was fleeing your homeland. Mine fleeing an assassin clan. We were forced to grow into adults immediately."

"I saw what you could do. What you did do so that you could escape Necogen," Eos said as he recalled the images of slain guards in fallen snow. He moved his hand on the railing of the balcony until it brushed against hers. They touched for a second before they both recoiled awkwardly.

She smiled sadly at him. "We're the same in many ways. We're survivors. It was no different than what you did to the soldier to save Axel Kane."

Eos tensed up at the memory. He decided to change the subject. "Someone Maxima and I met recently knows you. He wants to show us what's happening at the factories that is poisoning the water. It is my intent, and his, that we destroy them and free the people of Mircite from their water crisis. Then, there is something else he wants to show us. *Something bigger than the factories.*"

Jezca brushed the hair from in front of her eye so that nothing was hidden.

"So, you know my brother?"

"You-your brother?"

TUNNEL VISION

Jezca smiled with a sadness weighing on her lips.

$$\infty \qquad \infty \qquad \infty$$

"I can't be gone long. Archpriest Mellitus will be looking for me," Jezca said with a short breath as she followed Caldus alongside Eos and Maxima.

Caldus scoffed. "Finding you a few minutes late or a few hours late will make no difference. Besides, it's right over this peak. After that, you will see what the Mitad is working on *inside the mountain*."

Maxima added, "Scavok will be looking for us too. He's Father's master of assassins, so he'll be tracking us."

"This is too important. Now look out there." Caldus pointed as they stood atop the ridge that overlooked the Sepeleo river. The morning light crept between rocks and over crests, bleeding over the river in a golden blanket. The gray stone and raging water reflected it over natural beauty, but three structures cast long shadows below. They were unnatural, out of place, and from the looks of it...Earth-like.

"What are those?" Eos asked, shaken by the juxtaposition of manufacturing plants in Hyperborean nature.

"The only way to find out is to get inside. We've watched them move crates in and out of the north two. We think they're some kind of small metal cylinders. Nothing seems to come out of the south factory, but I know one thing for sure. The waste streaming out of the sides of those buildings is what poisons the water supply," Caldus said.

Eos observed the gushes of black-green sludge that poured into the river. He thought of all the bodies lying in wait for death to greet them...to take them from their agony. It was an agony that

∞ 363 ∞

CHAPTER TWENTY-THREE

punished them for the crime of trying to quench their thirst. He seethed with his vessels pulsing as he declared, "We need to destroy them. Whatever they're doing in there is guaranteed to be worse than the poison that they're dumping out. So it's better that they collapse before anyone finds out what the Mitad is working on!"

"Agreed. I have a plan, and we'll execute it in just a few days," Caldus said.

"Whoa! Slow down, Caldus," Jezca interjected. "You narrowly escaped one mirza because of your bounty. What makes you think that you can take on one of their strongholds?"

Maxima joined in the caution, "Perhaps we can take our time and determine the best strategy for stopping the pollution without having to fight high ranking members of the Mitad."

Caldus glowered. He stood before his sister. "People are dying every day. There is no time to slow down. The Red Corcinths raided the explosives yesterday. Eos and Maxima are powerful Soul Wielders. The time is now, and you don't have a say. You're either in or out—and before you say anything else, I want you to see this." He led them back into the mountain.

∞ ∞ ∞

Borne Ozen parted black hair from in front of his pale eye sockets to pull up binoculars. He gestured to the southeast, down a pass that led to Aritrea. "Down that pass," he slurred the words madly, "is-is-is where Saida will lead the troops. We'll arm them, and then they'll cross the river to complete their mission."

Zolo was annoyed as he looked through his brass binoculars at the gloom of early morning. The sun was just beginning to peek

TUNNEL VISION

into the river valley. "I still haven't heard exactly what that mission is."

Ozen revealed his sharp canines and said, "Their mission is Anite."

The word meant little more than *war* to Zolo. Anite could have been anywhere and anyone, but it meant that he was working closer than he would have liked to an invasion attempt. "Is our work part of that?"

"No. No. No. Unnecessary. Our work has a longer-term vision. Now, when Saida visits this-this-this morning, we must be ready with the presentation of our improvements in-in-in production." Ozen moved for the roof access door back into the building.

Zolo remained outside, scanning the mountains as he did many mornings. It had been the only comfort recently. The beauty of the snow-tipped peaks gave him peace as the work became more and more suspect to his morality. The problem—that aspect he loved. Working with soul energy materials and designing improvements to the factory process...that was fun. Borne Ozen was a genius to study under. However, the secrecy around their work and the prisoner they had locked away gave him nightmares. Durath Leorix was a shell of a human being after being trapped inside high quantities of the soul-negate. From his research, one-tenth of the material would have incapacitated the warrior son of Ramath. The amount that surrounded him now, he calculated, was zombifying his mind and will.

He moved the lenses across the river to the breaking first light of the east side of the river. The golden saturated peaks of blue-gray in a dazzling display.

Wait.

CHAPTER TWENTY-THREE

There!

Someone—no! One. Two. Three. Four.

Four people gathered on the east side peaks. Zolo squinted through the binoculars.

He saw a raven-haired young woman that he recognized.

"No..." he exhaled. The binoculars dropped in disbelief.

Could it be? Were Eos and Maxima here in the Mircite Valley? And who is with them?

"Zolo, are you coming. You-you-you dropped your binoculars. What's gotten into you this morning?" Ozen asked from inside the open door.

An hour later, Saida strutted around the factory methodically with Ares lingering behind him. He ran his hand through his hair and curled his lips. "You told me that we progressed well, so I better see results, Ozen."

The mirza researcher bowed low before Saida. "Yes, my lord. We have made great strides with Zolo's contributions. He-he-he has sped up our timeline a great deal."

Saida raised an eyebrow at Zolo. "Is that so?" His mustache wriggled as he sniffed the burnt electric smell that permeated the entire place. "It sure smells in here."

Zolo lowered his head, taking after Ozen's lead. "We were able to increase the efficiency of the production process by thirty percent and doubled purity of the metus stone at the same time. We've produced enough to manufacture another cage already."

Saida's face expressed an immense pleasure at the news as his smile twisted and his eyes crinkled. "For a young man such as yourself to accomplish this monumental feat, under the guidance of our esteemed Borne Ozen, of course," he added to not sleight the mirza, "is unheard of. You are gifted, Zolo. You manifested

TUNNEL VISION

your wielding ability at such a late age. You solve complex problems of science and Soul Energy..." He shook his head and stroked his chin. "It certainly wasn't your plain Earthling mother that gave you those genetics. No, I think not. Tell me, who was your father?"

Zolo hesitated. A heavy cloud seemed to hang on him as he thought about his next words. They were soft, wounded words. "Sir, I barely remember my name before Lord Vistomus renamed me Zolo. It is a passing memory that I was once called Jace. I knew my mother for only the early years of my life. My father...I never knew him."

"Well, Zolo. Jace. Whatever you prefer here on Hyperborea. Vistomus was sure sentimental when he gave you that name." Saida snickered at an amusement that only he understood about his fellow Mitad leader. "I suspect I will be giving you more responsibility soon, should you choose to accept it."

Zolo thought carefully and decided to take a risk. "Such an honor would please me, sir. However, in a role like that, I would bring up my concerns about our work to you."

"Oh, you have concerns now?"

"I do. The waste that we dump into the river...I have heard and seen of the sickness it causes in Mircite. We don't have to cause such suffering. We could dispose of it—"

Saida interrupted with a scoff and rolled his eyes. "Not this. Moving the toxins would be a drain on our resources. Plus, it has the added benefit of keeping the little Mircite pests too thirsty to get nosy. They're begging for their next drink instead of poking around in our work." He threw his head back and sighed, "Clearly, you spent too much time with Ares. His soft-heartedness rubbed off on you. I need you both to harden up if you want to be part of

CHAPTER TWENTY-THREE

the Mitad operations. Ares knows better. You get a pass for now. I'll hear no more of this heart bleeding nonsense."

With a sinking stomach, Zolo nodded. "Yes, sir." Inside, he grew angry. Just as Vistomus Fulmen had begun to operate with faltering morals, Saida seemed to magnify the same Mitad problem. It seemed only Ares was worthy of trust.

Saida marched before the machinery like a warlord. "In just a few days, our army will be coming here to carry munitions across the river. Then, they will make their way to Anite. We will topple our strongest enemy and advance our campaign." He turned to Ares. "You did well in negotiating with Salvaluc in Tenebrim. You redeemed yourself in convincing an inlume to betray his fellow inlume, Talus."

Ares did not show the slightest expression. "I made him aware of his choices. I made him choose his Order or his people. He was more than happy to pick."

"How uncharacteristic of Salvaluc. My old master is a fanatic that never budges, but I'll accept his submission gladly. Now, do you still want to meet *him*?"

Ares' pupils dilated. His lips quivered, but he maintained no emotion. "I have not changed my decision."

"So, you'll kill her then? You can sever that part of you and become what was always intended?"

"I will. When we discover her location, I will end her life."

Saida shared his news in a booming, boisterous voice, "You're in luck! The Bellators are in Mircite, according to my spies in the Monte kingdom. You'll have your chance to kill your past sooner than you thought. When you destroy Maxima, you'll get what you wanted."

TUNNEL VISION

Zolo's stomach churned. He had taken care of Maxima when Ares rescued her from Braxton on Earth. He had stood in front of a gun for her as a child. He had stolen the Mellizo Glyph from Vistomus Fulmen to aid in her safe return to her brother. And now…his eyes had not played tricks on him. Eos and Maxima were in the valley.

Does Saida know they were overlooking the factories at this very moment? Had Ares given in to hatred to such a degree? Or was it power-lust?

Zolo locked stares with his master.

Ares said through clenched teeth, "The opportunity couldn't come soon enough." Then he left the room.

There was a coldness in the air that made Zolo shiver. Suddenly he felt like the fleck of metus stone that Ozen held with gloves was much too close to him. It was draining all positive thoughts from him. He grabbed the horrible shard with his bare skin and squeezed it until it cut into his palm as he exited the factory.

The hell of the soul-negate nearly broke his will by the time he found Ares on the river bank.

Ares' looked ragged while he contemplated deeply over the *hurr* of the foaming water. His wavy locks of dark hair blew against his face as his amethyst eyes fixated on the far shore.

"You're going to kill your own sister?" Zolo snarled while holding his shortened little finger.

Ares nodded without speaking for a while.

Zolo seized Ares' hand and put the shard of metus stone into it.

The action snapped Ares out of his stupor.

He tossed the source of agony into the water.

CHAPTER TWENTY-THREE

"There is someone that I need to meet with. This path is the only way to get to him. You are my apprentice, Zolo...loyal as your finger has proven...so I will explain some of my plans to you. If you have the ears to listen."

∞　　∞　　∞

The tunnel that bore through the heart of the Sepeleo mountains was on a scale that Eos hadn't imagined. As they approached the incredible structure, held by support beams made of timber three feet thick, they saw only by a few light-stones activated along the way and the glow of Soul Spheres.

Eos sensed immediately upon his approach that there was something inside the cave-tunnel. It was alive but not conscious. It was many but of one mind. Above all, it was deep inside. What he sensed—Jezca sensed a hundred times over.

The Priestess halted and fell behind Caldus, Eos, and Maxima as they approached the opening of the hole in the heart of the mountain.

"Wait," Jezca said.

"Scared already?" Caldus joked.

"We all should be," Eos reinforced Jezca's warning.

Jezca closed her eyelids as if focusing. Her forehead wrinkled. "There's a force of Soul Energy inside. When I try to focus on it, the thing senses me...like a giant eye...or hundreds of eyes."

"Don't worry. They won't come unless they're called. The Red Corcinth's faced a swarm of the creatures already. They're made of Soul Energy and can explode on contact, but they stay sleeping unless called by a Mitad member."

TUNNEL VISION

Eos searched internally for direction. He knew. "We have to see what's inside and where the tunnel leads."

"No," both women chimed in harmony.

Eos knew how Jezca's ability worked. He had a hunch, but she could confirm it. So he asked, "Jezca, can you see the sources of the Soul Energy in the tunnel?"

She nodded.

"How far in do they go?"

"As far as I can see. Into the heart of the mountain...and beyond. I'd need to travel inside, to be precise."

Eos walked forward, slowly but steadily. He wanted to stay far away from the ghostly Soul Energy that emanated from deep inside, but he needed to be sure.

Maxima followed immediately and chastised her brother, "Scavok will be furious that we snuck out again. This is dangerous. We should report it to Father and leave it at that."

"I can't do that. I need to know what the Mitad is doing before it's too late. I can sense...that this tunnel has a specific purpose that...well, let's just see how far it goes. You're coming with me, right?"

Maxima sighed reluctantly. "I can't let you go in alone, having just gone unconscious recently."

Caldus chased after them. "Hey, I'm supposed to be leading this venture."

Jezca followed at a distance.

They walked for what seemed hours. Their steps were swallowed by the immensity of the cave—echoes that were forgotten forever in the stone walls. The light of their Soul Spheres created a shadow version of the group, framed behind pink and

CHAPTER TWENTY-THREE

sapphire and crimson. The colors blended into a colorful procession.

Step after step, they moved cautiously further into the body of the cave.

As they continued, Eos could sense the hostile, watching Soul Energy retreating before them.

It evaded their path, but just barely.

Then, their aura ceased moving and began building.

Eos halted. "Can you sense—"

"Yes. They're not running anymore," Jezca confirmed fearfully. "Oh no. They're moving towards us."

The four panicked and began backpedaling.

Eos asked before the overwhelming sense to flee seized him, "How far? Can you tell how far?"

Jezca pursed her lips and said shakily, "All the way. Or nearly. Far enough to be completed at any time. They just need to puncture the last length of rock. And then…"

"And then what?" Maxima asked knowingly.

"The tunnel breaks through to Anite," Eos finished. "They're making a tunnel that could move an army."

Rumble. Krattle-scree. Rumble.

The Soul Energy moved, not far away. It shook the tunnel with its monstrous size.

"I thought you said they didn't act unless provoked?" Jezca yelled as they shuffled out of the tunnel faster.

"They don't. They didn't. They haven't before." Caldus stuttered. The magnitude of the threat fell on him. This was bigger than what he and Alia had escaped from. Almost something different entirely.

The first glow became visible in the distance.

TUNNEL VISION

Then another.

Then one hundred.

The tunnel pulsed like an artery with a clog moving through it. It was impossible to count the crawlers as their arachnid-like legs scrambled over each other. They were a hive-minded network of Soul Energy moving like a wave towards the four intruders.

"Throw something at them, now!" Cladus screamed as he fled and pulled an amgrite stone from his pack. He charged it with Soul Energy while running and hurled it desperately behind him. The explosion was significant, and the static screech of the crawlers echoed around them as the first few in the wave became part of the blast.

Eos and Maxima sent Soul Spheres into the crawlers.

Jezca waved her hand, creating slashes of pink light that manifested at the head of the mass.

The creatures screamed in anger, rattled in a furious chase, and echoed with the static electric hiss of their existence. It wasn't clear if their attacks were increasing the distance between them and the monsters. Every assault required concentration and the slowing to turn and direct it.

The crawlers lurched over each other in a ten-foot-tall wave now.

Each explosion only destroyed the first few before the mob rolled over and consumed the fallen crawlers.

Then the electric popping and snapping sound grew louder. The sound of limbs dampened.

The four slowed to look at what was happening.

The crawlers bubbled as if exploding into a molten blast but instead melted into one another. Limbs spread into limbs, eyes sunk into bodies, and the gray light of the many morphed into one.

CHAPTER TWENTY-THREE

Finally, the huge crawler opened its smooth, blank eyes, each the size of a human being. It screeched in a way that brought a rain of rubble down from the ceiling.

Caldus threw an animus stone into the giant crawler.

The thing swallowed it into its body. The explosion was muffled. A few bubbles rippled from its skin...then it slowly moved its six legs and crawled forward.

Caldus' head sunk low. He knew what he had to do. "I brought you all here. So, I'll do this. Get out!"

"No," Jezca said. "We all chose freely to come—"

"Sister! I love you. Now, all of you need to go." Caldus set down his bag and opened it quickly. Amgrite stones filled it. He touched the pile of dozens of stones with his hands, and light spread blindingly into the cave.

Eos realized that while Caldus could only wield with what he could touch, his abilities were as profound as his sisters. The entire bag was ready to explode in a few seconds.

Lurch! The giant crawler scurried forward in a blinding movement and swatted the bag into the far side wall with its front leg. The amgrite stones shattered harmlessly. Caldus fell to his back.

A spiked leg lifted over him, ready to pierce his body.

Caldus was helpless.

The point leg of gray energy pierced down.

Boom.

A crimson Soul Sphere struck and gave the giant crawler a moment of pause as Eos dove in and pulled Caldus away. Then, on his feet again, Caldus ran back.

An angry growl came from behind them, "I'll handle this monstrosity. You four disobedient death-seekers get out of here." A silver mane and ponytail came from the shadows. The scarred

TUNNEL VISION

face of Scavok Alter showed no emotions at the situation. Instead, he pulled his short sword, *Safisay*, from his back-sheathe. It was made of high-quality anima stone and had a hilt like a wing, etched with layers of feathers.

Scavok Alter thrust the blade into the dirt floor as the creature barged toward him.

He clapped his hands together as if in prayer and then placed them on his sword's hilt.

"Go!" Scavok cried. A lattice network of ice-blue Soul Energy spread across the tunnel just as the giant crawler reached him. It threw itself into the Soul Energy wall.

It was a mesmerizing net, like a blanket of ice crystals, but Eos had no time to admire it. All four of them sprinted from their savior as commanded. They didn't stop until they reached daylight, their lungs ready to burst, and their feet blistered.

Jezca was not the first to recover her breath but was the first to speak. "Wasn't that enough for you, Caldus? Do you really think you can take on the creator of that creature and multiple other mirzas?"

Caldus was stunned. His pride was wounded, like when his sister had slapped him in the Necogen temple as children. Yet, his determination was intact. Alia and Philo's death would be memorialized by bringing change to the Mircite valley.

"I don't have to. *We* only have to destroy the factories and get away."

CHAPTER TWENTY-FOUR

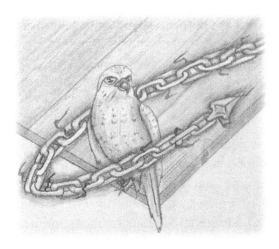

FIRST BOND : FINAL PRAYER

The border between Corleo and Monte territories was almost entirely mountains, but the flatland sliver that passed between the two was made of abandoned mines and small supply villages for travelers. The geography made the foothills on the east border of Corleo one of the most isolated locations in Corland. Talus watched from his perch as Ramath Leorix slowed his Soul Step to a halt and waited at his private meeting spot amidst the gray skyline and pines.

After waiting for half an hour, Ramath began to pace impatiently. He scratched at his forearms and rubbed his tired, baggy eyes.

"She's not coming," said a deep, familiar voice.

Ramath whipped around and saw what had to be a strung-out figment of his imagination—before him stood Talus Bellator

FIRST BOND : FINAL PRAYER

adorned in light battle clothes. Silver and gold accented metal came up around his neck, and the auburn braids of his instantly recognizable beard fell over his upper chest.

"You can't be here…am I…" Ramath wondered aloud.

Talus shook his head. "If you had been more forthcoming and truthful, Ramath, then I wouldn't have to be here like this. I'm the last friend you have on Corland. All others have given up hope that you are still an ally."

"Then, Riselda?" Ramath asked single-mindedly.

"Ah, yes. Scavok intercepted Riselda Beltra before she crossed the border. She was quite closed-lipped. It took some convincing to betray your meeting location," Talus said with a solemn face.

"You interrogated Astor Bruinsma's third in command? That's bold, Talus. Too bold. He'll make trouble for you."

"Perhaps," Talus said with a shrug. "I think not. We worked out a deal. I understand you meet her here for information as much as your monthly *fix*."

Ramath rolled his eyes. "So, she's not coming?"

"She's not coming," Talus confirmed.

Ramath's gray and black shoulder-length hair shook as he threw his head back and sighed with over-emphasized exaggeration. "You don't understand what I'm going through, Talus. If you did, the least you could do is leave me my drugs."

"Well, Brother, you'll have to make do until your next meeting."

"There isn't another meeting!"

"No?" Talus asked, confused.

"If you came for a fight, I'm too tired for that," Ramath said, gripping his face in stress at the thought of the withdrawals that would come if he didn't find another source to replace Riselda's delivery.

"I came for truth. So, let's talk. One message in the past year! *One!*" Talus growled. "And you tell me you've taken the mark, but not to worry? Then you avoid me when I come into the Winter Aisle."

"It's always about you, isn't it, Talus? Difficult for you, but me? It's been *really* easy. I've been walking on paths of gold here with Voro running around my kingdom, Saida breathing down my neck, as I'm sure you're aware, and I'm supposed to play both sides with perfect delicacy."

"And are you playing both sides perfectly?"

"NO! I'm losing my mind. Jaco Hetfel is looking for any opportunity to kill me. I have *an army* moving through my kingdom right now. *An enemy army, Talus!* Do you know what that's like? My counsel is ready to overthrow me. And my son is missing! Please tell me Riselda at least shared her intel with you?"

Talus was silent for a while. He spoke solemnly. "Saida took your son hostage. Durath is being held at the factory on the river."

"And what, besides an entire pride of corcinths, could hold my son hostage?" Ramath said with heavy breathing.

"I'm just as concerned as you are about the answer to that question, and I will help you get him back. Now, what have you done? Tell me about the curse mark and the Mitad's plans. They're already moving through Tenebrim for an attack on Anite."

Ramath's bearded mouth hung open. He swore under his breath. "Well. That…that's news to me. You're going to have a lot to deal with. I recommend you go home to your wife and prepare for that offensive. I will handle things down here."

FIRST BOND : FINAL PRAYER

"Are you handling them, Ramath? It sure seems like they're handling you."

"I'm tired, Talus. So incredibly tired," he said with slow pronunciation. "I ask for your trust in my darkest hour. I know what I am doing."

"I can't do that. You haven't earned that. I can't keep my children from investigating the factories themselves, let alone abandon this entire risky venture to your drug-addled plans."

"Eos and Maxima?" Ramath asked, suddenly excited. "They're alive?"

"Yes, they returned home to me. If you read my letters, you'd know that."

"All letters are shot down by my men in the north range well before they get near Corleo. The Mitad would read them first otherwise. By the stones, that great news, Talus. I prayed to the manus gods that they would come back to you one day." A strange look crossed his face. "Wait. Why did you bring them here? You shouldn't have done that."

"My son has taken the same mark that is on your neck. I needed to consult Priestess Jezca for her powers of sight," Talus revealed.

"Noooot good. That's not good. This mark is meant to consume the wearer. Someone's running the show for Saida and Fulmen. I don't know who, but it is *his mark*. And *he* plans to use the ones he chooses to bear this mark, whether alive or dead. Alive, you become like one of the Voro—a puppet. Dead...I don't want to think about it."

"Can you explain?"

"That's it. If I knew more, I'd tell you. All I can say is that you need to get that curse mark off of Eos at all costs. Now, I have to

CHAPTER TWENTY-FOUR

go, but if you don't trust me, then you can watch me honor the Bellators tomorrow. Watch the factories from a distance. I'm going to lead the tail end of an invasion force. It's going to look bad. But you have to let me act according to my plan. The Mitad is weakest at the moment they believe they are strongest."

"Let you lead an invasion force through the mountain? Are you mad?"

Ramath walked to Talus and bowed his head before him. "Yes. I'm mad but loyal. I'm still the brother who pulled you out of the emerald pools when we were young."

"You still have the Bellator branding?"

Ramath walked past Talus. "I asked for it and never had it altered. Now, I have to be back for a meeting with Saida soon, or they'll suspect me." He moved away from Talus. "You really could have left me Riselda's delivery. A man needs a bit of comfort in dark times."

"A bird on your back and a snake at your throat. Which one controls you?" Talus said just loud enough for Ramath to hear. "Will you choose the path of traitor or the path of a brother?"

Talus produced a sack from under his armor. He chucked it with anger at Ramath.

Selfish, reckless, foolish younger brother.

"Take them, you rock-head."

Ramath turned, flustered by the soft strike to the head. Then he saw what had fallen before him, and a pleased smile crossed his face for the first time that day. He grunted with a sad yet pleased tone, picked up the bag, and departed from Talus.

It was not long after when Ramath felt a call to turn back. Talus was gone; that much he could sense. This urge was ancestral. Primal. He drifted, unaware of where his feet were taking him. Up the foothills, he wandered with a vibrating tribal call pulsing in his chest that only he could hear.

The world around him shifted. It felt physical but unreal somehow.

The sensation was like a magnified version of what he felt during the coronation ceremony when he lit the horns in the foundation room. Then, with a sharp inhale, his eyes met the source of the call, and he knew why he was so irresistibly drawn.

A corcinth stood above him on a nearby cliff. Its legs were the height of the Corleo King, and its horns were a thick as a man's waist. There was a scarred patch of fur missing from its dull blue mane. This wound ran across much of its muscular gray torso. The majestic creature had been gravely wounded.

With a swish of its tale—it vanished.

Ramath's heart pounded. That was the king of a corcinth pride. It was a Crypt Keeper, a beast that legends said was more spirit than physical being. Never had he seen such a large corcinth.

Then it was before him in a swift movement. It appeared like a weightless boulder, hovering peacefully but threatening to crush everything below it.

The King of Corleo fell to a knee instinctually.

"Great spirit of my ancestors. Shabah alsalf tanwa albi," he recited a prayer that his mother would mumble when searching for answers. *Enlighten my heart.*

The corcinth let out a low rumble and flicked its tail calmly.

Bravely, resisting every awestruck urge to cower in fear, Ramath stood and made eye contact.

The noble animal bowed its head, signaling him to approach.

It was the urge that drew him, for his mind could not engage. He touched the mane of the corcinth king and spoke to it. The

CHAPTER TWENTY-FOUR

words were only in his mind, but they traveled between kings. He told of his troubles in resisting the Mitad in the ways he could, but now…now he was cornered. They had his son. *They had Talus' son, though I did not know it. The curse mark is upon him.* The corcinth communicated back with a shallow rhythm of Soul Energy from its horns. Ramath sensed its pain. He saw images of its pride defending the mountains from an impossible onslaught of the Overseer's crawlers.

"Please," he croaked as if dying. "I can't stand the thought of what I have to do. I will be gone soon, but if you can somehow…carry this message. I can't resist the curse, but maybe he can. Maybe he can save my son too."

It was a prayer of desperation to a wild mountain spirit…no to the spirit of his ancestors too.

A final prayer.

The coarse blue mane felt warm in his hand. It was the most life he had felt since the day his son was born. There was a flash of blinding light…like the entire vision had been a mirage that left only the pulsing white silhouette of horns in his eyelids.

Ramath was alone again.

∞　　　∞　　　∞

A flutter of white feathers was surrounded by the pale glow of Ares' Soul Chain. The energy moved around the perched bird as if deciding whether to constrict or dissipate.

"What does it say?" Bellia prompted.

Ares had a scroll laid out on the table. He read it by low lighting as he kept the white bird of his father's nation surrounded on the table.

FIRST BOND : FINAL PRAYER

"It appears Salvaluc has sent word to my mother that I went to Tenebrim."

Bellia let out a small gasp. "Did he give up the plans?"

"I can only imagine that he did, but he didn't implicate me…or at least my mother made no mention of it. She wrote about the matter of Grace Lapithos' journal. This is a twist that I had never expected from Terrava."

The gray light of his Soul Energy cast shadows about the room as the bird fluttered its wings anxiously. Feathered shapes danced on the wall, casting images similar to his father's crest over his room. He didn't like that.

"What would Terrava want with Grace's journal? We lost her so many years ago, but it seems like everyone is chasing her ghost."

Ares agreed with a nod. "You knew her better than I did."

"I traveled with her, but we only shared a few words."

Ares was pensive. "When I was a child, my mother would allow me a respite from my life of hiding. She would take me to her vacation house on the coast where I could be free for a few days a year." He paused for a long time. "She wants to meet me there."

"Will you meet her?"

The chains wove in a stalking pattern around the elsu. Each second, the implication of their contracting around the bird grew, but then the moment would breathe, and the chains would continue to circle for a bit longer.

"I've written her a response that agrees to meet her. However, if I am to continue down this path with the Mitad, I should burn this letter and tighten my chains."

Bellia came around the desk and put her arm on Ares. She said soothingly, "I'm here by your side no matter what." She took his hand in hers and placed it on her growing belly where new life was

CHAPTER TWENTY-FOUR

forming. "Perhaps there more to think about than only your path with the Mitad."

Contract.

Loosen.

Contract.

Loosen.

The chains wavered between outcomes.

"Bellia, it's time I tell you why we've been training the way we have recently. You're going to have to use it very soon, I believe."

∞   ∞   ∞

The warmth of the sun, the croak of stone-frogs, and the lilac scented air were the best relief Eos had felt since he had left on this journey to the Winter Aisle. It was only a subtle dash of peace after everything that had happened recently. Jezca, Caldus, and the Bellator siblings walked on the ridge above the Mircite shacks, leaving the dirty dwellings in the distance.

Scavok and Talus had chastised them for over an hour on the risks of what they did. The giant crawler was still alive, Scavok had said, and Talus seemed to have new information that worried him. He wouldn't share what it was, but they could tell that it distracted him from the full anger he could have directed at their recklessness. Still, after losing the Mellizo Glyph, Eos didn't know how much more he could disappoint his father, but he seemed to be finding new lows.

Maxima thought aloud, "Father agreed that the factories needed to be taken out. He seemed to know more about them than he let on."

"That's why we have to do it," Eos said with certainty.

FIRST BOND : FINAL PRAYER

"But he also said we were not to get near them no matter what," Maxima reminded him.

Caldus interjected, "The Red Corinths are prepared to move now. They await my orders to place the amgrite explosives next week. We can be done with the whole event in an evening and get out before we're ever discovered."

Maxima turned to Jezca and asked, "What do you say? We'll need you on our side, and you're my logical balance to these two impulsive boys."

Jezca hid behind the hair that covered her gemstone eye. "I prayed last night for hours, asking for direction. After contemplation, I believe that…taking down the factories would be serving the manus gods best. It is my duty."

There was a reluctant smile on Maxima's face. She did not want to disobey their father or run headlong into danger, but the matter seemed decided.

"Then, one week," Caldus declared.

They continued their walk until they left the Mircite Valley behind.

Eos felt a nagging pull on his back like his consciousness was warning him that the storm was approaching. Things were about to change in a way that he could never turn back.

What is this? We're just going to take down the factories…aren't we?

It was getting late when they decided to turn back. Dinner would be served soon, and they could not be missing for one minute without Scavok hunting them down.

The sound of a fifth pair of footsteps grinding the mountain gravel came alongside them.

CHAPTER TWENTY-FOUR

They turned at the noise. Maxima was the first to see—golden brown hair and green eyes. It was a familiar face, but one she had never expected to see on Hyperborea.

The sweet mountain air hung in stillness with the silence of the encounter, accented by the slightly sour note that they knew came from the factories not far away. The newcomer stood before them awkwardly, working out what to say.

"I saw you...by chance. When you were investigating the factories by the river, I had to follow you...and see you again. One more time. If you hadn't caused such a commotion in the mines, I wouldn't have ever found you, though."

"Jace? How are you here?" Maxima asked in disbelief.

Zolo smiled at his real name. No one ever spoke it except his long-ago foster siblings—nearly erased from memory. "Don't worry how I got here. I came to warn you—"

Maxima hugged Jace. He blushed.

"Who is this sneaking and tailing us?" Caldus demanded.

Parting from Maxima's embrace, slightly embarrassed, Jace introduced himself, "My name was Jace to them when we were living together as kids. Now, I'm known as Zolo. I came to warn you that a Mitad army has been marching through the mountain by night. It isn't large, but most of them have already traveled inside the tunnel you followed yesterday. It would be safest if you left Mircite just in case. I don't know what their plans are, but you should be far away from them. Saida knows you are in the valley..." he paused cautiously, "and, Maxima, he wants you dead."

Maxima was without words.

Eos suddenly understood the reason for his dread.

Caldus stood in front of Maxima and interrogated him. "And just how do you know all this?"

FIRST BOND : FINAL PRAYER

"Because I am," Jace began as he undid his tunic to expose his chest and ribs. The Mitad's two-headed serpent was inked over his heart. "I am part of the Mitad by circumstances beyond my control."

Caldus went for his daggers, but Jezca stopped him. "Brother, he is close to Eos and Maxima. Let's not be hasty. He just told us their plans."

Jace ignored Caldus and moved to Maxima. "I wanted to see you again. One more time. To say goodbye."

"Goodbye?" Eos asked.

"The rear guard is picking up the remaining ammunition manufactured in the factories...they move tomorrow night. They're carrying firearms from Earth for their attack. The rest of the attack force is already deep in the mines."

"Jace..." Maxima's voice trailed off. She could read in his expressions that he didn't intend to see them again.

"Eos. Maxima. I'd like to speak with you in private." Jace motioned to Caldus and Jezca casually.

Jezca took Caldus' arm. He was staring down Jace threateningly, but he followed his sister's lead and left the Bellators and Jace alone.

Their foster brother reached under his tunic and produced a small bottle.

"I stole this from master Ares, but I don't think he'll miss it." He smiled nostalgically as he held it up. "You remember? I was so excited to have a brother and sister."

Eos nodded. "We all shared the wine we found in your mom's basement."

Maxima's eyes winced with a mixture of happiness and longing at the memory. She said lowly, "What was it we said?"

CHAPTER TWENTY-FOUR

Jace recalled the three of them as children, sitting around the bottle inside the mostly fallen walls of an abandoned cottage near his mother, Lori's, house. They sat in the shadows and recited as the words that he spoke again now above the Mircite Valley, "After we drink together, you'll be my brother and sister. The three of us…need to become strong, and someday we'll go on adventures together."

There was a moment where it felt like electricity swam in the wind.

Jace took a drink and passed the bottle to Eos.

Eos drank, passed the bottle to Maxima, and said, "Well, we got an adventure. That's what we wanted, right? We got stronger."

Jace laughed dryly. "You know, I never met my dad, but my mom used to say that he *would glow like an orange sunrise* when it seemed like no one was looking at him. She would tell me how he could fix anything and was the strongest man she had ever met. I wanted to be like that. Now, I learned that I can wield Soul Energy like you can," Eos and Maxima's mouths opened in surprise, "and I need to learn why."

"You could escape and come with us as you search," Maxima implored him.

Shaking his head, Jace admitted, "I have to follow my own path. It's with the Mitad right now. With Ares."

"No!" Eos said instinctively.

"He's not all bad, you know? Misguided, but I think he wants to be better. Someone needs to keep an eye on him," Jace said with a shy shrug. "Oh, there's one more thing I have to tell you. The factories are making something else—not just bullets. The Mitad is making something that can cancel out Soul Energy. It's bad, like dying inside but being forced to live eternally. Stay away from the factories. *Please leave the valley.*"

Eos responded, "We got stronger for a reason. It wasn't to let them poison the river that poor miners use for drinking, or to manufacture weapons to attack our homeland, or create anti-Soul Energy."

Jace smirked uncontrollably. "You always were stubborn, Eos. I came and said what I wanted. I've warned you, but the choice is yours. I can't stop you." He stretched out his fist in front of his chest as they had after drinking the wine as kids. "You know...I think the alcohol tasted better when we were kids."

Eos and Maxima reenacted their childhood bonding ceremony and touched their fists to Jace's. The stone-frogs sang their throaty song of dusk like the voice of the mountain, but now it seemed to be screaming out a warning.

CHAPTER TWENTY-FIVE

RIVER BATTLE PANIC

The acrid smell of the metus stone manufacturing plant curled Durath Loerix's nose. Saida had allowed him to keep his maroon-dyed fur cape and regal attire when he had thrown him in the metus cage. Now he was led up the factory stair case like a zombified husk of a man. His battle-scarred chest was exposed between his unbuttoned vest as he slumped against the wall.

"Move your weak little legs up the stairs, or I will wield you like a puppet to the roof," Saida bellowed.

With a rebellious scowl, Durath said weakly, "Then do it and save me the trouble."

Saida gave a half-laugh. "No. I think you could use the exercise after all that time in the cage, but I will give you some incentive."

RIVER BATTLE PANIC

He snapped his fingers, and a string of violet energy prodded Durath from behind. The zap of Soul Energy singed his fur cape.

"Watch the clothes. I did a lot to earn this cape from my father."

"Then move faster, or I'll give it a few more holes. Besides, we're going to see your father."

Durath's eyes lit up from their glazed detachment.

"Don't worry. I wanted you to see Ramath as he betrayed his nation and his best friend. Your father is about to lead the final deployment of soldiers in an attack on Anite."

The glaze returned over Durath's eyes, and he resumed marching in front of his captor.

Saida smirked, "Good. We'll get you back in your cage, and you'll have a front-row seat at the downfall of the once honorable king, Ramath Leorix."

$$\infty \qquad \infty \qquad \infty$$

The sound of running water created a noise cover, giving Maxima the inner peace she desperately needed. It stifled her urge to panic. She recalled the note she had left for Scavok Alter, warning that they had gone to take down the Mitad's factories. By the time he read it, they would be nearly finished with their mission. It would be too late for him or Talus to intervene. They hadn't wanted to accelerate their schedule to such a rushed plan, but Jace's warning had left them no choice.

Caldus distributed bags between Jezca, Eos, Maxima, and five masked members of the Red Corcinths. They huddled behind a pass in the Sepeleo mountains just out of view of the three factories that sat on the river.

CHAPTER TWENTY-FIVE

"Everyone gets one bag. There are ten special amgrites in each. These are the most volatile kind of stones mined. Once set off with Soul Energy, they will take down the factories multiple times over. Wait for the signal from Eos. Remember, Red Corcinths will take the far factory. Talker, Jezca, and Maxima will take the middle. Eos and I will hit the south one." He breathed in and out deeply, trying to calm himself. "There are going to be mirza in there, so stay quiet, stay low, and be quick. A small army is coming, so we don't have much time."

They moved quietly, mostly behind cover, but the final stretch to the factories required them to cross through open space. Maxima watched as Eos and Caldus remained behind at the south factory and the Red Corcinths moved ahead to the furthest north. She and Jezca began placing the special amgrite stones around the base of the building. They moved in opposite directions to circle the building as fast as possible. Her heart was beating nervously, and her hands were struggling to grip the stones as her palms sweated.

Maxima peaked around the front of the factory and saw crates stacked to her chest height in rows. *That must be the ammunition.* She had two of her ten stones remaining.

Jezca circled back around. "That's it for me. Are you ready?"

Maxima contemplated. "No, I need to make sure those crates go down too." She dashed from behind the building to the first aisle of stacked ammunition and fell to the ground to avoid being seen. She rummaged quickly for the two remaining stones and placed them.

Booom. Krattle-scree. Krattle-scree. Boom.

Maxima froze. Shew knew those sounds from the cave.

RIVER BATTLE PANIC

Jezca turned to the source of the noise—the north building. A bald man with a chin beard stood behind her. He stood in a wide stance with his hand reaching over a silver-taloned staff.

From behind the crates, Maxima saw a fearsome sight. She remembered falling rocks and the finding of Benedir's body. Rohl Ford towered over Jezca.

A few screams could be heard from the source of the explosions.

"Sounds like the Overseer has done his work. I don't expect he left any survivors. Now, I've heard about you, Girl. You're the priestess, yes?"

Jezca's training took over. *The icebox. The whippings. The repeated drills that went for hours on end. She was a Necogen assassin as much as a priestess.* Her feet shifted into a fighting stance, and her hands glowed with a pink haze.

Maxima's heart beat even harder so that she could hear it in her eardrums as she hid behind the crates, her mind churning to determine the best option. She could intervene, but she saw how powerful Rohl Ford was. He had defeated Benedir and taken away his body before they could climb over fallen rocks. If she didn't act soon, Jezca would be dead.

A voice came from the end of the aisle of ammunition. It was mischievous and familiar. "Why must we meet on such tenuous circumstances, *dear Sister?*"

Her brother stood across from her with amethyst eyes sparkling in the evening light.

"Ares," Maxima said with surprise.

Eos and Caldus heard the sound of crawlers attacking in the distance.

Caldus cursed. "The Overseer is here. We have to go—"

CHAPTER TWENTY-FIVE

"Go?" came a gruff voice. Caldus saw large sideburns protruding from under a black hat with golden sabers on it. "I turned ya into the Monte's once and got my reward. I don't think they'll be paying a second time, so yer not going anywhere," Yann Kilsig said and drew one of his sabers.

"Eos!" Caldus yelled in panic. "This is the guy that killed Alia."

"We have bigger problems!" Eos backed into Caldus.

Caldus looked over his shoulder.

Saida stared them down with eyebrows raised in amusement. "I'd say you boys are beyond bigger problems. You walked right into the corcinth's den with no understanding of how sharp a corcinth's horns really are."

∞ ∞ ∞

There was a silver mist that hung in the air over the plains on the southeast border of Anite. The foot of the Tenebrim canyons was veiled from view, where they spilled into the land of elsu.

Aizo grumbled in his inlume battle armor: light chainmail wove around his chest that looked like silk. The links were thin, forged with veins of liquified anima stone. It would defend no sword or arrow but could amplify the speed at which he initiated Solido. A golden elsu spanned its wings from shoulder to shoulder on his grey armor. He sighed, "With a fog this heavy, I'd say the Great Soul wants to see us struggle."

Hariban Brasidas nodded in agreement as he watched the edge of the mist with unbreakable focus. "There are only three spillways large enough for an attacking force to move through. The Kyrja units have arrows aimed at all three."

RIVER BATTLE PANIC

Hariban Sulla strode up to Aizo, wearing the heavy armor of a knight prepared to do battle against manus weapons. His winged shoulder pads curled up, his helmet had a fierce beak, and his feet were covered in the form of metal talons. "Gondul and Skult have taken the head of this spillway with units following behind them. They will march after the archers lose their ranged advantage. The other members of the Vangar will do similarly at the other two points."

The bleak sky created a cloud of dread over the battlefield, and the scent of coming rain put everyone on edge.

"We will crush them," Sulla reassured.

Aizo dulled the confidence. "Don't be so sure. There will be Emir Grimshaw and his mirza. The rabble will be dealt with easily enough, but we know little of their leaders' wielding abilities."

"There!" Brasidas cried out.

At the border of the fog, a black-cloaked figure broke through. His skin was pale, his face sharp-featured and gaunt, and his hair was shaven on the sides and braided with red strands on the top. He stared at Aizo from a great distance. They could not see each other's eyes, but they could sense the other's Soul Energy. Both released a heavy aura of their power to warn the other.

Emir Grimshaw is no weakling. He could rival any inlume.

"Do we fire on him?" Brasidas asked.

"If it would do any good, he wouldn't be standing there," Aizo murmured. "Wait until we see the rear of their forces exit the canyon.

Grimshaw held his arm up to the sky.

Maroon energy rippled through the fog.

A partial dome began to form over the spillway.

CHAPTER TWENTY-FIVE

Aizo swore aloud. "He's putting up a barrier over their exit of the canyon. Tell the Kryja to focus everything they have on breaking it. The Vangar and swordsman will have to take care of everything else."

"If that's the case, I'll have our wielders pincer them from the sides the moment the shield breaks," Sulla decided.

What are they playing at? They came through the most obvious path with an invasion force that couldn't win.

∞   ∞   ∞

A slight rumble echoed in the Sepeleo mountain river pass. From atop the factory, Durath's heart sank. The distant marching attack force was too far away to discern clearly, but he could sense the immense presence of his father and the Overseer leading the last thousand troops to carry the ammunition into the tunnel through the Sepeleo mountains and into Anite.

His sensing abilities were like an out-of-tune instrument within the metus cage, but in glimpses of clarity, all doubt was erased. Tears weren't for a king's son. Durath's eyes held back from spilling tears as he whispered weakly, "Father…why? You loved Talus like a brother. You loved your kingdom more than your family. Yet, you let the Mitad infiltrate it." *Why?* The question rang out in his head as the only anchor to reality while the cage drained him of his senses. Below he could hear the out-of-focus sound of Saida confronting someone.

Saida stroked his mustache with his index finger as he contorted his right hand like orchestrating a puppet. Mauve strings of light left each finger and pinned Eos' limbs to the wall. Eos writhed and struggled to lift any portion of himself away. "You

RIVER BATTLE PANIC

boys made a big mistake—starting a fight way beyond your abilities. This isn't the same as getting lucky on Earth against your rage-induced half-brother and a few underlings while Vistomus was away on business. You're playing in the big leagues now, and if you miscalculate—you die."

Yann Kilsig sent a teasing blast from his saber. The gold beam of light seared Caldus' ear but missed purposefully.

Caldus let out a yelp of surprise but then allowed his fury to take over. "I'm happy to die right here if it means that I get to avenge, Alia."

"Stupid Boy, there is no avenging. There is no victory for ya. Defeat was inevitable the moment ya stepped foot here," Yann laughed.

The taunt was enough to incite Caldus into a head-on attack. He drove Amon's daggers into Yann, who brought his blade up to meet them casually. The animus blades glowed a fiery red in the last minute of the attack. For a brief second, the skull hilts stared at Yann with hollow eye sockets.

The attack broke his guard and drove him back. The slashing wave of energy took him by surprise and opened up his brass button jacket with a streak of blood.

Saida chided with amusement, "Watch yourself, Yann. The boy is a fool and without skill, but he's still Grace's son, and he is using two of the most powerful blades ever crafted. Speaking of, those are worth a fortune. Make sure you take them after he's dead."

Caldus' mind spun. *How did they know Mom's name?*

Eos manifested a crimson glow, but the moment he did, Saida tightened the strings around his wrists and snuffed out the attempt.

Saida closed the distance to Eos. "You're coming with me."

"You wish," Eos snarled.

CHAPTER TWENTY-FIVE

"Oh, I don't think you have much say in the matter. You're going to watch the final march that will cripple your father's territory. Then, we're going to have a chat about that sealed curse."

Eos couldn't so much as budge his restraints. The aura emitted from Saida was unlike anything he had ever felt. At such a close range to the man's strings of energy, it was as if he was wearing a lead vest. Everything was heavy, and the air was thick, making it hard to breathe.

Walking on platforms of Soul Energy, Saida headed straight for the roof. He dragged Eos with him, scraping his body against the rough wall in a show of excessive dominance. Up Eos went, helplessly watching as Yann Kilsig battled with Caldus. It appeared that Yann was not going to underestimate the boy a second time.

Yann drove Caldus back. Golden streams of light shot from his saber in rapid succession. They tore at Caldus' arms and legs as he tried to dance in a careful evasive maneuver. His quick footwork saved him from mortal wounds, but his body was being sliced, and Yann was keeping him well out of range to counter effectively.

With a curling of his fingers, Saida placed Eos on the roof. Before him were two cages. The right one was empty, while the left held a young man of a similar age to Eos. His hair was a deep brown mane that flowed into his maroon fur cape. Eos noticed that he had a pattern of vertical scars across his torso, but what should have been the disposition of an intimidating man was closer to a withering corpse.

Eos was floated towards the open second cage, forced to his knees by the strings of Soul Energy, and then slid into it. Helpless, his eyes caught the dull gray sheen of the other prisoner's eyes. He was impotent and broken mentally. Eos soon felt why.

RIVER BATTLE PANIC

Inside the metal bars, he felt the cold hand of spiritual death ease over him. It was not sharp or harsh but a slow drift into emptiness. Eos thought of what Jace had told them. This must be it. *The Mitad is making something that can cancel out Soul Energy.* He attempted to produce any hint of Soul Energy, but none would come. It was like drawing from a dry well.

The son of Talus Bellator watched as an army of Mitad soldiers crossed the river bridge made from Borne Ozen's energy.

A portion of the group broke off to load carts with the ammunition.

Eos watched with a sunken, detached vision.

"What's your name," Eos asked in a low voice.

"Durath," the other prisoner said tiredly. "Durath Leorix. King's Son of Ramath Leorix."

Eos nodded with understanding as he drooped against the bars that caged him.

The sound of Soul Energy being wielded in battle was all around him. He touched the scar under his eye and wondered about his sister. *She must be protected. But how? I can't get out of here.* He kicked the bars but found they didn't budge.

"There's no use. Can't physically break the metal. Can't wield inside either," Durath said with an exasperation that communicated his many attempts to do the same thing.

"My sister is down there. I have to get to her."

Durath shrugged.

With no other hope, Eos attempted making a Soul Sphere.

Again.

And Again.

All attempts were in vain.

CHAPTER TWENTY-FIVE

Then suddenly, his Soul Energy moved erratically in his core! He felt a disruption in his body, like he was going to vomit, and his skin tingled. Whatever prevented him from wielding was causing a reaction, and he began to be pulled out of consciousness. All he could think of…was his sister.

Maxima went to block Ares' chain with her sapphire energy, but it came at her too fast. The links swung, wrapping around her forearm, burning her skin.

Ares whipped his end of the pale chain. The glow moved in a wave that launched Maxima back, away from the ammunition stacks. She slid on her back across the rocks, and they tore into her skin.

Maxima stood, burned and bloodied, but unshaken. Her half-brother had taken her by surprise, but she had trained under her inlume mother since they last encountered each other. His advantage was played. Now skill would persist.

She split two Soul Spheres as Ares ran towards the river to direct the fight away from the stacks of crates. One sapphire light chased down her half-brother. It ruptured into a wave of blue harmlessly behind him but kept him running.

Ares spun and flicked his chain whip at her. It streamed out of his sleeve and pierced the air with a speed she could barely react to. Before it closed in on her, she cast her other sphere out and deflected the chain.

The smell of ionized air and burnt metal met Maxima's nostrils as the energies clashed. It was the smell of a wielding battle, and static charge clung to the atmosphere.

The glowing chain rerouted and lurched at her again.

RIVER BATTLE PANIC

She rolled to the ground to avoid it and sprang up with two more Soul Spheres. The practice with her mother had made the action effortless.

Solido protected Ares from a direct attack.

Bwoom!

He stepped through the remaining vapor of the blast, summoned his chain again, and swung it in circles casually as he approached.

"Why?" Maxima asked from under the blue light of her hand. "You had your motivations for the Mellizo Glyphs before, but you didn't want to kill me." She analyzed his movements as he turned her towards the river with his stalking advance.

"That was then. The conditions are different, Sister. You are interfering with a plan that has particular meaning to me." He tensed as if about to unleash an attack.

"Which is?"

"The fall of dearest Father's empire."

Maxima wrinkled her nose and huffed in anger. "Eos was right about you! I wanted to give you a chance since you're my brother, but—"

"Then you were foolish. If the attack tonight succeeds, Talus loses everything."

"Why is that so important to you? What did he do that could require this kind of hatred?"

Ares laughed dryly. "I made a promise to myself when I was a child…while I was locked in my room in Alasedis. I was kept like a beast that the royal family feared. An outcast! But Saida showed me another way while I was very young. I swore that Talus would one day respect me or *fear me!*"

CHAPTER TWENTY-FIVE

"All of this...this...violence and suffering is to make him acknowledge you?" Maxima asked in disbelief.

Ares was silent for a moment, thinking pensively with his chain *whooshing* as it cut the air. He thought of his own child inside of Bellia.

I'm going to be a father.

He snarled, "The only thing I want more than that, I have been promised...in exchange for your head."

The pale Soul Chain shot at Maxima!

As she calculated when to release her sphere to counter the attack, she caught the movements of Mitad members loading crates onto carts in her periphery. She also saw the flurried movements from Jezca's fight at the edge of her focus.

"I can see why you're so revered amongst wielders. Manifesting your soul so far away from your body is something only the Order's inlumes and our emir can dream of. You're gifted," Rohl Ford gave credit to Jezca. "I think we've seen enough. I have orders not to kill you, and I'd like to obey them. So, what do you say we sit this battle out, little lady?"

Jezca eyed the bald mirza furiously. She twisted her neck, cracking it loudly. "Well, that is going to make it hard for you to stay alive."

"That's not very priestly of you, Girl."

"My creed is to aid the poor and weak. The manus gods would be pleased with your blood, I believe," Jezca said sharply.

She did no more than blink and gestured her finger forward slightly. Rose-pink light appeared on Rohl's chest. The stripes of energy crackled and brimmed with charge as they clawed into his chest.

RIVER BATTLE PANIC

Rohl put up a defensive layer over himself, but it was too late to absorb the entirety of it. Three slashes, like an animal had mauled his chest, bled through his black jacket. "Hurramit! I will kill you if I have to, Jezca. The priesthood has sway, but their alliance only buys them so much."

Jezca brought forth another attack.

Rohl managed to cover himself this time. He came through the popping and snapping of energies clashing and swung his staff at the ground. Energy flushed from the bottom of his staff as it struck the rocks. A shockwave spread through the land and kicked up a wave of stones that flew at Jezca.

The Priestess covered her face. It was all she could do as the heavy debris struck her, pelting her ribs, bruising her forearms, and cutting her legs.

"Ah, no defensive techniques whatsoever. See, this isn't a fight you can win. Now settle down and—"

Jezca gave his right rib cage four more stripes as she grunted in pain.

"You little b—"

He silenced himself in time to protect his throat from being torn open by another series of Jezca's assassin techniques.

Rohl howled in pain and frustration. "What kind of priestess knows how to go for the kill like that? You are one psychotic little girl."

"The kind that was raised in Necogen but escaped."

His brown eyes froze, and his pupils dilated. *Necogen. This is more dangerous than I thought.* Rohl realized the girl fully intended to kill him if he did not deal with her.

The Mirza thrust his staff out and sent a concussion of Soul Energy her way.

CHAPTER TWENTY-FIVE

Talus and Scavok were met with the site of a battle from high above the river and factories. Many battles. It seemed the entire valley was lit with Soul Energy. Their finely tuned senses could make out many players of immense skill in the fighting below.

"Saida," Talus barked.

"And Ares, it seems," Scavok added as he chased Talus down the mountain on a stream of Soul Energy.

They descended in a blur of speed towards the marching Mitad unit as it crossed the bridge.

The Overseer, Jaco Hetfel, glided forward at the head of the group with a dozen ghostly crawlers trailing behind him. The seven-foot-tall man's helmet gazed over the mountain with a single slit too narrow to see from. Scavok had learned from reconnaissance that the Voro leader did not see at all. Instead, the blind wielder had some network of creatures that allowed him to sense the world.

Talus honed in on Ramath walking alongside the Overseer. He moved with the aura of a broken man. His face was gaunt, his anxiety was apparent in every sullen step, but he still carried his three-pronged royal scepter with animus stone held in the center.

Ramath and the Overseer stopped after crossing the bridge at the sight of two men Soul Stepping at them with urgency.

"Scavok, we have to be quick. I may leave them to you, depending on how this goes. The kids are in trouble," Talus said as he sprinted.

The master assassin agreed, "Do as you must. I can't take them both on, but I can delay them perhaps."

Talus and Scavok landed before the Mitad march.

The sound of clashing Soul Energies hummed through the mountains and mixed with the static growl of the raging river.

RIVER BATTLE PANIC

"Talus, I warned you, my old brother. You've defied my advice, and you can't be permitted to walk away from this," Ramath said.

"You know that I don't intend to. Only one of us may leave."

"I know," Ramath answered with a head bowed in internal conflict.

The Overseer's southern kingdom drawl interjected, "We will unseat Anite from power, but we didn't expect to be gifted the King, his hariban assassin, the King's Son, and King's Daughter before we even made our attack. You make it too easy, Talus Bellator."

Scavok's silver ponytail whipped in the wind as he said, "No. You will find nothing easy about what's to come."

From behind the draping pieces of metal that covered the albino face, the Overseer declared, "Then, let's find out if that's true. We'll let old friends settle their duel while we determine how long you can delay our passage into the mountain."

CHAPTER TWENTY-SIX

SHADOW RISING

Talus closed his eyes and breathed in the air, full of regret shared between him and Ramath. As he exhaled, taming his brimming Soul Energy, an array of crimson feathers was summoned around him. They shimmered like a curtain of jewels.

"I can't let you go any further," he told Ramath with the conviction willing to end his dear friend. "I trusted you for so many years as you slipped into their grasp. Now you lead the final march against my kingdom?"

Ramath stamped his scepter near his foot. The animus stone lit up as a spiral of deep green energy circled the staff and took form above the three prongs.

"I have to make this look good, Talus. It's nothing personal."

"No. I imagine it couldn't be any more personal."

SHADOW RISING

"I told you to leave it to me and not come here."

"You knew I couldn't do that."

Ramath nodded slowly. "I knew. I broke our trust beyond that point."

Talus' voice cracked, "Is it because of Durath?"

"It's because I know how to do what is required. I'm not as soft-hearted as you. That was always your weakness." When Ramath finished the words, the green vapor crackled and morphed into a set of corcinth horns.

The green and crimson faced off for a moment of suspended potential violence as emotions frothed to the surface in both men.

Pop!

The horns burst forth with bottled-up tension and rushed at Talus, leaving a stream of tinted air in their wake.

The feathers around Talus rotated as if magnetized towards the horns and flew to meet them.

The energies met in the no-man's-land between the two. The rupture of their clash rippled out and knocked many of the Mitad soldiers off their feet behind Ramath. Talus slid back in a braced stance from the recoil.

A few of the trailing feathers avoided the explosion by altering course above the battle and then redirecting at Ramath. They dove down, locking in on the Corleo King. In return, he sent coiled spirals of energy from his scepter that precisely shot down each of Talus' crimson attacks.

The interplay of red and green sprayed about like fireworks that could kill either man, and yet both held something back to prevent any finality to their carefully calculated game.

Ramath considered aloud, "We've played this out many times in our youth."

CHAPTER TWENTY-SIX

The Bellator King agreed, "Yes, and I'd love to see whose skill has grown more since those days, but I must get to my children."

"Aye. I believe that would be wise," Ramath said.

Nearly one hundred feathers appeared.

The shimmering green stardust, in the form of a corcinth, condensed above the staff in response.

Scavok became distracted by the eruption of hundreds of Talus' feathered projectiles. He knew the battle was wearing on Talus emotionally. That attack must have drained a great deal of willpower to attempt a takedown of his brother gone astray. The moment of distraction was unprofessional for a master assassin.

Half a dozen crawlers sprang on him. Their rattling limbs propelling them into the air above. Scavok swung his short sword, Safisay, just in time to cast out a net of ice-blue lattices. They enveloped the overhead attackers and detonated them harmlessly overhead. It was a move that saved him, but they had been a distraction. A lone crawler had taken to the ground and was nearly on him.

It detonated itself early.

The round body contorted like a spontaneous bubbling of cancerous growths until it exploded half a second later.

Scavok raised his Solido, but couldn't absorb the entire attack in time. Blood ran down his arm in a warm trickle. A portion of his neck was burned, but the old gray fox shrugged it off with trained concentration. He needed to unsettle the Overseer.

"You and Saida are two of a kind, aren't you?"

The Overseer cackled as crawlers streamed from his sleeves, ran down his limbs, and grew to full size around him. "Perhaps we are."

SHADOW RISING

Scavok continued as he prepared his Soul Energy for the next move, clearing his internal gates in preparation for partial Severance. He taunted, "Few have betrayed an inlume and fallen from the Order. But you took it to another level. Only you fell so far."

"By killing my master?"

Scavok grunted angrily.

Fifty crawlers swarmed around the Overseer now. He was ready.

So was Scavok, who thrust his blade into the ground.

The Overseer took the distraction and said, "Kairus had served his purpose. The old Visrex knew he was beyond his prime. He taught me to see again. For that, I'm eternally grateful. However, he also taught me to see the hypocrisy of the Order of Soul Wielders. In that way…Saida and I are the same."

"So, you heartlessly murdered the man who saved you?"

"Kairus taught me that principles must be paramount. My eyes don't work for vision, but they still function for tears. It was not an easy choice to kill my hero, but it had to be done."

Scavok snarled, "I'm going to try to enjoy killing you more than you can enjoy fighting me."

"You may try." The Overseer raised a hand in command and sent the wave of crawlers out.

A wall of icy energy crystalized and spread out from the short sword.

Krattle-scree. KRATTLE-scree. KRATTLE-SCREE!

The monstrosities approached.

They slammed into the net of energy that Scavok had formed. The things hurdled over each other to throw themselves into the barrier. As they did, spikes of energy like icicles leaped from the

CHAPTER TWENTY-SIX

wall and pierced the creatures made of Soul Energy. Each detonated one after another atop the hoard.

Scavok advanced and pushed the net forward as he moved.

The Overseer could see that his crawlers were not enough on their own to overwhelm Anite's master assassin. More flowed from his sleeves and circled his feet.

Scavok closed in.

Over one hundred crawlers fought to stand atop the pile before the Overseer.

Then they lost form. The individual legs morphed into the mass.

The eye indentions became indiscernible, a few at a time.

The giant crawler was forming.

It loomed over Scavok, taller than ten men, as the barrier approached. This time, it was bigger than what he had faced in the cave. There was more room for it to move out in the open too.

This fight will not be the same.

Scavok prepared for the clash. Off to the north, he could make out the form of a corcinth head made of green energy enveloping Ramath and Talus.

The Anite King seemed to hold the immense pressure of Ramath's energy at bay with crimson wings that sprouted over him. The two men were indiscernible, but Scavok watched their silhouettes.

Ramath leaned into Talus' ear.

The energies dissipated.

Talus sprinted on planes of energy towards the factories, and Ramath resumed his march, leading the Mitad towards the tunnel. There was nothing Scavok could do. His attention had to be entirely on the Overseer, or he would be crushed. He knew Visrex Kairus' killer outmatched him.

Inside the metus cage, Eos' body was motionless. There was the stillness of death.

Durath peered between bars and called to him, "Hey, kid. Tattoo hand. You okay? I think you pushed yourself too hard." He waited for a response, but none came.

Saida laughed and said, "Fool of a boy. He better learn to use what I gave him."

The laugh echoed quietly between the sounds of battle. Where Eos was, the sound was subtle. It reverberated in his muddled state of mind. The chilling sounds of the Mitad leader shook off of blue-gray mountains that weren't real rock structures—not real in the physical sense, at least.

Eos stood and shook off a groggy feeling. He knew where he was. The slight tingle at the back of his brain told him something was off about this version of the Sepeleo mountains. A notion played with his mind: time was not operating correctly. It was like this in training with Aizo. The mirror in Fanum Ortus had been the same. So too was the reaction to Jezca's probing in the temple. This was his Soul Void.

As he wandered the void, he wondered why he had been pulled in this time. Previously it had been for training or a reaction to stimulus. The soul-canceling that Jace had warned about must have triggered this trip.

He didn't have time for this. Maxima was in danger, and he needed to figure out how to get out of the cage...and get past Saida. The hopelessness of the situation settled on him.

First, get out of the Soul Void. Then get out of the cage. Then get everyone I can out of the river valley.

CHAPTER TWENTY-SIX

Things had turned so quickly for the worse.

Eos walked into the shadow of something huge. The temperature changed under the darkness—more than he thought a shadow could cause. He looked up.

Before him was a corcinth, and not just any corcinth. He could sense by the stature of the blue-maned beast that this was a leader amongst the others. Yet, like everything else in the void, he felt that it was not real in any physical way. That didn't prevent cold fear from locking Eos in place as he watched the spirit-beast approach with a casually swinging tail.

There was a sense of being in the presence of royalty but more than that. He was before royalty amongst higher beings—a spirit guide. It forced him to fall to a knee and bow out of instinct.

The corcinth's horns glowed.

Eos' eyes locked on the sight.

A sphere of light formed between the spikes of the horns.

Eos shook but sensed that he wasn't supposed to back away.

There was a crackle like the sky was being torn apart.

The sphere pulsed. Then it shot out in a beam and struck Eos in the forehead.

Unable to breathe, he prepared for the worst.

Can I die in the Soul Void?

No pain came. He only felt a warmth spread over his body. Something was being imparted on him, like a gift of guidance. Images of Maxima's notebook, routes of vein-like energy pathways, and the curse mark on his arm all filled his head. He couldn't comprehend it with his logic, but somehow…he understood…something that he couldn't put into words.

The corcinth let out a mighty roar as the beam dissipated. Then, it was gone. It left Eos as quickly as it had appeared. He reflected on what had happened but couldn't find any thoughts that would solidify. Notions came to him in incomplete bits. He should keep his gates perfectly purified, or else the curse would have an opportunity to seize him. Maxima's invented techniques from her notebook were important.

The ideas were poorly formed, clinging to his subconscious.

"So, you return to me, crownless and unworthy as before."

Eos whipped around to find the masked figure in a black cloak before him.

"I haven't…had…t-t-time," Eos tried to explain.

"You've had all the time you needed to lose the Mellizo Glyph. You've had all the time you needed to destroy thousands of years of customs and culture in the temple when you lost control. All the time you needed to allow all your friends and loved ones to face certain death at the Mitad factories."

Eos shook his head in denial. "I've met you many times now. Who are you?"

"I am you. The side of your soul that you keep repressed. I am your alternate path, your potential, the king lying in wait to take the throne."

Eos snarled in annoyance at the cryptic riddle. "Not much of a name."

"You may call me Zala Alsar if you wish. You may call yourself that as well."

"Okay, Zala. Why are you here?"

Zala's cloak rippled at his feet as he walked up to Eos. "Better to ask that of yourself. You are here before me because you lack the killer instinct. You're in danger, and so is everything you hold dear, but you lack the conviction to do something about it."

CHAPTER TWENTY-SIX

"What would you know about my conviction? I'll do anything to stop the situation out there."

"Anything?" Zala asked with interest.

Eos answered with a fierce glowering gaze.

Zala's eyes smiled from behind the white mask. "Then use your curse. Give in to it and allow your murderous instinct to take control. It is the only way. Last time you didn't have conviction, and we were interrupted by the memory swap with the Priestess."

The situation was laid plainly before him. If he didn't learn to use the curse mark now, he would not be able to fight Saida or aid Maxima in her battle against Ares.

"Will it help me break the cage?"

"No, you already have what you need to do that."

Eos didn't understand but said, "I accept. I will do what it takes to defeat Saida." He reached out his hand.

The blackened hand was slapped away.

Zala cackled. "You misunderstand. I've allowed you to put us in danger too many times. When the body wakes…I will wake in it and take control."

"I can't allow that," Eos growled.

"Then you better prove yourself to be the Master. Show me you are worthy of leading."

Eos brought forth a crimson elsu.

Zala mirrored him with an ink-black bird.

A moment of shock passed over Eos as he wondered, "That's…my technique. How…?"

"I told you. It is very simple. I am just a part that you choose to repress."

"Then I'll just have to defeat you and keep you repressed."

A sneer came from behind the mask, "You don't get it."

SHADOW RISING

Eos cast his elsu forward. Its wings streaked across the Soul Void.

"Good, Eos. Show me your instinct to kill," Zala cried out as he sent his elsu at Eos.

There was no clash. Eos' energy was ripped in two—split by the shadow version of itself. It struck him squarely in the chest, sending him flying into the mountain wall. The excess energy rolled off of him and pulverized the mountain.

Slabs of stone fell around him.

Heaving and bloody, Eos leaned against a pile of rubble.

"Eos, you're trying to keep me locked inside, but it is *you* who are the imitation. You're weak, and your time as master is over," Zala said and appeared in front of him.

Another crimson elsu came to life in defense.

Zala plunged his hand into the creature.

Red gave way to black. The waves of the curse mark poisoned the elsu and consumed its color.

It turned on Eos.

"You're really going to face me without a weapon to fight back with?" Zala teased. "You lack the required murderous intent."

The shadow elsu dove into Eos' abdomen, piercing him all the way through.

Blood dribbled from his lips.

The ink-like energy remained on both sides of his body.

Above the river, Talus charged at the rooftop with two cages on it. He could sense a faint trace of Eos' Soul Energy. However, it was faint, and Durath was on the building as well. As he reached the cages, a line of mauve-colored strings made of Soul Energy blocked his path.

Talus had no time to react and charged directly into them.

CHAPTER TWENTY-SIX

They burnt his skin and shocked his senses. His vision went white from the immense power of the technique. He was sent tumbling towards the river, only catching himself in the final seconds before meeting the water.

Saida descended on him as the purple strings of Soul Energy faded.

"Talus, old friend, you're looking a tad frantic. Why don't we slow down and have a talk?"

The two men stood on platforms of Soul Energy above the river.

"The time for talk is years behind us."

Saida sighed, stroking his dark hair and casting out his pointed fingers in preparation. He smirked. "Can't you humor my banter, old man?"

"If you call off your mirza and let my children go, I'll humor you all you want."

Saida made a tsking sound and clicked his tongue. "No can do, oh great Visrex." He contorted his fingers as strings shot out with electric crackling from all five fingers.

Purple clashed with crimson as the attack struck a curtain of feathers.

Light zoomed before the two men, clashing, recoiling, and buzzing.

Feathers shot out to deflect lines of Saida's attack.

Strings cut across the air to slice attacking feathers.

The two master wielders sparred in an expert array of skills.

The burning metallic smell of the struggling Soul Energies tinged the air.

SHADOW RISING

Talus knew he couldn't continue the battle without showing more of his hand against the Mitad leader. So, he reached within and summoned an even greater technique.

The feathers shimmered out of existence, and a set of massive red wings sprouted from Talus' back. The energy's wingspan reached thirty feet across and made the air sizzle around it.

The Soul Wings beat and closed in around Saida.

The Mitad leader was forced to clench both hands in a contortion. Ten strings shot out and braced against the wings.

Zmmm. Vmmm.

The energies hummed magnetically. They repelled each other, but the sensation that they would explode violently was increasing with each moment.

Talus' wings squeezed inward. The strings shrank as Saida struggled against the Bellator King.

"Don't forget," Saida warned with a diabolical smile.

One line of mauve light abandoned the defense and pierced backward.

Talus' attention followed the distraction as Saida had expected. The attack bolted towards the cages on the roof. The right wing faltered, split, and a myriad of feathers broke off of it to chase the attack on Eos.

It was an excessive response—more than required, but Talus would not risk harm befalling his children.

The gust of red light swarmed in front of the cage and reflected the attempted attack on Eos' motionless body.

Talus had done it. He had successfully protected Eos, but his defense was malformed now.

The strings tugged on it like collapsing a puppet down into a heap.

CHAPTER TWENTY-SIX

In the instant that it gave way, the tenth string of light reappeared.

It came like a razor wire and ripped into Talus' right shoulder.

The sensation was a paradox—the heat was so intense that it felt like painful ice melting down his arm. It cleaved through him.

The limb came off and plunged into the river.

No blood came. The wound was seared closed immediately.

"Poor Talus. Wounded, losing, and it appears as if preventing one child from being attacked wasn't enough…" Saida said and gestured to the middle factory.

Maxima sprinted on planes of sapphire energy up to the roof, fleeing her half-brother's pursuit.

Sweat drenched her as panic set in. Ares seemed intent on ending her life. He had not landed an attack but was wearing her down and toying with her.

She tumbled onto the top of the factory. Out of the corner of her eye, she saw another person. It was a feminine figure, hooded and behind the brick structure that led to the roof from inside. As Maxima rolled to her feet, she caught the familiar blonde hair and amethyst eyes: *Bellia.*

There was no time for wondering why the female Mitad member was also here.

Maxima turned to see Ares closing down on her.

The Soul Chain swung threateningly. Beads of energy dripped from the pale weapon.

Instantly, a Soul Sphere came to being in Maxima's hand. It split into two, like a cell replicating and dividing. Her physical limit from the battle so far was weighing. She had run too hard, dove too many times, thrown too many spheres. There was only one option—she had to put everything into this last attack.

SHADOW RISING

Ares moved towards her and said, "Maxima, you look tired. Why don't you take a rest up here with me?" His chain hovered before him and then tilted to point at her.

Maxima's back heel shifted to distance herself but it met the edge of the building. She was trapped.

It has to be now.

The two blue orbs floated before her as her hands separated from them.

Then, the replication began.

Her eyes were focused, and her breathing steadied as she cleared her mind of distractions in the material world.

Two became four.

Four became eight.

Sapphire lights stretched and pulled away from themselves until they snapped into two weapons.

Ares cursed his luck. "You and Eos are always pulling new tricks out against me."

Eight became sixteen. She felt the drain on her reservoir—the internal pathways felt thin and overdrawn. She looked across the gap between factories and saw Eos, caged and unmoving. No one would save her from this. No one needed to. She would open Eos' prison as soon as she had dealt with Ares.

The ghostly white chain struck out at Maxima. It collided with the Soul Spheres, causing small explosions over the river that required the chain to regenerate constantly.

The spheres moved at Maxima's will and swarmed Ares.

His chain was effective in dealing with them, but only one at a time. The first struck him.

CHAPTER TWENTY-SIX

Ares lost his balance for a brief moment as he realized his breathing was heavy from constantly repairing his weapon after every collision with Maxima's duplicating energy.

Bellia was behind him. He knew he had to act quickly as ten orbs swirled around.

Black marks like the ink of a tattoo crawled up his neck as another attack struck. Perhaps he could deal with his sister's new technique with only his first two Soul Gates open. However, his plan didn't allow for the wasted time or uncertainty.

The chain morphed. The droplets of Soul Energy wriggled and transformed as the color of the curse mark overtook Ares' weapon and crept up his neck and face.

The chain became the body of a great beast. A snout and fangs formed like a hybrid between a wolf and dragon, black as the color of death's greeting. Its jaw snapped, and whiskers twisted about as it swallowed Maxima's spheres whole.

Are's held the tail of the creature as it wrapped around his arm, still a hybrid between chain whip and full beast. It lashed out wildly with the scream of uncontrollable vibrations sparking in the sky. He kept it small. The head was not much more than human size, but this way he could maintain sanity as he used the curse mark.

The battle for control of his mind was more exhausting than wielding.

He felt his consciousness fading in favor of something else.

The image of the Overseer, the Pursuer, and the Negotiator flashed in his eyelids.

Ares was determined: he would not become one of the Voro. He had to maintain control and be quick. His thoughts went through many distractions, but they rested on a lone idea.

I am going to be a father. I must do what is best for my child.

SHADOW RISING

Maxima grunted. She had no more to give as the spheres failed to stretch enough to form new weapons. Their circling of Ares and his monster slowed. One by one, they were consumed in the fangs of the dark shadow dragon.

"I want you to know," Ares said with a struggle, "that I cared about you, Maxima. I was never planning to hurt you, but then…I was given this offer. There's one thing that I've always wanted."

"And killing me will achieve it?" Maxima asked.

"There is someone that I need to kill. You're only a step in my path to fulfilling that. Unfortunately, my path…is in the darkness."

Ares wound his arm back and whipped it forward. His dragon attacked!

Maxima tried to move, but her legs shook wearily.

Her Soul Energy was depleted.

Behind her, she found only a steep fall into the river.

She knew what came next was unavoidable.

Inside the Soul Void, Eos peered down at his pierced abdomen, bleeding and charred.

Zala chided, "Now you realize your place. There can only be one ruler. I have the killer instinct to keep us alive, and you must step aside."

It took everything Eos had to reach down and find the strength to plunge his hand into the shadow elsu that had pierced him. He thought of disappointing his father, failing to protect Maxima, all the people poisoned by the Mitad's factory, and the attack on his homeland that was being carried out now. He had only just arrived on Hyperborea, yet everything he had worked to find was being torn apart before him.

All of his desires, pain, and hopes swirled. He cast them into the shadow elsu.

CHAPTER TWENTY-SIX

Crimson came to life in the bird.

The curse mark's color retreated.

Zala backed away in disbelief.

Eos forced himself to walk forward, summoning the crimson elsu to go before him.

"I don't need your lust for violence. My will to protect my family and dreams is more than enough to defeat you," Eos said through gritted teeth and blood.

His reclaimed elsu soared forward and collided with Zala.

Black Soul Energy ascended into the sky. Zala Alsar faded into defeated wisps. Before he was completely overcome, he muttered with a laugh that was both sad and proud, "I guess you had it after all."

The Soul Void became like a scene set in smoke. It faltered, wavered, and began to drift.

Eos' mind came back to reality, where he was unharmed. He found himself still in the cage. Below him, his father fought with Saida. To the north, he saw Maxima and Ares in battle.

Maxima looked to be in trouble.

A sinking feeling hit Eos. He reached through the bars to his sister to try and prevent what he could see was inevitably coming as Ares' black dragon attacked. After victory in the Soul Void, he had hoped that he could somehow wield his way out of the cage. His attempts were in vain, and the bars would not break.

It was hopeless.

Maxima watched the serpentine shape come at her.

At that moment, she knew there was no stopping what came next. There was a brief crackling that preceded the impact. Then, in less than a second, it was upon her.

SHADOW RISING

Ares' dragon tore through her chest like lightning finding a path to the ground.

It didn't hurt. Maxima was surprised by that fact.

It was painless…like it was only a dream.

The dragon's whiskers came out the other side of her body; then, the entire thing ran her through.

She was sure that her face was one of lamenting curiosity at the unexpected feeling of death. Just a slight pull of the eyebrows and purse of the lips. She looked across at Ares' amethyst eyes.

He closed the distance between her and wrenched his weapon back out of her body.

Still, she never felt a thing.

There was regret in Ares' eyes—it was a tortured sadness of a young boy trapped in an adult's body that was moving down a path he couldn't reverse.

"It's not personal."

Ares lifted a foot and kicked Maxima off the ledge.

Eos watched her fall through the bars of his cage.

He screamed.

It was a blood-curdling scream wishing for anything to alleviate the agony. Only the continued straining of his throat could numb his mind to what he saw as Maxima's body splashed into the water.

She never resurfaced.

The scream went silent, Eos' hands ceased gripping the bars, and he fell back defeated.

CHAPTER TWENTY-SEVEN

TORN APART

The dome of maroon Soul Energy had eventually broken, but Aizo suspected it was a decision not to expend any more, rather than exhaustion that caused it. The vast reserve of energy that Emir Grimshaw possessed was frightening. The pincer maneuver had mixed success. The mirzas emboldened the Mitad soldiers at the front of their ranks.

In the distance, Gondul's black blade was sending massive waves out to clash with another mirza to the west. Karo and Skult were joining forces in a battle with the mirza on the east. The sounds of swords and arrows clattering against Soul Energy and armor hummed through the area. The smell of blood and sweat hovered in everyone's nostrils.

If Aizo had been forced to guess, he would say that the Anite forces were losing, but just barely.

TORN APART

Grimshaw swaggered forward with one hand in his pocket. He was tired from the duel but gave off an aura of calm and indifference.

"You're the legend they talk you up to be, Aizo Mudar."

Aizo wiped the sweat from his brow and grunted in acknowledgment.

"Too bad you're old. In your prime, you would have been a good fight."

"Don't let the overconfidence of youth deceive you. We're just testing the waters so far," Aizo said. His heavy build was a detriment against Grimshaw's ranged attacks. It forced him to use Solido more than he preferred. He had to admit that it was wearing him down.

Grimshaw raised his free hand nonchalantly. His index finger was turned sideways as it pointed at Aizo.

A concentrated bead of energy formed at his fingertip. It was a dull red droplet of light, but Aizo had learned what came next. He put up his orange defensive layer, which ran through the manus stone-infused chainmail and amplified both the durability of his technique and its speed to release.

It was not a moment too soon.

The bead of Soul Energy turned into a projectile blast that would have otherwise left a hole in Anite's defender.

Aizo slid back, his boots sinking into the dirt as he braced against the shot.

Grimshaw breathed arrogance as he threw up his chin and said, "Now, what happens when I do this?" Then, without ever dropping his pointed index finger, he added the middle finger to the gesture.

CHAPTER TWENTY-SEVEN

The immense pressure from the slight movement made Aizo's eyes widen. He threw up his Solido and dove for the ground simultaneously.

A shot with double the strength pierced the distance between the two.

It clipped Aizo's shoulder. Orange light shattered. The beam deflected off him and left a one-hundred-meter skid mark across the ground.

"You're mismatched against me," Grimshaw shrugged. "Time to end this." He raised a third finger.

"Is that so?" Aizo asked with wild amusement in his voice.

Sever.

He cast out his mental net, mingling his Soul Energy with the air molecules around him. They bumped and vibrated against other pockets of air and spread. A sunset hue shimmered faintly all around Grimshaw.

A curious look was painted on Grimshaw's face. He raised an eyebrow, sensing the change but unsure of its implication.

He lowered his raised eyebrow and allowed overconfidence to decide for him. The three fingers released an enormous blast that weighed down on everyone near the duel.

The maroon erupted against the Soul Energy that Aizo had planted all around Grimshaw.

The Emir was engulfed in the chain reaction of micro-explosions that grew atop each other.

Aizo switched his energy to an awareness of the life forms around him. Anite and Mitad numbers were dropping around him. They were losing. He hadn't expected that, and he could sense that Grimshaw weathered the blast.

TORN APART

Not sure how much longer he could last, Aizo considered revealing his strongest technique, but a bellow from a war horn distracted his reading of the situation.

It was a sound that he knew was not the Mitad's. Nor was it his own army's.

An immense presence stepped through the canyon spillway. The Soul Energy was on another scale compared to Grimshaw's.

A glittering emblem painted the sky over the warzone. Thousands and thousands of dazzling white specs formed a sun icon with a stream of rays pouring down from it.

Relief came over Aizo.

Salvaluc's banner was over them all now.

The warriors of Tenebrim moved in behind the Mitad forces, pouring from the edge of the canyon territory.

Salvaluc could not claim to be neutral anymore, and Aizo thanked the Great Soul for the blessing. The Inlume had trapped the Mitad forces.

Grimshaw looked up at the white light that covered him from the sky.

Aizo hummed and made a pleased noise. "I believe you should consider this your one chance to retreat. The warriors of the canyon will be on you soon. Salvaluc will make short work of you all."

Grimshaw held up three fingers threateningly. Then all five. "Perhaps he too is just an old washed-up remnant of the Order? It makes no difference to me. My mission is a success. Your armies have gathered on the wrong border. Alasedis is vulnerable to our true attack."

Aizo's arms fell in disbelief.

CHAPTER TWENTY-SEVEN

The Emir snarled viciously. "Anite will fall as Ramath Leorix leads the Mitad to crush Anite."

∞   ∞   ∞

A possession took hold of Eos. *Revenge. Search the river.* Those thoughts alternated. But first, he had to break out of the cage. *How?*

Wielding wouldn't help. Zala had said that much in the Soul Void.

"Will it help me break the cage?"

"No, you already have what you need to do that."

All he knew was that his sister, an initiated member of the Order of Soul Wielders and gifted prodigy of wielding, was under the water. Seconds were critical.

Durath squinted from his cage. "Who was that girl?"

"My sister," Eos seethed. He thought of Maxima as she had looked in his moment of jealousy. It was his greatest regret. He had been jealous when his sister had been given what she rightfully deserved, when she had looked so elegant and beautiful under her anatus crown of sapphire light.

"King's Daughter?" Durath shook his head at the grave news. "If only we were strong enough to bend these bars…"

Eos remembered the moment that he should have been proud and celebrated with Maxima as a tear rolled down his eye and over the scar Saida had given him. He realized—there was a way to be stronger!

"This Blood Ascension, have you tried it?"

"No. I'm still working out the details. In its original conception, an attempt would take a decade off your life span, if not kill you immediately after.

TORN APART

There's cellular damage to arteries that I'm still trying to prevent. I believe I solved it in my notes, but I need to think it through more to be sure."

Shortened life span was no concern in a moment like this, and Eos repeated the writing from Maxima's notes in his head. It was simple enough. He allowed a momentary purge of emotions as he fixated on his Soul Reservoir. He could sense it, but controlling it was nearly impossible due to the metus stone. The energy within him churned and struggled to comply. Manifesting it exteriorly would be impossible…but internally…he would be able just barely to manage it.

Soul Energy surged through the meridians of his body.

There was a rush of increased blood flow and oxygen delivery.

The technique was unstable, and the metus stone was working against him. It would last only seconds. The long-term consequence on his life span in exchange for those seconds was unknown. Nevertheless, he trusted that Maxima's brilliance had worked through the majority of the side effects.

His veins bulged as the vascularity increased throughout his entire body, rippling under his skin.

Eos seized the bars and tore at the cage with all his might.

Creak. Crack.

The bars gave way. Eos lurched out and did the same to Durath's bars. His skin burned, and his heart seemed to beat too fast and too vigorously for his body to contain, but he managed an opening wide enough for Durath to escape.

Instantly, Eos sprinted down with Soul Step and dove into the water.

He went under until he could hold back his lungs no longer and swallowed water. Bobbing up and down, he repeated the search, but Maxima was nowhere to be found. Eventually, he

CHAPTER TWENTY-SEVEN

realized that he was being carried with the current. Whatever had happened to her body, it was far downriver.

Eos understood that truth but didn't stop his dive until he was nearly forced back into the mountain range. Then, he used Soul Step to escape the raging water, emerged from white foam, and fell to his knees onshore.

Maxima is gone.

Eos sat, stunned, as he became entranced in the unstoppable movement of the current.

Down the shoreline, Jezca stood over Rohl Ford.

"You people will not harm the innocents of Mircite anymore," she declared.

Rohl's eyelids shut permanently as the majority of his blood escaped around him from the gashes left by Jezca's instantaneous and boundary-breaking attacks. The young Priestess had been far more than he expected. The underestimation cost him his life.

Jezca breathed steamy gasps for air as she calmed down from her fight. She knew she should have felt remorse. Sadness and regret should have been her response, but the Necogen training was rooted in her. Instead, all she felt was a battle well won.

From behind a set of hanging jowls, a voice quivered, "Oh dear...you shouldn't have done that. It is against the ways of the manus gods. Much penance will be required to amend this."

Jezca couldn't believe her ears. The voice—it was Archpriest Mellitus, but he should still be in Mircite. She faced him, fearing the implications.

"Father Mellitus! Why are you...?"

"Dear child, the Mitad have asked me to offer you terms of surrender."

TORN APART

"The Mitad? You…you're…but…" Jezca shook in disbelief that the holy man who helped raise her could utter such words.

"Don't act so surprised. The priesthood can't maintain power unless we cooperate with power itself."

"The manus gods would never allow such a thing!"

Mellitus rolled his eyes. "Jezca, the High Priest and his archpriests are the living will of the manus gods. Do not question such complex matters—"

"NO!" Jezca's voice cracked in a pure scream of horror.

Down the river, she saw Yann Kilsig pointing a saber down at Caldus' face. Her brother was helpless and cornered on his back.

"It's too late for him," Mellitus muttered.

Yann Kilsig's saber glowed.

A sphere of light formed at the tip.

Then it burst into a beam that pierced her brother before she could move.

She couldn't hear anything. The shock of the death left her reeling on her hands and knees. She knew she was screaming until her voice was nearly gone from strain. She stood, clenching her hands with fury. Her Soul Energy was prepared to manifest as Yann Kilsig glowered at her tauntingly.

"Let him live, Priestess. Your brother chose his fate long ago when he abandoned the priesthood. Vengeance is not the way of the gods. Recall the parable of the—"

"Don't you ever speak to me about my brother again!" Jezca said.

Her violet Soul Energy came to life at a distance greater than she had ever managed before. Light slashed at Yann's face. He clutched his face as the pain came.

"Cease this at once, Jezca!"

CHAPTER TWENTY-SEVEN

"Whys would I listen to you?" She proceeded towards another blow.

"Because the Mitad has your mother."

Jezca paused.

Mellitus smiled, knowing he had won. "Grace Lapithos lives."

There must be truth in the words. The half-journal that Jezca held was a testament that Grace had continued work long after disappearing.

Ramath Leorix hurled to the ground from the top of the factory with minimal Soul Step to slow his speed. Emerald light emitted from his fist as he brought a massive punch down. His maroon cape fluttered above him as he fell, highlighting his path behind him.

The vague, ghost-like image of a corcinth formed in the light as the punch collided with Yann Kilsig.

The Mirza had no time to anticipate the attack.

Yann Kilsig was crushed in a single strike from Durath Leorix.

"You see?" Mellitus spoke smoothly, "The manus gods right the world in their own way. Through simple-minded beings like that wild animal. You are a woman of higher substance."

Jezca barely heard him as she tried to comprehend the loss of her brother.

Caldus!

She saw Durath pick up Caldus' twin daggers. Her instinct was to fight for them immediately.

Mellitus stepped in front of her. His robes shattered her fixation. He spoke sharply, "You will follow me, and the Mitad shall lead you to where they keep your mother, or else Saida will kill you, and there is nothing I or the priesthood can do to stop him."

TORN APART

Durath approached. "Do you need help, Girl?"

Jezca knew how she must respond. There was no other way. She had only one living family member, and the Mitad held her captive. She responded despondently, "No, thank you. P-p-please...take good care of those daggers. They meant...a lot to Caldus."

Behind Durath, Jezca saw Ares standing atop the roof with cursed Soul Energy wrapped around his forearm. She knew that she couldn't act freely.

"Let's go, Father Mellitus. Take me to my mother," Jezca said with finality.

The black dragon haunted Eos' vision. He saw it burned into his eyelids when he tried to shut it out. He saw Maxima falling off the building, clutching her chest. Adrenaline poured through him, and he forgot his exhaustion in favor of rage.

The speed with which he moved was like nothing he had ever done before. In his possessed state, he was using Soul Step on par with Scavok Alter, but it came at a cost. Black tainted the platforms that he ran on. His curse was running freely through his body—and he accepted its aid willingly.

Blinding hatred warped Eos' sense of time. He stepped foot on the roof without recalling how he got there. Ten shadow elsu flew around him and hovered before Ares' dragon.

"Brother, how good to see you," Ares said with amusement. "I'm guessing you're not going to listen to an explanation of what you just saw?"

There was no response. Eos lifted his right arm and cast out his first elsu.

Shadow wielding met shadow wielding. Cursed energies clashed.

CHAPTER TWENTY-SEVEN

Vmmmm.

The elsu nosedived down into the open jaws of Ares' weapon. The resulting explosion erupted for the entire river valley to see.

Ares braced through the smoke of the blast in a sheen of Solido.

"Didn't think we could talk this one out," Ares sighed sarcastically. "We'll have to take this where we can be more destructive." He dashed from the roof with Eos in pursuit. The curse mark ran up his neck and face, moving erratically towards his eyes. It matched Eos' advancing curse.

The brothers stared each other down, hovering above the river.

Maxima fell below where I stand. The one who did it is desecrating this space. I will erase him.

No words left Eos' lips, but he circled his eslu.

Ares summoned his dark dragon at full size as the curse threatened to consume both of them. The beast's head was taller than Ares' entire body. It snapped its teeth and snarled amidst the hum of electrified air.

The shadow dragon made the first attack.

Two elsu soared to meet it.

Ares wasn't holding back now. His attack snapped through the two elsu, only slowing for a second. The resilience of the dragon took Eos by surprise. The dark energy reached him with teeth bared.

An elsu rushed to deflect it.

The bird managed to prevent a head-on collision, but Eos still absorbed some of the blow. He was sent tumbling from his Soul Step and slid across the rock floor violently. His six remaining elsu did not fade. The curse overwrote his need for concentration, and the pain that would have broken apart his wielding technique now only aggravated him.

All six remaining elsu turned about and broke for Ares.

Eos glared vengefully.

The first attack struck Ares' dragon in the side of the head. It wavered and shuttered but turned and wrapped its teeth around the second elsu that approached. The attack was snuffed out; its explosion was exhaled like smoke through the wolf-like snout of the creature.

Three and four struck the body, which writhed at the attacks.

The fifth went high, turning for the sky.

Ares gave chase. Black ink pursued black ink in the air over the river.

The distraction had worked. The sixth and final elsu sped around from the side and went for Ares. The dragon swallowed the elsu in the sky, but Ares could do nothing about the one coming directly at him.

Gray Solido marbled with darkness protected Ares.

Bwooom!

The eruption engulfed him.

Eos saw shards of Solido flake off in the smoke.

Ares peered through it at his brother with a cracked defensive shell around him.

"I really do owe you a beating that you won't forget, Eos. But this isn't the opportune moment."

Eos' mind was too far gone to react smartly. If he had not been consumed by hate, he would have been able to maintain his control and decision-making better. This much he knew from his lesson from the corcinth in the void. There was something else…another

CHAPTER TWENTY-SEVEN

way to maintain his dominance over the curse, but he couldn't grasp it at that moment.

The curse worked instead of him. Despite his shaking body and skin that felt on fire, another ten shadow elsu were born. The act made his bones feel brittle, and his veins seem to shrivel.

Ares smiled. He was tempted to continue and had been so looking forward to this fight. "Unfortunately, we'll have to complete this match another time. I have someone that I can't let get away. Bellia, it's time."

"Don't you dare try and run away from what you did!" Eos spoke for the first time.

"Believe me; I'm not. I'd love to listen to your whimpers as I crush you, but alas...Perhaps you should tend to our dearest father. He seems to be in trouble." Ares chuckled as he released his Soul Step and plunged towards the ground. Violet light tore open the fabric of space below him.

Bellia! Eos was furious that he had not thought of the Mitad woman's ability as the curse mark made its way towards his eyes in tongues like dark flames.

Ares was gone.

Processing the words, Eos looked for Talus, who he found engaged with Saida. The man he believed to be an invincible force was clutching his shoulder where his right arm should have been. The massive wings of Soul Energy were shrinking as they fought Saida's array of strings.

Saida was not having an easy time. His clothes were torn and tattered, and he bled from numerous wounds. He breathed heavily as his brown hair fell in disarray over his face.

TORN APART

Eos wasted no time in comprehending his father's wound. He ran towards the scene with his elsu leading the way. They blindsided Saida in a barrage.

The Mitad leader was sent flying across the battlefield. He rolled in violent bumps to a stop after the impact of Eos' attack. Blood trickled from his lips as they curled into a gleeful smile.

"You finally did it! What a boost it has provided the pitiful child-powers you wielded before."

"These factories are coming down, Saida. The pain you cause on everything you touch will end soon," Eos said with matter-of-factly.

"You think so? How about this proposition?" Saida said as he wiped the blood from his mouth, "I kill the King of Anite like Ares did your sister, rule the Winter Aisle, and cripple the Anite empire with a secret army that breaks through the mountains while all defenses are fighting a false invasion on the east border." The arrogance twisted his mustache up his cheeks.

Eos lashed out thoughtlessly. All five of his remaining elsu attacked.

"No, Eos. Think," Talus said but saw that his words fell on a young man possessed by his curse.

A wall of mauve strings surrounded Saida and then proceeded towards the shadow elsu.

The beams of light sliced through the winged attacks, making a mural in the sky of Eos' diced energy before it exploded.

The wall of stringed light advanced rapidly on Eos and Talus.

There was only time for Talus to wrap the two of them in the protection of his crimson wings.

Zmmmmm!

CHAPTER TWENTY-SEVEN

Saida's fingers contorted to manipulate his weapons. They hummed against the wings and filled the air with a burnt scent. It was so strong that Eos could taste it like a film of ash on his tongue.

The wings exploded out like a giant elsu spreading for flight. Both Soul Energy forms vaporized from the deflection.

"Eos! Run for Mircite!"

"No, Father. I won't let you fight him alone."

"I'm running with you. Now!" Talus was desperate.

Eos looked where his father was staring.

Scavok was sprinting towards them.

"Go! Go. Go," Scavok cried.

A tsunami of crawlers followed him as if the giant crawler had multiplied ten times over and broke apart again. Thousands of the creatures hurdled over each other after him.

The grip of the curse faded as Eos shifted from an offensive mindset to survival.

They turned to flee.

"Oh no, you don't," Saida said and produced a myriad of strings.

The horns of a pine-green corcinth glowed from behind Saida. Durath landed from a mighty leap over the river and struck him. The attack was more impactful than Eos could have imagined— far beyond anything he could do without his curse's assistance.

The strings faded as Saida was temporarily crushed to the ground.

Durath ran over Saida and joined Eos and Talus in their exit from the river valley.

"That could have gone better," The Leorix King's Son panted.

Scavok joined them. "A Voro who can create an army is not a strong matchup for an assassin. I could hold him back no longer."

TORN APART

Eos saw a gash in the master assassin's shoulder and chest. Even through the adrenaline, the pain from his use of the curse was overwhelming. He knew he wasn't going to make it to the mountain cover. His legs were as stable as malleable rubber and his skin and organs felt like they were falling apart. Whether it was from the use of the Blood Ascension technique, the curse, or both, he wasn't sure.

The multiple waves of pale glowing light swam through the horizon at them, filling the floor, the air above, and the periphery.

Eos fell. His body wouldn't move. He had no command over his limbs anymore.

"Bellator kid, get up!" Durath urged without stopping.

Scavok cursed. He went back and picked Eos up with Talus following.

The horde was nearly upon them.

Krattle-scree. KRATTLE-SCREE!

"Go, Scavok. I'll finish this. Maxima died trying to stop the Mitad and their factories. My daughter's death will not be remembered for failing at her goal."

"No, I can't leave my king to be sacrificed. Your kingdom needs you alive more. Missing an arm and the King's Daughter is enough of a loss."

"I'm only buying time," Talus said with certainty. "This will be everything I have. I will only be able to run away after this. Make use of it."

The crimson wings grew from behind his shoulders.

Talus closed his eyes. "I'll meet you back in Anondorn."

The Soul Energy grew.

The wingspan reached thirty feet.

Then larger than the torrent of crawlers that closed in.

CHAPTER TWENTY-SEVEN

Then larger than the factory.

Brilliant streaks of red painted the entire valley as Talus severed part of his soul.

It took flight—breaking through the crawlers and bathing everything in Talus' light like a nuclear flash.

The river surged above the ground as if gravity was reversed when the feathers swooped over it.

The factories crumbled and fell.

Bellator energy laid claim over the entire area for a brief instant.

The Overseer and Saida used Solido to survive the attack.

Talus turned. He was relieved to see that the others had disappeared into the mountains, and he followed. His path was not straight back to Anondorn, however.

Tears streamed down his face as he made his way into the mountain. He thought of his daughter—so newly returned to him. Yet, the Great Soul had reclaimed her after such a short reunion. There was a void of memories he should have had with her and never would. That fact hurt as much as anything else. However, the task at hand distracted him slightly from this pain.

His dear friend was now leading the last of a Mitad attack force on a march to invade Anite while it was weakest. He remembered the instructions that Ramath had given him as they stood in the middle of mixing Soul Energies in the river valley.

Ramath had stood across from Talus amidst a torrent of green and crimson. There had been a shared understanding…a trust. It was a feeling branded on Ramath's back and in Talus' heart. Ramath had lost control, given in to the Mitad's influence, and handed over his freedom and kingdom. But he had done it in coordination with Talus initially. Talus knew he bore some of the responsibility. They had wanted to infiltrate the Mitad to get a better understanding of their movements and motives.

Much later, Talus entered Morax's abandoned mine. He was guided by the meager light of a dying Soul Sphere. It was all he could muster. Fond memories of his adopted brother flooded his weary head: battles won, fights forgotten over laughs and drinks, dares and competitions, tears of joy and sorrow…

Talus activated his inlume crown. The wreath lit his way, consuming less energy than the Soul Sphere—he needed every last bit to complete the mission. He had lost much and needed to protect what remained: his kingdom, his wife, his son, and the home that they all would reunite in.

Eventually, he reached a massive support beam with the cross-sectional area that would allow the multiple royal transport wagons like the one Appocles carried him in to pass through easily. It was an unbelievable feat of engineering. Under the faint glow of the inlume crown, Talus saw a sign that gave him confidence. A hurriedly carved symbol of an elsu was engraved in the beam.

It was the second major support that he was seeking. When he found it, his heart ached with what he must do.

The tunnel went utterly dark as Talus extinguished his light and waited.

The darkness enveloped him, and he sat alone with his suffering, recalling the last words Ramath would ever speak to him.

"There are weak points in the tunnel to Anite. I am prepared to take out two at the far end. The second major support on the Monte side must be destroyed by another. It should have been Durath, but he was captured before I could relay the plan. It has to be you now, Talus."

The distortions of battle and noises of the vortex of Soul Energies hid the conversation.

CHAPTER TWENTY-SEVEN

"You'll be inside when it comes down?" Talus asked with crinkled eyes.

"Aye. I'll be inside. So will nearly all of the Mitad soldiers."

"There has to be another—"

"No. I'm a dead man anyway. The curse mark has consumed me. I'm too weak of mind to fight it. The drugs have destroyed me. They were my coping mechanism knowing my body would soon fail."

Talus nodded solemnly. "Then this is it?"

"This is it. I've left something for Eos. I hope my corcinth friend finds him in whatever realm it chooses."

Talus didn't understand but thanked his friend for whatever the parting gift was meant to be.

Ramath swallowed like he was dying of dehydration. "Please…save Durath. Get him out of here, and don't let him come back. Give him a life like your father, Bekrin, gave me."

"I swear it."

"Good. I can't wait any longer. The march will get too far ahead of me, and I need to be at the front of it before they break through to Anite. Eos needs you now."

Talus understood. "Goodbye…old friend. You were always loyal. Even after everything you went through."

"No. Not always. Not entirely. But in the end."

There was a tremendous rumble that all the corcinths on Hyperborea couldn't have caused.

It was the signal Ramath had foretold. The two Anite-side major supports had fallen.

The entire north Sepeleo mountain range creaked and groaned like an ancient creature taking its final steps on broken legs. Talus let a flicker of crimson out one last time and snapped the beam before him to pieces with his only arm.

TORN APART

The tunnel failed. Kingdoms shook. The mountain screamed out.

Talus only whispered to himself as the world threatened to tear to pieces.

"Goodbye, old friend. You chose the path of a lost brother."

∞   ∞   ∞

The mid-day sun blared in Terrava's eyes. She was filled with dread—not at the coming battle—but a motherly instinct that she hadn't been able to shake for hours. She worried for her children.

Xaro Monte stroked his white mane and blew smoke from his pipe as they stood on a balcony at the boundary of West Avem, overlooking the distant foothills of the Sepeleo mountains.

"It seems absurd to think that the Mitad could move their forces through the mountains. Are you certain this is where our focus should be at a critical time like this?" he asked.

Spintha spoke on behalf of Terrava as she seemed in no mood to be challenged. "King Talus sent his messenger elsu, Hermios, to tell us that they have found a way to attack. There can be no mistake."

"Well, I stand ready to assist should this attack actually play out, Queen."

There was something not genuine in Xaro's voice, but Terrava knew that his strength was almighty. The vast majority of the Anite army and wielders were on the eastern border at the Tenebrim spillway. The Ignoble Lord's assistance would be critical in fending off a surprise attack.

Rumble.

CHAPTER TWENTY-SEVEN

The mountain gurgled like pockets of air escaping from underwater.

Something is coming.

Terrava scanned the horizon line, watching every inch of the mountain for signs of a breach.

Crumble. Crash.

A wall of the foothills broke into pieces, allowing a force of hundreds to pour out. The leader at the head of the Mitad attack had a tremendous presence. Terrava could feel his Soul Energy all the way on the wall of the West Avem lookout.

There was a flare of pressure from the man's power. He wanted there to be no mistake in identifying him. Terrava recognized it well.

Ramath, the betrayer, led the strike on Anite. Talus' trust was misplaced.

"Impossible!" Xaro exclaimed. "They couldn't have tunneled through the Sepeleo. That would take far too long…and without being noticed."

Ramath was a blurred shape from a distance, but he made a clear gesture—he put his hand over his heart as soldiers streamed by him like he was a rock in a river.

The hand fell from his heart, and he turned. The King of Corleo went back into the tunnel.

Terrava let her eyelids fall wearily. The intuition that she should fear for her children's life was multiplied by what she saw before her. There was not enough military force to hold back a small army from entering West Avem. She and Xaro would have to fight them off alone.

There should have been a feeling of rage channeling through her to defend her borders, but instead, there was only profound tiredness. She had lost Rebus, then her children, and then her dearest friend Grace. Now she sensed that her children's return had been short-lived. Either they, the kingdom, or both were in mortal danger. The peril overwhelmed her, but she needed to defend her people.

No more than a few hundred Mitad foot soldiers had exited the tunnel when the mountain began to speak in groans and rumbles. The earth shook with a pained tremble.

A ripple of noise, like a great monster tunneling through the mountain, reverberated back from Anite into the heart of the Sepeleo.

Almost as if answering the sound, another far greater shaking came from the Corleo side.

The new opening in the foothills collapsed.

Stone fell on the Mitad soldiers underneath it.

The collapsing weight of a mountain as old as Hyperborea itself could be heard echoing across south Anite and through north Corelo.

"Collapse?" Spintha asked with confusion.

The men at the mountain base turned frantically, trying to analyze what happened when their numbers were cut off, and they were without a leader.

"It would seem so. Remain here, Queen Terrava. I will clean up this pathetic show of an attack. What a waste of resources. It would appear the Mitad is not the threat we feared," Xaro moved to leap off the balcony and into battle.

"I will join you," Terrava ignored Xaro's request. She knew that the cause of the pit in her stomach was Saida's doing. Any vengeance she could deliver should be done in person, after everything he had done to alter her life. "I don't think this tunnel

CHAPTER TWENTY-SEVEN

collapse happened without steep consequences. I sense many losses were the payment. Both in Corleo and East Avem."

"My Queen!" Spintha protested Terrava's joining the battle.

It was too late. Xaro and the Queen of Anite launched themselves towards the Mitad on planes of Soul Energy.

The monstrous strength of Xaro Monte was legend—and the myths built around him may not have done him justice. Terrava was an inlume of much esteem, yet she couldn't crush the enemy forces anywhere near as quickly as the Ignoble Lord did.

The Mitad numbers were decimated with precision and finality. None were left by the end of the hour.

When peace was restored in the valley, Terrava was once again on the balcony. But, this time, she pushed aside the doting aid of medics and advisors who worried over her post-battle wounds and decisions.

She threw them all out and closed the doors of the balcony with a wall of sapphire light.

Only Spintha remained.

"I don't need to tell you that it was reckless for the Queen to fight when the King is away," The old inlume chided.

"I defended my home."

Spintha nodded.

An elsu arrived, but Terrava barely noticed. There was a great joy to be had in the message she received, but her focus only acknowledged it as something occurring in another world. She was worried for her family.

"Aizo has written us. Salvaluc came to our assistance. Anite has won the battle of East Avem."

Spintha allowed a yellow inlume crown to glow over her head and touched each of the three broken swords with reverence. "The

TORN APART

Great Soul has guided us to victory. Salvaluc will be remembered for his loyalty."

Terrava didn't recall how she had responded. Words of relief and gratitude left her lips, but they were only partially genuine. She could not be at peace until her family returned.

She needed to see Talus walk back into Alasedis with Eos and Maxima.

She tapped her fingers on the porcelain-white railing and looked out at the collapsed rubble.

Her family needed to be whole, or her heart would break irreparably.

CHAPTER TWENTY-EIGHT

OTHER WORLD CALLING

Seven dark days had passed since Maxima had fallen into the Sepeleo river. The remaining Bellator family and the Winter Aisle travelers had spent the time in Anite, tending to their quiet sadness. For Eos, the halls of Alasedis seemed less white, the sky grayer, and the people duller. Life was missing the spark that sustained meaning for all the past years of his life.

That spark had been sapphire blue.

The stained-glass of Talus' private study chamber was creating a drifting kaleidoscope on the table as the sun set. The light made Eos consider wielding for the briefest of moments. He had not produced a spark of Soul Energy in the last week. It was not that he couldn't, but his desire was nonexistent. The haunting memory of the curse nearly consuming him made the prospect unappealing.

OTHER WORLD CALLING

The image of Talus handing him the Mellizo Glyph appeared like a mirage in the hazy stained-glass light. That too, had been lost.

"It was all failure," Eos mumbled to himself.

"Not all," Talus said.

Eos wasn't sure how long his father had been watching him from the doorway.

Talus sat in the empty chair beside Eos. They both sunk into the cushions and were silent for some time, stewing in the heavy cloud of depression that seemed to permeate the castle.

"You know…I used to tell everyone in Anite that you two were still alive…out there somewhere waiting to be found and return home. Some believed for a while, but after twelve years, I was the only one who held on to true hope and belief. I *knew* you were alive… Holding my children again was the greatest moment of my life."

Eos asked lowly, "Do you think Maxima's still alive?"

Talus winced and exhaled slowly, "I…I could sense her Soul Energy as she fell into the river. There was a strange moment when I felt a surge in energy there, but I was sure that the Soul Energy was gone after a moment. Completely. Extinguished."

"Ares!" Eos growled weakly.

"You must understand…Ares is not like others. His birth was not like anyone else, and his mind has been corrupted."

"That doesn't change anything that he's done!"

"No. It doesn't. He was born under the same curse mark that you have. That much you must understand. His true essence has been hidden behind the influence of Saida's control. He's never been free of it nor had a seal to protect him."

"The curse mark won. He can't be forgiven," Eos said with certainty.

CHAPTER TWENTY-EIGHT

"No. It hasn't won, and it is always possible to forgive. It doesn't mean we should forgive him, but there is room in the heart for perspective. How much did you control your actions when the curse took hold?"

Eos did not respond. The truth of the words ground his hateful and suffering thoughts to a halt. Eventually, he pondered, "I wonder what my friends on Earth would say about this?" Major Clark and Colonel Kane would surely have some wise words. Draven, Malin, Devers, Skye, and Grant would know how to cope with loss.

Talus continued, "I doubt I'll ever forgive him for taking my daughter away from me..." his voice creaked with weariness. "I may kill him the next time I see him. However, I understand that he has lost himself to darkness. There was a young boy that showed me his first Soul Sphere, and he probably still exists somewhere inside Ares."

The white pattern of the elsu in the window drifted in front of them as the day's light fell.

Talus changed the subject, "I think it's time, my son."

"Time for what?" Eos raised an eyebrow.

"That you join the Order of Soul Wielders."

"How can you say that? I lost the Mellizo Glyph. I didn't protect Maxima. Caldus died during our attack on the factories. Jezca is missing. Benedir died too!" Eos' voice cracked as he listed the tragedies.

"You may add to that list: Julian Cassion is calling for an immediate emergency reelection after all that's happened and the loss of his son," Talus grumbled and rubbed his forehead.

"Will he succeed?"

OTHER WORLD CALLING

"I don't believe he has the votes, and we fended off the Mitad successfully…so I pray he does not. Now, among all those failures, remember the words of the Order.

I believe in the Divine Soul, which all mankind may glimpse in their own reflection.

I believe in the right for all to make for themselves a free life.

I will use wisdom granted by the Divine Soul to guide my wielding towards this belief.

I will set aside the influences of nations and kingdoms when they are destructive to mankind.

I will transform chaos into order.

I will pursue the path of light.

I will uphold the Order of Soul Wielders so that they may defend all others.

Did you uphold those principles? Recklessly without a doubt. But so has every inlume in their younger days. It's time for you to join the tradition. You fought valiantly, overcame incredible odds, freed all the people of Mircite from poison and crawlers, and together we stopped the production of bullets and metus stones on the Corland. We foiled the plans the Mitad have been prepared for years. Thousands of their numbers have been defeated and Anite was unharmed by their assault. Not all is failure, and not all is lost. We do not understand the workings of the Great Soul. All we can do is accept what has been and work towards what we can control."

His father's words shook Eos. He couldn't hide that being compared to a young inlume, though a reckless one, had given him the first hint of a smile in days.

"I do mean it. Tomorrow we will head to the Turrim Cartus and initiate you as an anatus…if you accept."

Unable to speak, Eos shook his head vigorously in agreement.

CHAPTER TWENTY-EIGHT

"Then it is settled."

Footsteps came frantically into the room as a heavy body waddled in.

Scipio panted as he exclaimed, "King Talus! King Talus! There is a visitor that collapsed at the gate. He claims to know your children and come from a land that no one in the castle has ever heard of, called *Earth*."

Eos and Talus entered the north wing of the castle where the Sanofem medical quarters resided. They walked under the engraving of two strands of Soul Energy forming a helix around a chalice and into a room filled with white curtains.

The Sanofem walked in gray dresses with their faces covered by translucent silks that hid their eyes and could be seen through only one way. Talus had explained that the Sanofem were women who wished only to show the exterior world their medical prowess. Their dedication to the art of healing was all-consuming.

Many women walked about the room, but the one nearest them introduced herself as Sirona, the senior healer on duty. Her blond hair was in a tight bun like all the other members of the Sanofem. Her lips and lower face were the only other features that showed.

"The stranger from outside the gate is here," Sirona led them to the far end of the white brick room. She stopped them in front of closed curtains. "I must warn you that he suffered from severe exhaustion, dehydration, and battle wounds. The fact that he made it to our care is an act of the Great Soul. Please respect his sleeping and do not disturb him."

Sirona pulled back the curtains.

It was like a window into the past opened before Eos. It seemed so long ago that Eos was on Earth, but the fluttering of the silver curtains revealed a sight that reminded him less time had passed than he felt. Strawberry blond hair lay disheveled against the pillow in the bed. Scabbed lips, a scarred face, and a long beard made the face nearly unrecognizable.

How?

It shouldn't be possible that *he* was here—on Hyperborea.

Eos remembered what Aizo had done during their last hours on Earth.

"This is my thanks to you. I wish I had more to give, but all I can offer is to bring them back to visit soon." Aizo motioned to the object in Glenn's hand. "That is insurance that you'll see them again."

Eos and Maxima's old guardian and dear friend, Glenn, rested in the bed.

"He was carrying this," Sirona picked up a dirty desert shawl from the bedside table. "Forgive me for speaking so boldly about a tender wound…but I believe he wanted your daughter to have it, my King." She held out her hands with the dirt-caked scarf spread over them.

Talus took it with a perplexed look.

"That was…" Eos failed to finish his sentence as tears came to his eyes. "That was Maxima's. On Earth. She always wore it."

Talus rubbed the cloth with his thumb. "Then we shall treasure it. And him?"

"This is Glenn. He took care of us while Aizo was imprisoned with General Braxton."

"He shall receive the best care," Talus commanded.

A powerful elderly female voice joined the conversation, "He brought one more thing with him." A pure white gown walked up to them with the same facial covering as the Sanofem. Her dress had a wreath of golden feathers sewn around the chest and

CHAPTER TWENTY-EIGHT

shoulders. The woman's age showed in the wrinkles around her lips, but the fitness of her body did not match the age that her voice revealed. She extended a hand, and Talus received it.

Tiny chain links flowed from the King's palm.

Eos saw the Mellizo Glyph in his father's hand. A look of understanding crossed both of them.

"Thank you, my lady Artisis. This artifact is more important than you know."

Sirona's head was bowed. Artisis, the head of the Sanofem, spoke with careful wisdom, "I examined it. Its power is apparent, though its purpose is less so. The King's secrets shall remain his."

Glenn cracked open his eyes enough to see. He spoke with the voice of a dying man, weary and pained, "Eos...so...so good to see you. I didn't think...think...I would make it. Earth...fallen. Emir Raggan...attacked." There was a pause before their old protector spoke his last sentence, "Where...where's Maxima? I didn't shave...just for...her." The cracked lips ceased to move.

"Glenn!" Eos moved to hold the man who had been like a father to him for the majority of his life.

Sirona put her arm out. "He's only sleeping. This is too much excitement for him now. He must rest."

Artisis walked them out of the medical care wing.

Eos' heart ached with a hollow brittleness that he had never felt before.

∞   ∞   ∞

The late-day sun cast long shadows on the three swords of Fanum Ortus. They sprawled out, long clawing blotches on the rocks pointing to the pedestal that held every energy signature of the Order of Soul Wielders.

Aizo, Talus, and Terrava stood behind the tapered geometric stone pedestal. The dark blue veins of anima stone that ran up the sides mesmerized Eos. The distraction was a kind reprieve from mourning. He felt a tinge of hope.

"Are you ready?" Talus asked.

"One second," Eos paused the ceremony.

Streaks of white clouds brightened the lively blue of the sky, moving like lazy spirits, and the angle of the sunlight gave them an outline of gold. Eos breathed in slowly to process the moment. Fresh spring air brushed against his cheeks. The mossy scent of the Iussum mountains filled his nose, and the image of Maxima painted his eyelids. He pulled her scarf from his tunic and tied it around the base of the Turrim Cartus.

Now she was present to witness the initiation—both her memento and her Soul Energy, which was forever part of the Record of the Order.

"I'm ready, Father." Eos nodded.

"It is not me who will initiate you today," Talus said hesitantly.

Eos eyes darted in a confused panic.

"Do not worry," Talus comforted Eos. "I realized on our journey that we both desperately want to make up for lost time, but it can't be done. The past remains and cannot be changed. I am your father, but...I am not your inlume teacher."

Eos tried to interject, but Aizo beat him to it.

"You didn't think you could get rid of me that easily, did you?" Aizo laughed mischievously.

CHAPTER TWENTY-EIGHT

It was in that crazed laugh that Eos understood what he had been trying to suppress. Aizo had always been his teacher despite his efforts to change that to Talus.

"Aizo protected you on Earth when we could not," Terrava added. "He sacrificed his life on Hyperborea for you, is the one who sealed your curse, and who taught you to perform partial Severance."

Aizo teased, "Of course, you must willingly accept me. It is not the way of the Order to force a student with a master."

Eos vigorously shook his head in an agreeing motion.

"Let's begin then," Aizo said. "Place your hand over the Record of the Order and repeat the oath after me."

Eos would never forget the sky that day, the scent of the mountains, and the faces of his parents, but the words repeated would become a blurred memory. He memorized the feeling of the last sentence leaving his lips and the light coming from Talus and Terrava's expression of pride.

"I will uphold the Order of Soul Wielders so that they may defend all others."

A stream of crimson Soul Energy sifted from his palm and fell over the slightly convex dome of anima stone atop the Turrim Cartus. The sapphire light trickled down the veins throughout the rock, and the scarf at the base whipped in the wind, brushing against him.

A wreath of crimson light twisted around his crown. The single sword-like cross floated above his forehead, and he knew—he was an anatus of the Order of Soul Wielders.

Talus smiled from behind his braided beard and bellowed, "Welcome to the Order, Son."

OTHER WORLD CALLING

Eos embraced Talus and Terrava to receive a warmth that he had desperately needed.

"Mom...Dad..." Eos pressed carefully.

"Yes, Son?" Terrava asked.

"I made an oath just now, but the meaning of it...the test of it came before I said the words. Glenn came because Earth is in trouble. He's family too."

Pain creased in Terrava's eyes as she knew her son was going to depart from her again soon.

Solemn eyes fell as Talus stroked his beard thoughtfully.

"I cannot ask you to stay. You've spent more time there than in Anite. You are a young man with two homes."

"I want to stay here. My home is with you..." Eos paused before staying, "but a piece of me is there. Glenn raised me—"

"Just don't think that you get to make the return trip alone!" Aizo broke in.

Just then, Eos wished he could remain at Fanum Ortus and perfectly preserve everything about the first time he had entered it with his parents and sister. If only he could bottle the tranquility of that moment...but duty summoned him on the strings of unseen will. His path was not destined. He sensed a web of futures that were not yet realized, but all of them compelled him on this road. There were pockets of time possible where he could remain on Hyperborea instead, but they only led to ends obscured in shadows. It was unclear what he was seeking, but it lay at the end of this thread of choices.

Eos looked out at the three swords of his ancestors plunged into the edge of the cliff. He knew there were unknown forces behind him in time that compelled him forward.

"No, Aizo. I wouldn't dream of making the journey without you."

52268192R00270